BRET BAIER

THE HISTORY CLUB

A GRAPHIC NOVEL

ILLUSTRATED BY
MARVIN SIANIPAR

DUEL ACROSS TIME

ALADDIN
NEW YORK   LONDON   TORONTO   SYDNEY   NEW DELHI

ALADDIN · AN IMPRINT OF SIMON & SCHUSTER CHILDREN'S PUBLISHING DIVISION · 1230 AVENUE OF THE AMERICAS, NEW YORK, NEW YORK 10020 · FIRST ALADDIN HARDCOVER EDITION NOVEMBER 2023 · TEXT COPYRIGHT © 2023 BY BRET BAIER · ILLUSTRATIONS COPYRIGHT © 2023 BY MARVIN SIANIPAR · LETTERING BY DAMIAN CANTA · ILLUSTRATION ON PAGES 25, 51, 89, 117, AND 128 BY SLIM3D/ISTOCK · ALL RIGHTS RESERVED, INCLUDING THE RIGHT OF REPRODUCTION IN WHOLE OR IN PART IN ANY FORM. · ALADDIN AND RELATED LOGO ARE REGISTERED TRADEMARKS OF SIMON & SCHUSTER, INC. · FOR INFORMATION ABOUT SPECIAL DISCOUNTS FOR BULK PURCHASES, PLEASE CONTACT SIMON & SCHUSTER SPECIAL SALES AT 1-866-506-1949 OR BUSINESS@SIMONANDSCHUSTER.COM. · THE SIMON & SCHUSTER SPEAKERS BUREAU CAN BRING AUTHORS TO YOUR LIVE EVENT. FOR MORE INFORMATION OR TO BOOK AN EVENT CONTACT THE SIMON & SCHUSTER SPEAKERS BUREAU AT 1-866-248-3049 OR VISIT OUR WEBSITE AT WWW.SIMONSPEAKERS.COM. DESIGNED BY KARIN PAPROCKI · THE ILLUSTRATIONS FOR THIS BOOK WERE RENDERED DIGITALLY. · THE TEXT OF THIS BOOK WAS SET IN CC MEANWHILE AND ASTOUNDER SQUARED. · MANUFACTURED IN CHINA 0723 SCP · 10 9 8 7 6 5 4 3 2 1 · LIBRARY OF CONGRESS CONTROL NUMBER 2023933150 · ISBN 9781534485594 (HC) · ISBN 9781534485617 (EBOOK)

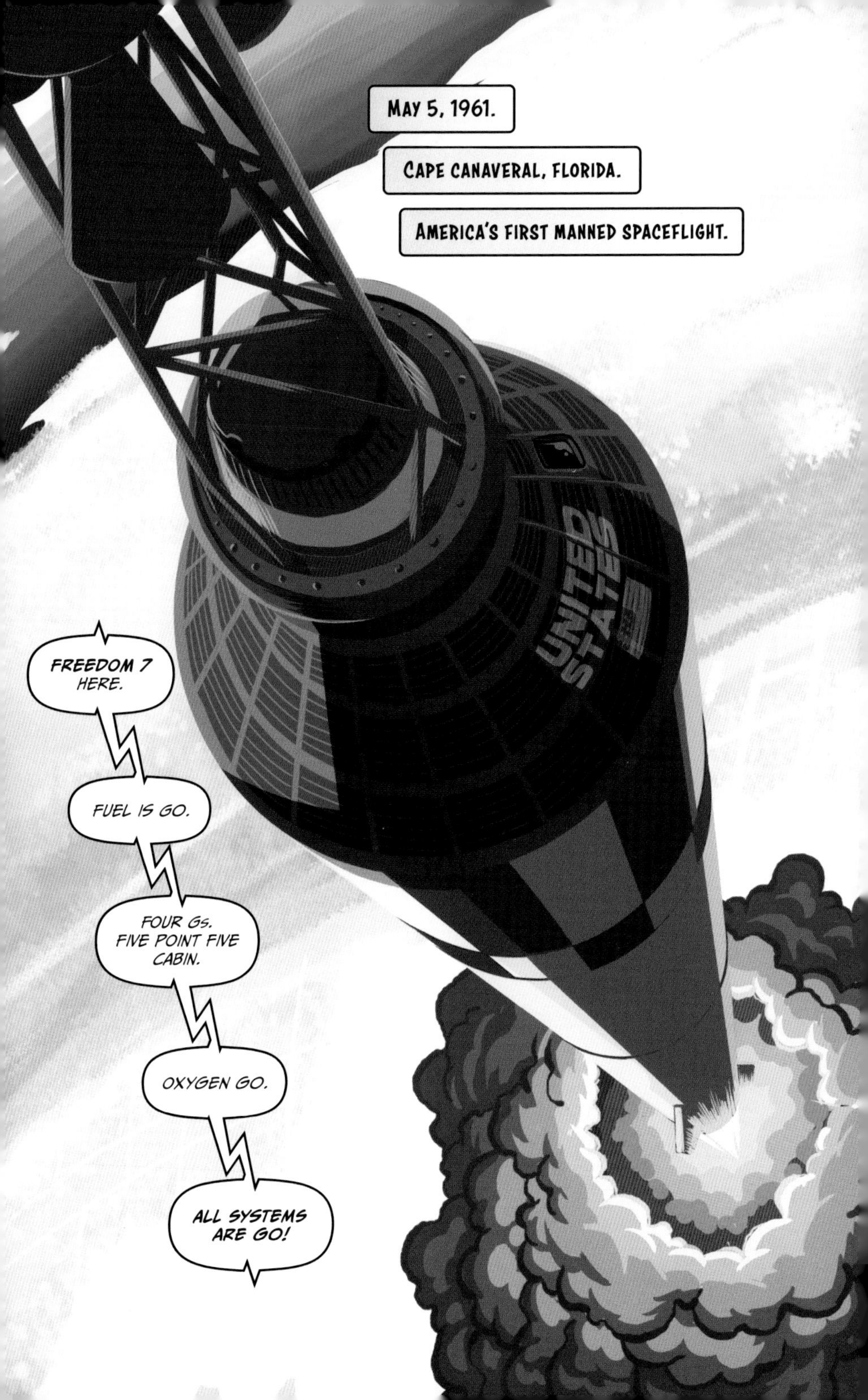
MAY 5, 1961.
CAPE CANAVERAL, FLORIDA.
AMERICA'S FIRST MANNED SPACEFLIGHT.
UNITED STATES
FREEDOM 7 HERE.
FUEL IS GO.
FOUR Gs. FIVE POINT FIVE CABIN.
OXYGEN GO.
ALL SYSTEMS ARE GO!

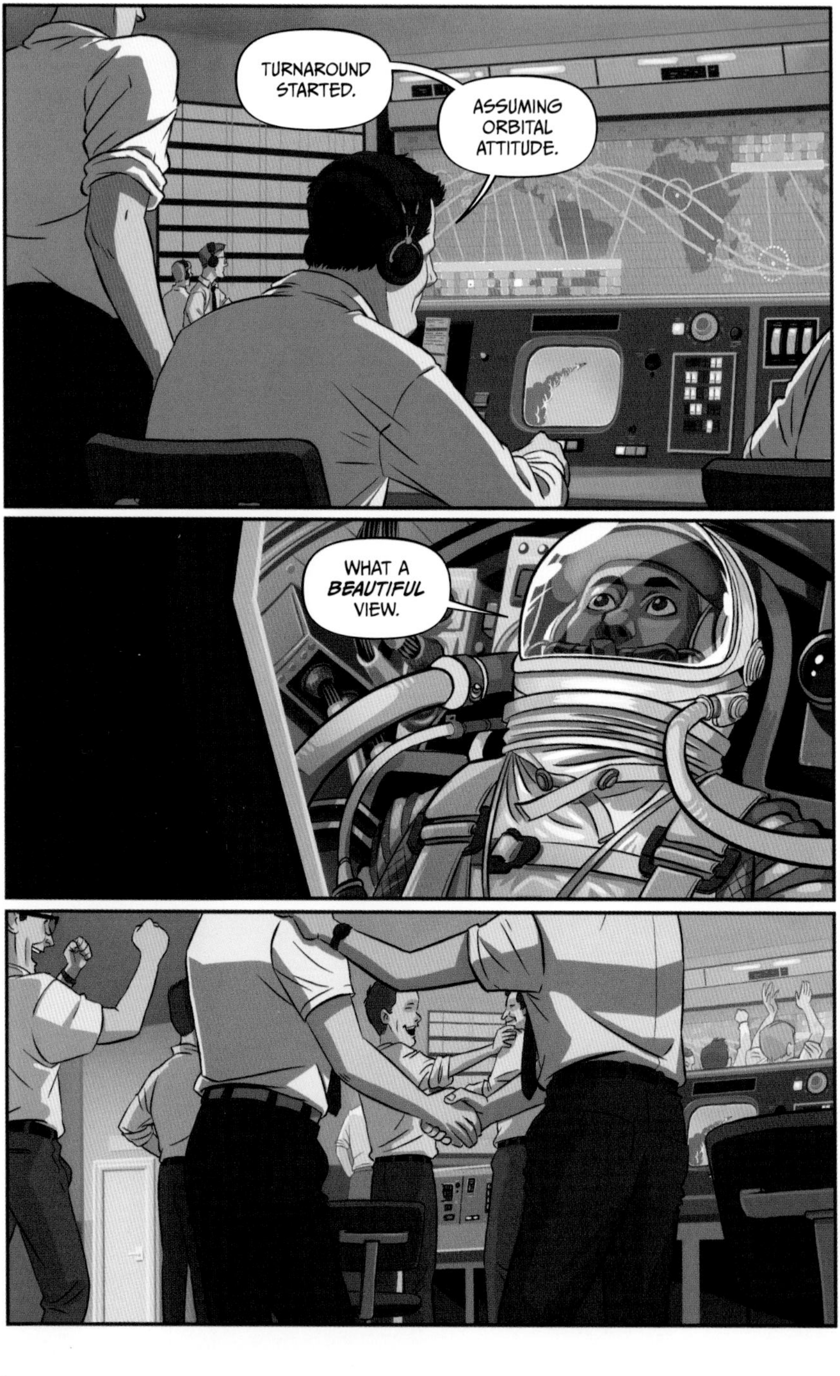
TURNAROUND STARTED.
ASSUMING ORBITAL ATTITUDE.
WHAT A *BEAUTIFUL* VIEW.

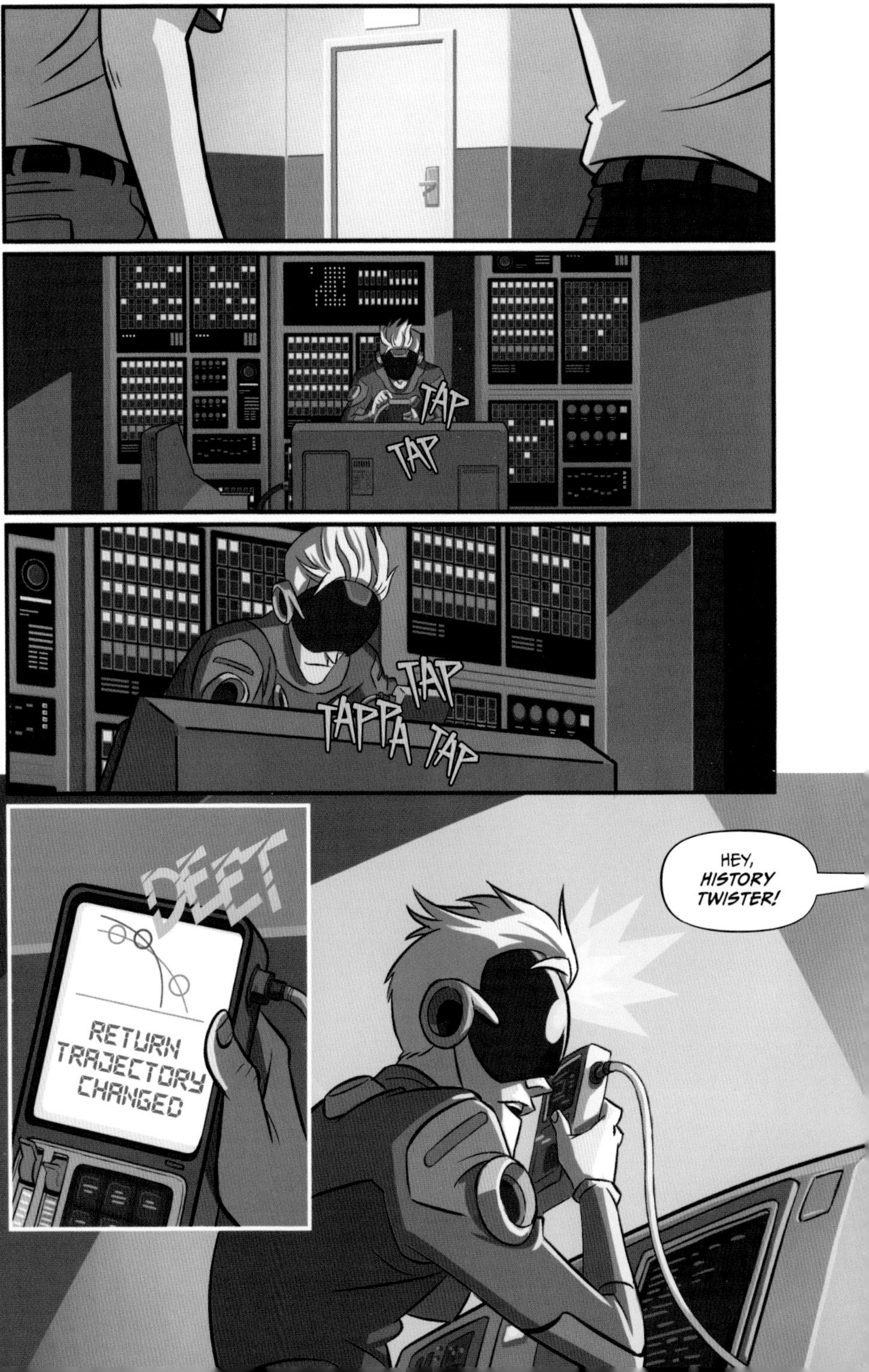

TAP
TAP
TAP
TAPPA TAP
DEET
RETURN TRAJECTORY CHANGED
HEY, HISTORY TWISTER!

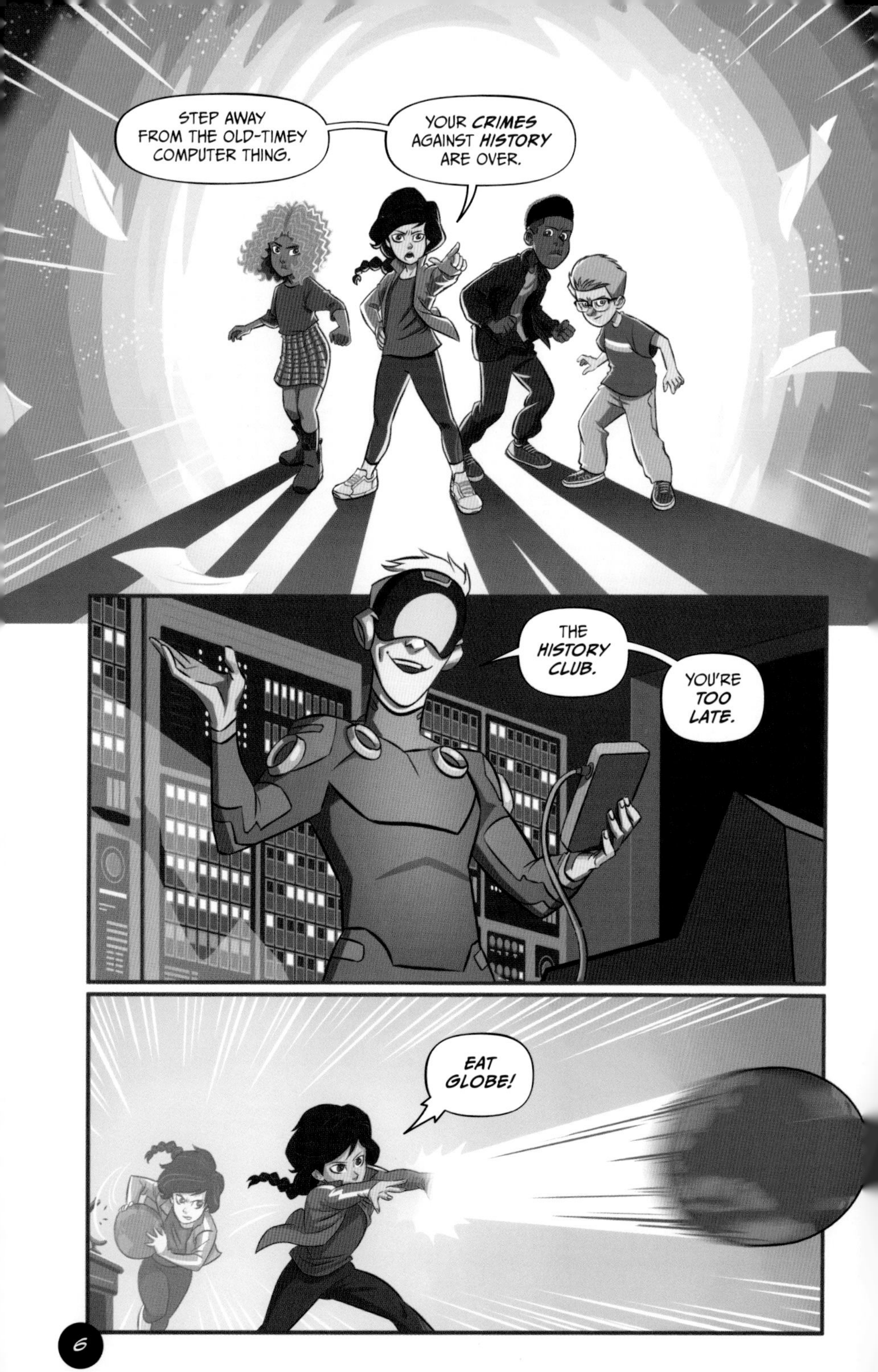
STEP AWAY FROM THE OLD-TIMEY COMPUTER THING.
YOUR CRIMES AGAINST HISTORY ARE OVER.
THE HISTORY CLUB.
YOU'RE TOO LATE.
EAT GLOBE!

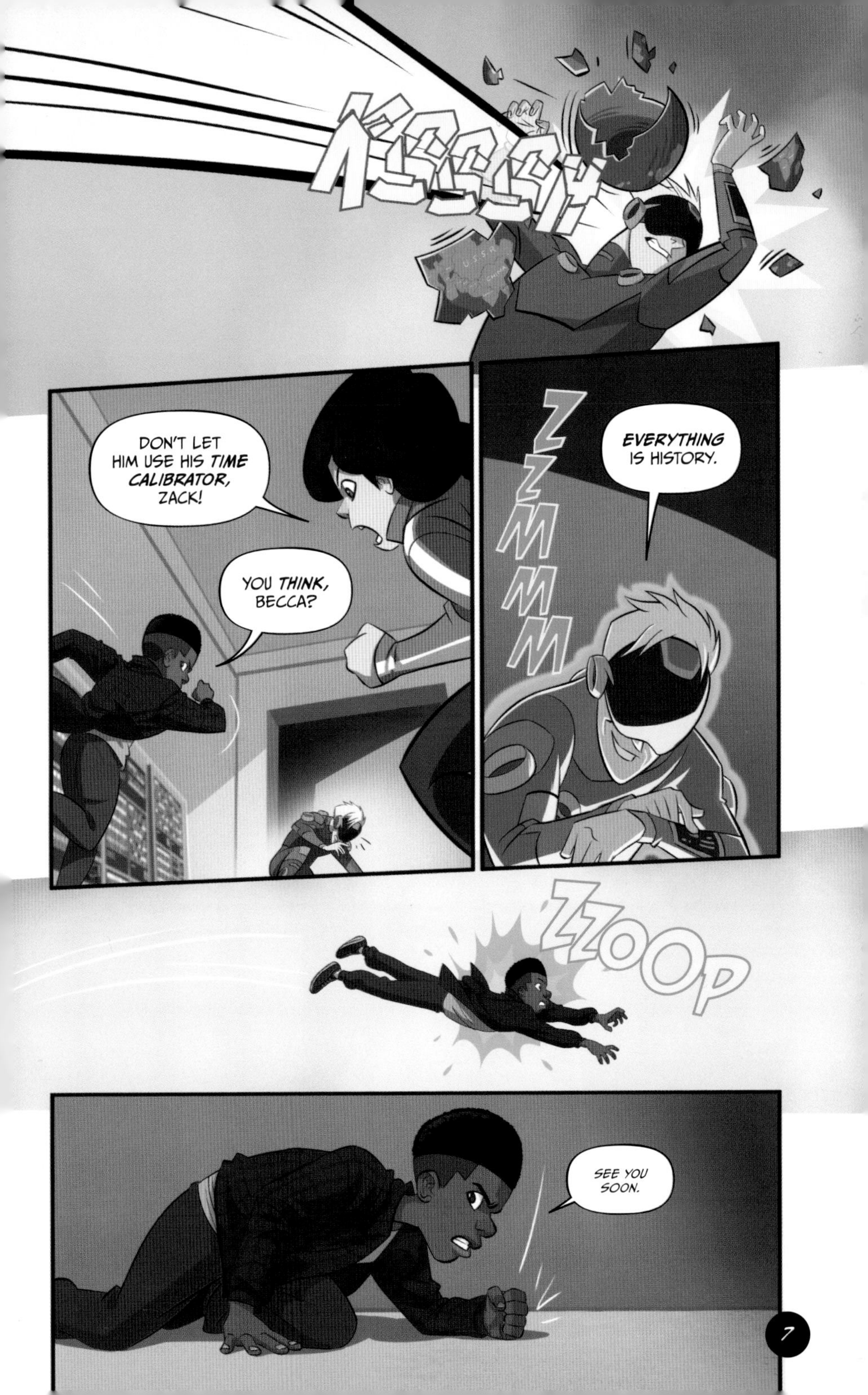
KRSSSH
DON'T LET HIM USE HIS *TIME CALIBRATOR*, ZACK!
YOU *THINK*, BECCA?
ZZMMMM
EVERYTHING IS HISTORY.
ZZOOP
SEE YOU SOON.

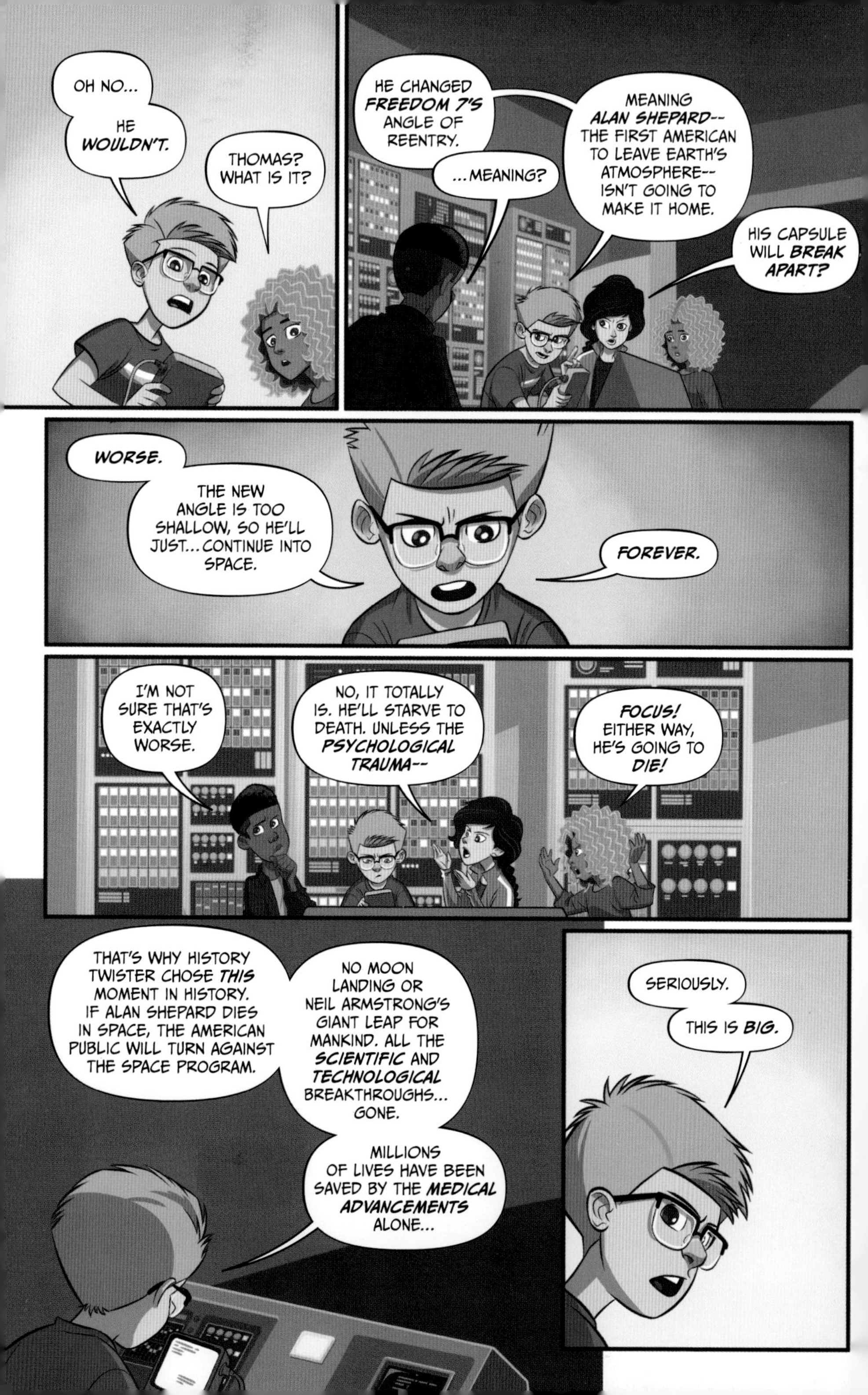
OH NO...
HE WOULDN'T.
THOMAS? WHAT IS IT?
HE CHANGED FREEDOM 7'S ANGLE OF REENTRY.
...MEANING?
MEANING ALAN SHEPARD-- THE FIRST AMERICAN TO LEAVE EARTH'S ATMOSPHERE-- ISN'T GOING TO MAKE IT HOME.
HIS CAPSULE WILL BREAK APART?
WORSE.
THE NEW ANGLE IS TOO SHALLOW, SO HE'LL JUST... CONTINUE INTO SPACE.
FOREVER.
I'M NOT SURE THAT'S EXACTLY WORSE.
NO, IT TOTALLY IS. HE'LL STARVE TO DEATH. UNLESS THE PSYCHOLOGICAL TRAUMA--
FOCUS! EITHER WAY, HE'S GOING TO DIE!
THAT'S WHY HISTORY TWISTER CHOSE THIS MOMENT IN HISTORY. IF ALAN SHEPARD DIES IN SPACE, THE AMERICAN PUBLIC WILL TURN AGAINST THE SPACE PROGRAM.
NO MOON LANDING OR NEIL ARMSTRONG'S GIANT LEAP FOR MANKIND. ALL THE SCIENTIFIC AND TECHNOLOGICAL BREAKTHROUGHS... GONE.
MILLIONS OF LIVES HAVE BEEN SAVED BY THE MEDICAL ADVANCEMENTS ALONE...
SERIOUSLY.
THIS IS BIG.

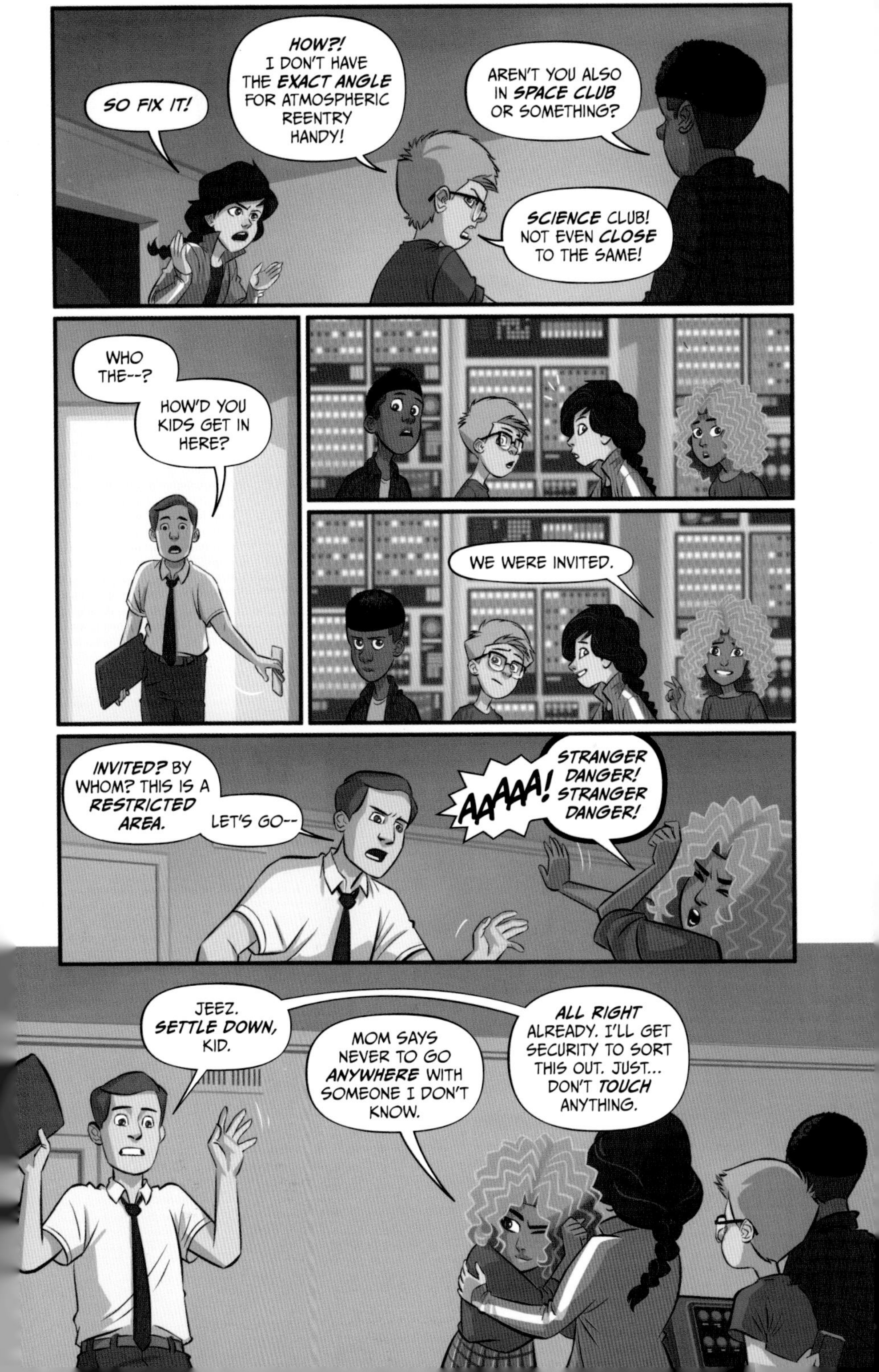
SO FIX IT!
HOW?! I DON'T HAVE THE EXACT ANGLE FOR ATMOSPHERIC REENTRY HANDY!
AREN'T YOU ALSO IN SPACE CLUB OR SOMETHING?
SCIENCE CLUB! NOT EVEN CLOSE TO THE SAME!
WHO THE--?
HOW'D YOU KIDS GET IN HERE?
WE WERE INVITED.
INVITED? BY WHOM? THIS IS A RESTRICTED AREA.
LET'S GO--
AAAAA!
STRANGER DANGER! STRANGER DANGER!
JEEZ. SETTLE DOWN, KID.
MOM SAYS NEVER TO GO ANYWHERE WITH SOMEONE I DON'T KNOW.
ALL RIGHT ALREADY. I'LL GET SECURITY TO SORT THIS OUT. JUST... DON'T TOUCH ANYTHING.

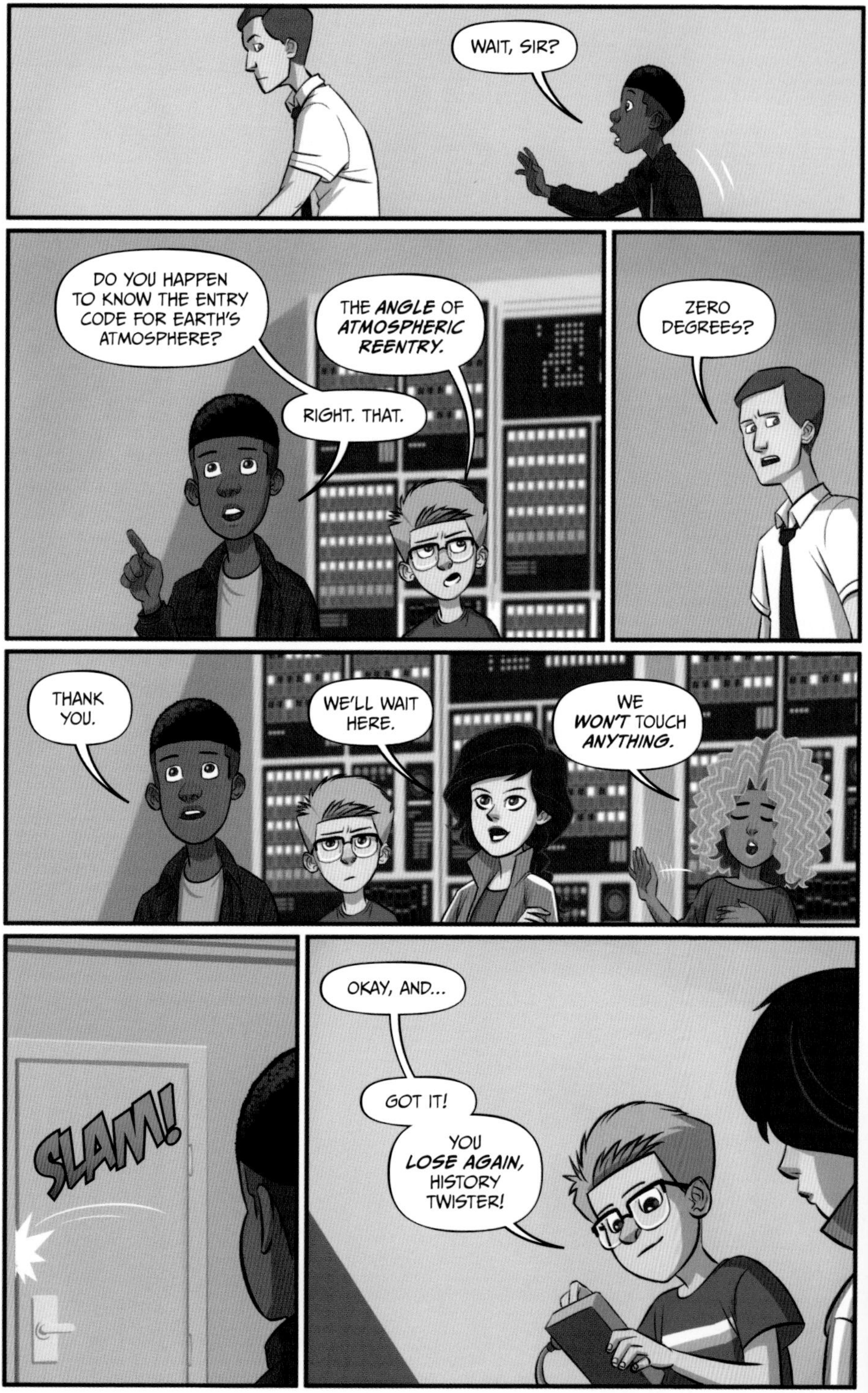
WAIT, SIR?
DO YOU HAPPEN TO KNOW THE ENTRY CODE FOR EARTH'S ATMOSPHERE?
THE *ANGLE* OF *ATMOSPHERIC REENTRY.*
RIGHT. THAT.
ZERO DEGREES?
THANK YOU.
WE'LL WAIT HERE.
WE *WON'T* TOUCH *ANYTHING.*
SLAM!
OKAY, AND...
GOT IT!
YOU *LOSE AGAIN,* HISTORY TWISTER!

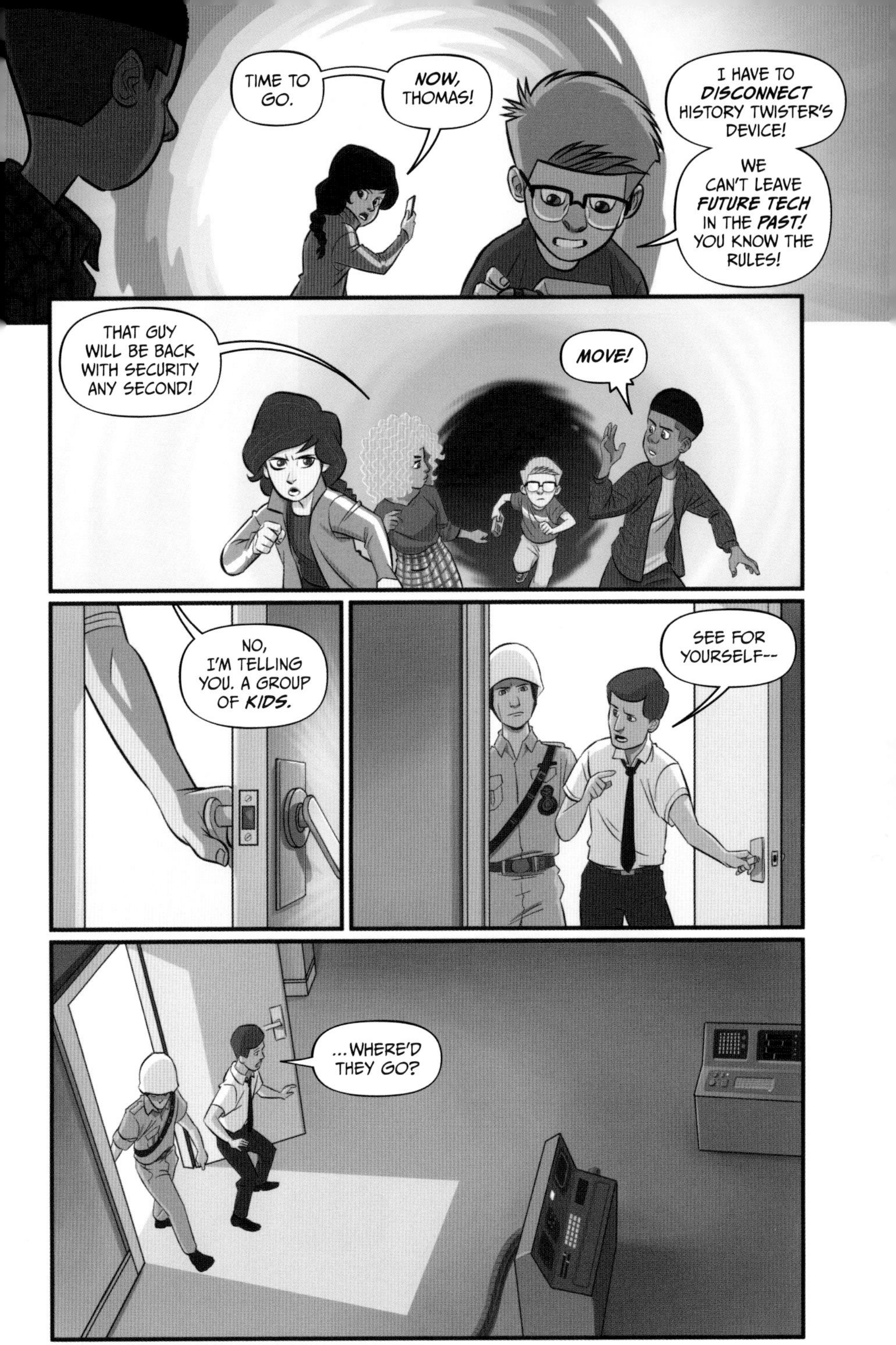
TIME TO GO.
NOW, THOMAS!
I HAVE TO DISCONNECT HISTORY TWISTER'S DEVICE!
WE CAN'T LEAVE FUTURE TECH IN THE PAST! YOU KNOW THE RULES!
THAT GUY WILL BE BACK WITH SECURITY ANY SECOND!
MOVE!
NO, I'M TELLING YOU. A GROUP OF KIDS.
SEE FOR YOURSELF--
...WHERE'D THEY GO?

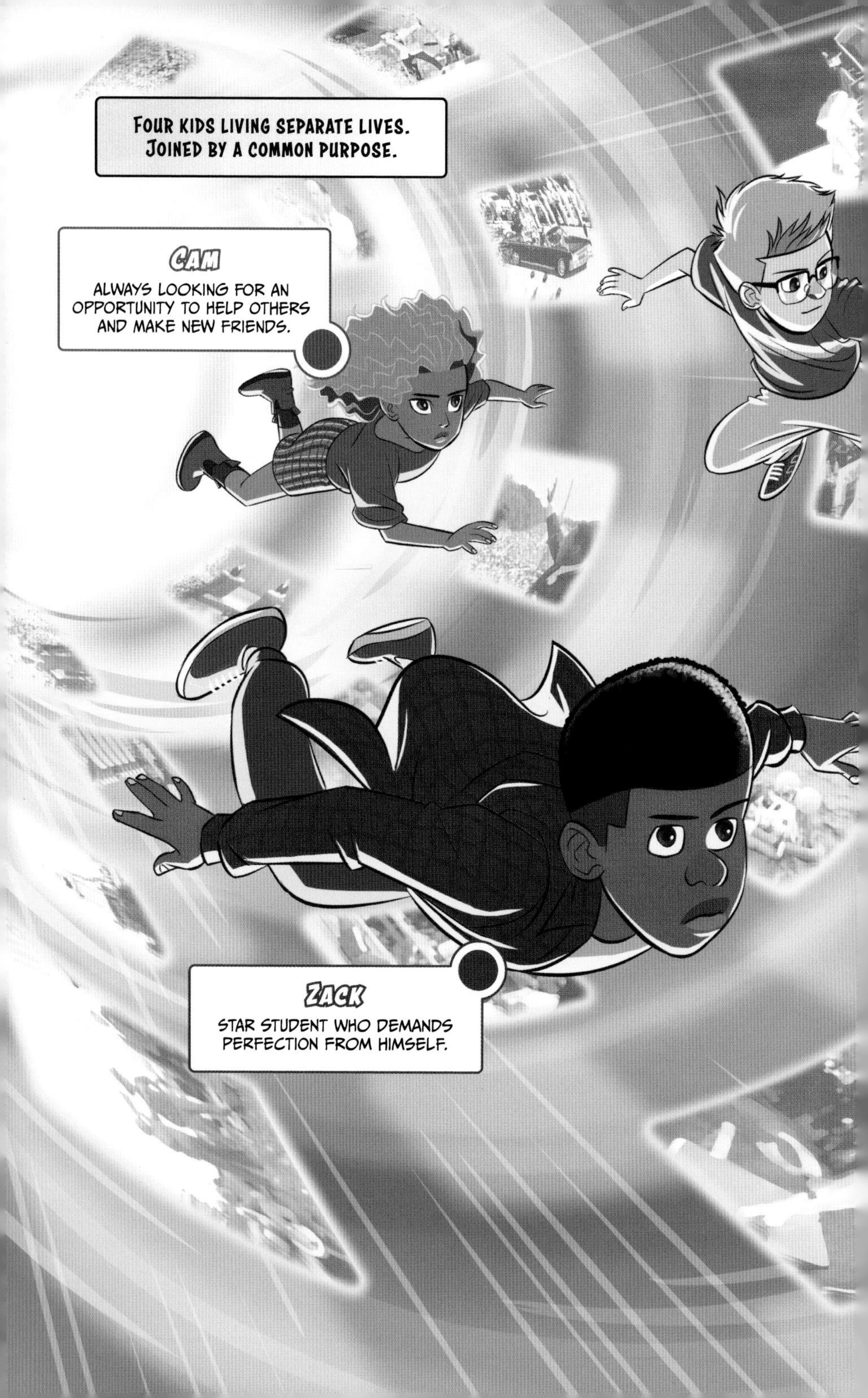

FOUR KIDS LIVING SEPARATE LIVES. JOINED BY A COMMON PURPOSE.
CAM
ALWAYS LOOKING FOR AN OPPORTUNITY TO HELP OTHERS AND MAKE NEW FRIENDS.
ZACK
STAR STUDENT WHO DEMANDS PERFECTION FROM HIMSELF.

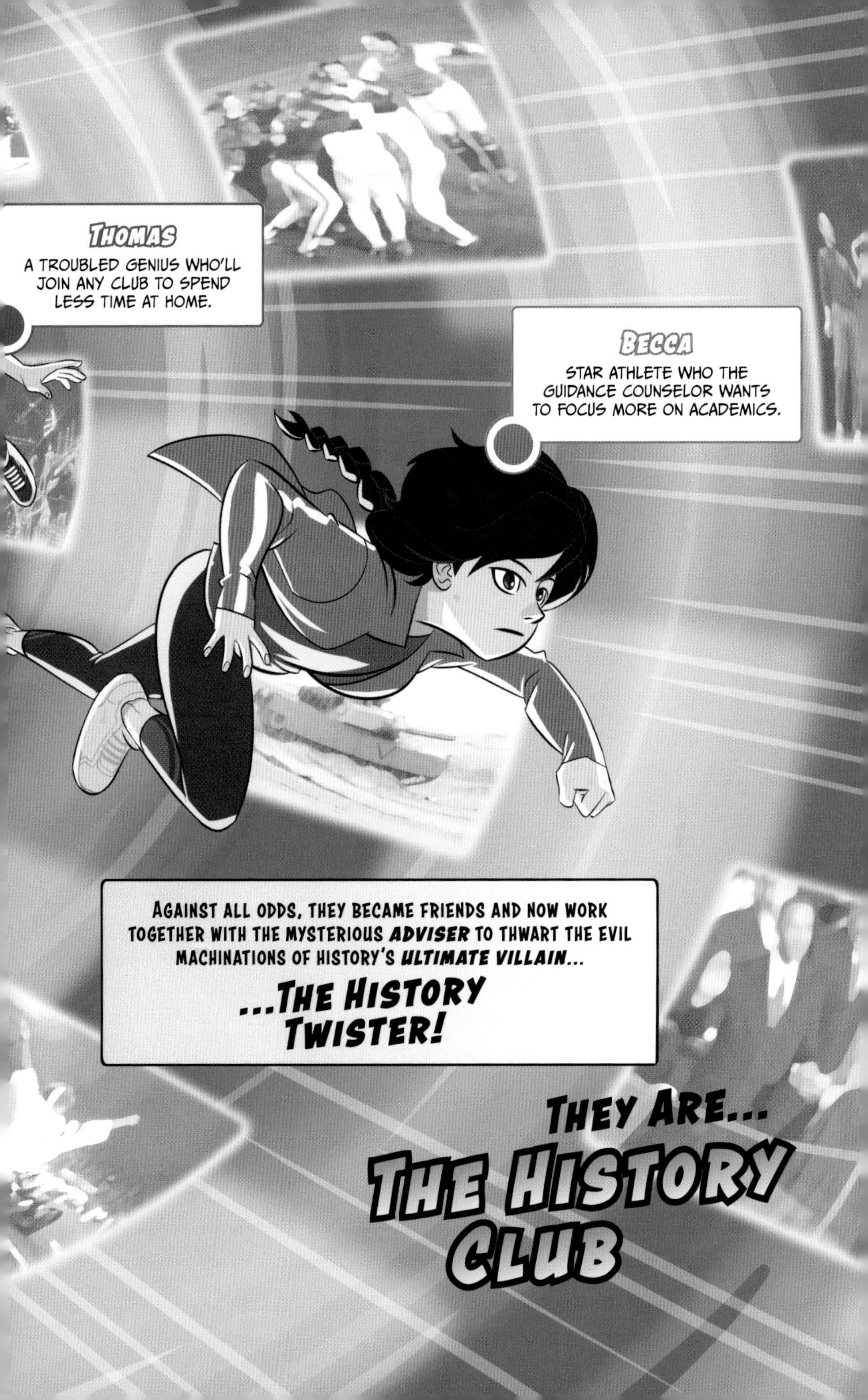
THOMAS
A TROUBLED GENIUS WHO'LL JOIN ANY CLUB TO SPEND LESS TIME AT HOME.
BECCA
STAR ATHLETE WHO THE GUIDANCE COUNSELOR WANTS TO FOCUS MORE ON ACADEMICS.
AGAINST ALL ODDS, THEY BECAME FRIENDS AND NOW WORK TOGETHER WITH THE MYSTERIOUS ADVISER TO THWART THE EVIL MACHINATIONS OF HISTORY'S ULTIMATE VILLAIN...
...THE HISTORY TWISTER!
THEY ARE...
THE HISTORY CLUB

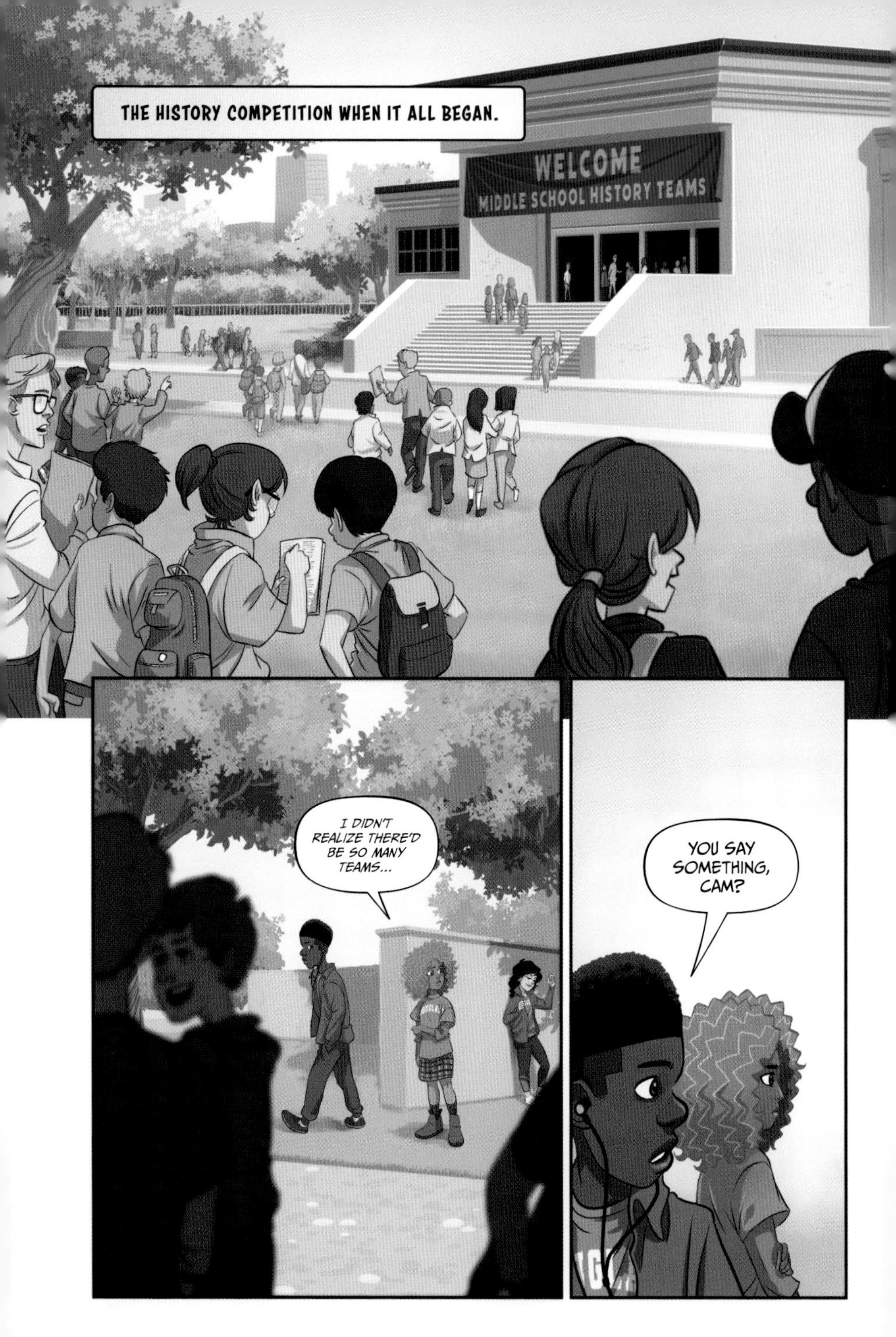
THE HISTORY COMPETITION WHEN IT ALL BEGAN.
WELCOME
MIDDLE SCHOOL HISTORY TEAMS
I DIDN'T REALIZE THERE'D BE SO MANY TEAMS...
YOU SAY SOMETHING, CAM?

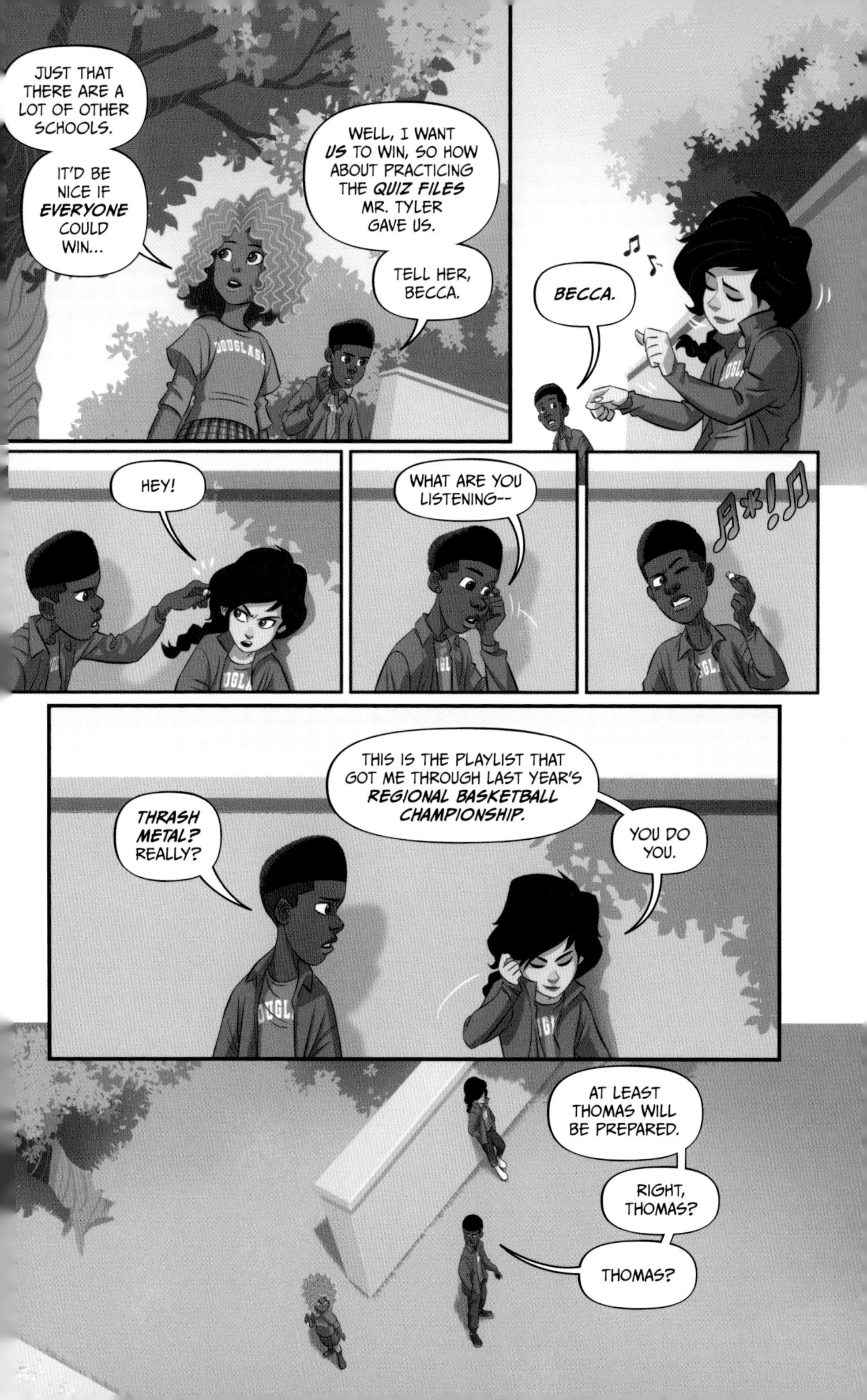
JUST THAT THERE ARE A LOT OF OTHER SCHOOLS.
IT'D BE NICE IF EVERYONE COULD WIN...
WELL, I WANT US TO WIN, SO HOW ABOUT PRACTICING THE QUIZ FILES MR. TYLER GAVE US.
TELL HER, BECCA.
BECCA.
HEY!
WHAT ARE YOU LISTENING--
THIS IS THE PLAYLIST THAT GOT ME THROUGH LAST YEAR'S REGIONAL BASKETBALL CHAMPIONSHIP.
THRASH METAL? REALLY?
YOU DO YOU.
AT LEAST THOMAS WILL BE PREPARED.
RIGHT, THOMAS?
THOMAS?

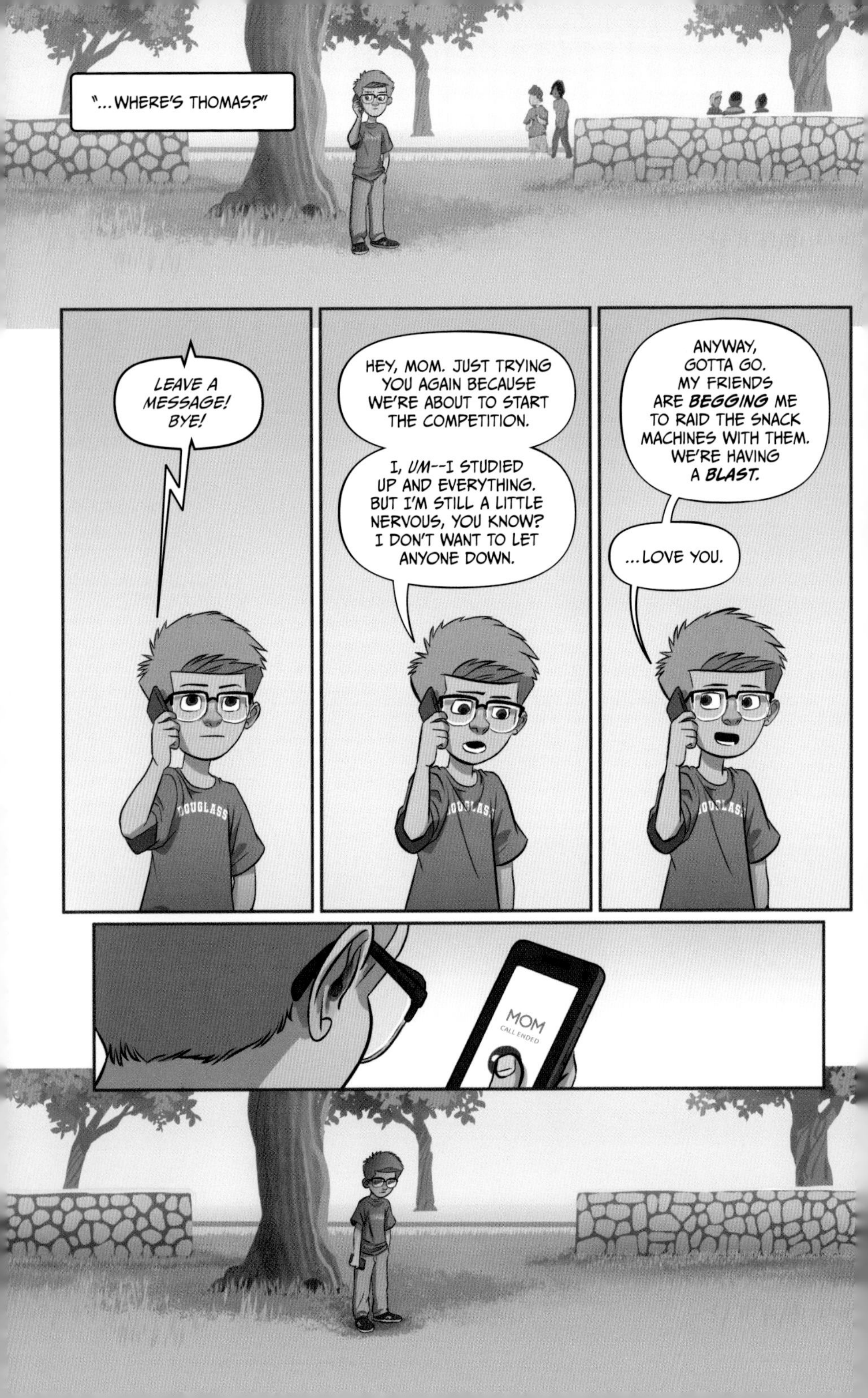
"...WHERE'S THOMAS?"
LEAVE A MESSAGE! BYE!
HEY, MOM. JUST TRYING YOU AGAIN BECAUSE WE'RE ABOUT TO START THE COMPETITION.
I, *UM*--I STUDIED UP AND EVERYTHING. BUT I'M STILL A LITTLE NERVOUS, YOU KNOW? I DON'T WANT TO LET ANYONE DOWN.
ANYWAY, GOTTA GO. MY FRIENDS ARE ***BEGGING*** ME TO RAID THE SNACK MACHINES WITH THEM. WE'RE HAVING A ***BLAST.***
...LOVE YOU.
DOUGLASS
MOM
CALL ENDED

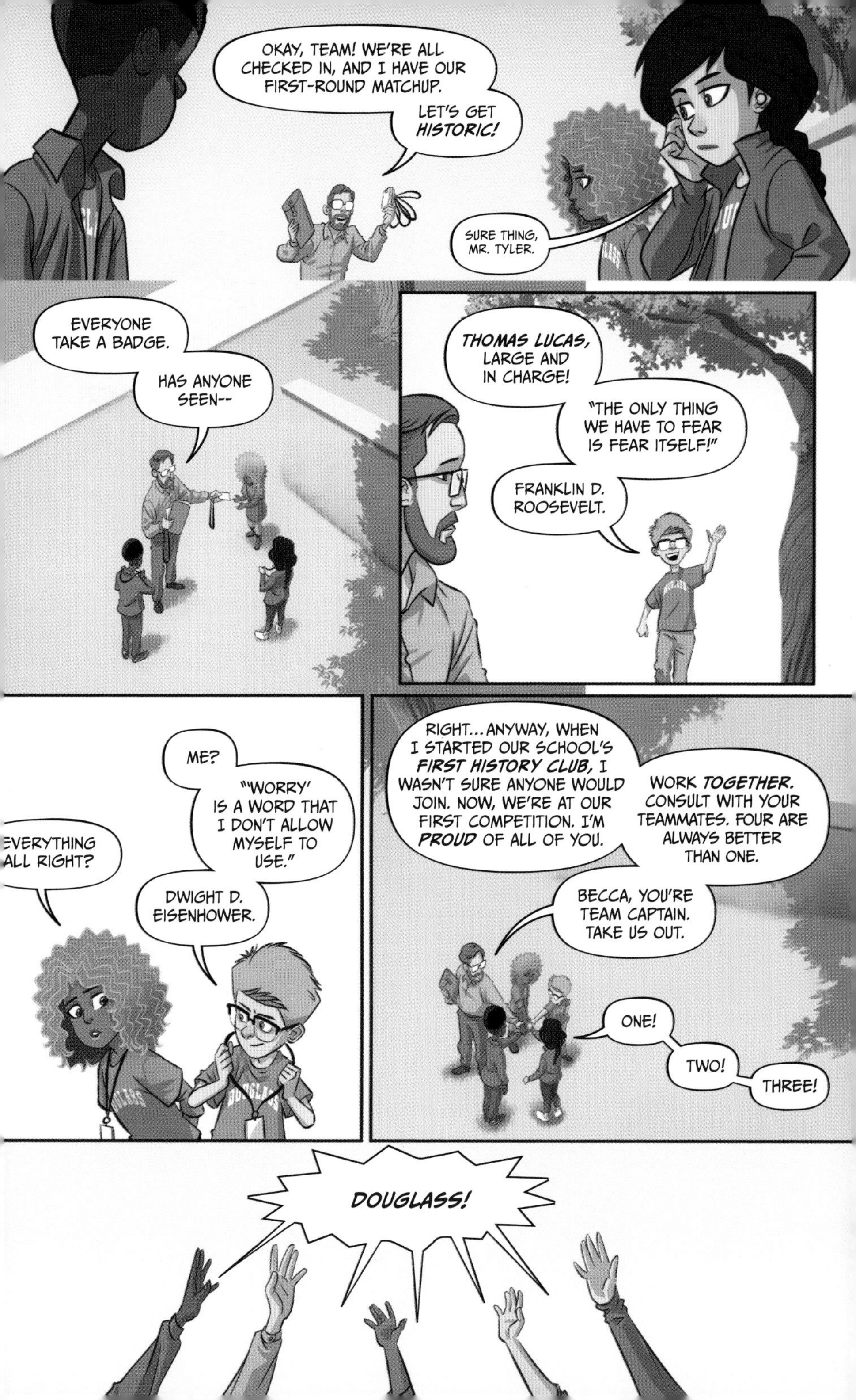
OKAY, TEAM! WE'RE ALL CHECKED IN, AND I HAVE OUR FIRST-ROUND MATCHUP.
LET'S GET *HISTORIC!*
SURE THING, MR. TYLER.
EVERYONE TAKE A BADGE.
HAS ANYONE SEEN--
THOMAS LUCAS, LARGE AND IN CHARGE!
"THE ONLY THING WE HAVE TO FEAR IS FEAR ITSELF!"
FRANKLIN D. ROOSEVELT.
EVERYTHING ALL RIGHT?
ME?
"'WORRY' IS A WORD THAT I DON'T ALLOW MYSELF TO USE."
DWIGHT D. EISENHOWER.
RIGHT... ANYWAY, WHEN I STARTED OUR SCHOOL'S *FIRST HISTORY CLUB,* I WASN'T SURE ANYONE WOULD JOIN. NOW, WE'RE AT OUR FIRST COMPETITION. I'M *PROUD* OF ALL OF YOU.
WORK *TOGETHER.* CONSULT WITH YOUR TEAMMATES. FOUR ARE ALWAYS BETTER THAN ONE.
BECCA, YOU'RE TEAM CAPTAIN. TAKE US OUT.
ONE!
TWO!
THREE!
DOUGLASS!

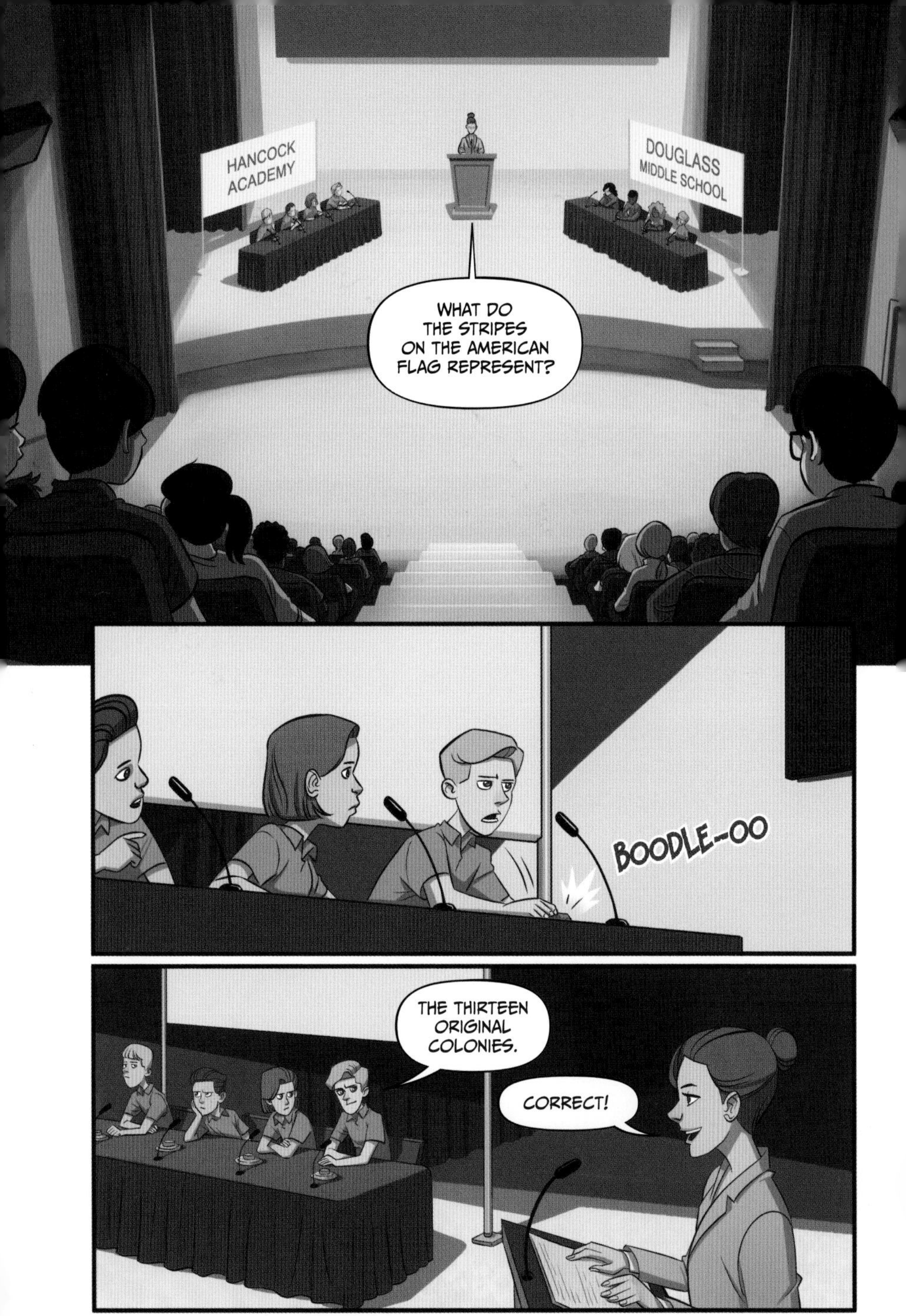
HANCOCK ACADEMY
DOUGLASS MIDDLE SCHOOL
WHAT DO THE STRIPES ON THE AMERICAN FLAG REPRESENT?
BOODLE-OO
THE THIRTEEN ORIGINAL COLONIES.
CORRECT!

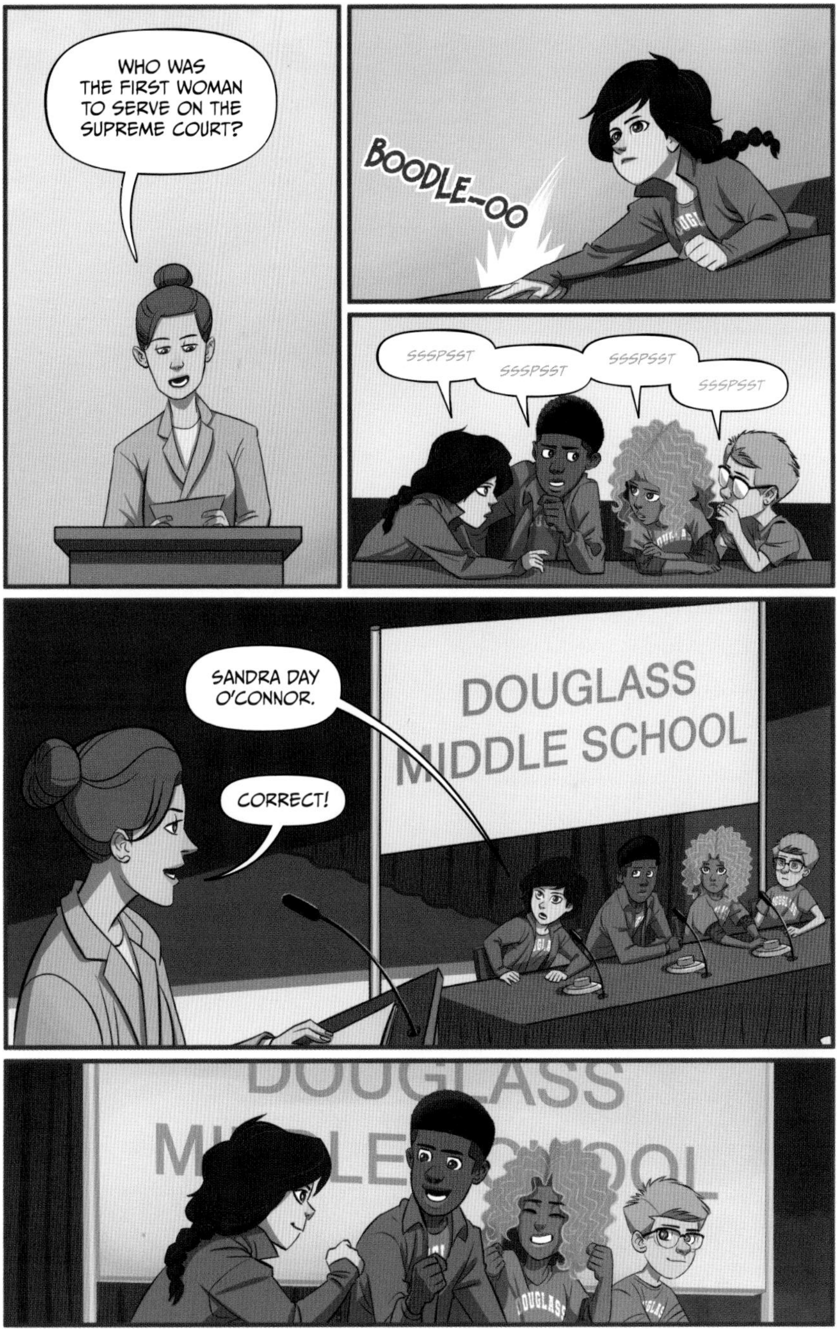
WHO WAS THE FIRST WOMAN TO SERVE ON THE SUPREME COURT?
BOODLE-OO
SSSPSST
SSSPSST
SSSPSST
SSSPSST
DOUGLASS MIDDLE SCHOOL
SANDRA DAY O'CONNOR.
CORRECT!
DOUGLASS

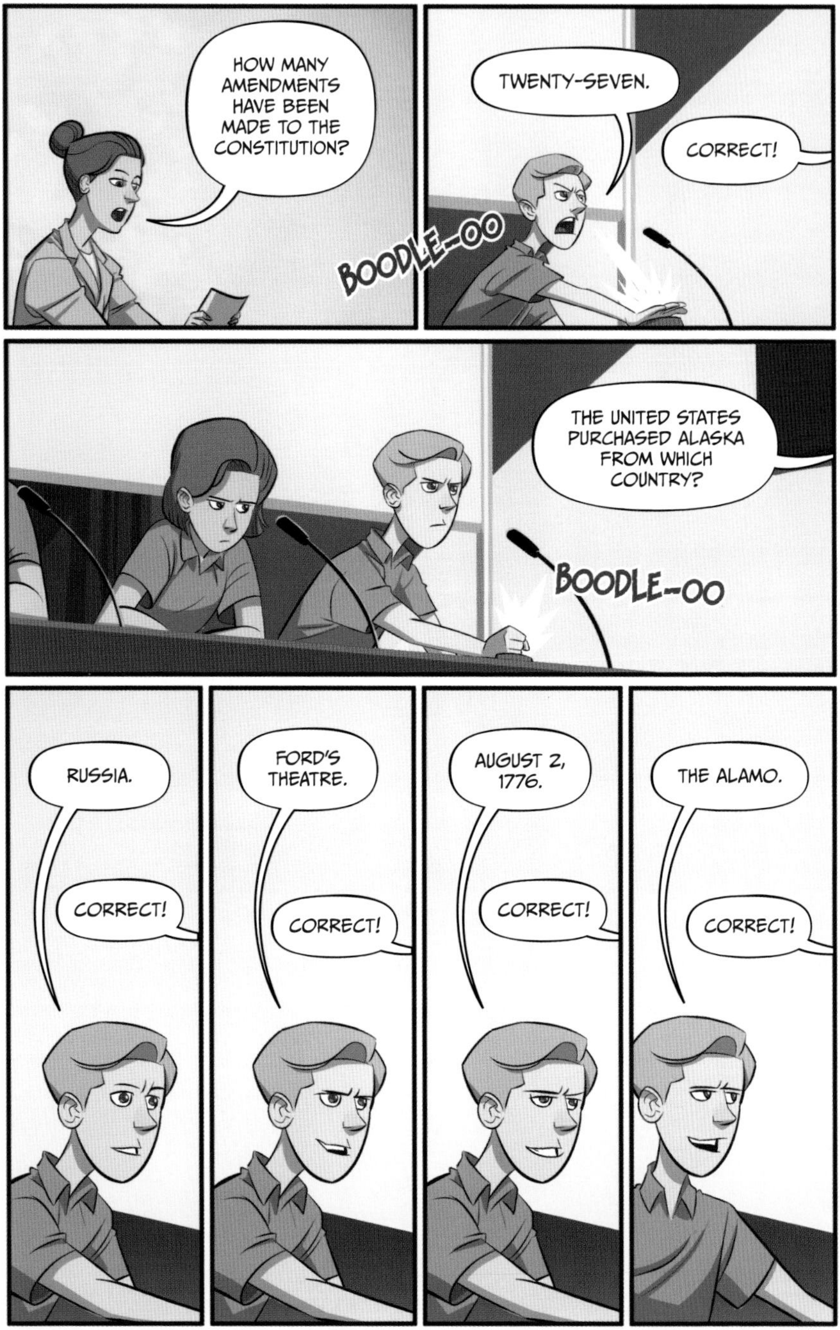
HOW MANY AMENDMENTS HAVE BEEN MADE TO THE CONSTITUTION?
TWENTY-SEVEN.
BOODLE-OO
CORRECT!
THE UNITED STATES PURCHASED ALASKA FROM WHICH COUNTRY?
BOODLE-OO
RUSSIA.
CORRECT!
FORD'S THEATRE.
CORRECT!
AUGUST 2, 1776.
CORRECT!
THE ALAMO.
CORRECT!

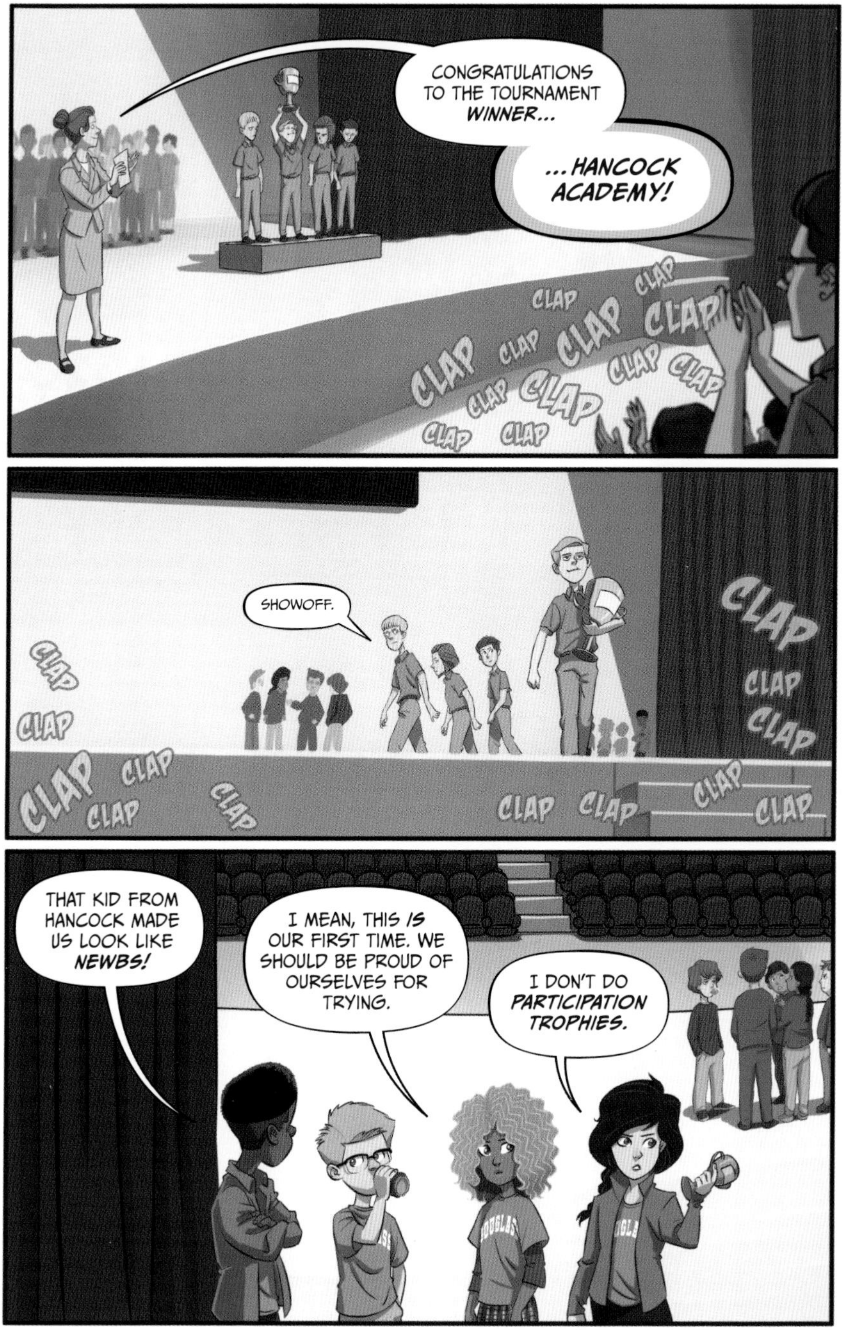
CONGRATULATIONS TO THE TOURNAMENT WINNER...
...HANCOCK ACADEMY!
CLAP CLAP CLAP CLAP CLAP CLAP CLAP CLAP CLAP CLAP CLAP CLAP
SHOWOFF.
CLAP CLAP CLAP CLAP CLAP CLAP CLAP CLAP CLAP CLAP CLAP CLAP CLAP
THAT KID FROM HANCOCK MADE US LOOK LIKE NEWBS!
I MEAN, THIS IS OUR FIRST TIME. WE SHOULD BE PROUD OF OURSELVES FOR TRYING.
I DON'T DO PARTICIPATION TROPHIES.

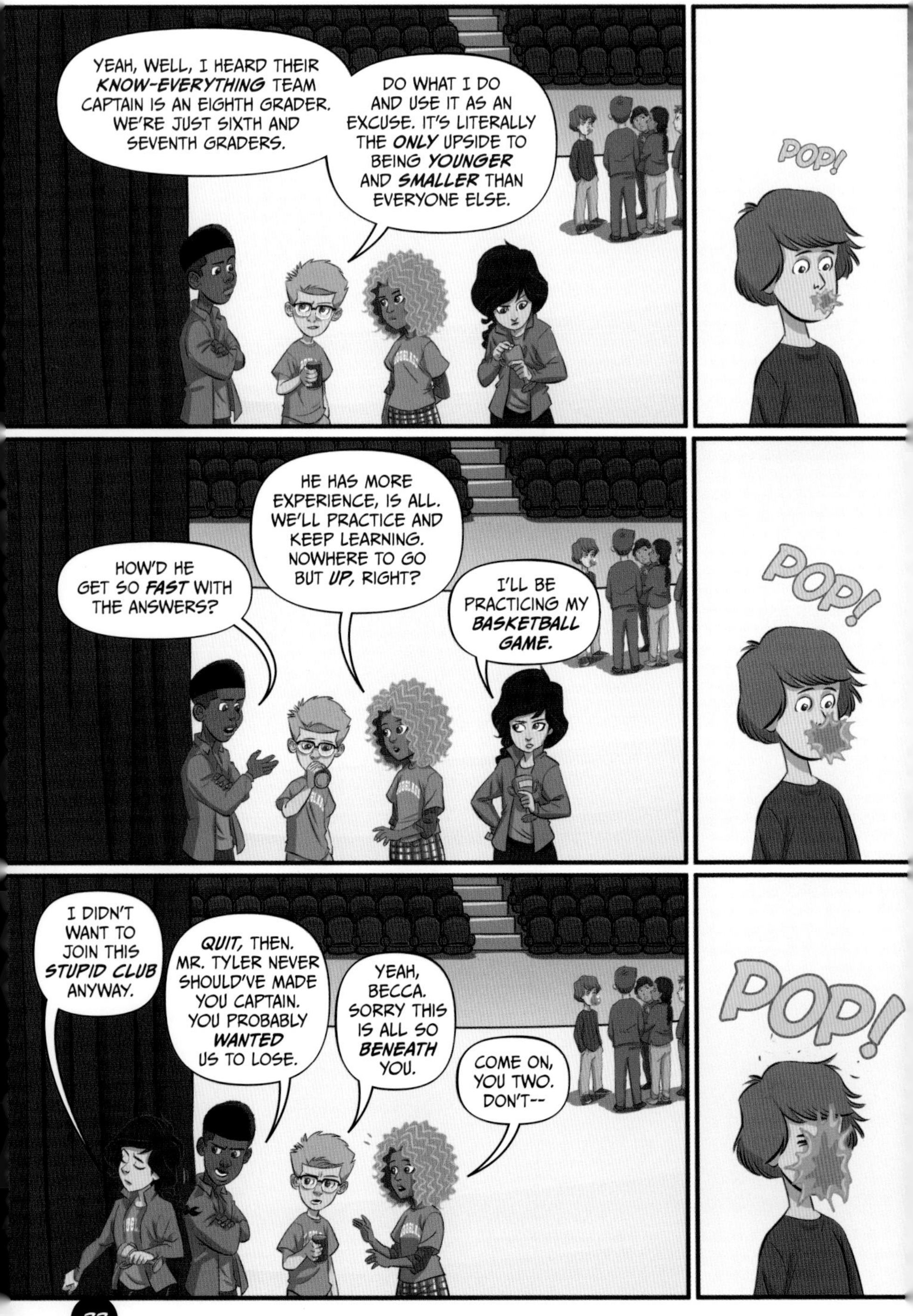
YEAH, WELL, I HEARD THEIR KNOW-EVERYTHING TEAM CAPTAIN IS AN EIGHTH GRADER. WE'RE JUST SIXTH AND SEVENTH GRADERS.
DO WHAT I DO AND USE IT AS AN EXCUSE. IT'S LITERALLY THE ONLY UPSIDE TO BEING YOUNGER AND SMALLER THAN EVERYONE ELSE.
POP!
HOW'D HE GET SO FAST WITH THE ANSWERS?
HE HAS MORE EXPERIENCE, IS ALL. WE'LL PRACTICE AND KEEP LEARNING. NOWHERE TO GO BUT UP, RIGHT?
I'LL BE PRACTICING MY BASKETBALL GAME.
POP!
I DIDN'T WANT TO JOIN THIS STUPID CLUB ANYWAY.
QUIT, THEN. MR. TYLER NEVER SHOULD'VE MADE YOU CAPTAIN. YOU PROBABLY WANTED US TO LOSE.
YEAH, BECCA. SORRY THIS IS ALL SO BENEATH YOU.
COME ON, YOU TWO. DON'T--
POP!

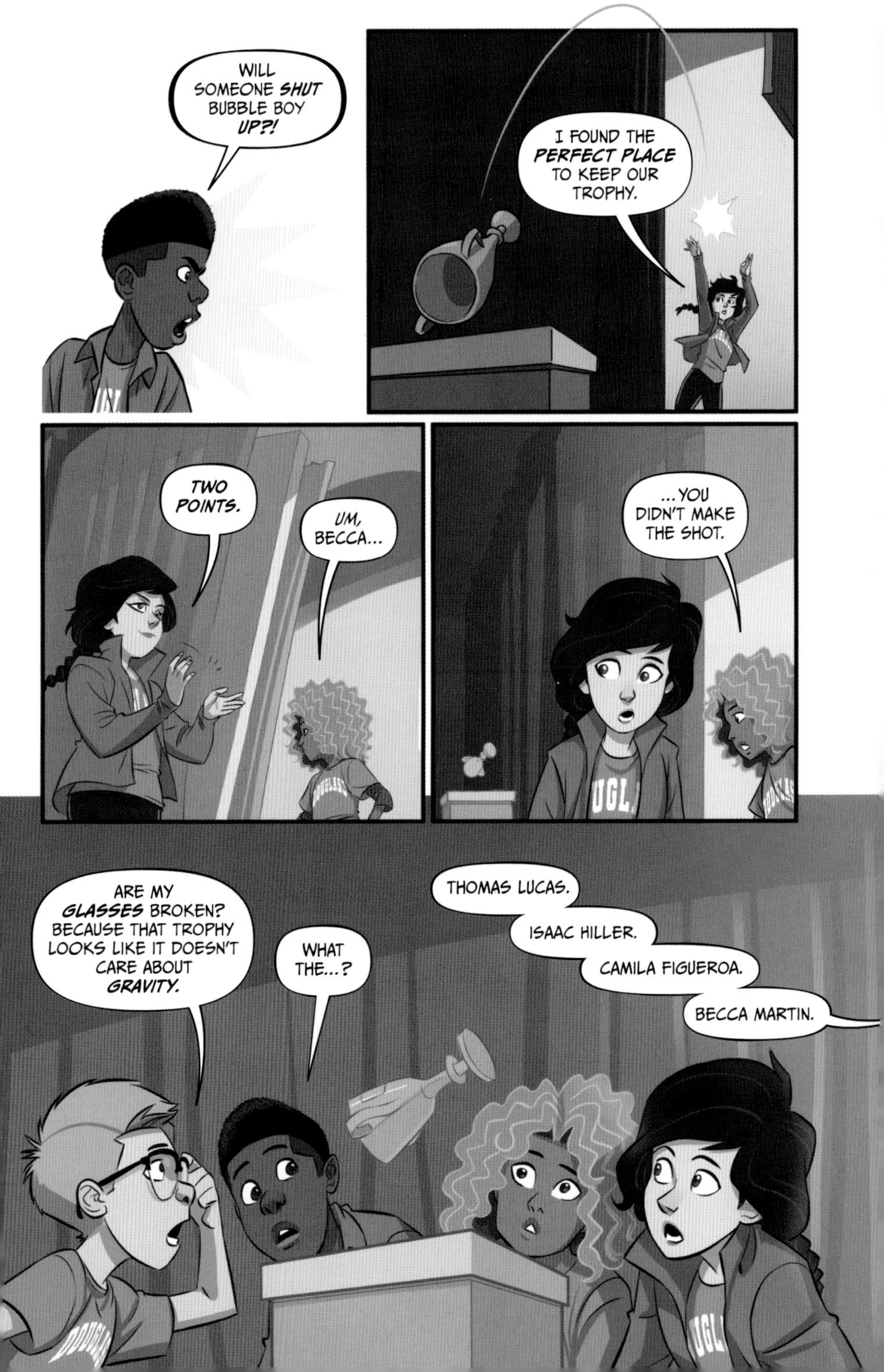
WILL SOMEONE SHUT BUBBLE BOY UP?!
I FOUND THE PERFECT PLACE TO KEEP OUR TROPHY.
TWO POINTS.
UM, BECCA...
...YOU DIDN'T MAKE THE SHOT.
ARE MY GLASSES BROKEN? BECAUSE THAT TROPHY LOOKS LIKE IT DOESN'T CARE ABOUT GRAVITY.
WHAT THE...?
THOMAS LUCAS.
ISAAC HILLER.
CAMILA FIGUEROA.
BECCA MARTIN.

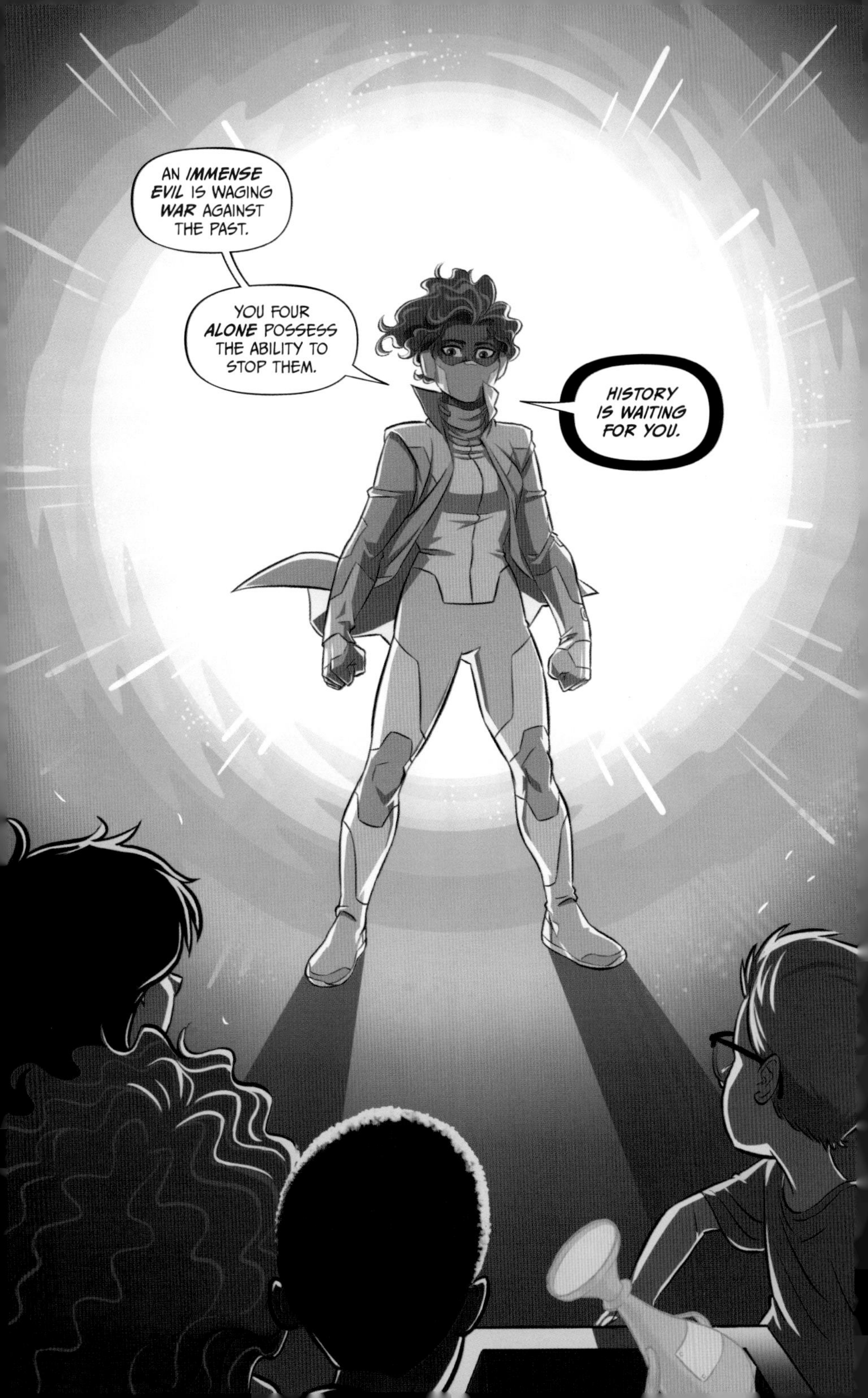
AN IMMENSE EVIL IS WAGING WAR AGAINST THE PAST.
YOU FOUR ALONE POSSESS THE ABILITY TO STOP THEM.
HISTORY IS WAITING FOR YOU.

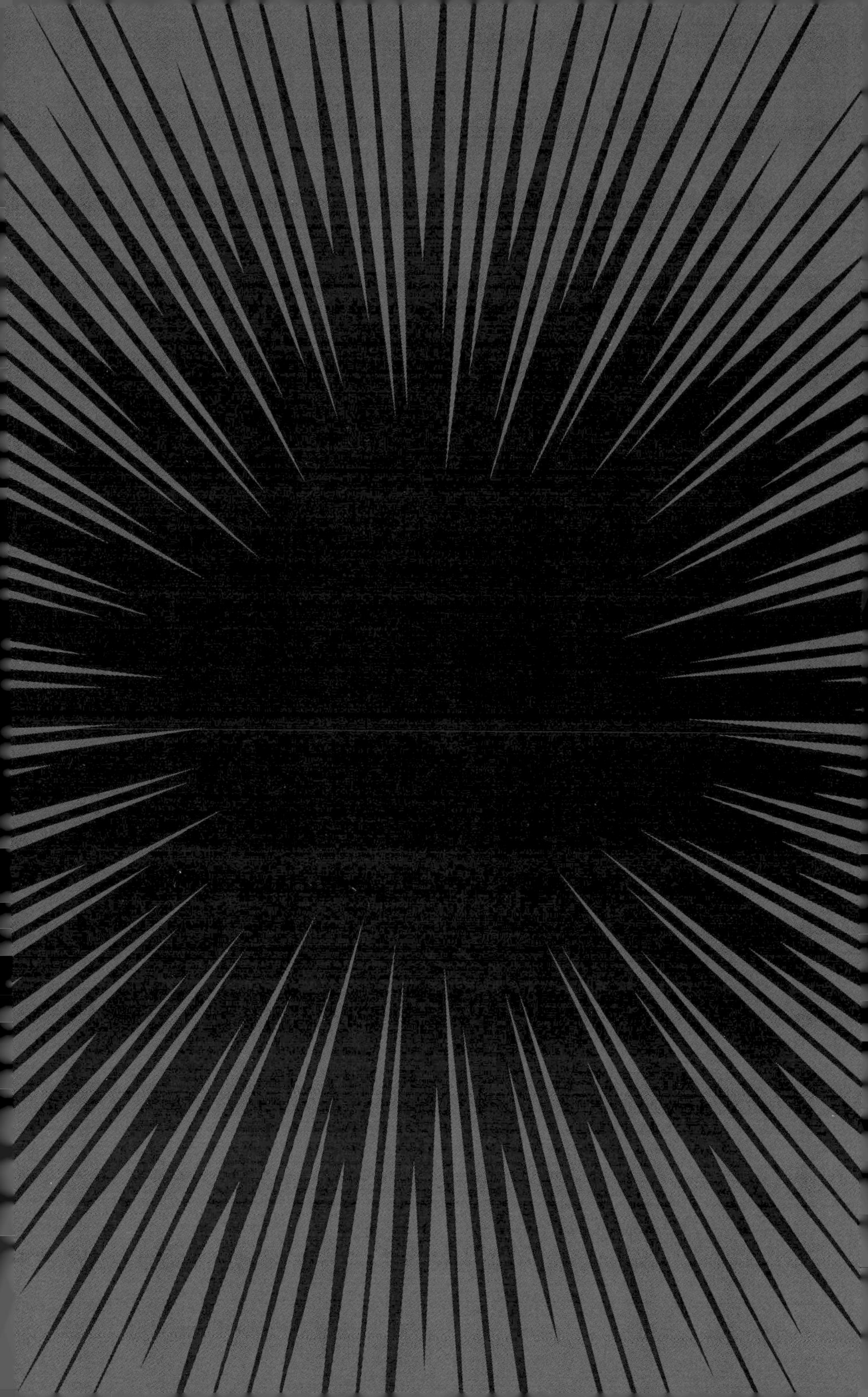

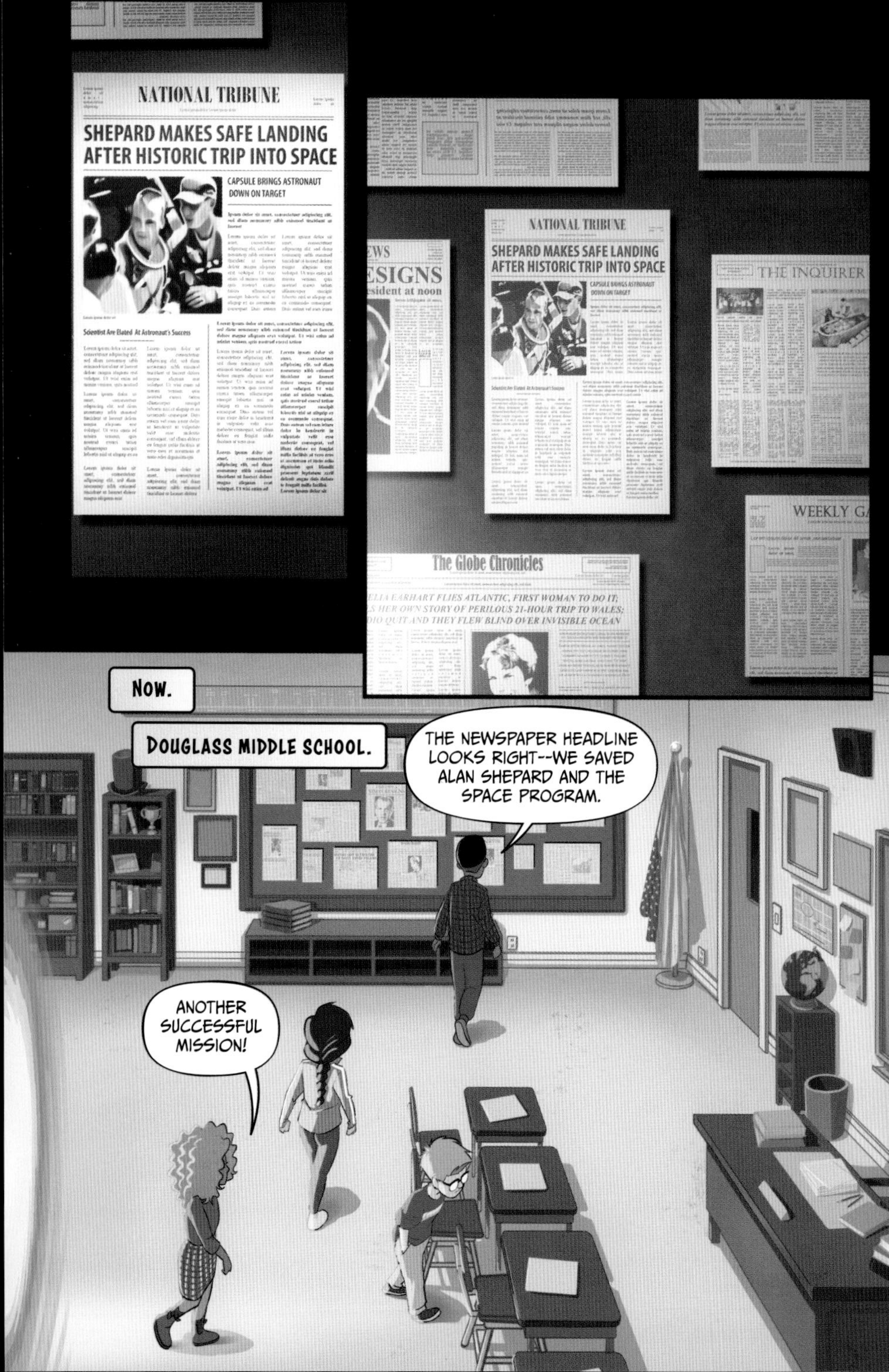
NATIONAL TRIBUNE
SHEPARD MAKES SAFE LANDING AFTER HISTORIC TRIP INTO SPACE
CAPSULE BRINGS ASTRONAUT DOWN ON TARGET
Scientist Are Elated At Astronaut's Success
NATIONAL TRIBUNE
SHEPARD MAKES SAFE LANDING AFTER HISTORIC TRIP INTO SPACE
CAPSULE BRINGS ASTRONAUT DOWN ON TARGET
THE INQUIRER
WEEKLY GA
The Globe Chronicles
ELIA EARHART FLIES ATLANTIC, FIRST WOMAN TO DO IT;
LS HER OWN STORY OF PERILOUS 21-HOUR TRIP TO WALES;
DIO QUIT AND THEY FLEW BLIND OVER INVISIBLE OCEAN
Now.
Douglass Middle School.
THE NEWSPAPER HEADLINE LOOKS RIGHT--WE SAVED ALAN SHEPARD AND THE SPACE PROGRAM.
ANOTHER SUCCESSFUL MISSION!

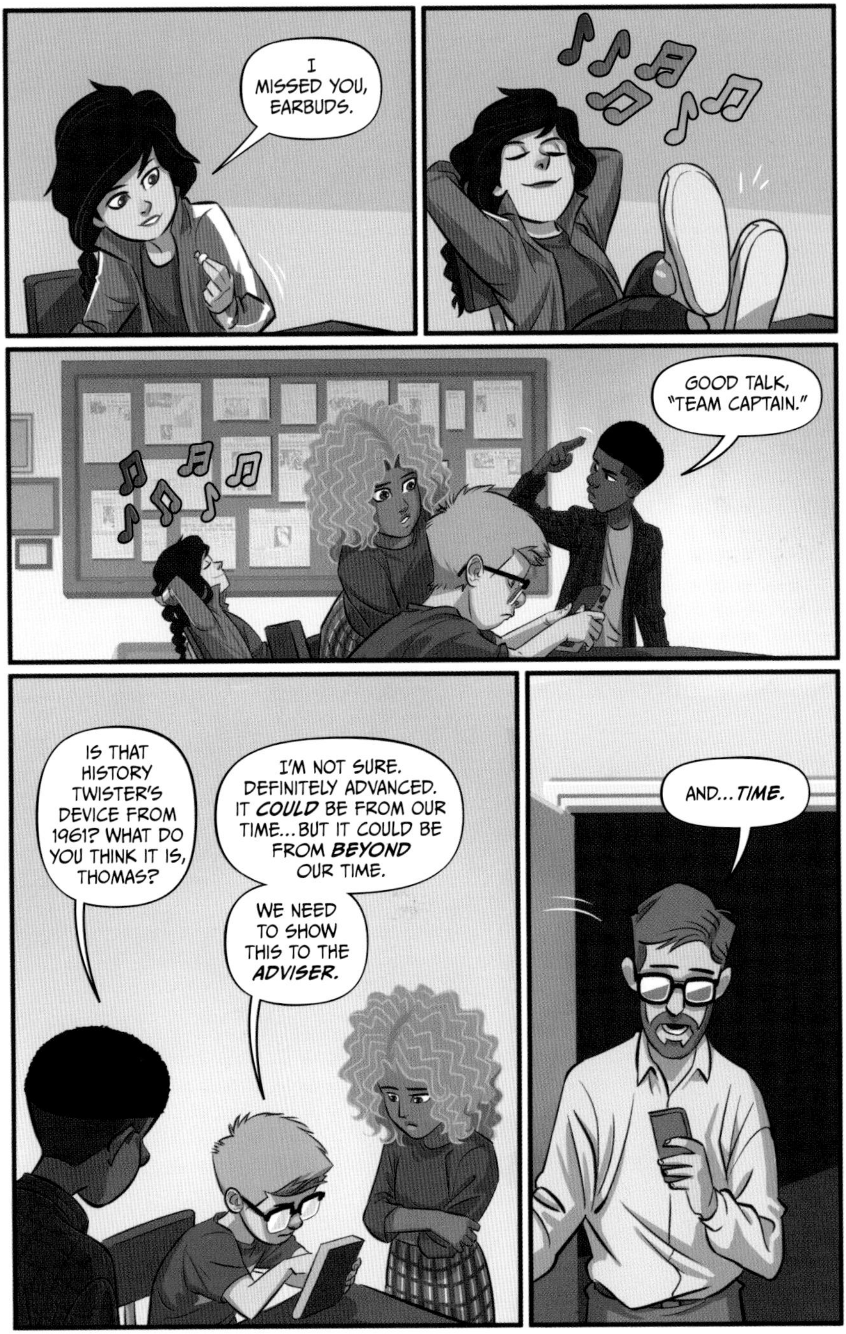
I MISSED YOU, EARBUDS.
GOOD TALK, "TEAM CAPTAIN."
IS THAT HISTORY TWISTER'S DEVICE FROM 1961? WHAT DO YOU THINK IT IS, THOMAS?
I'M NOT SURE. DEFINITELY ADVANCED. IT *COULD* BE FROM OUR TIME...BUT IT COULD BE FROM *BEYOND* OUR TIME.
WE NEED TO SHOW THIS TO THE *ADVISER.*
AND...*TIME.*

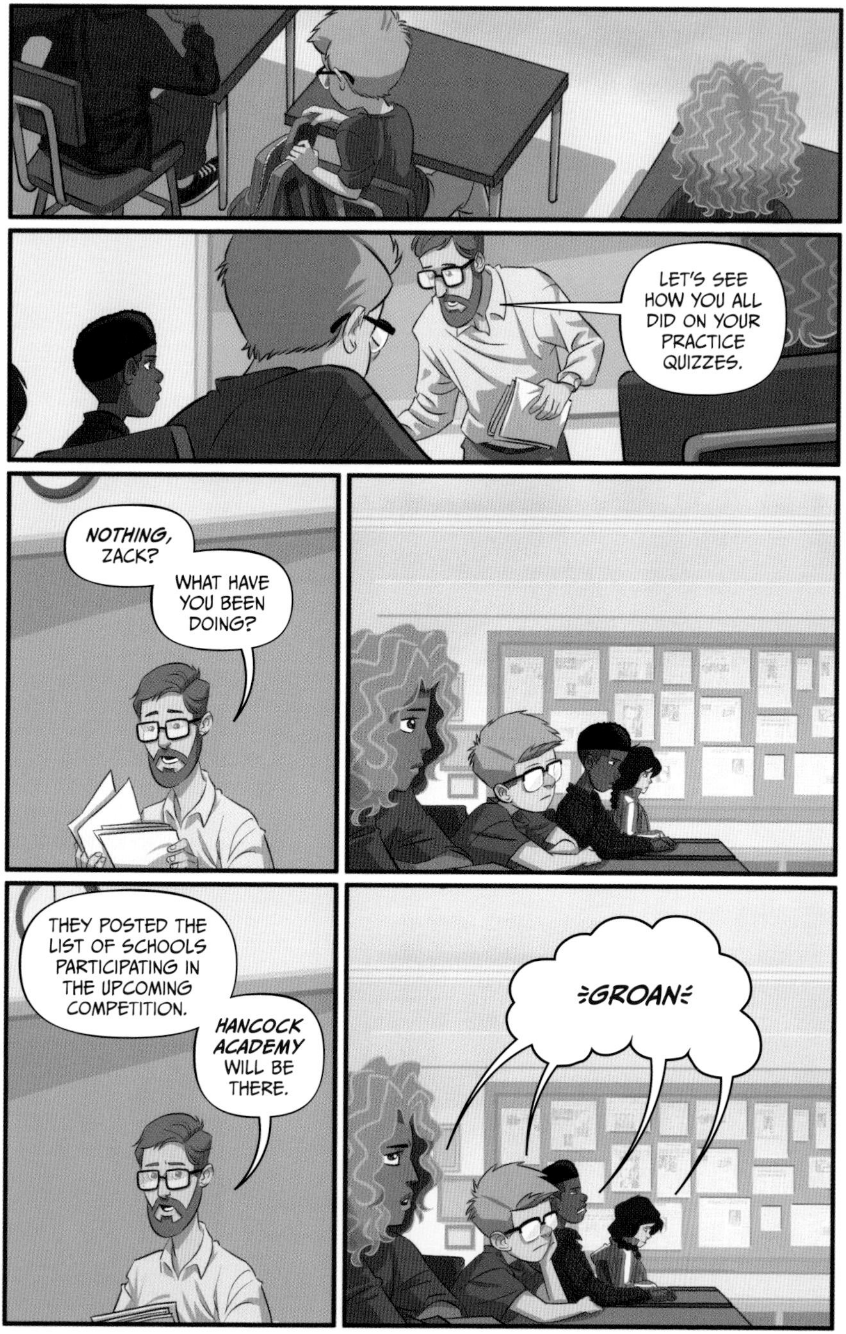
LET'S SEE HOW YOU ALL DID ON YOUR PRACTICE QUIZZES.
NOTHING, ZACK?
WHAT HAVE YOU BEEN DOING?
THEY POSTED THE LIST OF SCHOOLS PARTICIPATING IN THE UPCOMING COMPETITION.
HANCOCK ACADEMY WILL BE THERE.
GROAN

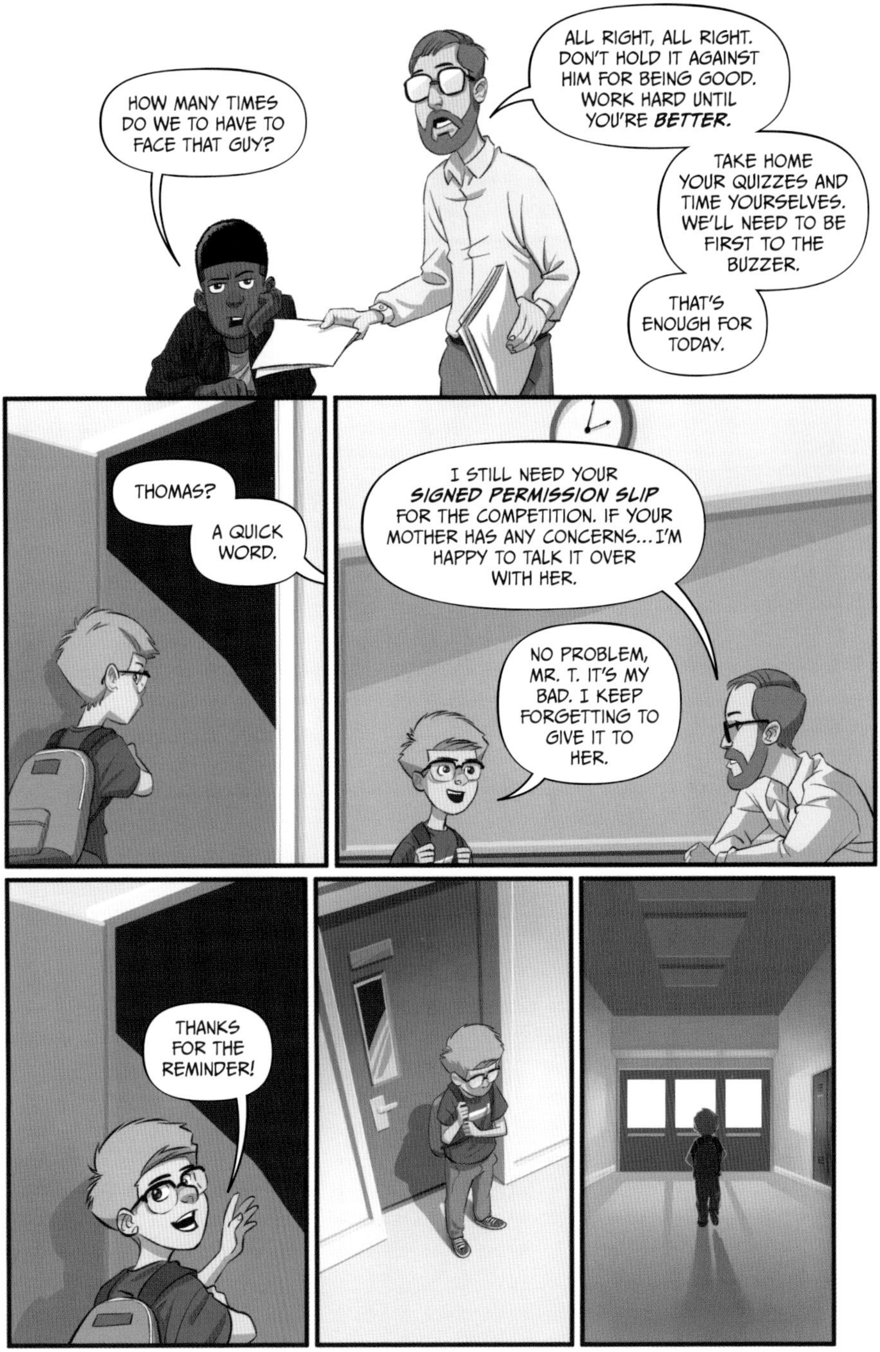
HOW MANY TIMES DO WE TO HAVE TO FACE THAT GUY?
ALL RIGHT, ALL RIGHT. DON'T HOLD IT AGAINST HIM FOR BEING GOOD. WORK HARD UNTIL YOU'RE ***BETTER.***
TAKE HOME YOUR QUIZZES AND TIME YOURSELVES. WE'LL NEED TO BE FIRST TO THE BUZZER.
THAT'S ENOUGH FOR TODAY.
THOMAS?
A QUICK WORD.
I STILL NEED YOUR ***SIGNED PERMISSION SLIP*** FOR THE COMPETITION. IF YOUR MOTHER HAS ANY CONCERNS...I'M HAPPY TO TALK IT OVER WITH HER.
NO PROBLEM, MR. T. IT'S MY BAD. I KEEP FORGETTING TO GIVE IT TO HER.
THANKS FOR THE REMINDER!

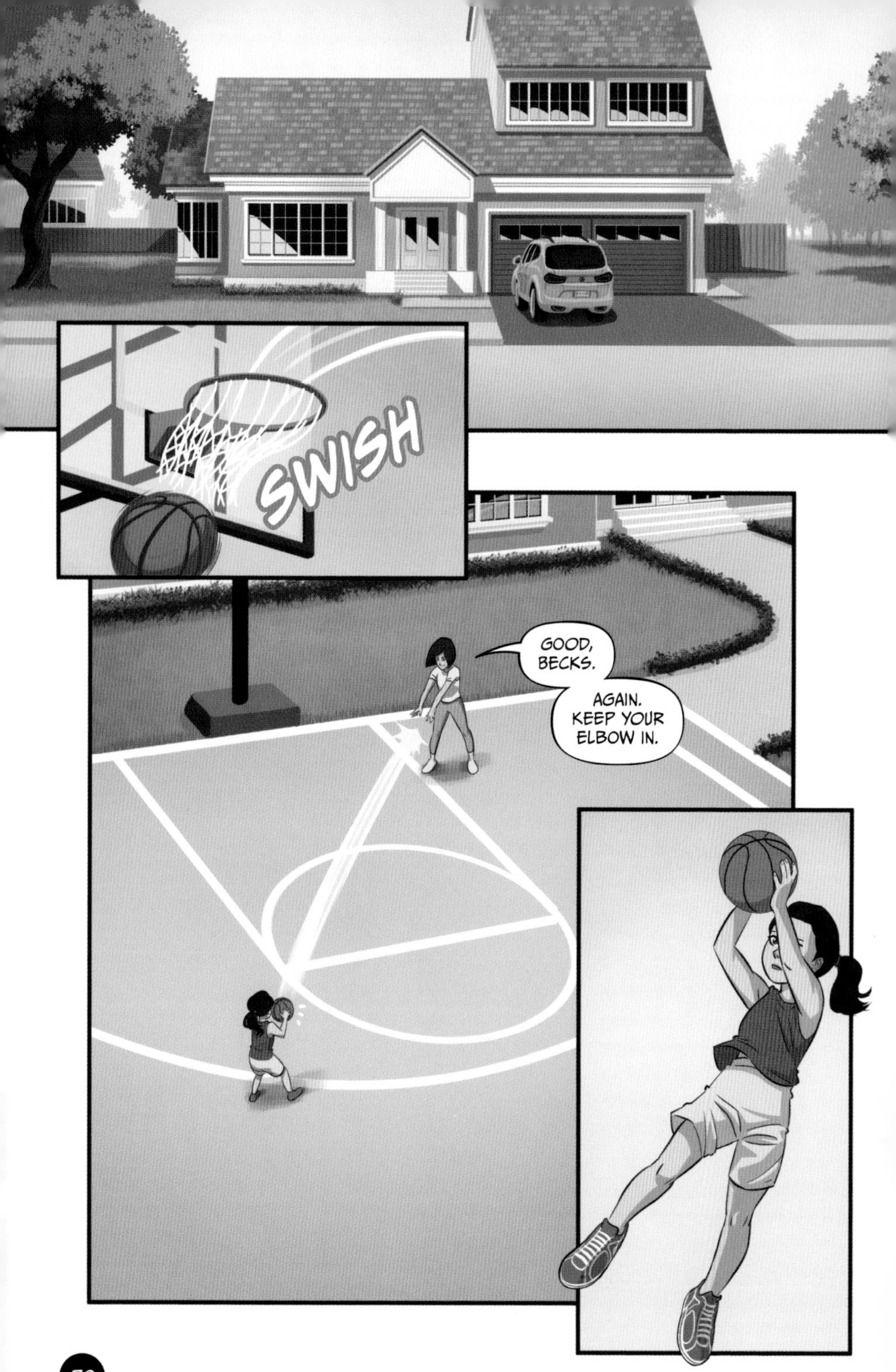
SWISH
GOOD, BECKS.
AGAIN. KEEP YOUR ELBOW IN.

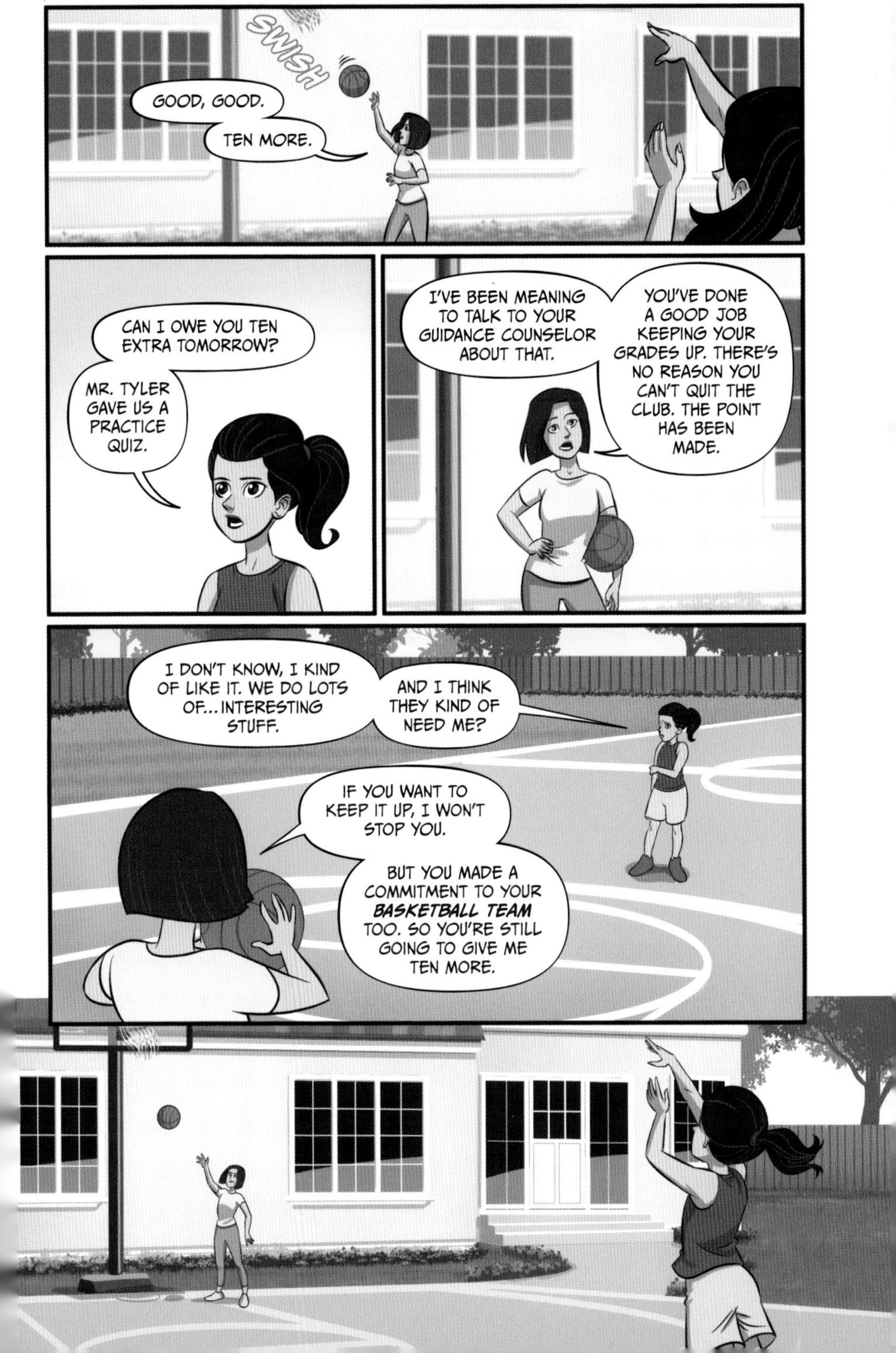
SWISH
GOOD, GOOD.
TEN MORE.
CAN I OWE YOU TEN EXTRA TOMORROW?
MR. TYLER GAVE US A PRACTICE QUIZ.
I'VE BEEN MEANING TO TALK TO YOUR GUIDANCE COUNSELOR ABOUT THAT.
YOU'VE DONE A GOOD JOB KEEPING YOUR GRADES UP. THERE'S NO REASON YOU CAN'T QUIT THE CLUB. THE POINT HAS BEEN MADE.
I DON'T KNOW, I KIND OF LIKE IT. WE DO LOTS OF... INTERESTING STUFF.
AND I THINK THEY KIND OF NEED ME?
IF YOU WANT TO KEEP IT UP, I WON'T STOP YOU.
BUT YOU MADE A COMMITMENT TO YOUR ***BASKETBALL TEAM*** TOO. SO YOU'RE STILL GOING TO GIVE ME TEN MORE.

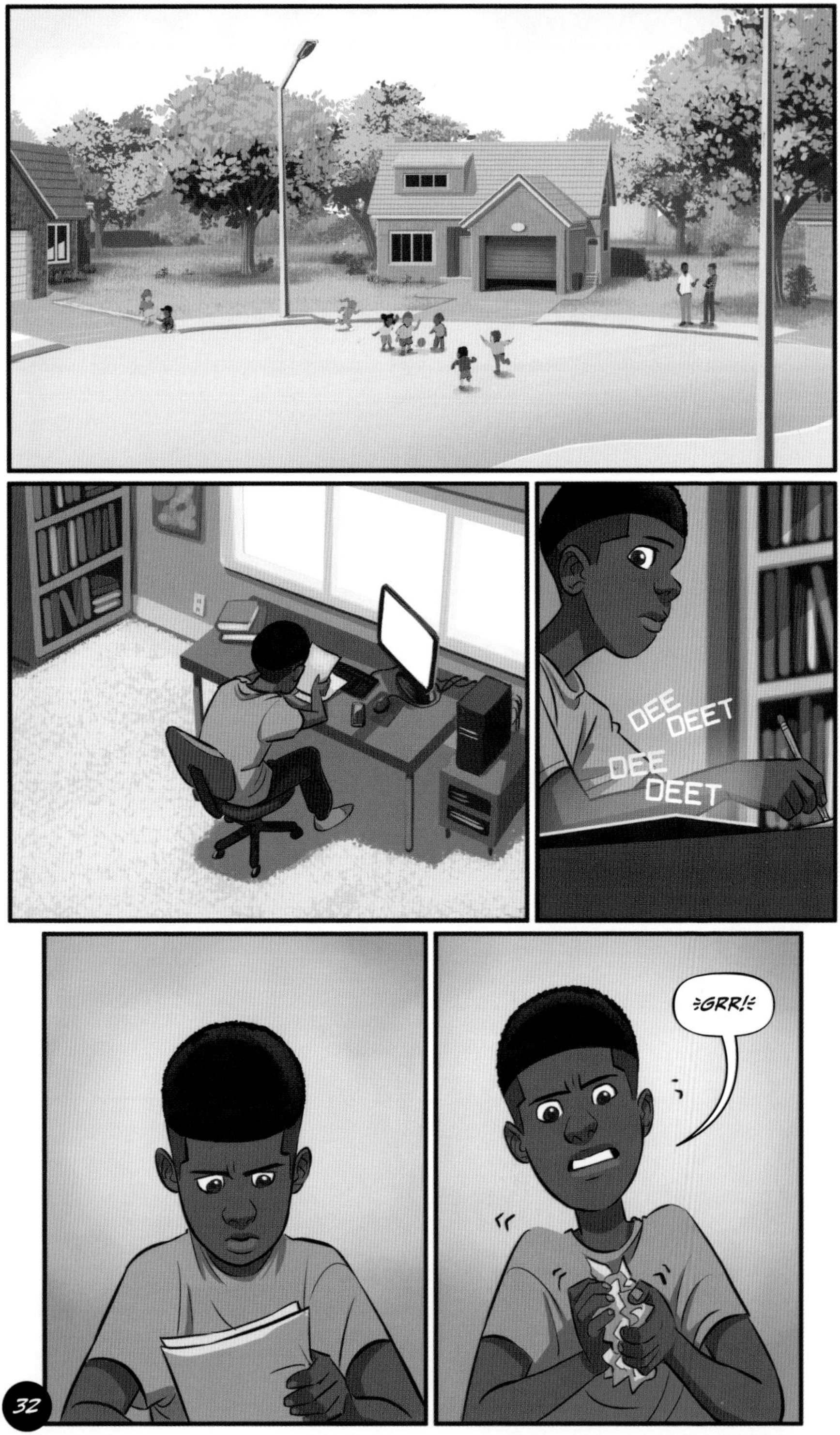
DEE DEET
DEE DEET
GRR!

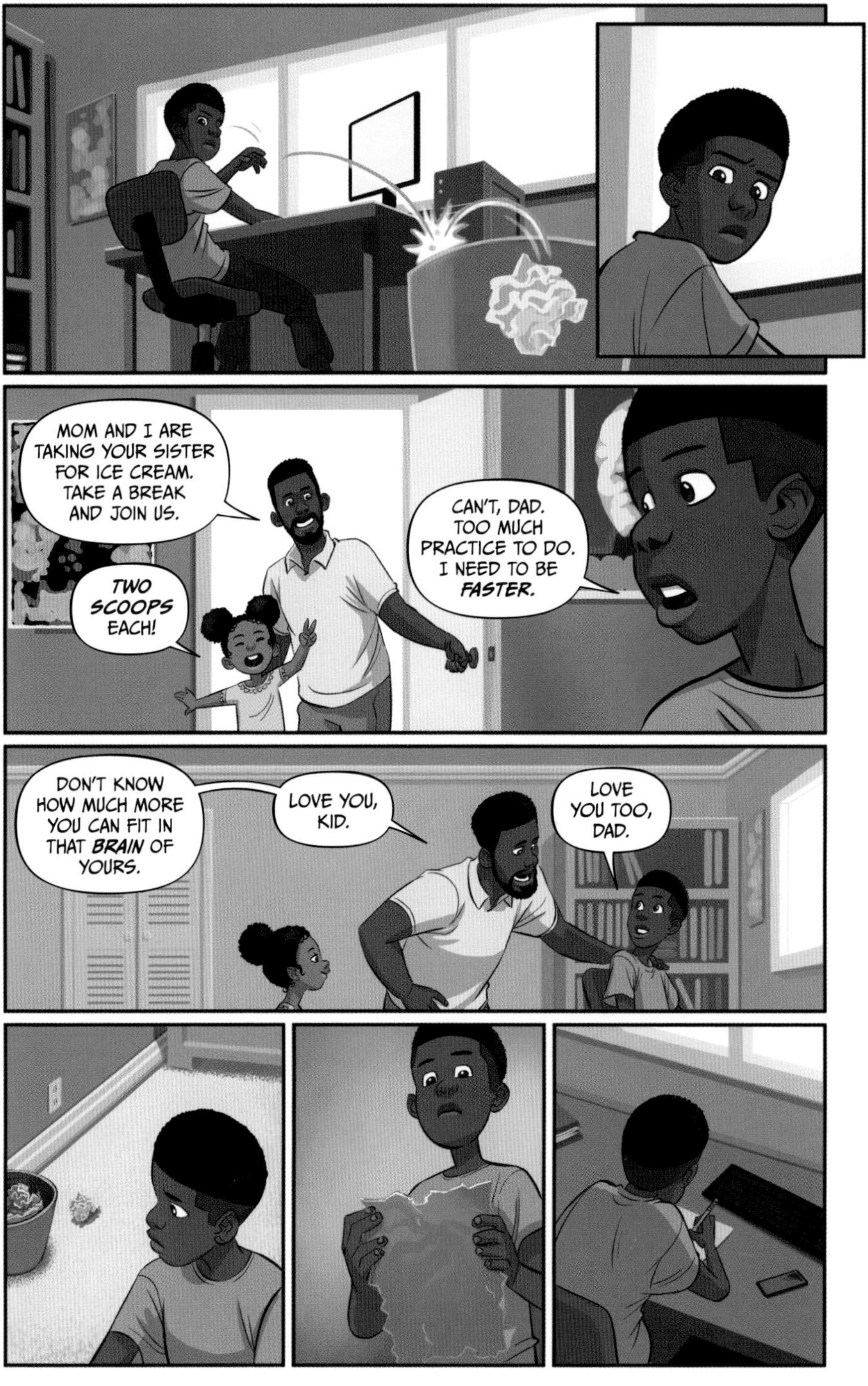
MOM AND I ARE TAKING YOUR SISTER FOR ICE CREAM. TAKE A BREAK AND JOIN US.
TWO SCOOPS EACH!
CAN'T, DAD. TOO MUCH PRACTICE TO DO. I NEED TO BE FASTER.
DON'T KNOW HOW MUCH MORE YOU CAN FIT IN THAT BRAIN OF YOURS.
LOVE YOU, KID.
LOVE YOU TOO, DAD.

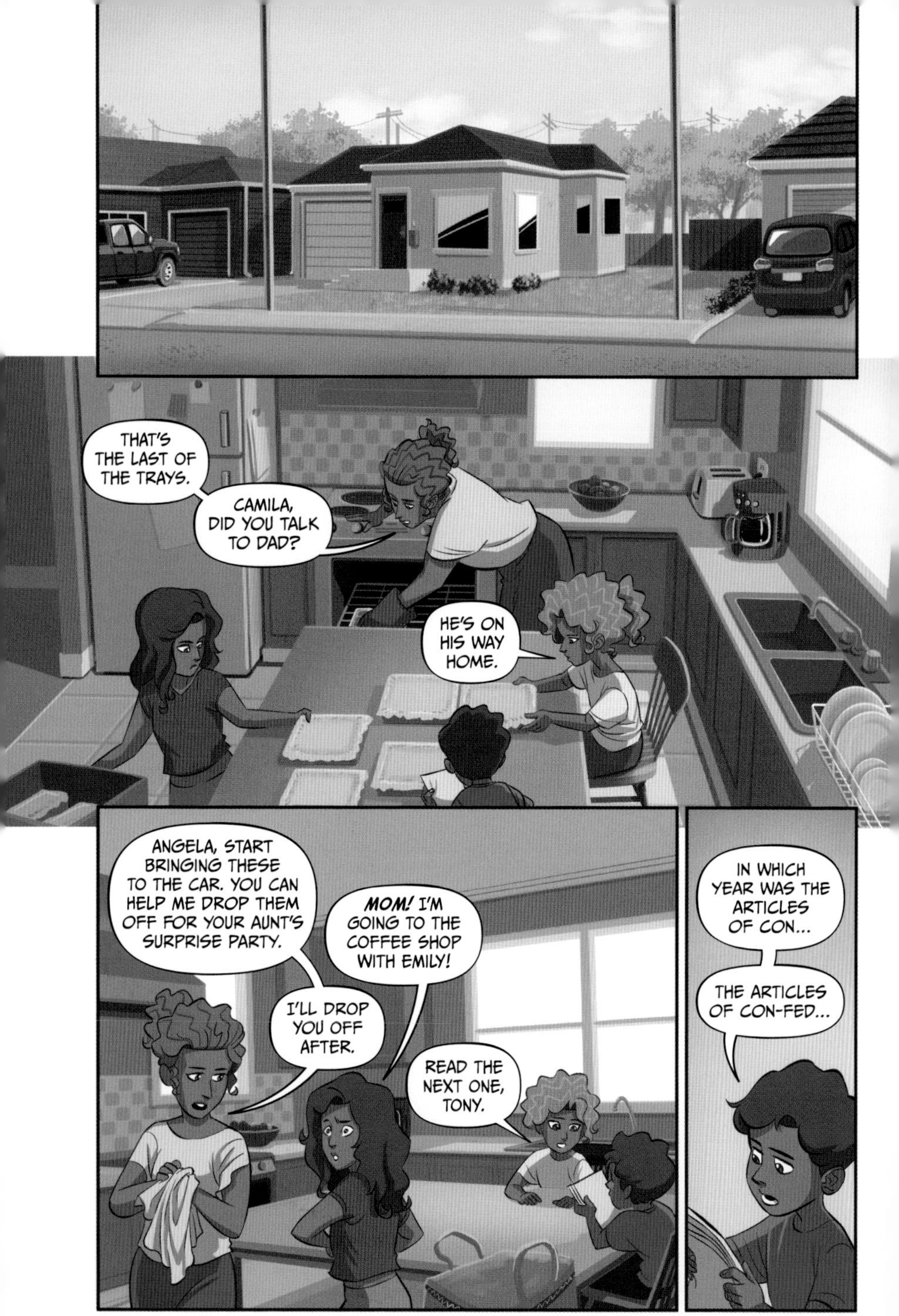
THAT'S THE LAST OF THE TRAYS.
CAMILA, DID YOU TALK TO DAD?
HE'S ON HIS WAY HOME.
ANGELA, START BRINGING THESE TO THE CAR. YOU CAN HELP ME DROP THEM OFF FOR YOUR AUNT'S SURPRISE PARTY.
MOM! I'M GOING TO THE COFFEE SHOP WITH EMILY!
I'LL DROP YOU OFF AFTER.
READ THE NEXT ONE, TONY.
IN WHICH YEAR WAS THE ARTICLES OF CON...
THE ARTICLES OF CON-FED...

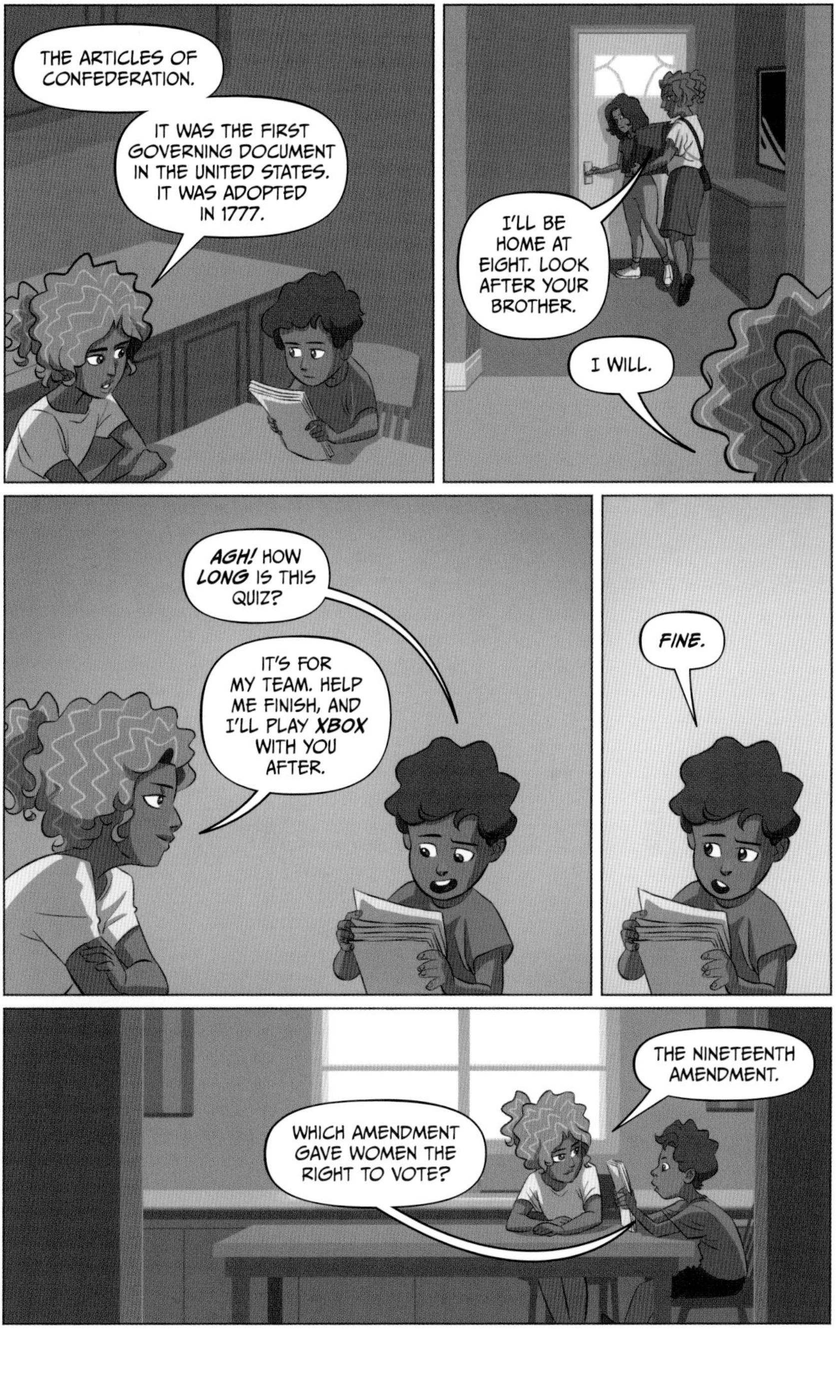
THE ARTICLES OF CONFEDERATION.
IT WAS THE FIRST GOVERNING DOCUMENT IN THE UNITED STATES. IT WAS ADOPTED IN 1777.
I'LL BE HOME AT EIGHT. LOOK AFTER YOUR BROTHER.
I WILL.
AGH! HOW LONG IS THIS QUIZ?
IT'S FOR MY TEAM. HELP ME FINISH, AND I'LL PLAY XBOX WITH YOU AFTER.
FINE.
WHICH AMENDMENT GAVE WOMEN THE RIGHT TO VOTE?
THE NINETEENTH AMENDMENT.

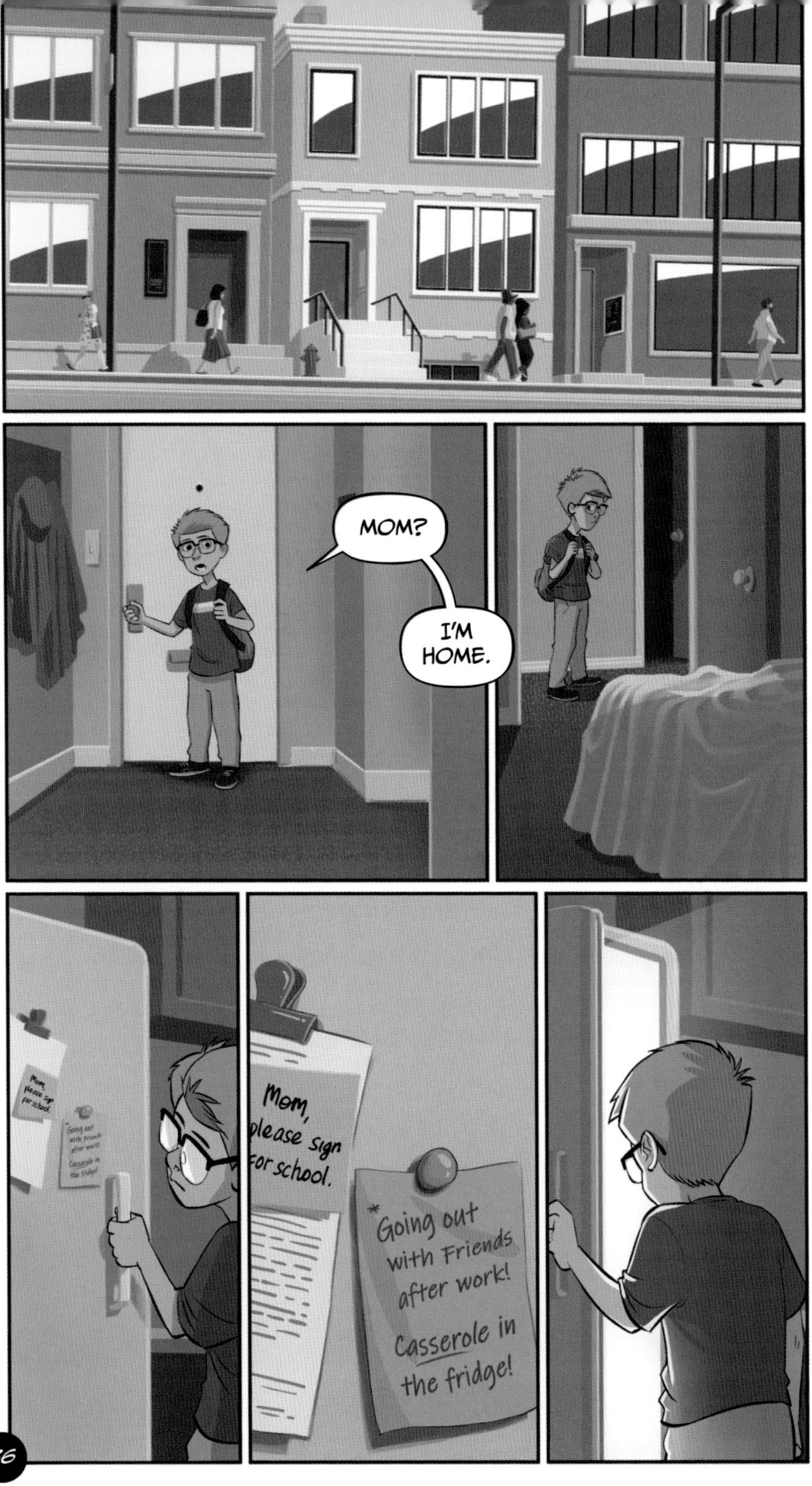
MOM?
I'M HOME.
Mom, please sign for school.
Going out with Friends after work!
Casserole in the fridge!

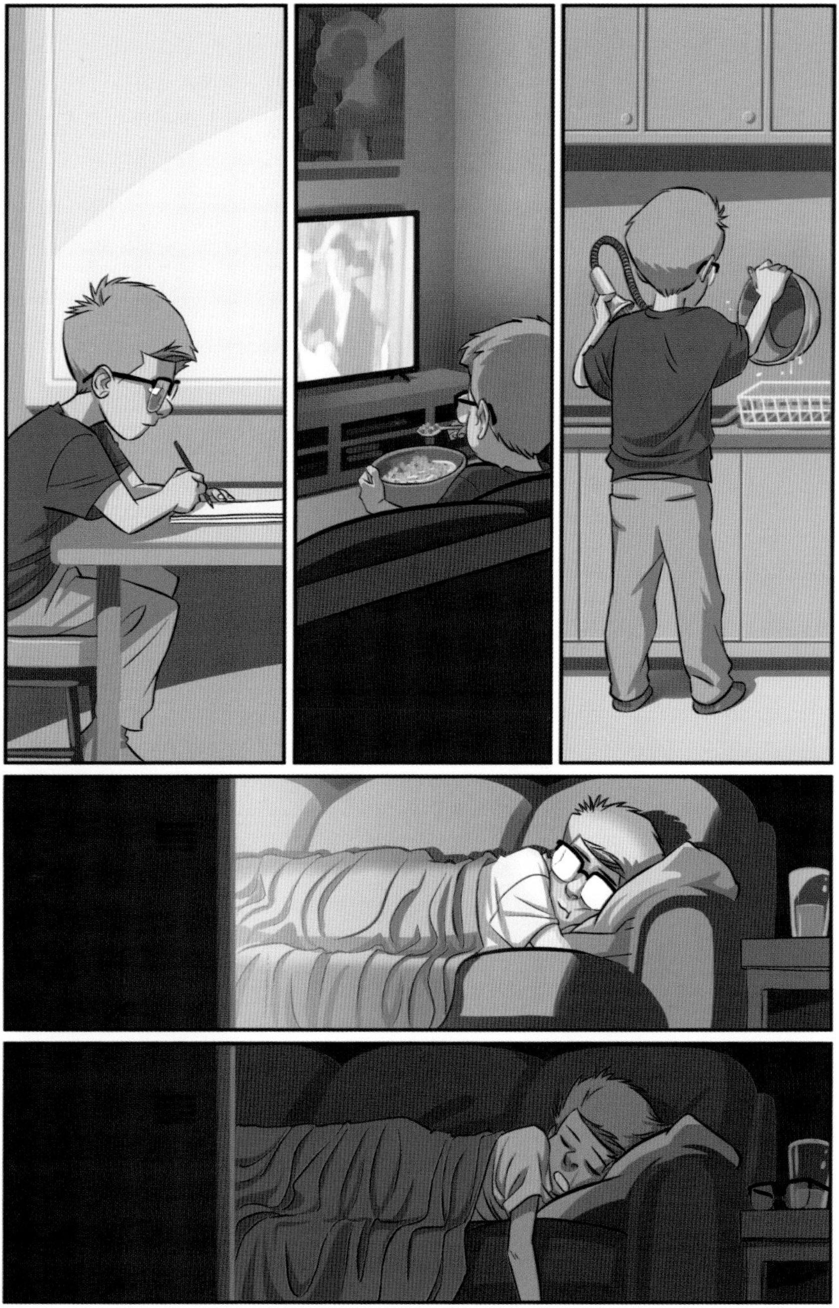

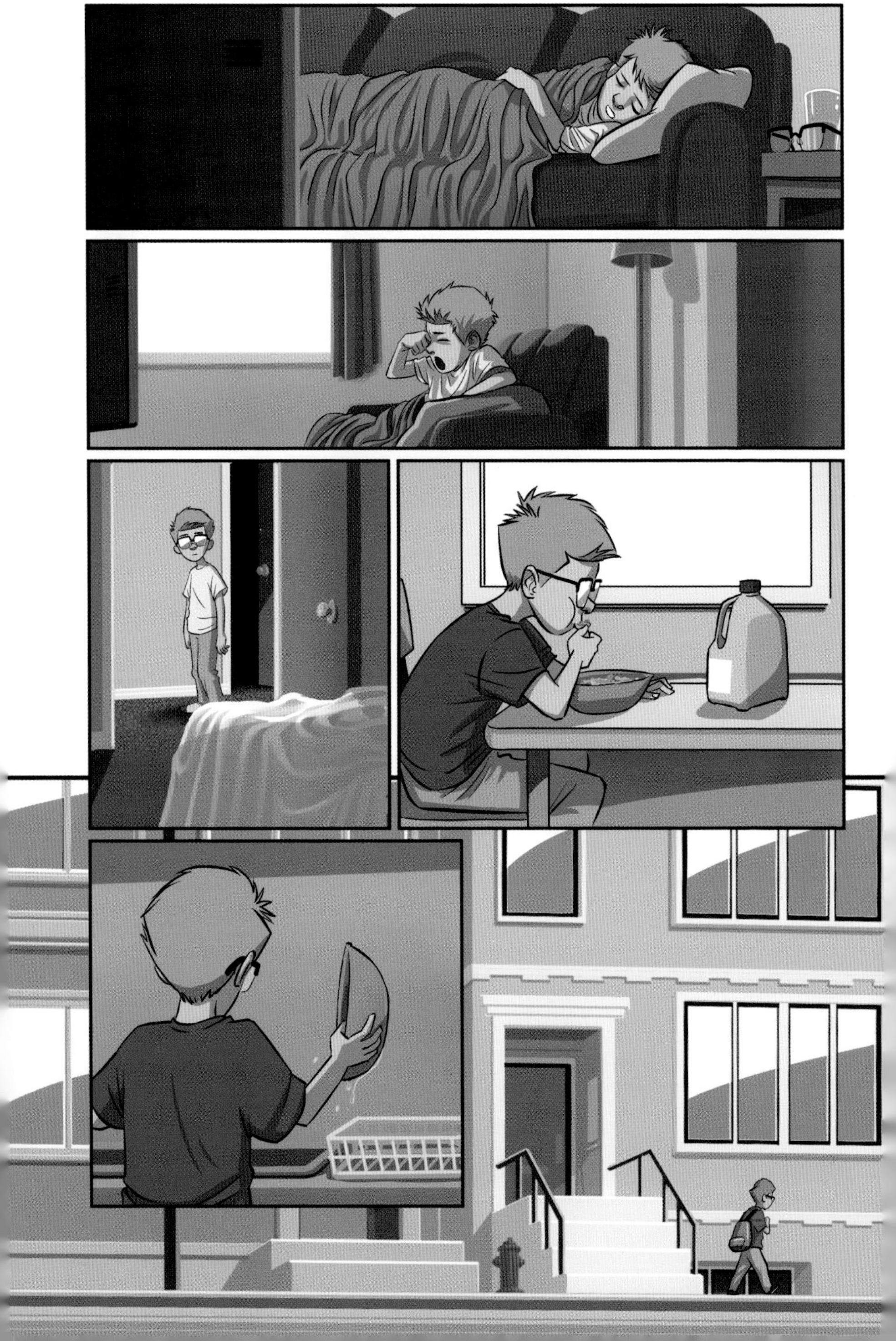

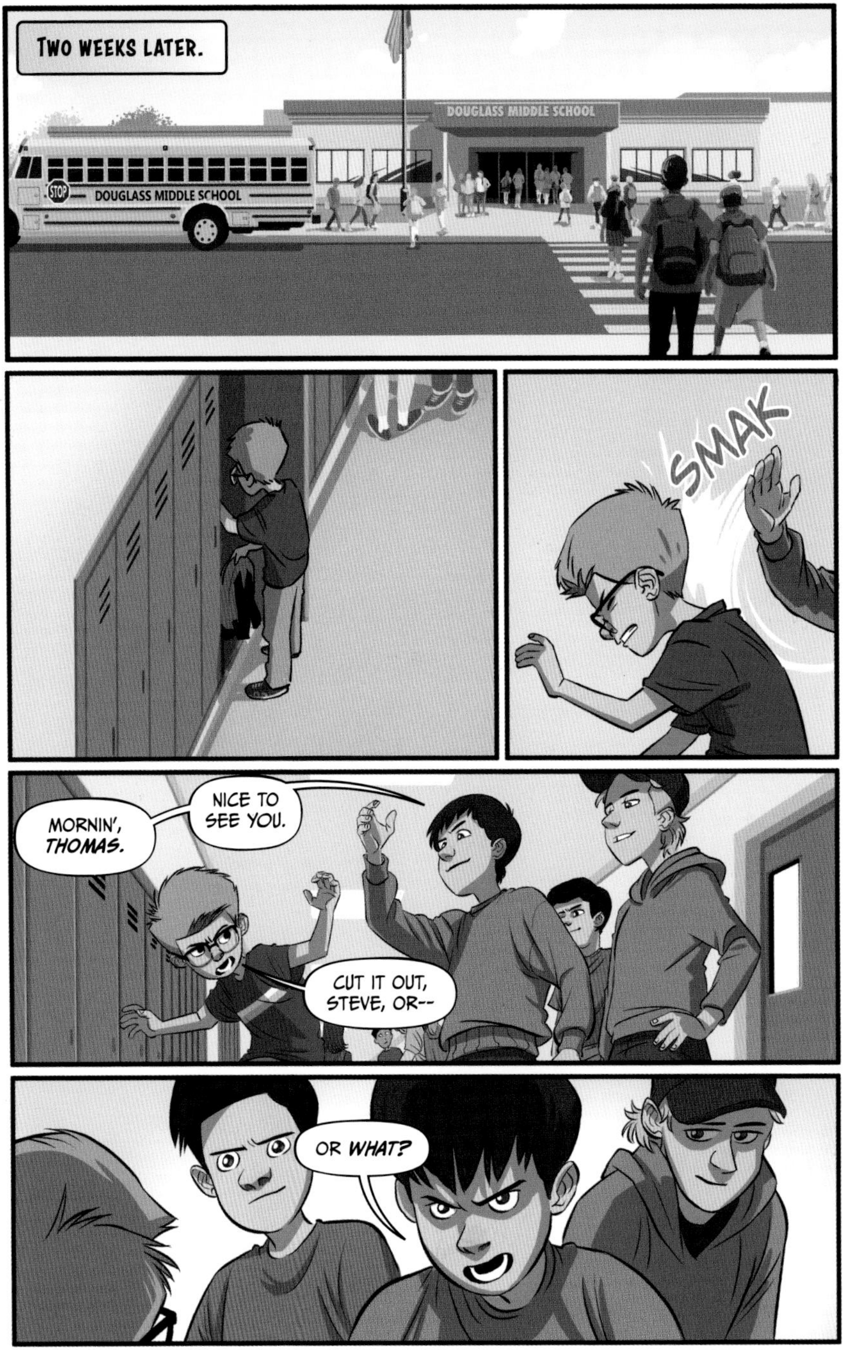
TWO WEEKS LATER.
DOUGLASS MIDDLE SCHOOL
STOP
DOUGLASS MIDDLE SCHOOL
SMAK
MORNIN', *THOMAS.*
NICE TO SEE YOU.
CUT IT OUT, STEVE, OR--
OR *WHAT?*

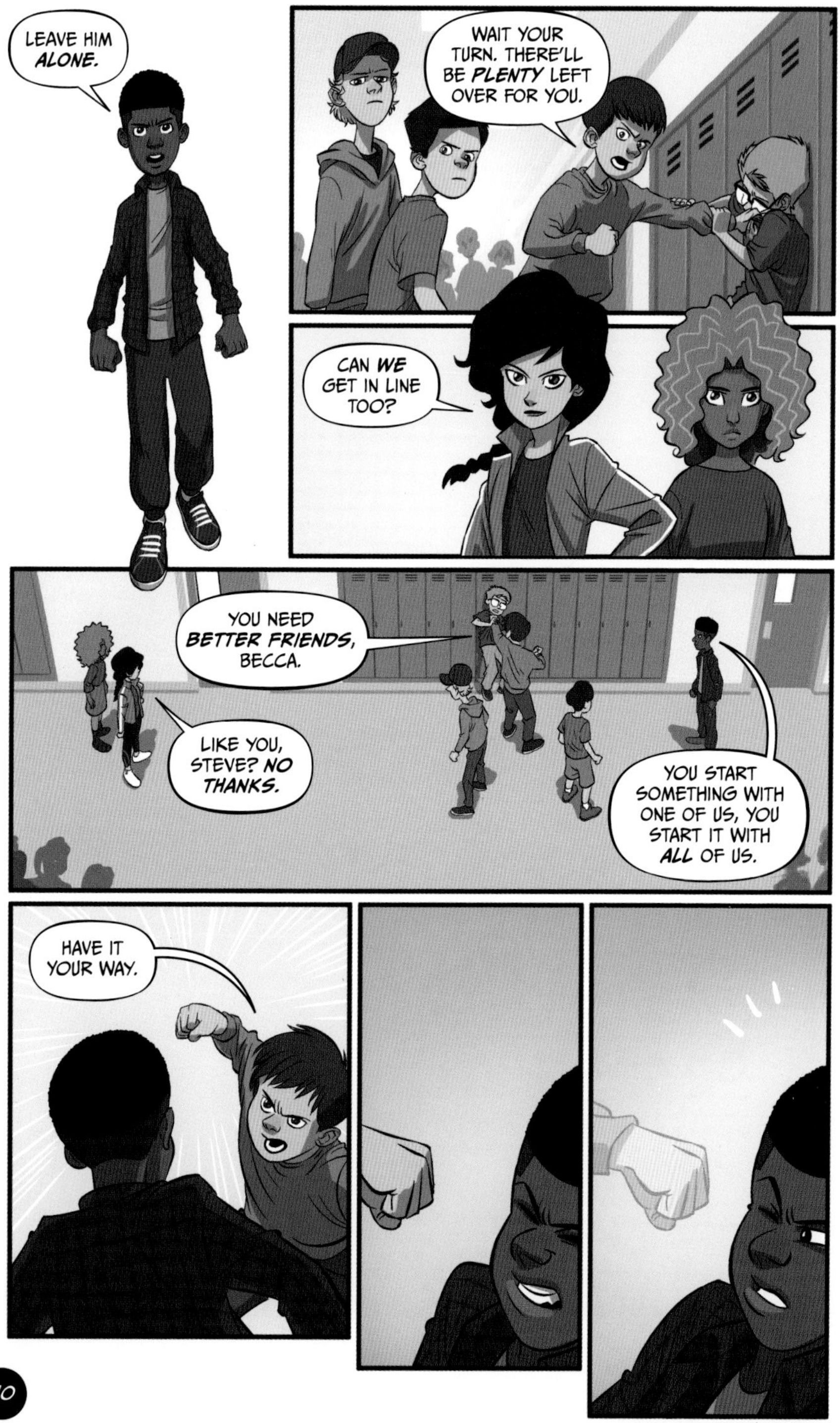
LEAVE HIM ALONE.
WAIT YOUR TURN. THERE'LL BE PLENTY LEFT OVER FOR YOU.
CAN WE GET IN LINE TOO?
YOU NEED BETTER FRIENDS, BECCA.
LIKE YOU, STEVE? NO THANKS.
YOU START SOMETHING WITH ONE OF US, YOU START IT WITH ALL OF US.
HAVE IT YOUR WAY.

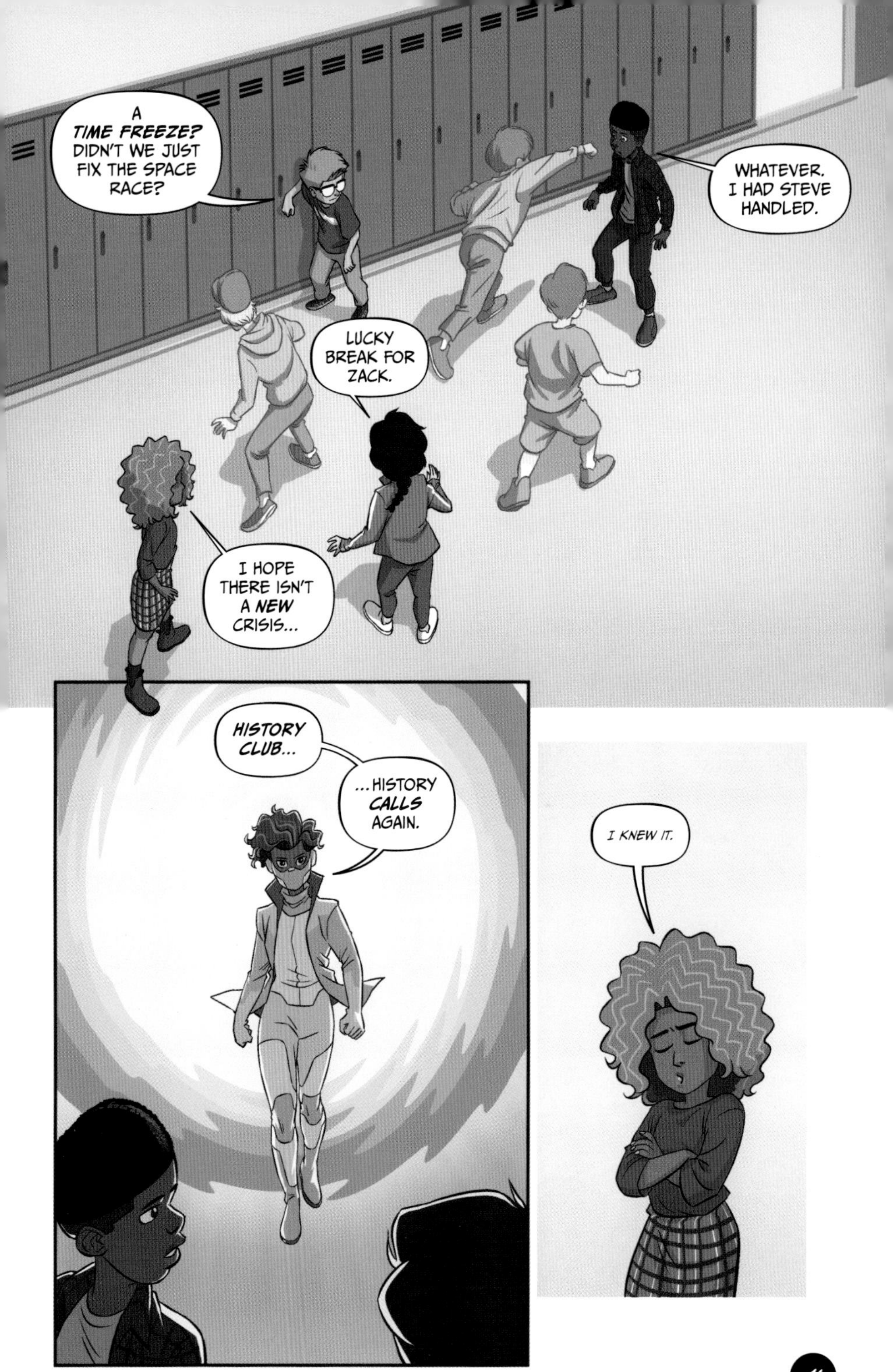
A *TIME FREEZE?* DIDN'T WE JUST FIX THE SPACE RACE?
WHATEVER. I HAD STEVE HANDLED.
LUCKY BREAK FOR ZACK.
I HOPE THERE ISN'T A *NEW* CRISIS...
HISTORY CLUB...
...HISTORY *CALLS* AGAIN.
I KNEW IT.

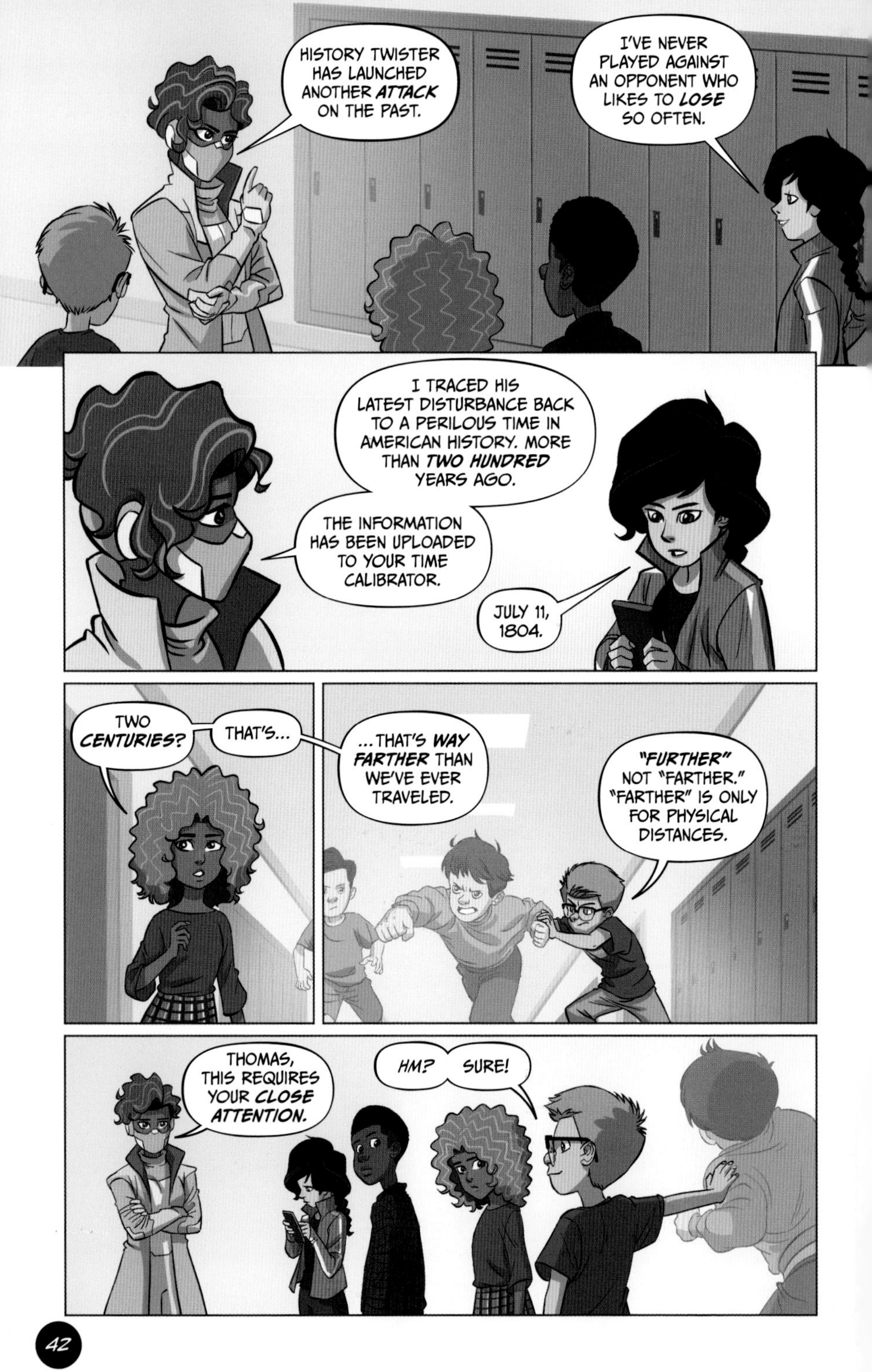
HISTORY TWISTER HAS LAUNCHED ANOTHER ATTACK ON THE PAST.
I'VE NEVER PLAYED AGAINST AN OPPONENT WHO LIKES TO LOSE SO OFTEN.
I TRACED HIS LATEST DISTURBANCE BACK TO A PERILOUS TIME IN AMERICAN HISTORY. MORE THAN TWO HUNDRED YEARS AGO.
THE INFORMATION HAS BEEN UPLOADED TO YOUR TIME CALIBRATOR.
JULY 11, 1804.
TWO CENTURIES?
THAT'S...
...THAT'S WAY FARTHER THAN WE'VE EVER TRAVELED.
"FURTHER" NOT "FARTHER." "FARTHER" IS ONLY FOR PHYSICAL DISTANCES.
THOMAS, THIS REQUIRES YOUR CLOSE ATTENTION.
HM?
SURE!

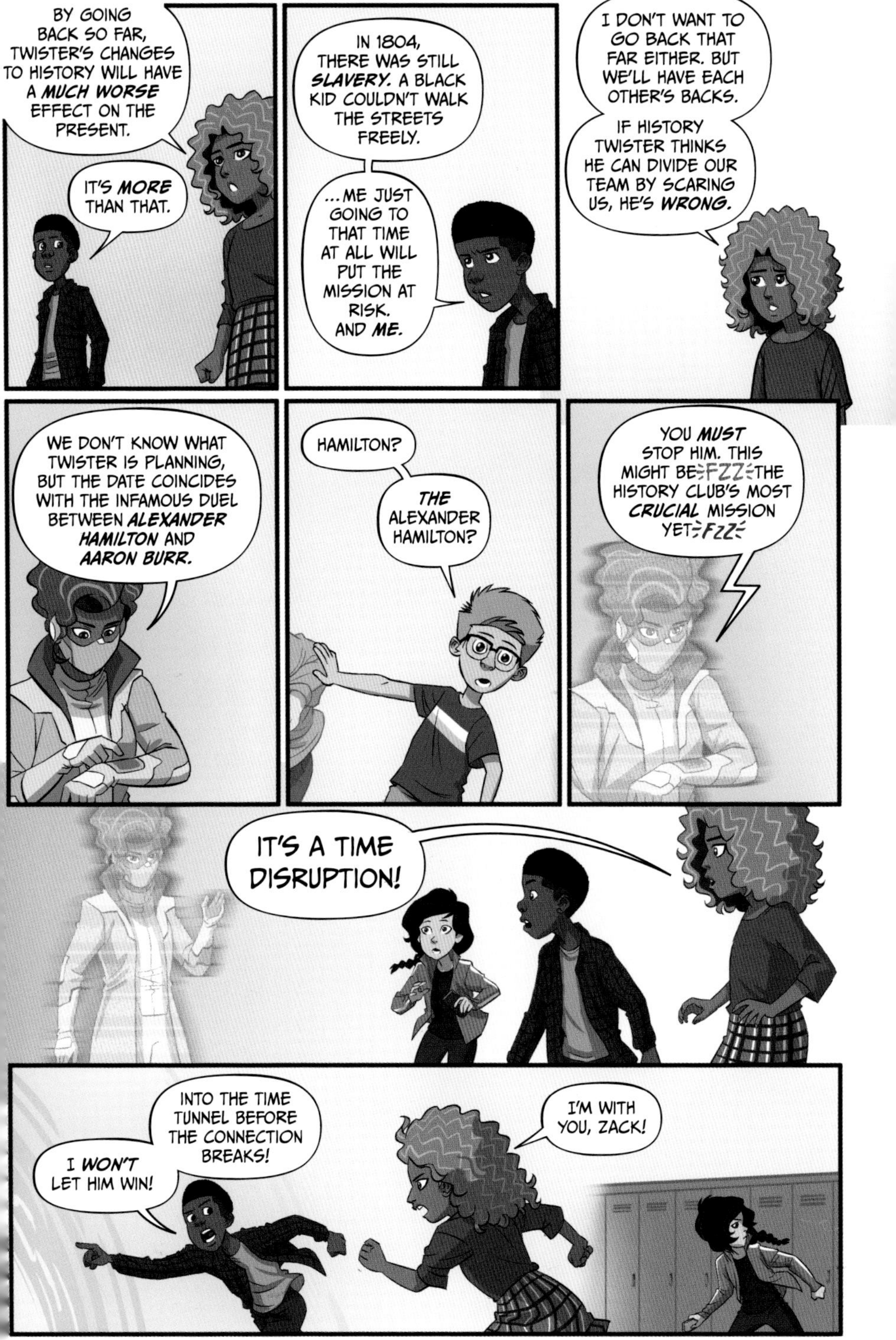
BY GOING BACK SO FAR, TWISTER'S CHANGES TO HISTORY WILL HAVE A MUCH WORSE EFFECT ON THE PRESENT.
IT'S MORE THAN THAT.
IN 1804, THERE WAS STILL SLAVERY. A BLACK KID COULDN'T WALK THE STREETS FREELY.
...ME JUST GOING TO THAT TIME AT ALL WILL PUT THE MISSION AT RISK. AND ME.
I DON'T WANT TO GO BACK THAT FAR EITHER. BUT WE'LL HAVE EACH OTHER'S BACKS.
IF HISTORY TWISTER THINKS HE CAN DIVIDE OUR TEAM BY SCARING US, HE'S WRONG.
WE DON'T KNOW WHAT TWISTER IS PLANNING, BUT THE DATE COINCIDES WITH THE INFAMOUS DUEL BETWEEN ALEXANDER HAMILTON AND AARON BURR.
HAMILTON?
THE ALEXANDER HAMILTON?
YOU MUST STOP HIM. THIS MIGHT BE FZZ THE HISTORY CLUB'S MOST CRUCIAL MISSION YET FZZ
IT'S A TIME DISRUPTION!
I WON'T LET HIM WIN!
INTO THE TIME TUNNEL BEFORE THE CONNECTION BREAKS!
I'M WITH YOU, ZACK!

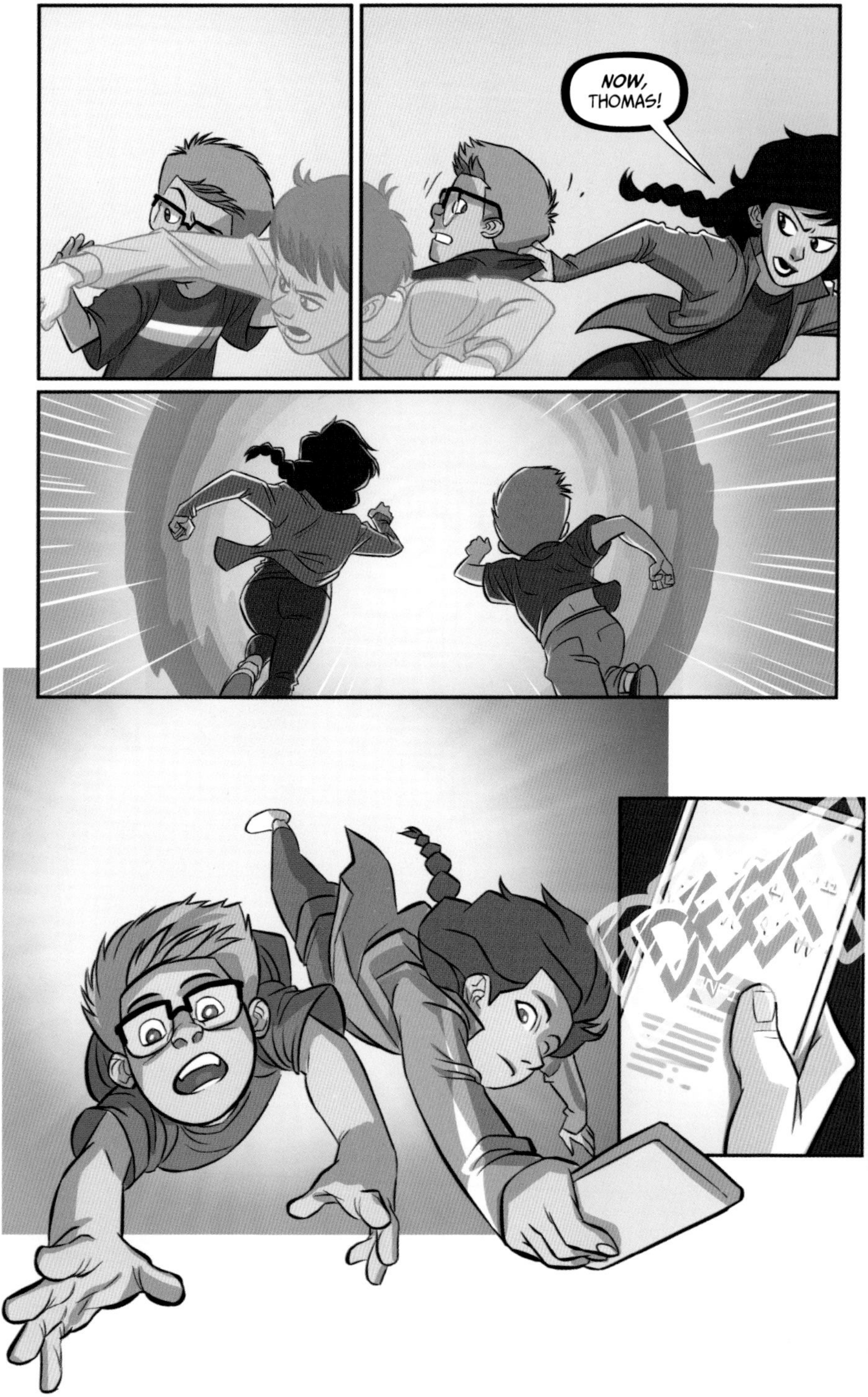
NOW, THOMAS!

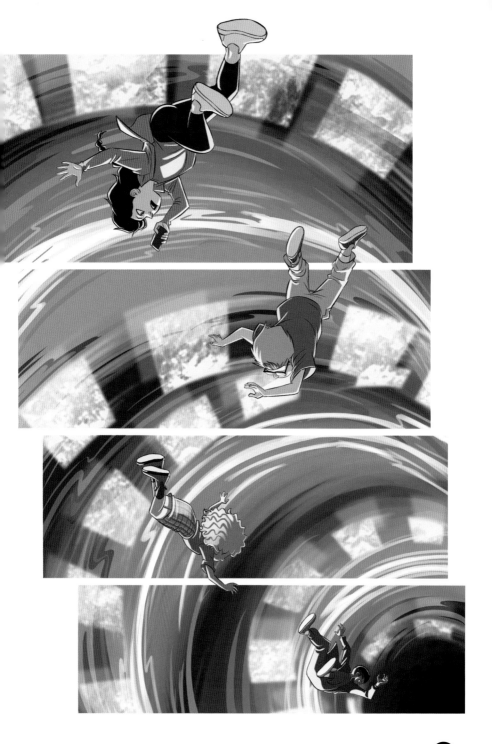

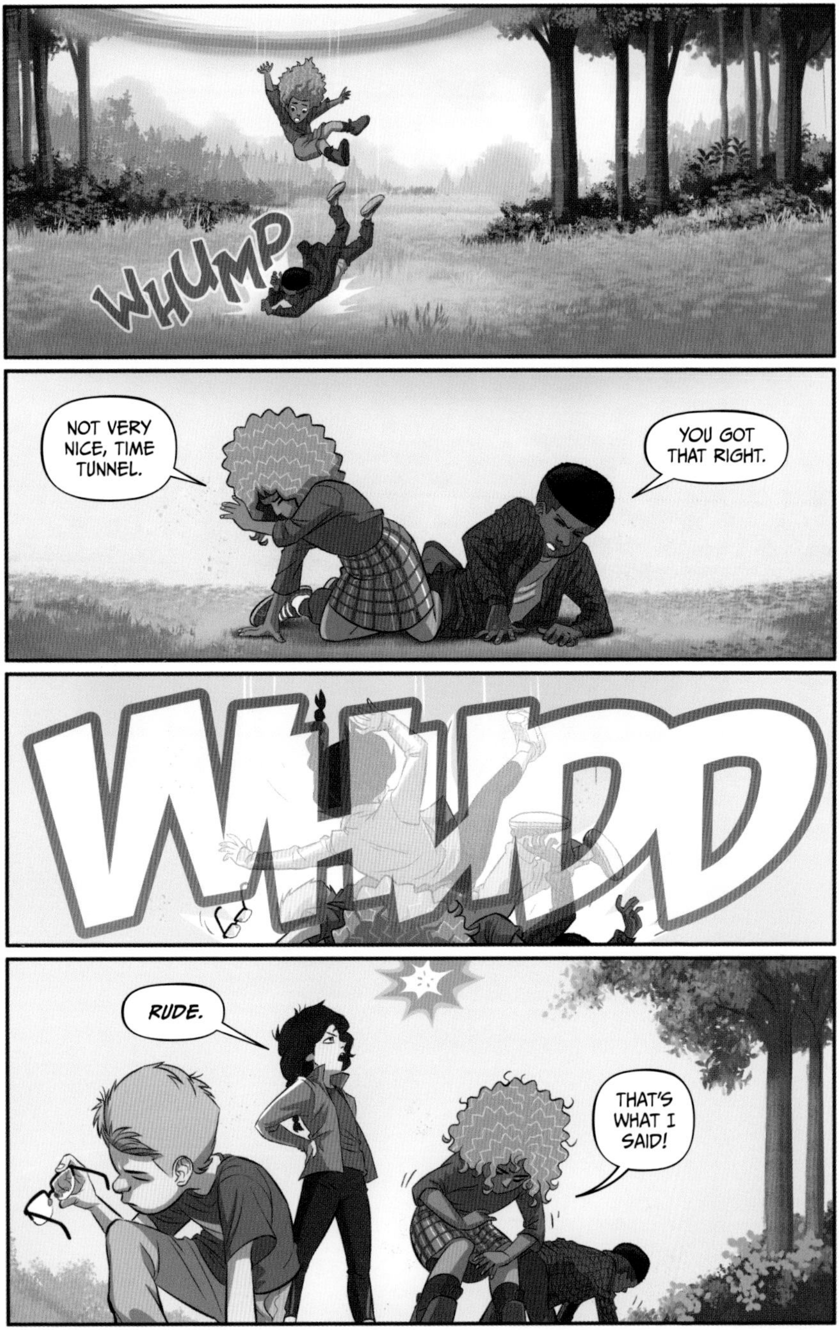
WHUMP
NOT VERY NICE, TIME TUNNEL.
YOU GOT THAT RIGHT.
WHUDD
RUDE.
THAT'S WHAT I SAID!

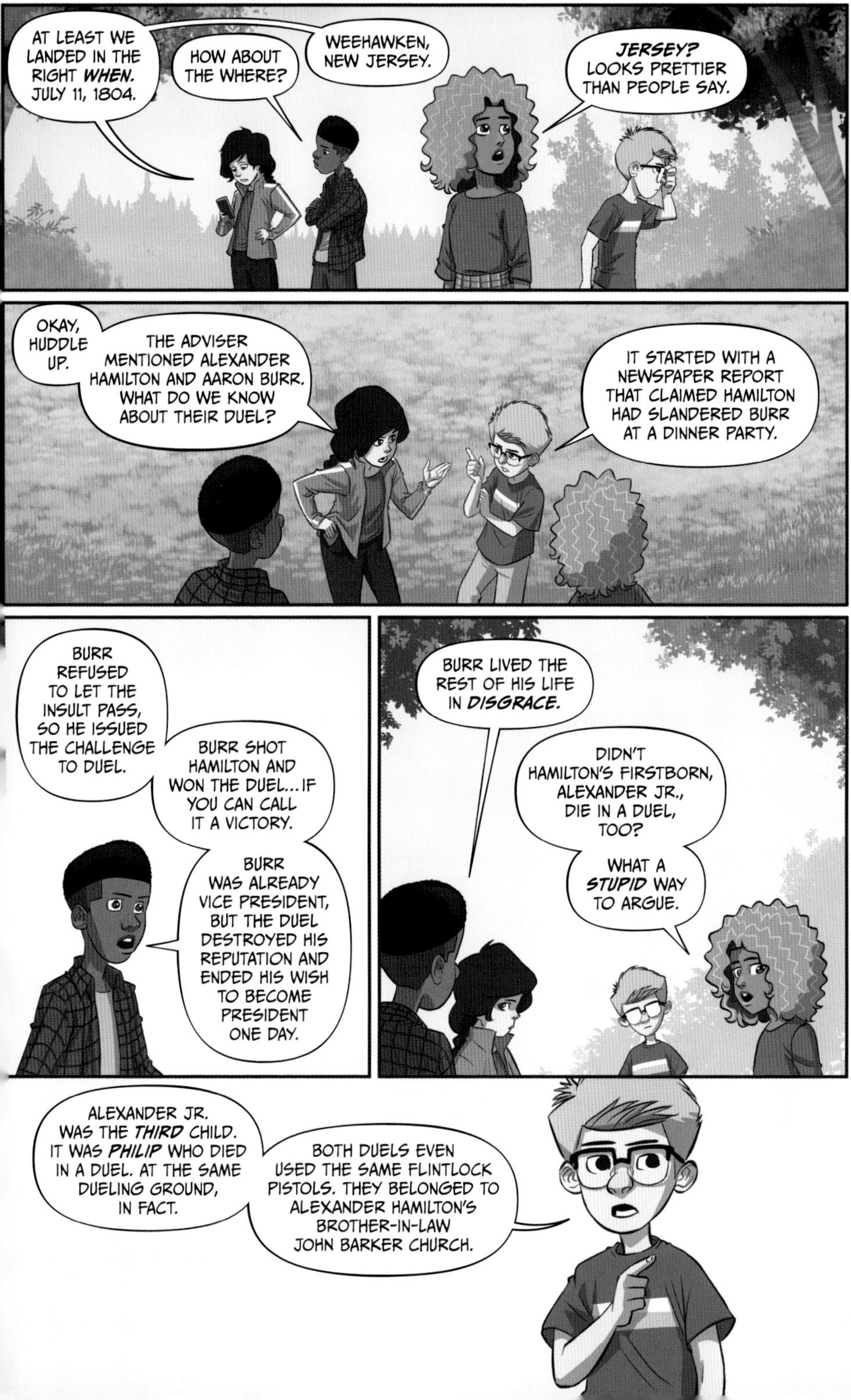
AT LEAST WE LANDED IN THE RIGHT *WHEN.* JULY 11, 1804.
HOW ABOUT THE WHERE?
WEEHAWKEN, NEW JERSEY.
JERSEY? LOOKS PRETTIER THAN PEOPLE SAY.
OKAY, HUDDLE UP.
THE ADVISER MENTIONED ALEXANDER HAMILTON AND AARON BURR. WHAT DO WE KNOW ABOUT THEIR DUEL?
IT STARTED WITH A NEWSPAPER REPORT THAT CLAIMED HAMILTON HAD SLANDERED BURR AT A DINNER PARTY.
BURR REFUSED TO LET THE INSULT PASS, SO HE ISSUED THE CHALLENGE TO DUEL.
BURR SHOT HAMILTON AND WON THE DUEL... IF YOU CAN CALL IT A VICTORY.
BURR WAS ALREADY VICE PRESIDENT, BUT THE DUEL DESTROYED HIS REPUTATION AND ENDED HIS WISH TO BECOME PRESIDENT ONE DAY.
BURR LIVED THE REST OF HIS LIFE IN *DISGRACE.*
DIDN'T HAMILTON'S FIRSTBORN, ALEXANDER JR., DIE IN A DUEL, TOO?
WHAT A *STUPID* WAY TO ARGUE.
ALEXANDER JR. WAS THE *THIRD* CHILD. IT WAS *PHILIP* WHO DIED IN A DUEL. AT THE SAME DUELING GROUND, IN FACT.
BOTH DUELS EVEN USED THE SAME FLINTLOCK PISTOLS. THEY BELONGED TO ALEXANDER HAMILTON'S BROTHER-IN-LAW JOHN BARKER CHURCH.

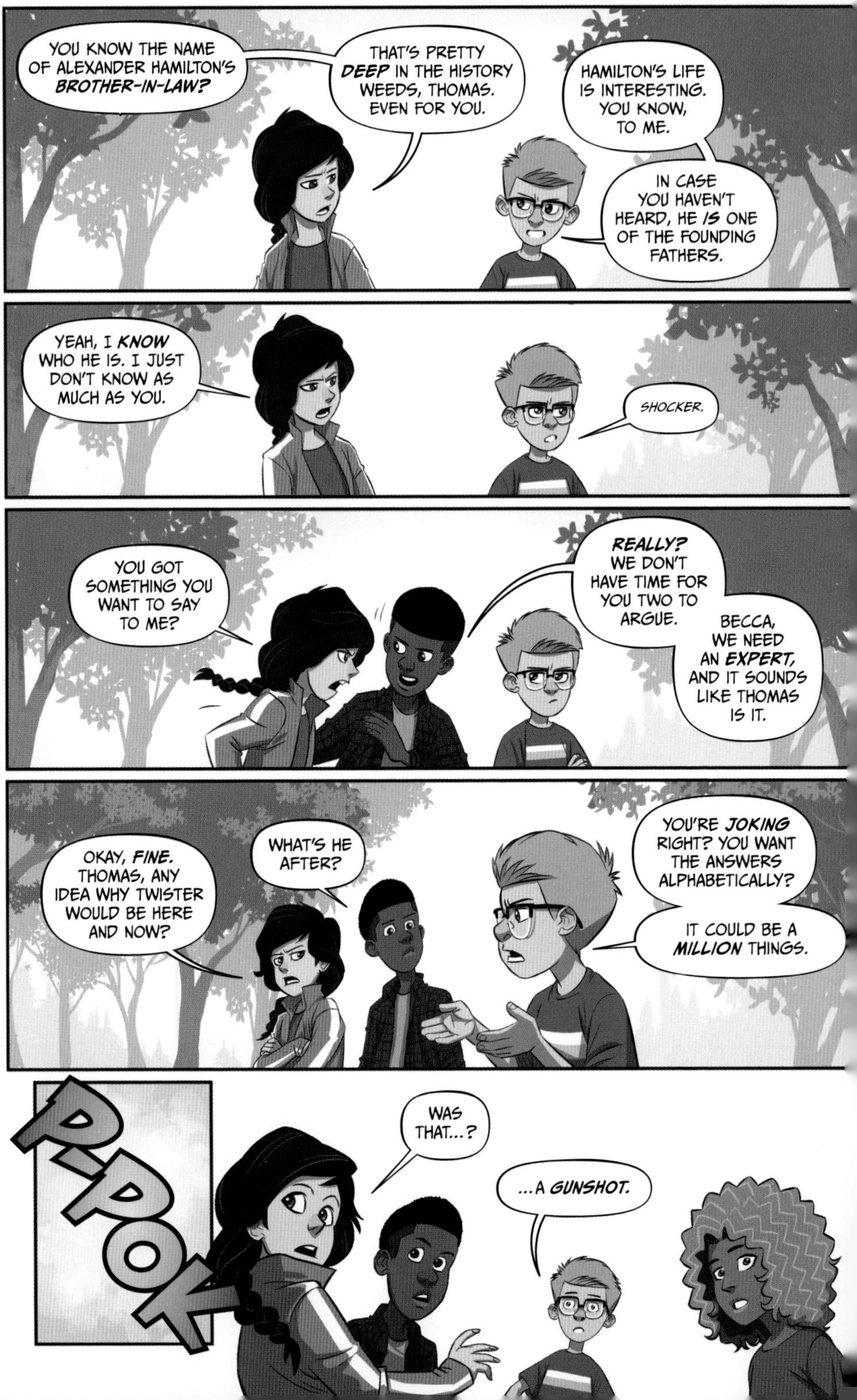
YOU KNOW THE NAME OF ALEXANDER HAMILTON'S BROTHER-IN-LAW?
THAT'S PRETTY DEEP IN THE HISTORY WEEDS, THOMAS. EVEN FOR YOU.
HAMILTON'S LIFE IS INTERESTING. YOU KNOW, TO ME.
IN CASE YOU HAVEN'T HEARD, HE IS ONE OF THE FOUNDING FATHERS.
YEAH, I KNOW WHO HE IS. I JUST DON'T KNOW AS MUCH AS YOU.
SHOCKER.
YOU GOT SOMETHING YOU WANT TO SAY TO ME?
REALLY? WE DON'T HAVE TIME FOR YOU TWO TO ARGUE.
BECCA, WE NEED AN EXPERT, AND IT SOUNDS LIKE THOMAS IS IT.
OKAY, FINE. THOMAS, ANY IDEA WHY TWISTER WOULD BE HERE AND NOW?
WHAT'S HE AFTER?
YOU'RE JOKING RIGHT? YOU WANT THE ANSWERS ALPHABETICALLY?
IT COULD BE A MILLION THINGS.
P-POK
WAS THAT...?
...A GUNSHOT.

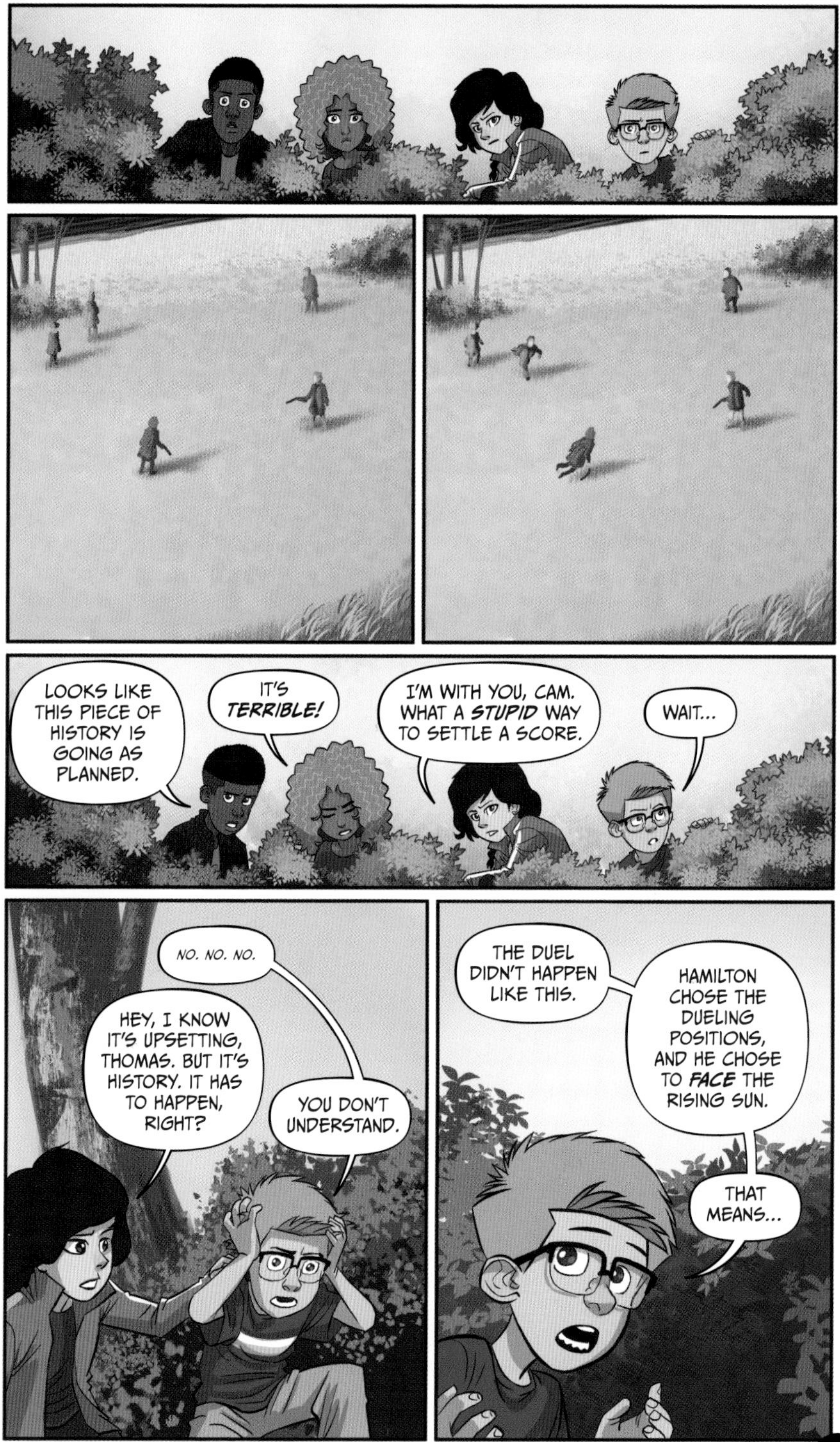

LOOKS LIKE THIS PIECE OF HISTORY IS GOING AS PLANNED.
IT'S *TERRIBLE!*
I'M WITH YOU, CAM. WHAT A *STUPID* WAY TO SETTLE A SCORE.
WAIT...
NO. NO. NO.
HEY, I KNOW IT'S UPSETTING, THOMAS. BUT IT'S HISTORY. IT HAS TO HAPPEN, RIGHT?
YOU DON'T UNDERSTAND.
THE DUEL DIDN'T HAPPEN LIKE THIS.
HAMILTON CHOSE THE DUELING POSITIONS, AND HE CHOSE TO *FACE* THE RISING SUN.
THAT MEANS...

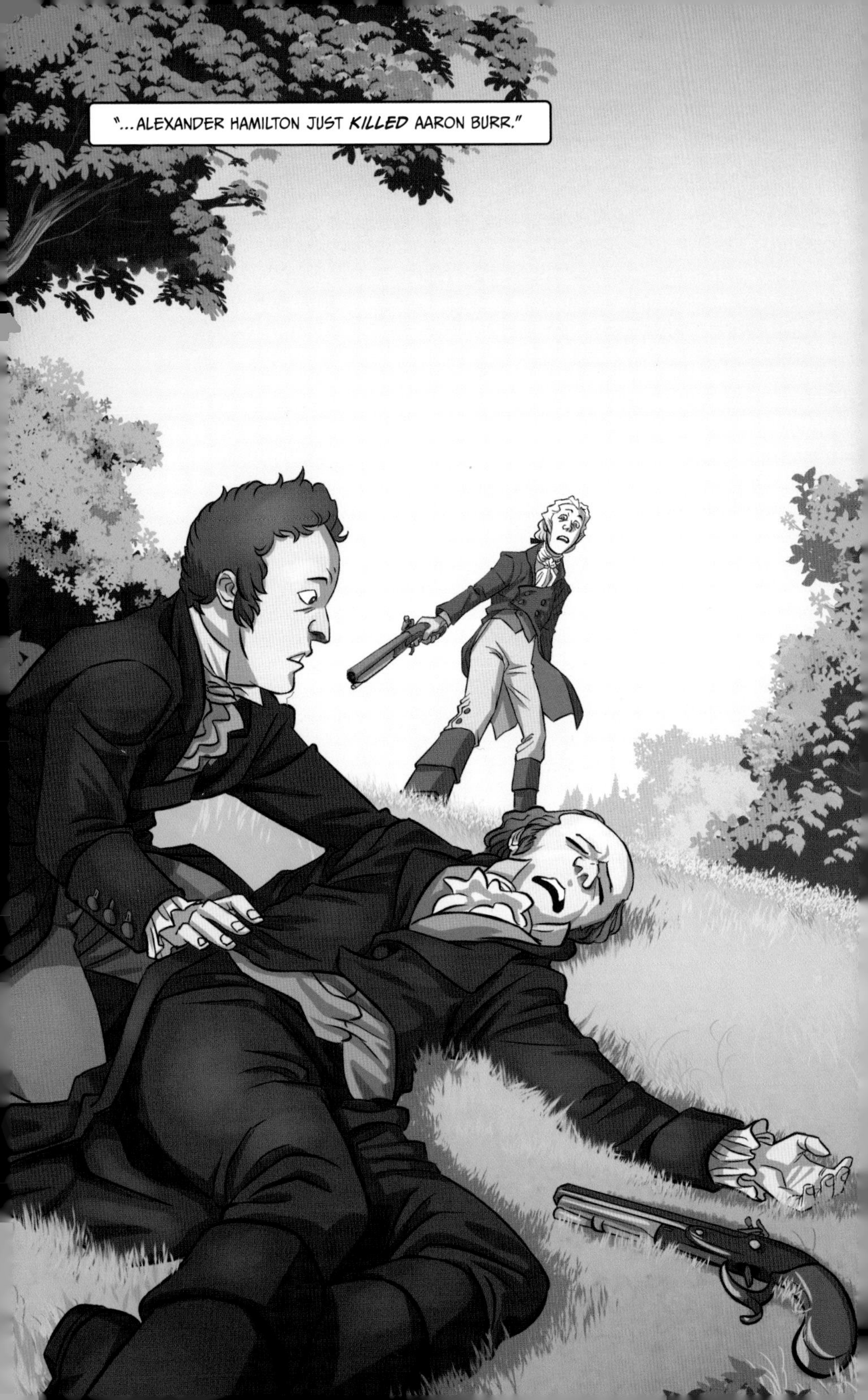
"...ALEXANDER HAMILTON JUST KILLED AARON BURR."

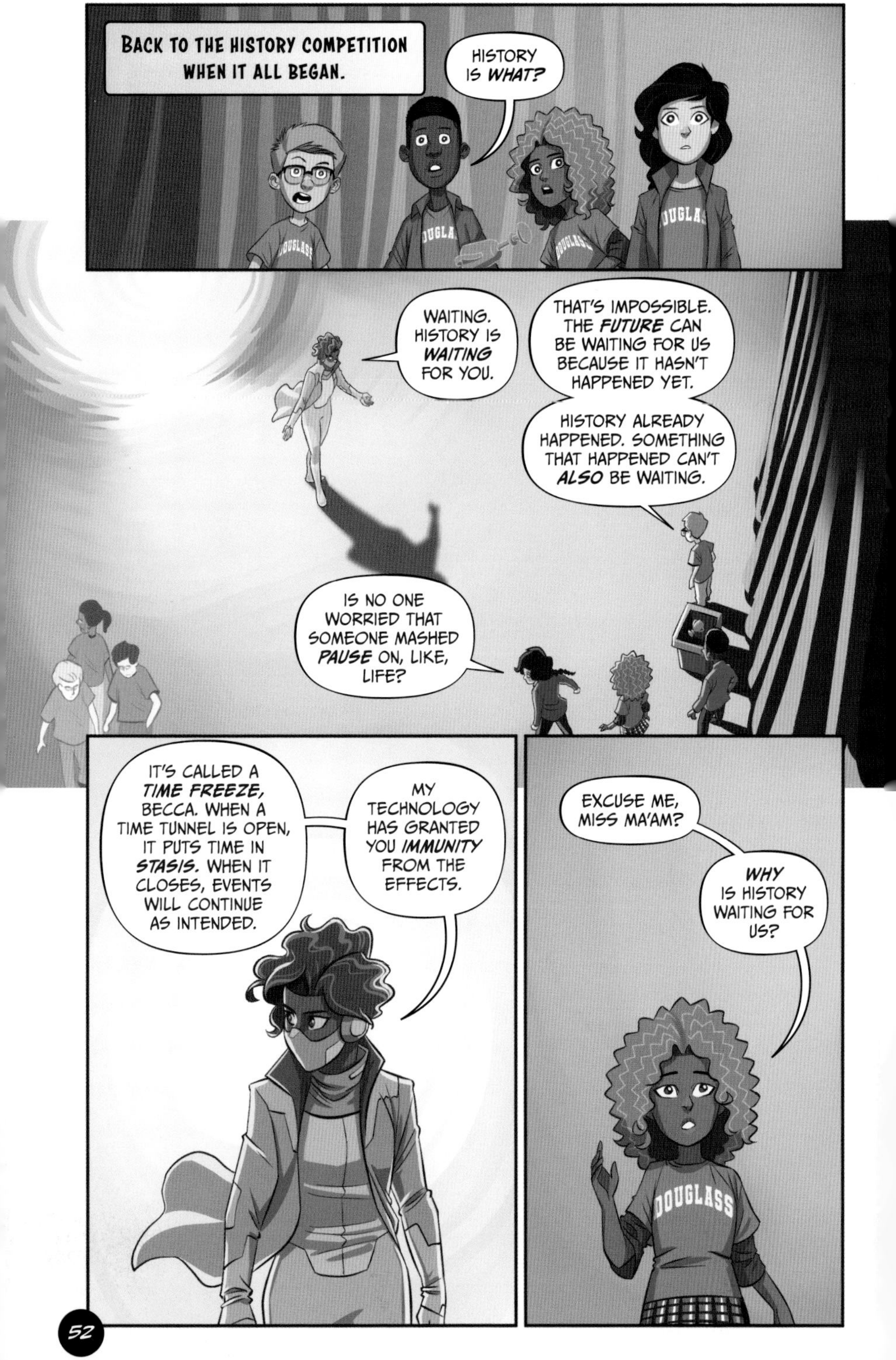
BACK TO THE HISTORY COMPETITION WHEN IT ALL BEGAN.
HISTORY IS *WHAT?*
DOUGLASS
WAITING. HISTORY IS *WAITING* FOR YOU.
THAT'S IMPOSSIBLE. THE *FUTURE* CAN BE WAITING FOR US BECAUSE IT HASN'T HAPPENED YET.
HISTORY ALREADY HAPPENED. SOMETHING THAT HAPPENED CAN'T *ALSO* BE WAITING.
IS NO ONE WORRIED THAT SOMEONE MASHED *PAUSE* ON, LIKE, LIFE?
IT'S CALLED A *TIME FREEZE,* BECCA. WHEN A TIME TUNNEL IS OPEN, IT PUTS TIME IN *STASIS.* WHEN IT CLOSES, EVENTS WILL CONTINUE AS INTENDED.
MY TECHNOLOGY HAS GRANTED YOU *IMMUNITY* FROM THE EFFECTS.
EXCUSE ME, MISS MA'AM?
WHY IS HISTORY WAITING FOR US?
DOUGLASS

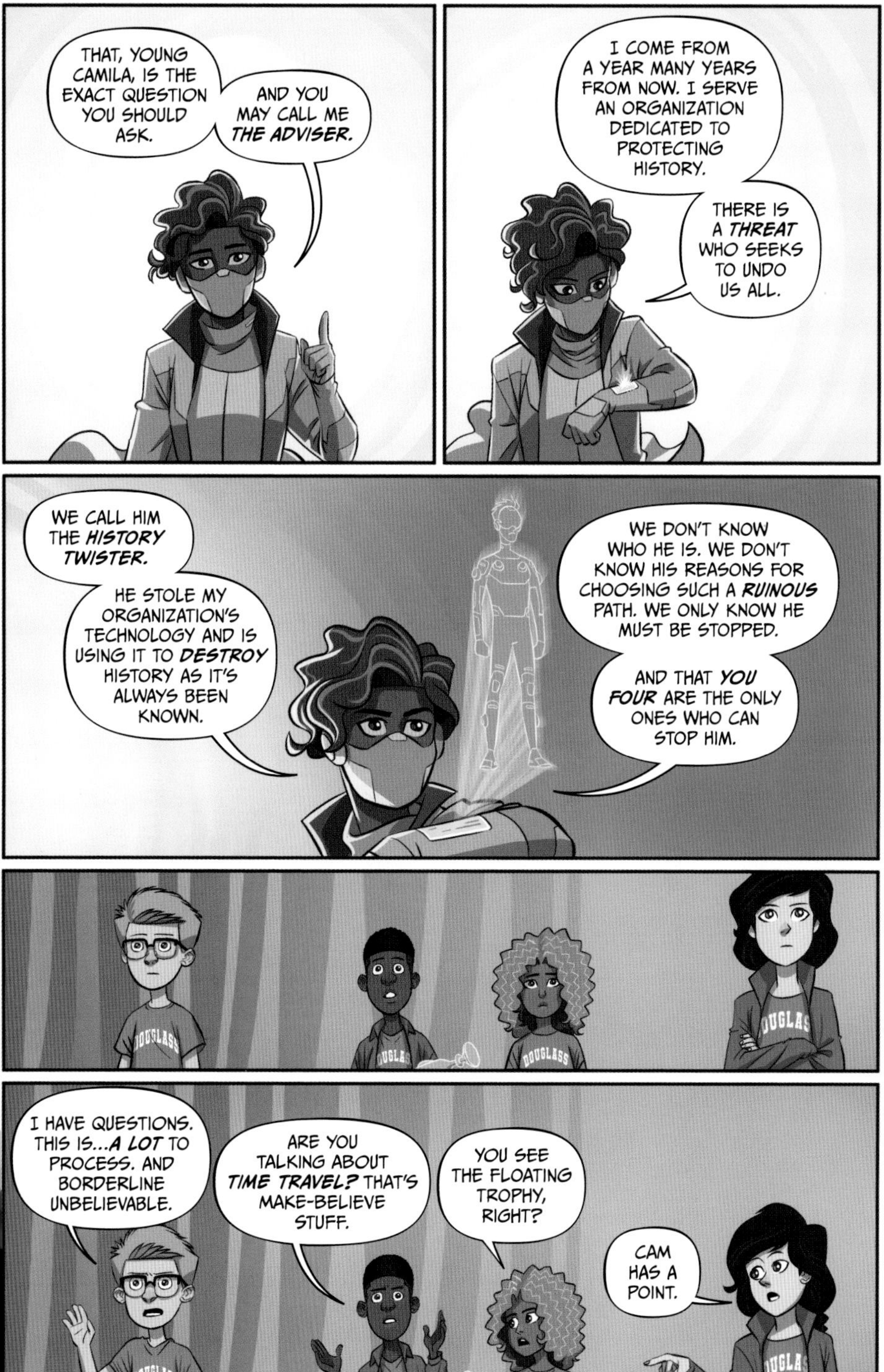
THAT, YOUNG CAMILA, IS THE EXACT QUESTION YOU SHOULD ASK.
AND YOU MAY CALL ME *THE ADVISER.*
I COME FROM A YEAR MANY YEARS FROM NOW. I SERVE AN ORGANIZATION DEDICATED TO PROTECTING HISTORY.
THERE IS A *THREAT* WHO SEEKS TO UNDO US ALL.
WE CALL HIM THE *HISTORY TWISTER.*
HE STOLE MY ORGANIZATION'S TECHNOLOGY AND IS USING IT TO *DESTROY* HISTORY AS IT'S ALWAYS BEEN KNOWN.
WE DON'T KNOW WHO HE IS. WE DON'T KNOW HIS REASONS FOR CHOOSING SUCH A *RUINOUS* PATH. WE ONLY KNOW HE MUST BE STOPPED.
AND THAT *YOU FOUR* ARE THE ONLY ONES WHO CAN STOP HIM.
DOUGLASS
DOUGLASS
DOUGLASS
DOUGLAS
I HAVE QUESTIONS. THIS IS...*A LOT* TO PROCESS. AND BORDERLINE UNBELIEVABLE.
ARE YOU TALKING ABOUT *TIME TRAVEL?* THAT'S MAKE-BELIEVE STUFF.
YOU SEE THE FLOATING TROPHY, RIGHT?
CAM HAS A POINT.
DOUGLASS
DOUGLAS
DOUGLASS
DOUGLAS

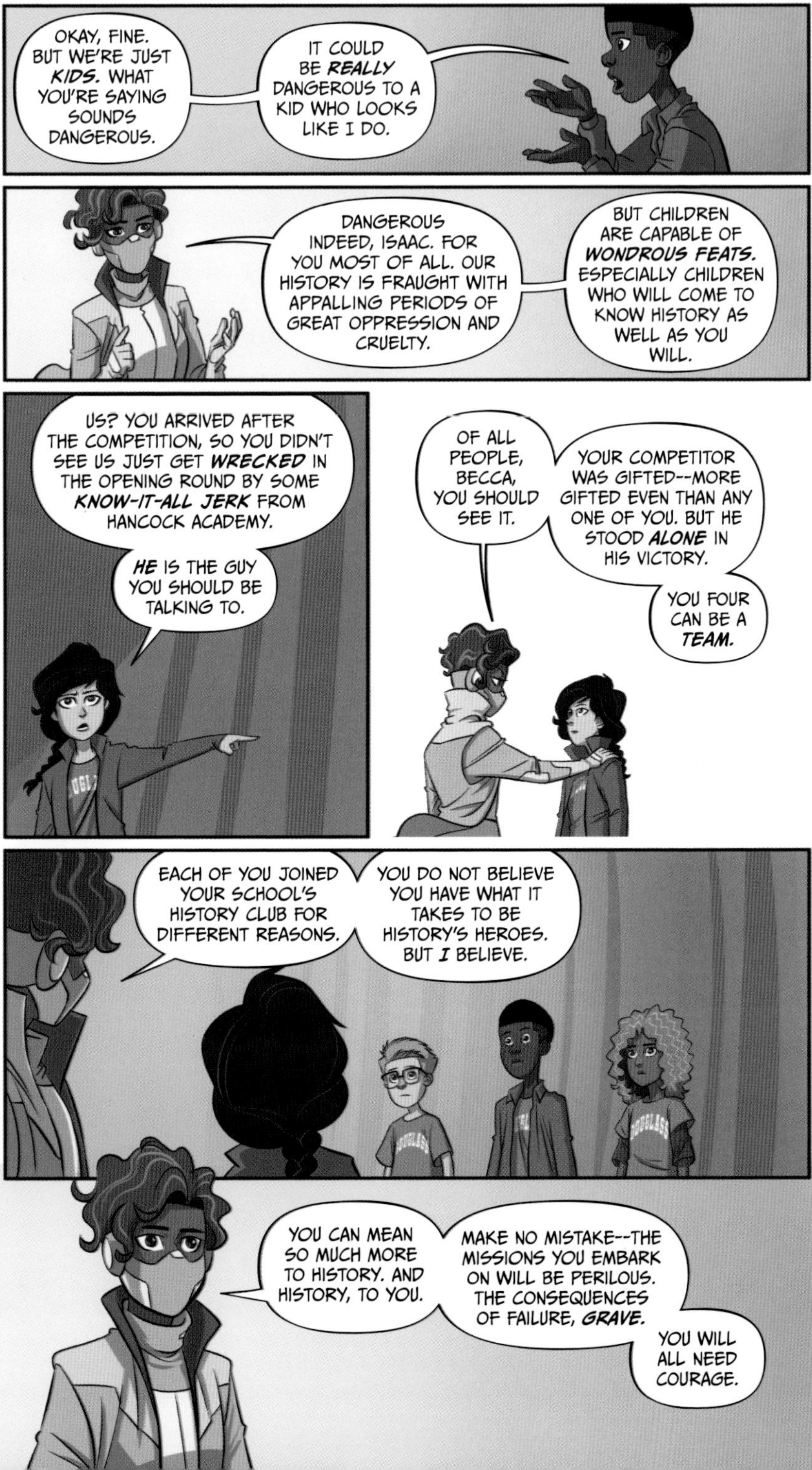
OKAY, FINE. BUT WE'RE JUST *KIDS.* WHAT YOU'RE SAYING SOUNDS DANGEROUS.
IT COULD BE *REALLY* DANGEROUS TO A KID WHO LOOKS LIKE I DO.
DANGEROUS INDEED, ISAAC. FOR YOU MOST OF ALL. OUR HISTORY IS FRAUGHT WITH APPALLING PERIODS OF GREAT OPPRESSION AND CRUELTY.
BUT CHILDREN ARE CAPABLE OF *WONDROUS FEATS.* ESPECIALLY CHILDREN WHO WILL COME TO KNOW HISTORY AS WELL AS YOU WILL.
US? YOU ARRIVED AFTER THE COMPETITION, SO YOU DIDN'T SEE US JUST GET *WRECKED* IN THE OPENING ROUND BY SOME *KNOW-IT-ALL JERK* FROM HANCOCK ACADEMY.
HE IS THE GUY YOU SHOULD BE TALKING TO.
OF ALL PEOPLE, BECCA, YOU SHOULD SEE IT.
YOUR COMPETITOR WAS GIFTED--MORE GIFTED EVEN THAN ANY ONE OF YOU. BUT HE STOOD *ALONE* IN HIS VICTORY.
YOU FOUR CAN BE A *TEAM.*
EACH OF YOU JOINED YOUR SCHOOL'S HISTORY CLUB FOR DIFFERENT REASONS.
YOU DO NOT BELIEVE YOU HAVE WHAT IT TAKES TO BE HISTORY'S HEROES. BUT *I* BELIEVE.
YOU CAN MEAN SO MUCH MORE TO HISTORY. AND HISTORY, TO YOU.
MAKE NO MISTAKE--THE MISSIONS YOU EMBARK ON WILL BE PERILOUS. THE CONSEQUENCES OF FAILURE, *GRAVE.*
YOU WILL ALL NEED COURAGE.

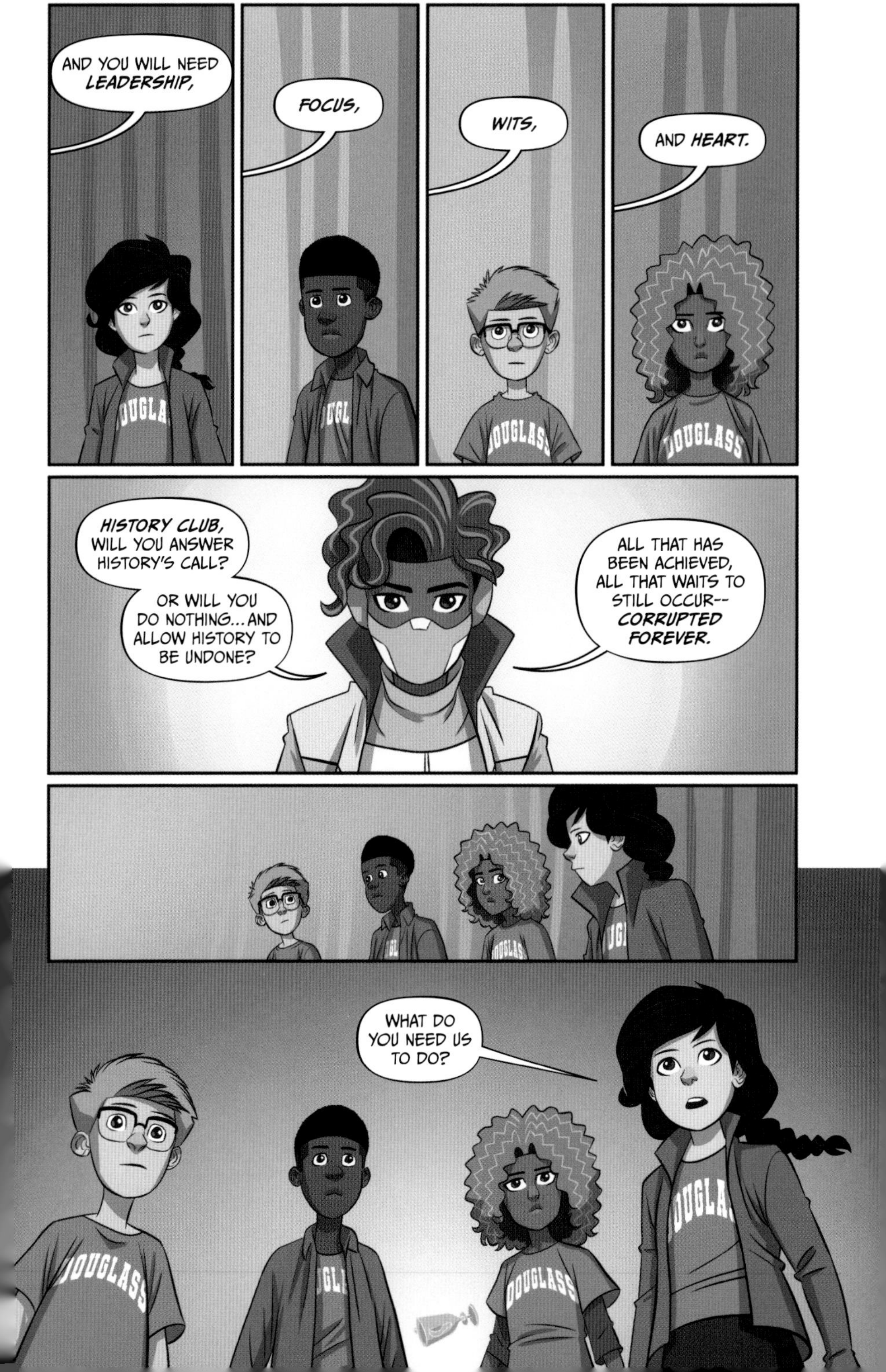
AND YOU WILL NEED *LEADERSHIP,*
FOCUS,
WITS,
AND *HEART.*
HISTORY CLUB, WILL YOU ANSWER HISTORY'S CALL?
OR WILL YOU DO NOTHING...AND ALLOW HISTORY TO BE UNDONE?
ALL THAT HAS BEEN ACHIEVED, ALL THAT WAITS TO STILL OCCUR-- *CORRUPTED FOREVER.*
WHAT DO YOU NEED US TO DO?

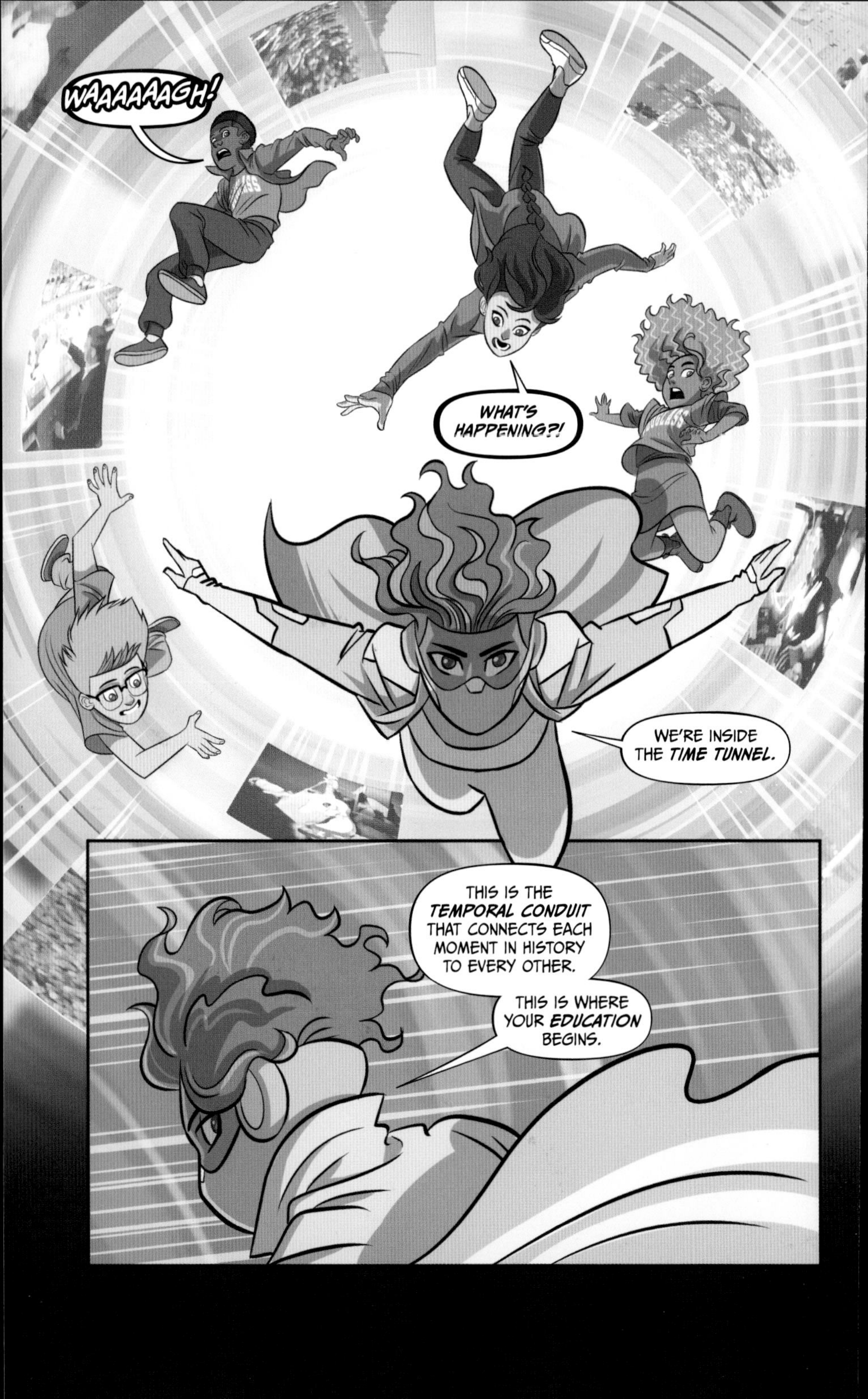
WAAAAAAGH!
WHAT'S HAPPENING?!
WE'RE INSIDE THE *TIME TUNNEL.*
THIS IS THE *TEMPORAL CONDUIT* THAT CONNECTS EACH MOMENT IN HISTORY TO EVERY OTHER.
THIS IS WHERE YOUR *EDUCATION* BEGINS.

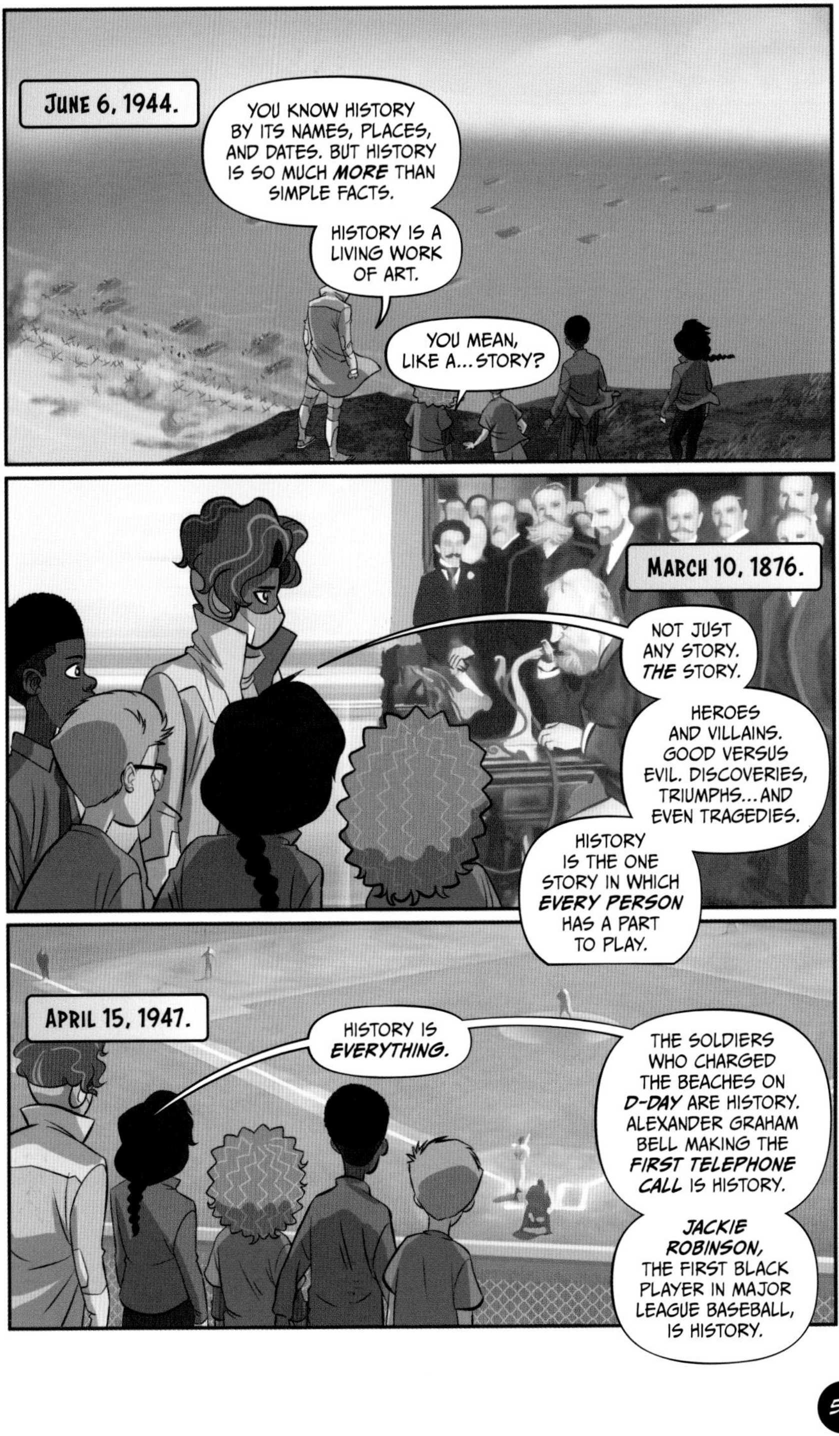
JUNE 6, 1944.
YOU KNOW HISTORY BY ITS NAMES, PLACES, AND DATES. BUT HISTORY IS SO MUCH *MORE* THAN SIMPLE FACTS.
HISTORY IS A LIVING WORK OF ART.
YOU MEAN, LIKE A... STORY?
MARCH 10, 1876.
NOT JUST ANY STORY. *THE* STORY.
HEROES AND VILLAINS. GOOD VERSUS EVIL. DISCOVERIES, TRIUMPHS... AND EVEN TRAGEDIES.
HISTORY IS THE ONE STORY IN WHICH *EVERY PERSON* HAS A PART TO PLAY.
APRIL 15, 1947.
HISTORY IS *EVERYTHING.*
THE SOLDIERS WHO CHARGED THE BEACHES ON *D-DAY* ARE HISTORY. ALEXANDER GRAHAM BELL MAKING THE *FIRST TELEPHONE CALL* IS HISTORY.
JACKIE ROBINSON, THE FIRST BLACK PLAYER IN MAJOR LEAGUE BASEBALL, IS HISTORY.

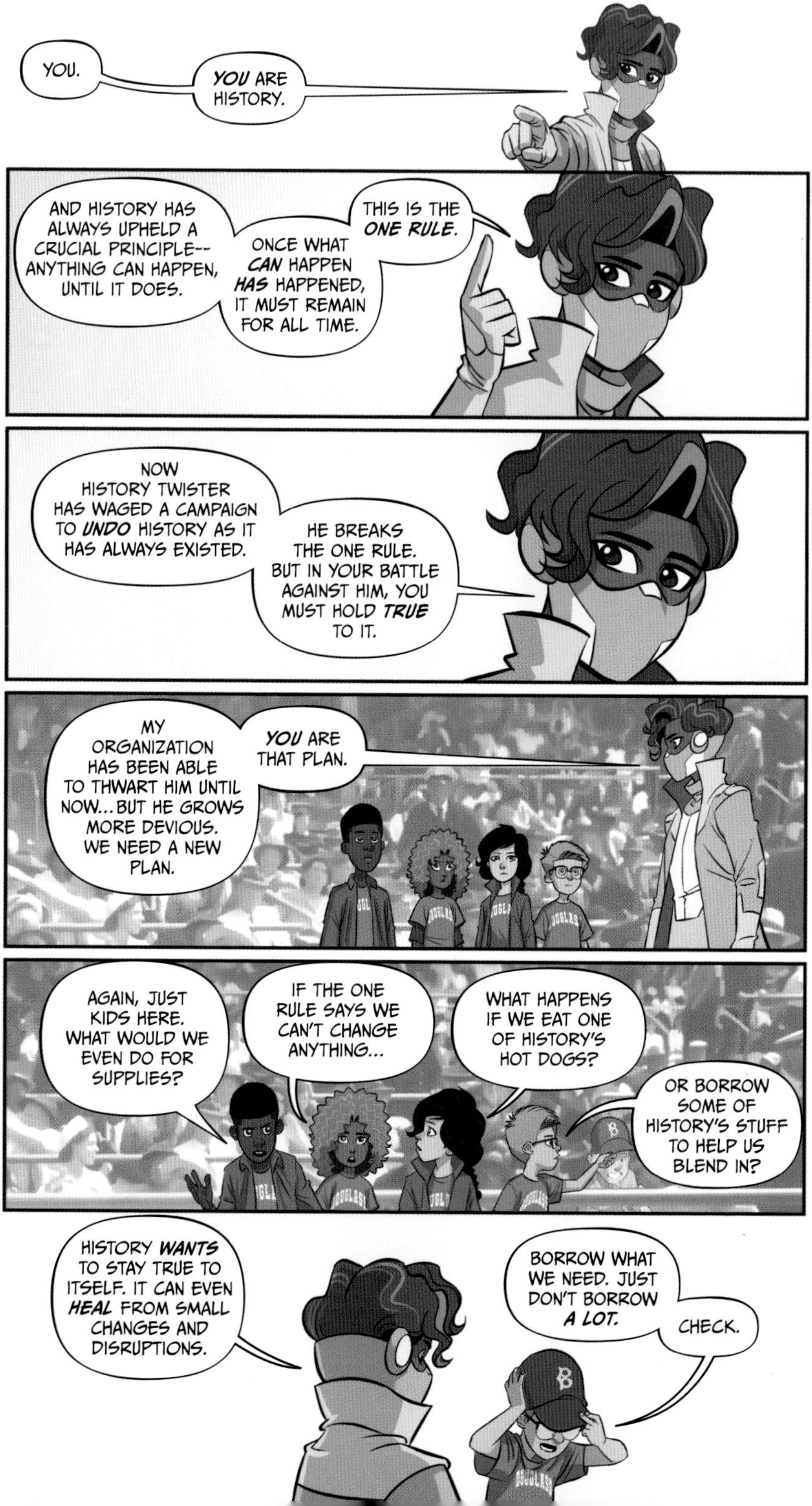
YOU.
YOU ARE HISTORY.
AND HISTORY HAS ALWAYS UPHELD A CRUCIAL PRINCIPLE-- ANYTHING CAN HAPPEN, UNTIL IT DOES.
THIS IS THE ONE RULE.
ONCE WHAT CAN HAPPEN HAS HAPPENED, IT MUST REMAIN FOR ALL TIME.
NOW HISTORY TWISTER HAS WAGED A CAMPAIGN TO UNDO HISTORY AS IT HAS ALWAYS EXISTED.
HE BREAKS THE ONE RULE. BUT IN YOUR BATTLE AGAINST HIM, YOU MUST HOLD TRUE TO IT.
MY ORGANIZATION HAS BEEN ABLE TO THWART HIM UNTIL NOW...BUT HE GROWS MORE DEVIOUS. WE NEED A NEW PLAN.
YOU ARE THAT PLAN.
AGAIN, JUST KIDS HERE. WHAT WOULD WE EVEN DO FOR SUPPLIES?
IF THE ONE RULE SAYS WE CAN'T CHANGE ANYTHING...
WHAT HAPPENS IF WE EAT ONE OF HISTORY'S HOT DOGS?
OR BORROW SOME OF HISTORY'S STUFF TO HELP US BLEND IN?
HISTORY WANTS TO STAY TRUE TO ITSELF. IT CAN EVEN HEAL FROM SMALL CHANGES AND DISRUPTIONS.
BORROW WHAT WE NEED. JUST DON'T BORROW A LOT.
CHECK.

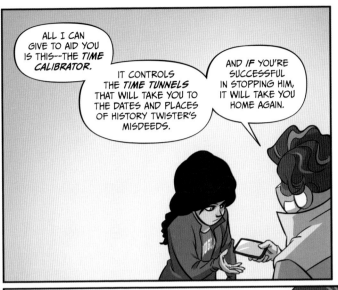

ALL I CAN GIVE TO AID YOU IS THIS--THE *TIME CALIBRATOR.*

IT CONTROLS THE *TIME TUNNELS* THAT WILL TAKE YOU TO THE DATES AND PLACES OF HISTORY TWISTER'S MISDEEDS.

AND *IF* YOU'RE SUCCESSFUL IN STOPPING HIM, IT WILL TAKE YOU HOME AGAIN.

AND...IF WE'RE NOT SUCCESSFUL?

HISTORY TWISTER WILL *WIN.*

THE STORY WILL BE *REWRITTEN,* AND EVERYTHING WE HAVE EVER KNOWN ABOUT OURSELVES WILL *CEASE* TO BE.

THESE ARE THE STAKES.

NO PRESSURE.

BUT, WAIT.

IF THE STORY OF HISTORY HAS ALREADY BEEN WRITTEN...AND IF YOU'RE FROM THE FUTURE...THEN YOU ALREADY *KNOW* HOW ALL THIS ENDS.

SO...HOW DOES IT?

I *DO* KNOW WHAT HAPPENS. JUST AS I KNEW YOU WOULD ASK ME TO TELL YOU, THOMAS.

BUT I CAN'T. I, TOO, MUST UPHOLD THE *ONE RULE.*

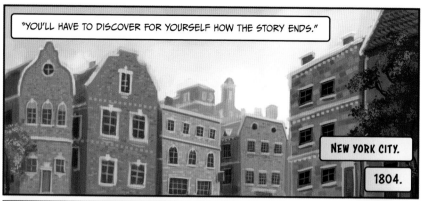

"YOU'LL HAVE TO DISCOVER FOR YOURSELF HOW THE STORY ENDS."

NEW YORK CITY.

1804.

SO THIS IS THE BIG APPLE BACK WHEN IT WAS, YOU KNOW, *LESS BIG*.

AND LESS CLEAN. WHAT'S THAT *REEK?*

HORSES. OR, MORE TO THE POINT, HORSE--

GOT IT. THANKS.

IT ISN'T SAFE FOR ME TO BE OUT IN THE OPEN.

LET'S GET OFF THE STREET.

ALLEY. *GO.*

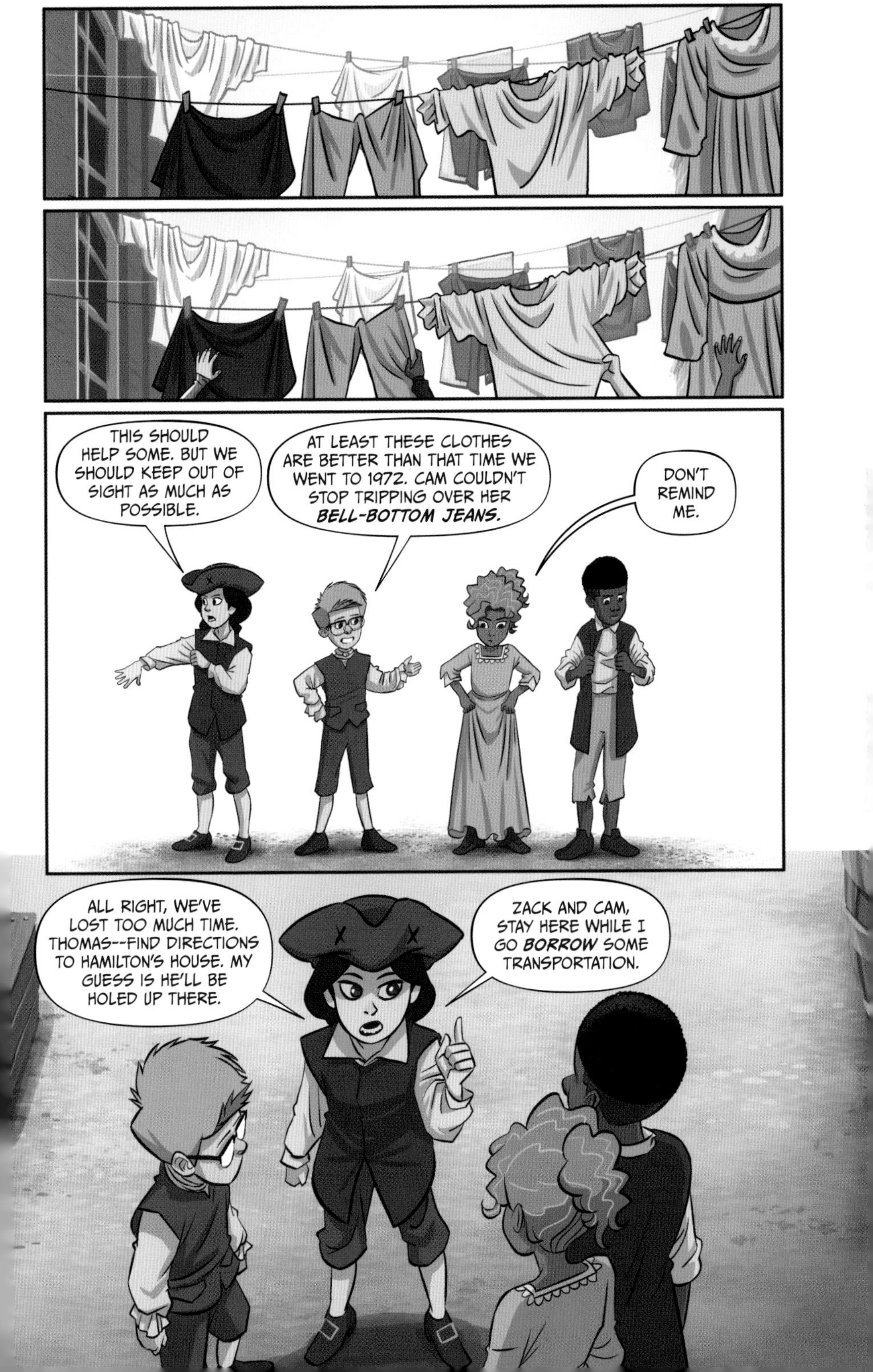
THIS SHOULD HELP SOME. BUT WE SHOULD KEEP OUT OF SIGHT AS MUCH AS POSSIBLE.
AT LEAST THESE CLOTHES ARE BETTER THAN THAT TIME WE WENT TO 1972. CAM COULDN'T STOP TRIPPING OVER HER ***BELL-BOTTOM JEANS.***
DON'T REMIND ME.
ALL RIGHT, WE'VE LOST TOO MUCH TIME. THOMAS--FIND DIRECTIONS TO HAMILTON'S HOUSE. MY GUESS IS HE'LL BE HOLED UP THERE.
ZACK AND CAM, STAY HERE WHILE I GO ***BORROW*** SOME TRANSPORTATION.

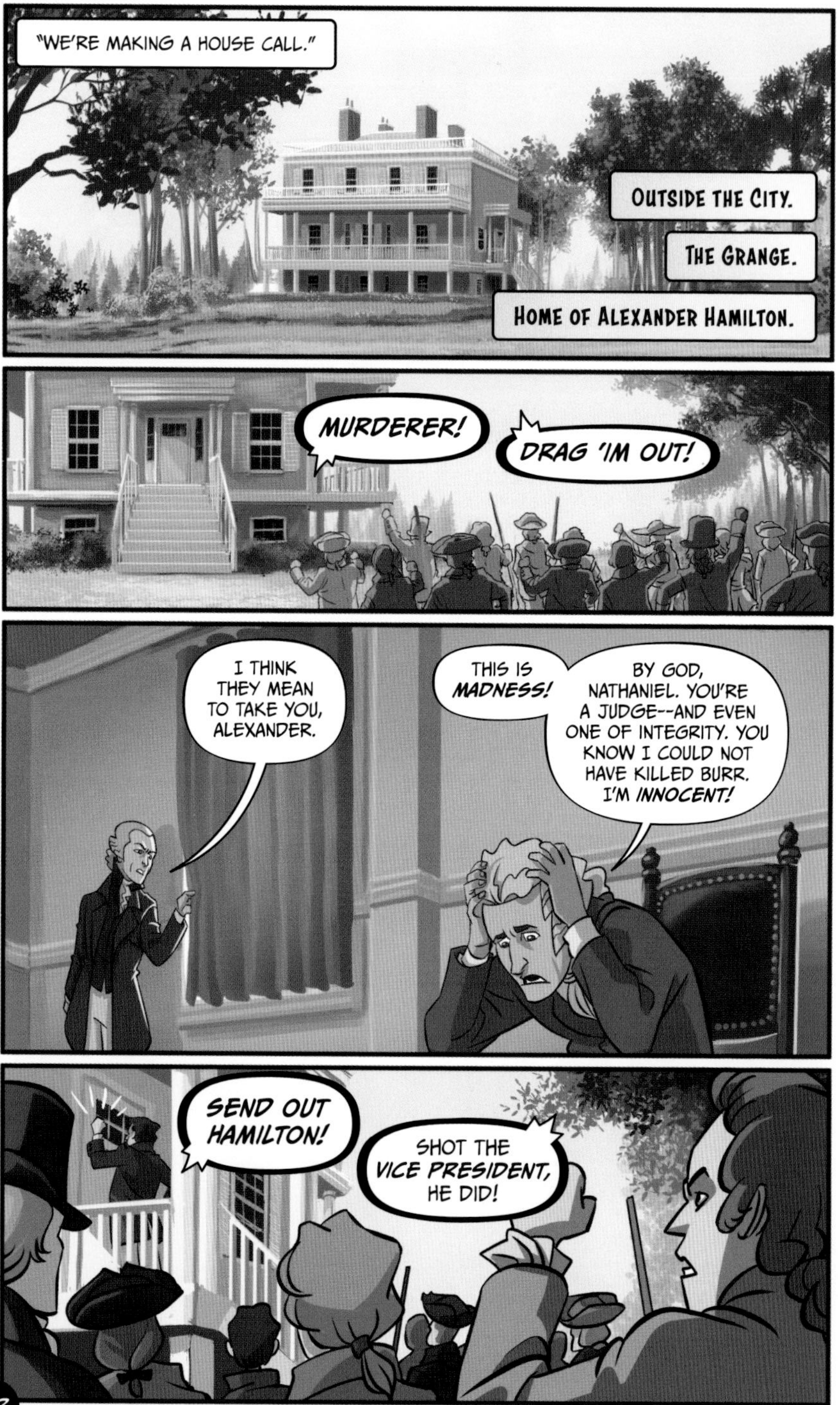
"WE'RE MAKING A HOUSE CALL."
OUTSIDE THE CITY.
THE GRANGE.
HOME OF ALEXANDER HAMILTON.
MURDERER!
DRAG 'IM OUT!
I THINK THEY MEAN TO TAKE YOU, ALEXANDER.
THIS IS MADNESS!
BY GOD, NATHANIEL. YOU'RE A JUDGE--AND EVEN ONE OF INTEGRITY. YOU KNOW I COULD NOT HAVE KILLED BURR. I'M INNOCENT!
SEND OUT HAMILTON!
SHOT THE VICE PRESIDENT, HE DID!

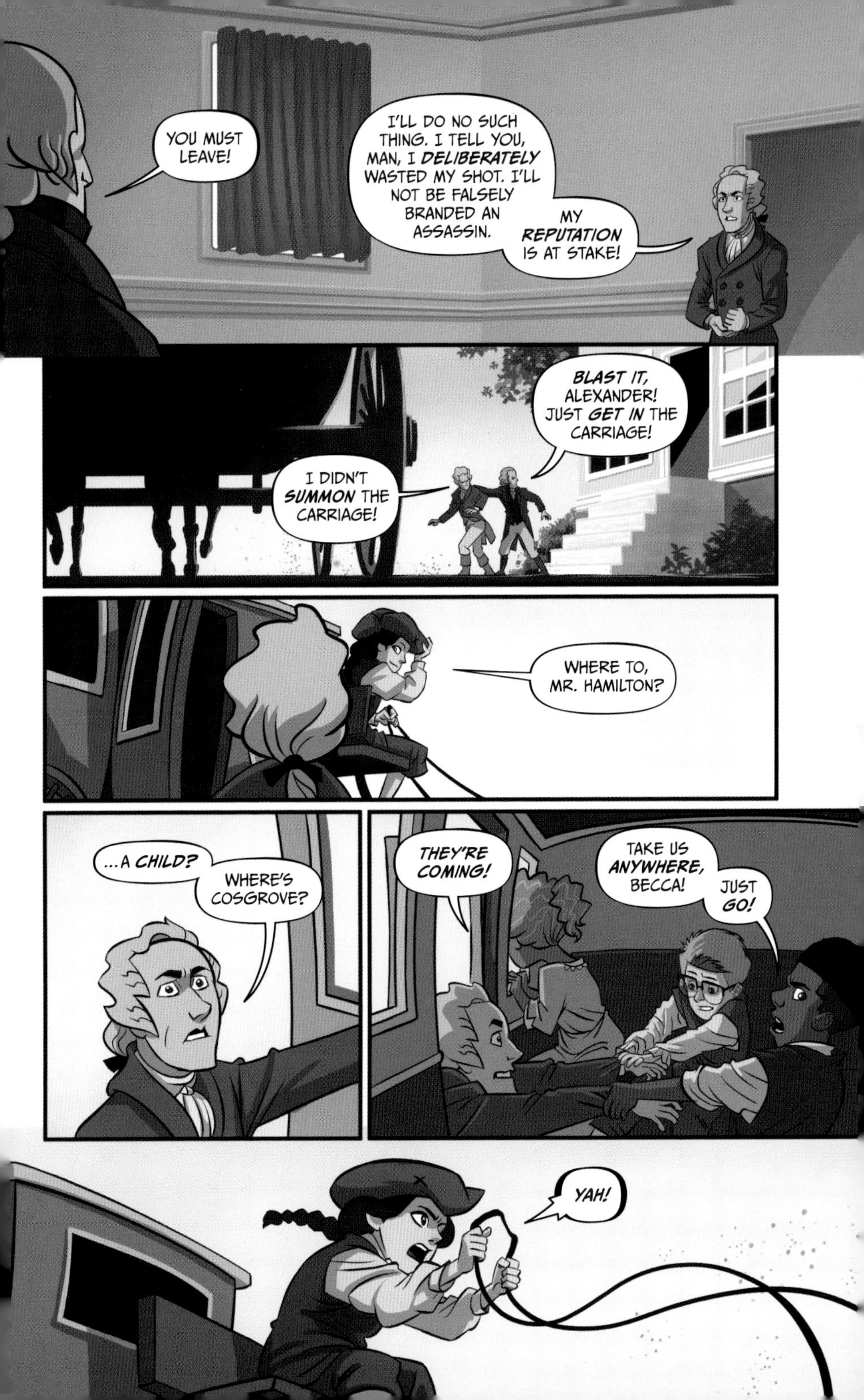
YOU MUST LEAVE!
I'LL DO NO SUCH THING. I TELL YOU, MAN, I DELIBERATELY WASTED MY SHOT. I'LL NOT BE FALSELY BRANDED AN ASSASSIN.
MY REPUTATION IS AT STAKE!
BLAST IT, ALEXANDER! JUST GET IN THE CARRIAGE!
I DIDN'T SUMMON THE CARRIAGE!
WHERE TO, MR. HAMILTON?
...A CHILD?
WHERE'S COSGROVE?
THEY'RE COMING!
TAKE US ANYWHERE, BECCA!
JUST GO!
YAH!

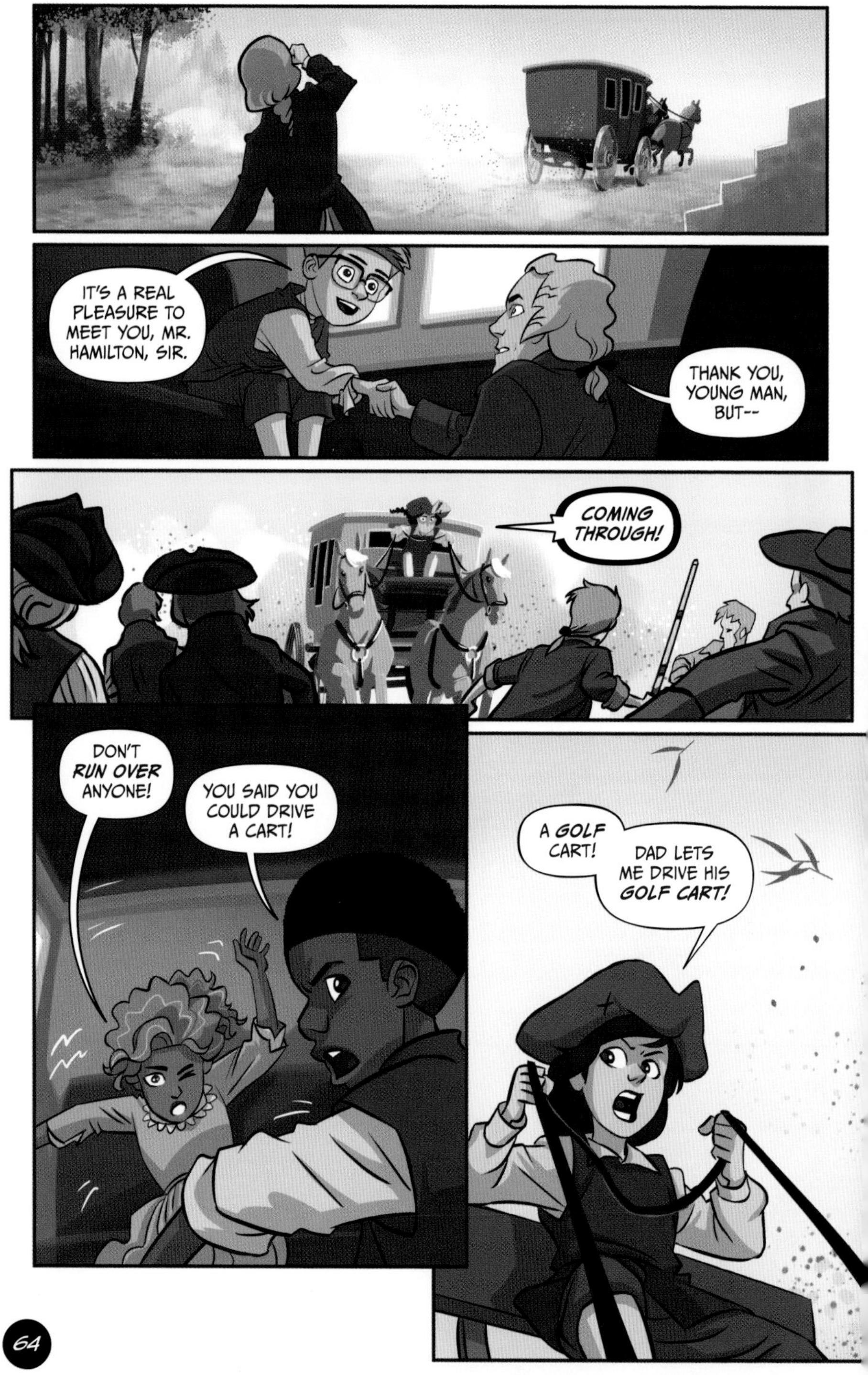
IT'S A REAL PLEASURE TO MEET YOU, MR. HAMILTON, SIR.
THANK YOU, YOUNG MAN, BUT--
COMING THROUGH!
DON'T RUN OVER ANYONE!
YOU SAID YOU COULD DRIVE A CART!
A GOLF CART!
DAD LETS ME DRIVE HIS GOLF CART!

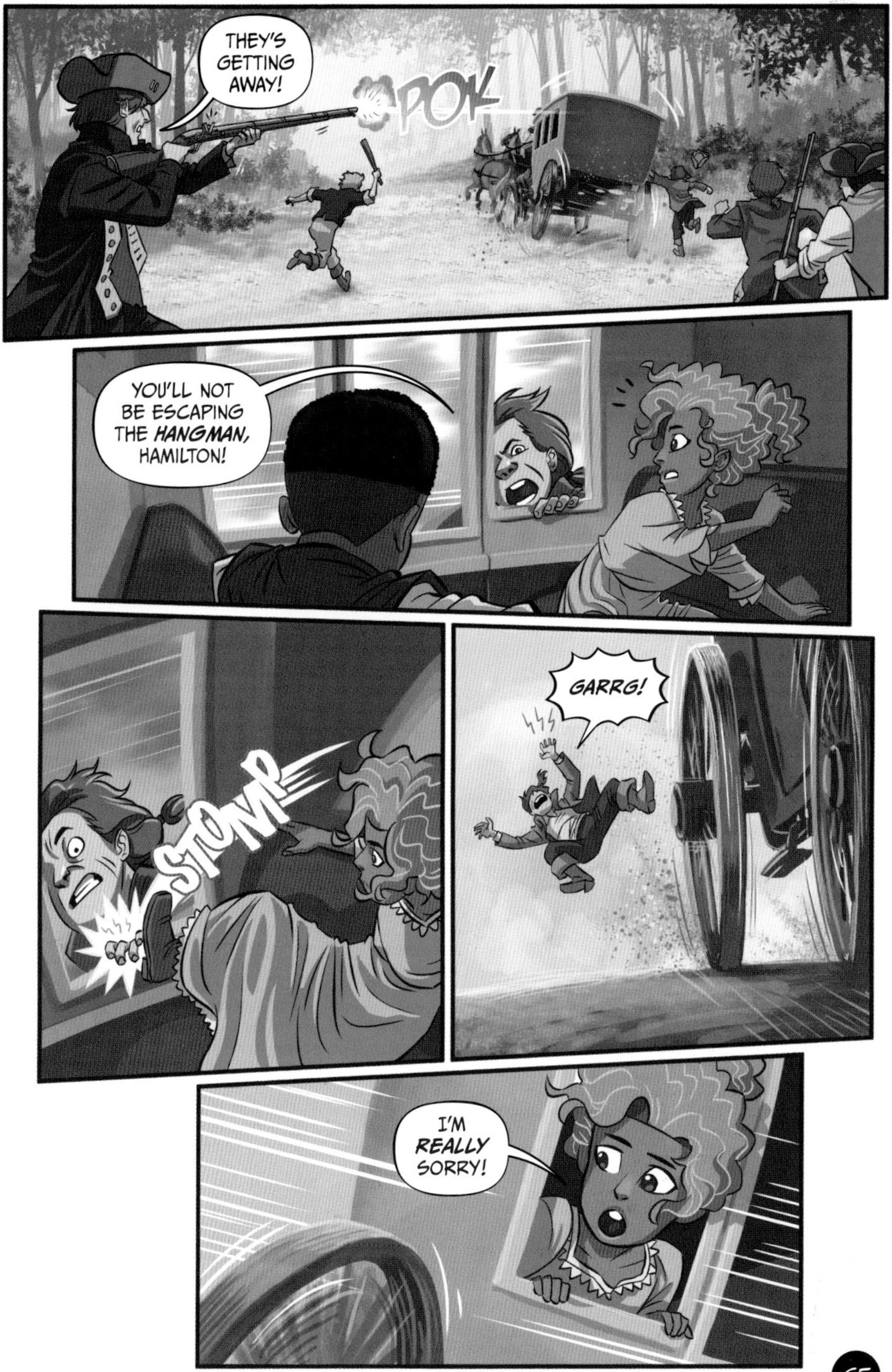
THEY'S GETTING AWAY!
POK
YOU'LL NOT BE ESCAPING THE HANGMAN, HAMILTON!
STOMP
GARRG!
I'M REALLY SORRY!

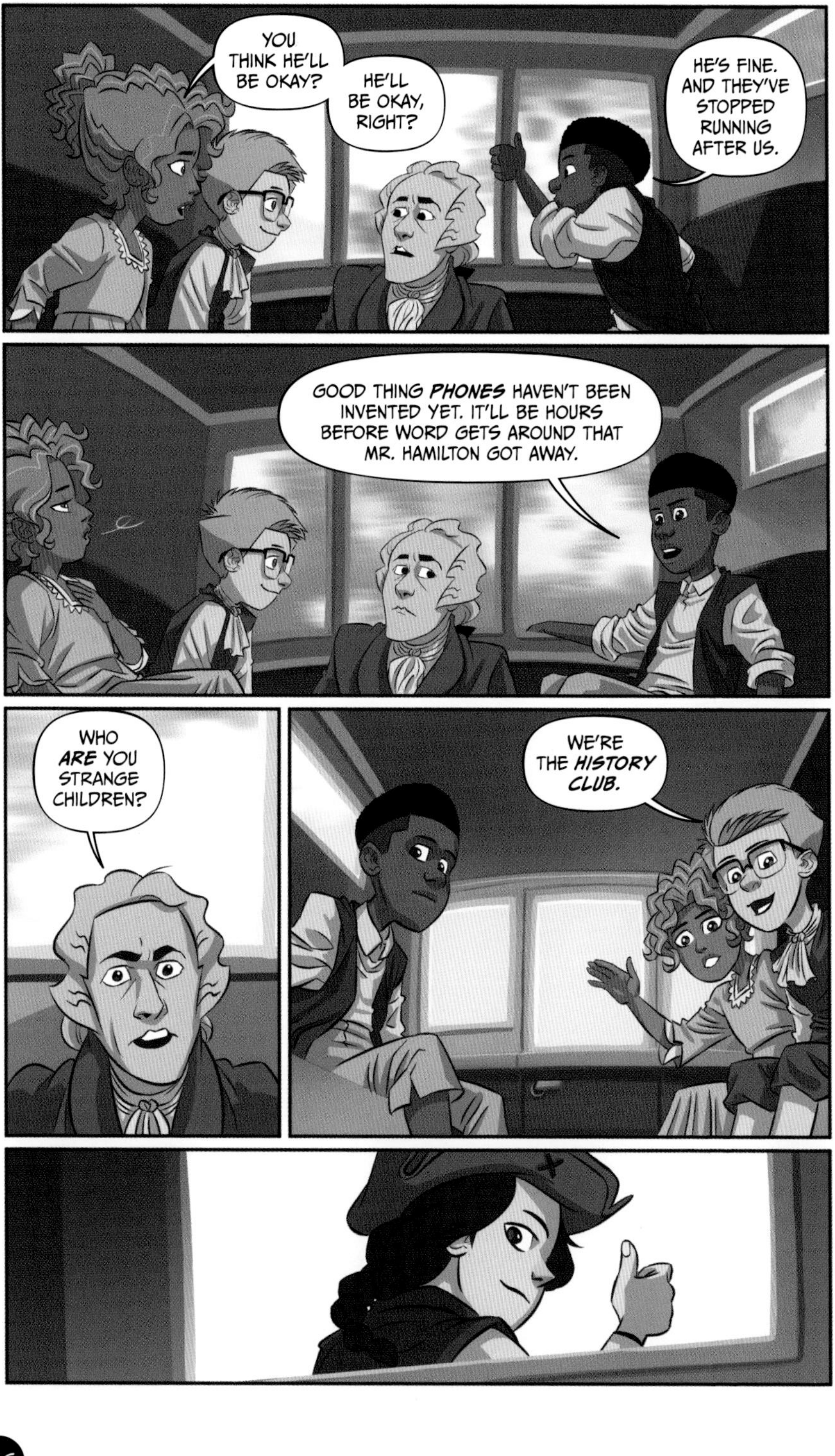
YOU THINK HE'LL BE OKAY?
HE'LL BE OKAY, RIGHT?
HE'S FINE. AND THEY'VE STOPPED RUNNING AFTER US.
GOOD THING PHONES HAVEN'T BEEN INVENTED YET. IT'LL BE HOURS BEFORE WORD GETS AROUND THAT MR. HAMILTON GOT AWAY.
WHO ARE YOU STRANGE CHILDREN?
WE'RE THE HISTORY CLUB.

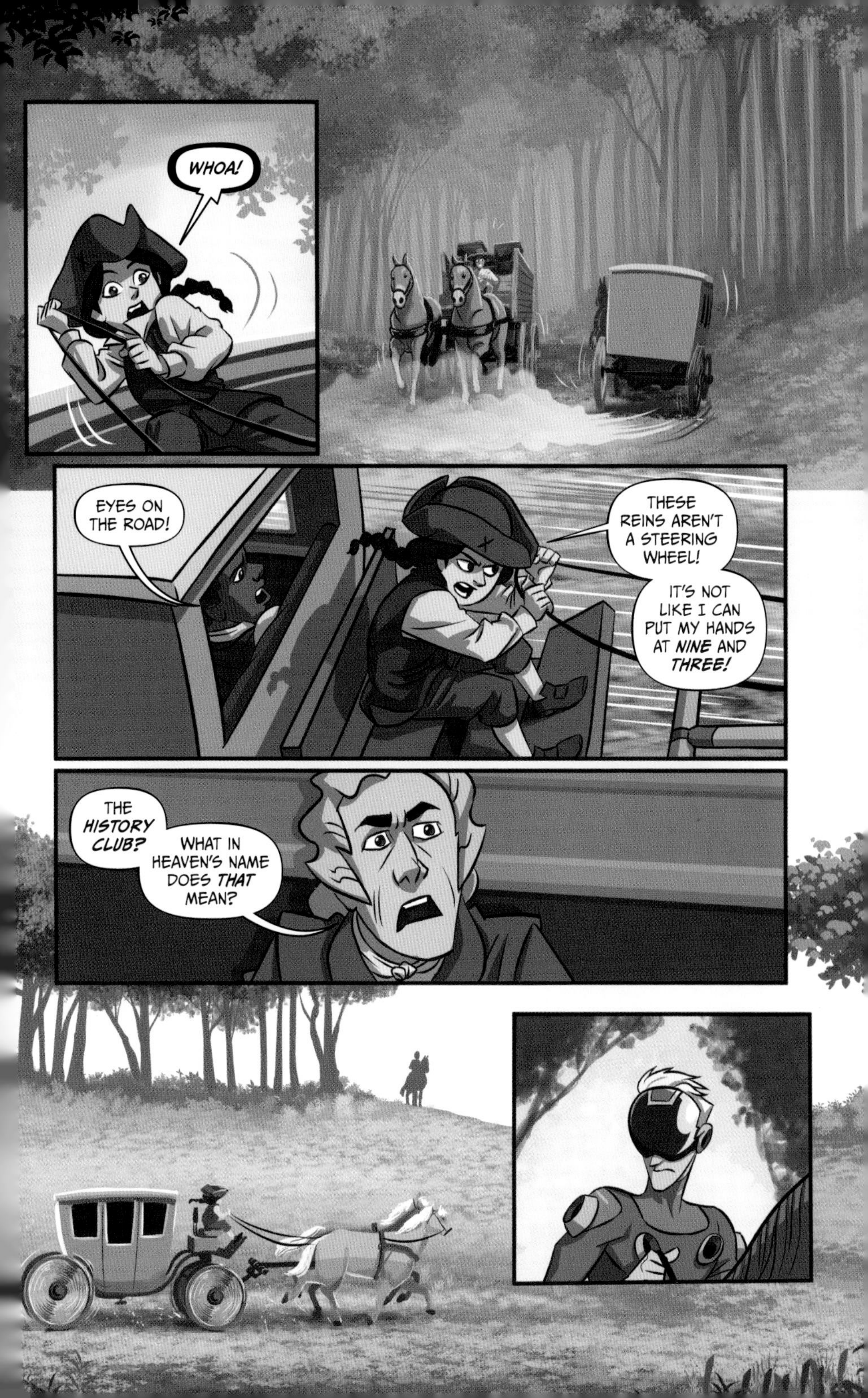
WHOA!
EYES ON THE ROAD!
THESE REINS AREN'T A STEERING WHEEL!
IT'S NOT LIKE I CAN PUT MY HANDS AT *NINE* AND *THREE!*
THE *HISTORY CLUB?*
WHAT IN HEAVEN'S NAME DOES *THAT* MEAN?

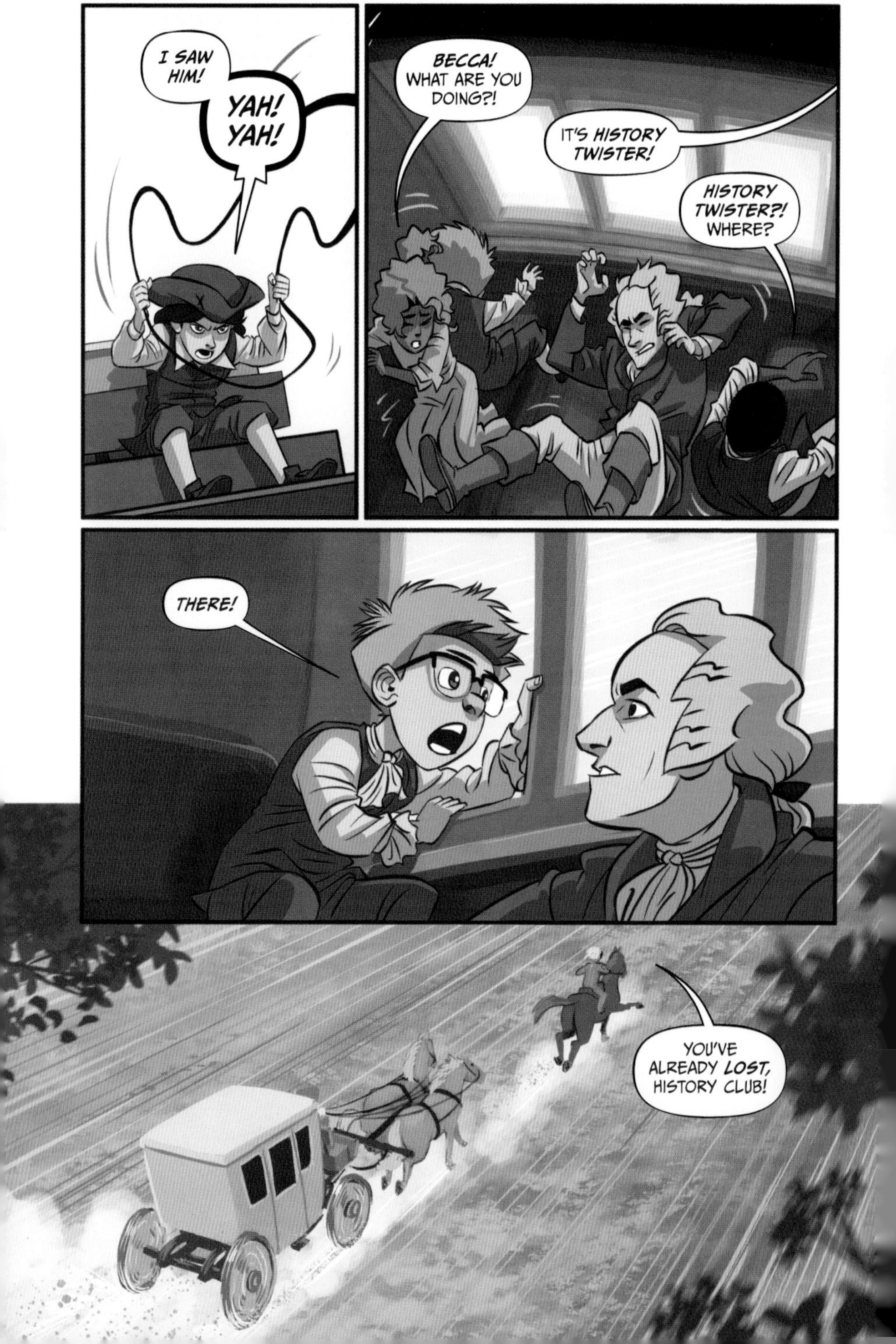
I SAW HIM!
YAH! YAH!
BECCA! WHAT ARE YOU DOING?!
IT'S HISTORY TWISTER!
HISTORY TWISTER?! WHERE?
THERE!
YOU'VE ALREADY LOST, HISTORY CLUB!

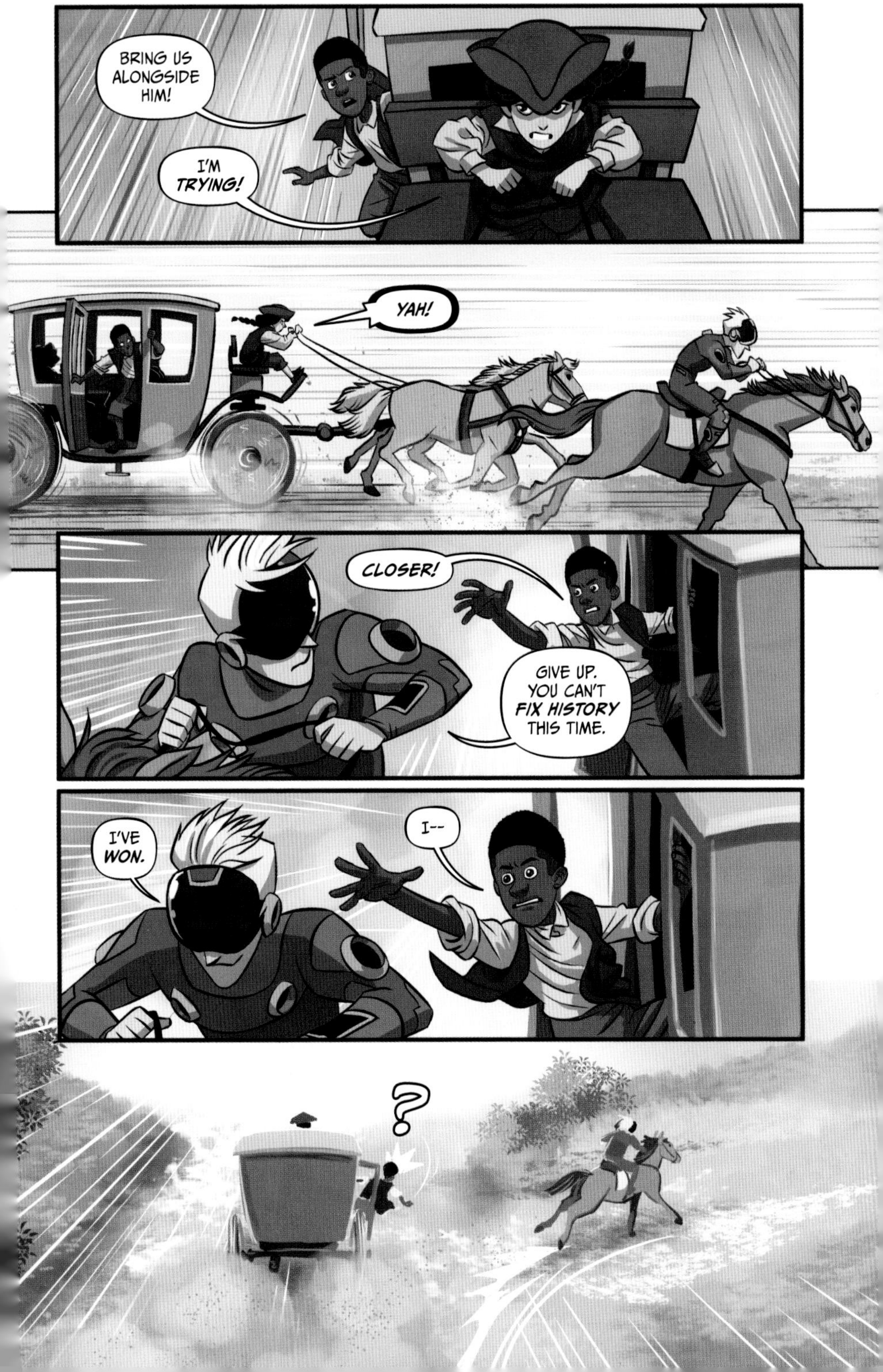
BRING US ALONGSIDE HIM!
I'M *TRYING!*
YAH!
CLOSER!
GIVE UP. YOU CAN'T *FIX HISTORY* THIS TIME.
I'VE *WON.*
I--
?

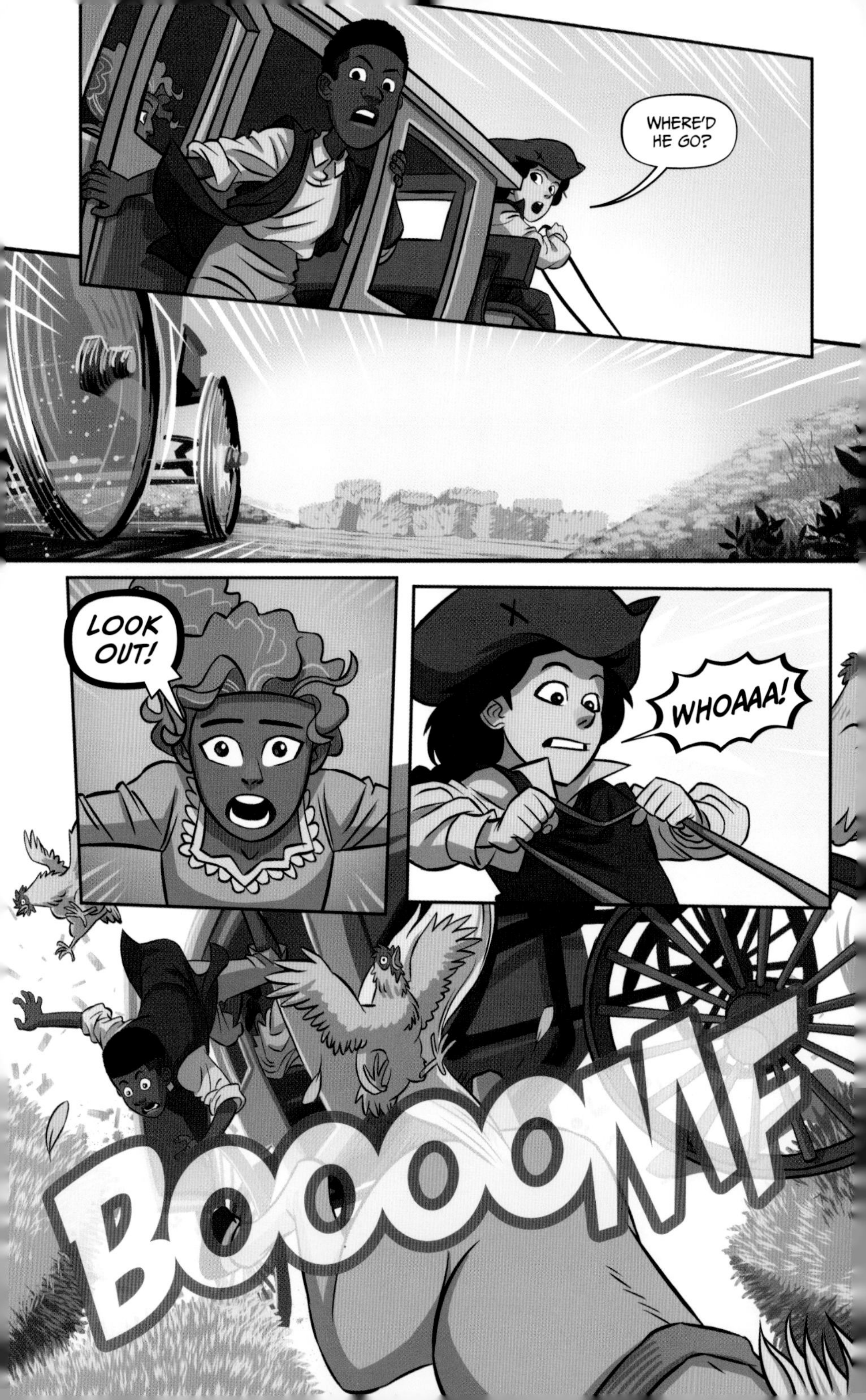
WHERE'D HE GO?
LOOK OUT!
WHOAAA!
BOOOOMF

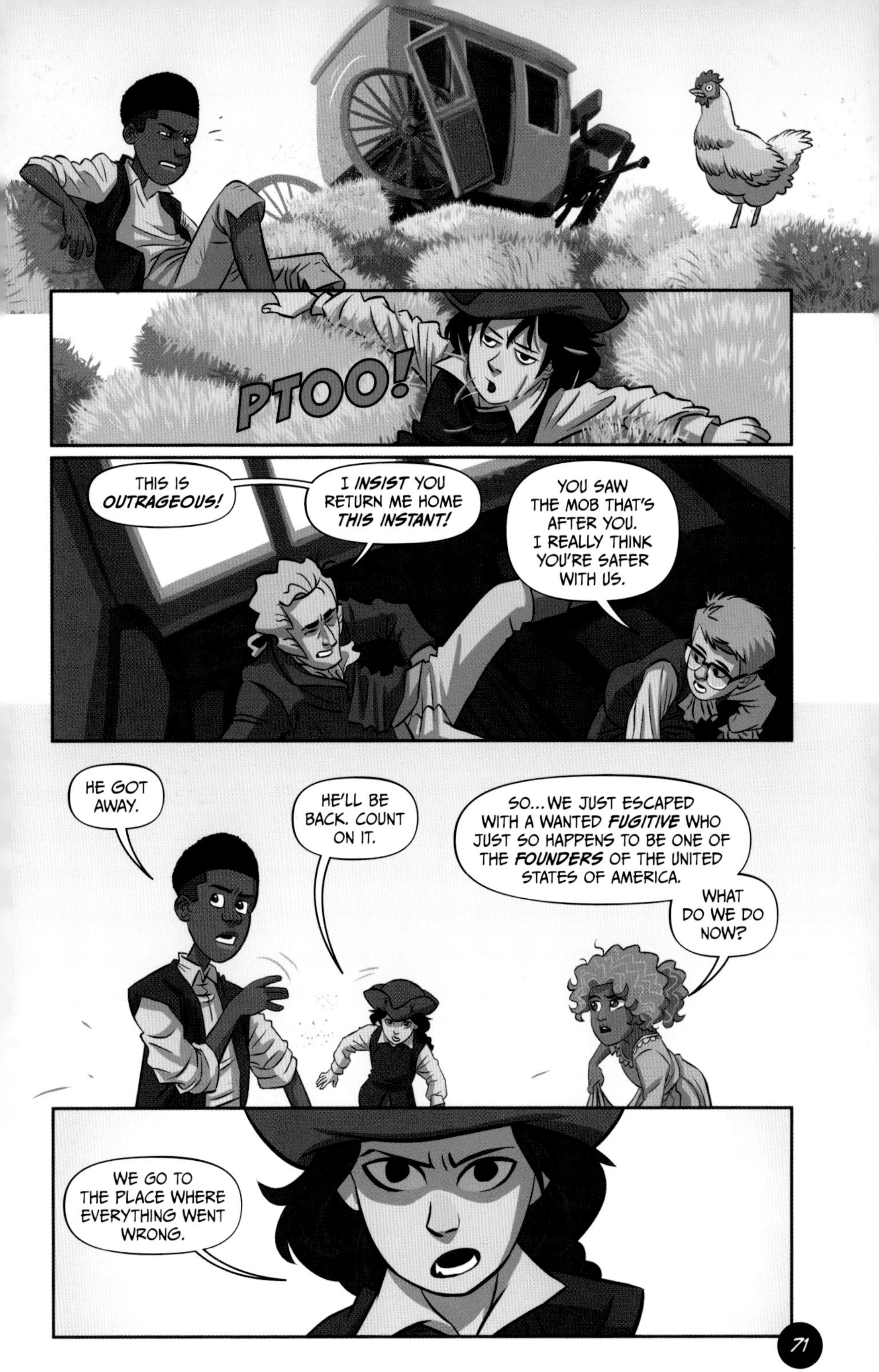
PTOO!
THIS IS OUTRAGEOUS!
I INSIST YOU RETURN ME HOME THIS INSTANT!
YOU SAW THE MOB THAT'S AFTER YOU. I REALLY THINK YOU'RE SAFER WITH US.
HE GOT AWAY.
HE'LL BE BACK. COUNT ON IT.
SO...WE JUST ESCAPED WITH A WANTED FUGITIVE WHO JUST SO HAPPENS TO BE ONE OF THE FOUNDERS OF THE UNITED STATES OF AMERICA.
WHAT DO WE DO NOW?
WE GO TO THE PLACE WHERE EVERYTHING WENT WRONG.

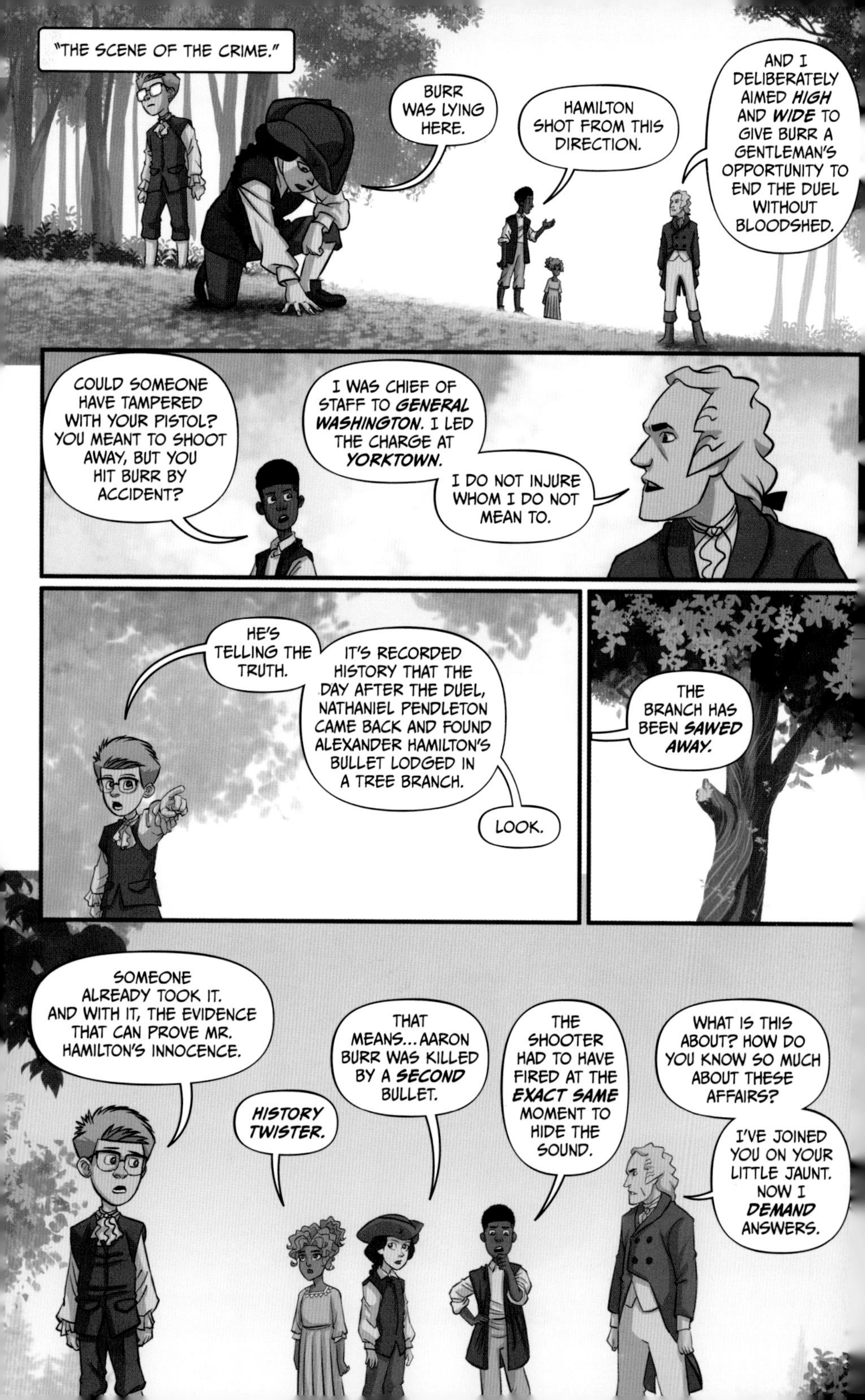
"THE SCENE OF THE CRIME."
BURR WAS LYING HERE.
HAMILTON SHOT FROM THIS DIRECTION.
AND I DELIBERATELY AIMED HIGH AND WIDE TO GIVE BURR A GENTLEMAN'S OPPORTUNITY TO END THE DUEL WITHOUT BLOODSHED.
COULD SOMEONE HAVE TAMPERED WITH YOUR PISTOL? YOU MEANT TO SHOOT AWAY, BUT YOU HIT BURR BY ACCIDENT?
I WAS CHIEF OF STAFF TO GENERAL WASHINGTON. I LED THE CHARGE AT YORKTOWN.
I DO NOT INJURE WHOM I DO NOT MEAN TO.
HE'S TELLING THE TRUTH.
IT'S RECORDED HISTORY THAT THE DAY AFTER THE DUEL, NATHANIEL PENDLETON CAME BACK AND FOUND ALEXANDER HAMILTON'S BULLET LODGED IN A TREE BRANCH.
LOOK.
THE BRANCH HAS BEEN SAWED AWAY.
SOMEONE ALREADY TOOK IT. AND WITH IT, THE EVIDENCE THAT CAN PROVE MR. HAMILTON'S INNOCENCE.
HISTORY TWISTER.
THAT MEANS...AARON BURR WAS KILLED BY A SECOND BULLET.
THE SHOOTER HAD TO HAVE FIRED AT THE EXACT SAME MOMENT TO HIDE THE SOUND.
WHAT IS THIS ABOUT? HOW DO YOU KNOW SO MUCH ABOUT THESE AFFAIRS?
I'VE JOINED YOU ON YOUR LITTLE JAUNT. NOW I DEMAND ANSWERS.

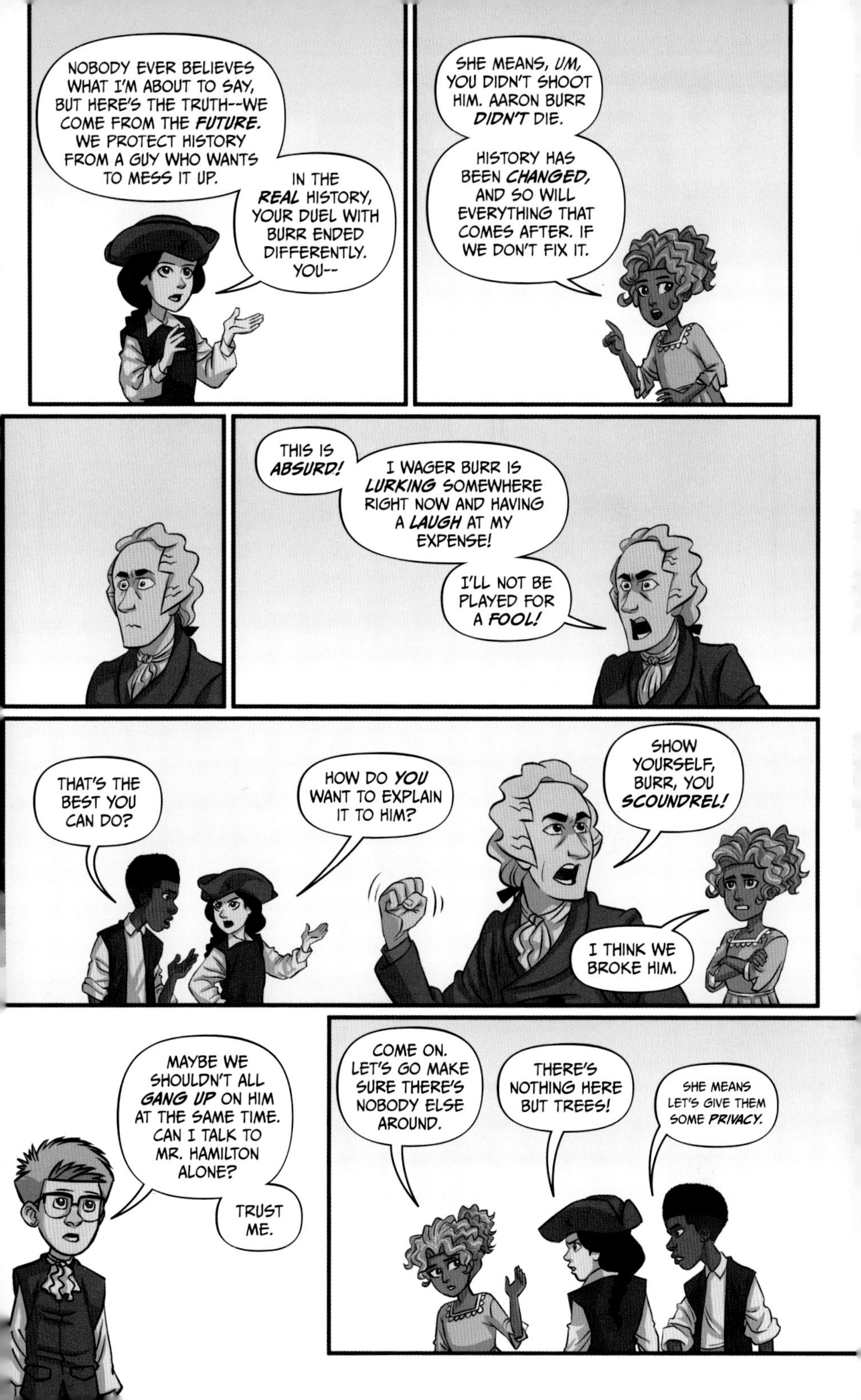
NOBODY EVER BELIEVES WHAT I'M ABOUT TO SAY, BUT HERE'S THE TRUTH--WE COME FROM THE *FUTURE.* WE PROTECT HISTORY FROM A GUY WHO WANTS TO MESS IT UP.
IN THE *REAL* HISTORY, YOUR DUEL WITH BURR ENDED DIFFERENTLY. YOU--
SHE MEANS, *UM,* YOU DIDN'T SHOOT HIM. AARON BURR *DIDN'T* DIE.
HISTORY HAS BEEN *CHANGED,* AND SO WILL EVERYTHING THAT COMES AFTER. IF WE DON'T FIX IT.
THIS IS *ABSURD!*
I WAGER BURR IS *LURKING* SOMEWHERE RIGHT NOW AND HAVING A *LAUGH* AT MY EXPENSE!
I'LL NOT BE PLAYED FOR A *FOOL!*
THAT'S THE BEST YOU CAN DO?
HOW DO *YOU* WANT TO EXPLAIN IT TO HIM?
SHOW YOURSELF, BURR, YOU *SCOUNDREL!*
I THINK WE BROKE HIM.
MAYBE WE SHOULDN'T ALL *GANG UP* ON HIM AT THE SAME TIME. CAN I TALK TO MR. HAMILTON ALONE?
TRUST ME.
COME ON. LET'S GO MAKE SURE THERE'S NOBODY ELSE AROUND.
THERE'S NOTHING HERE BUT TREES!
SHE MEANS LET'S GIVE THEM SOME *PRIVACY.*

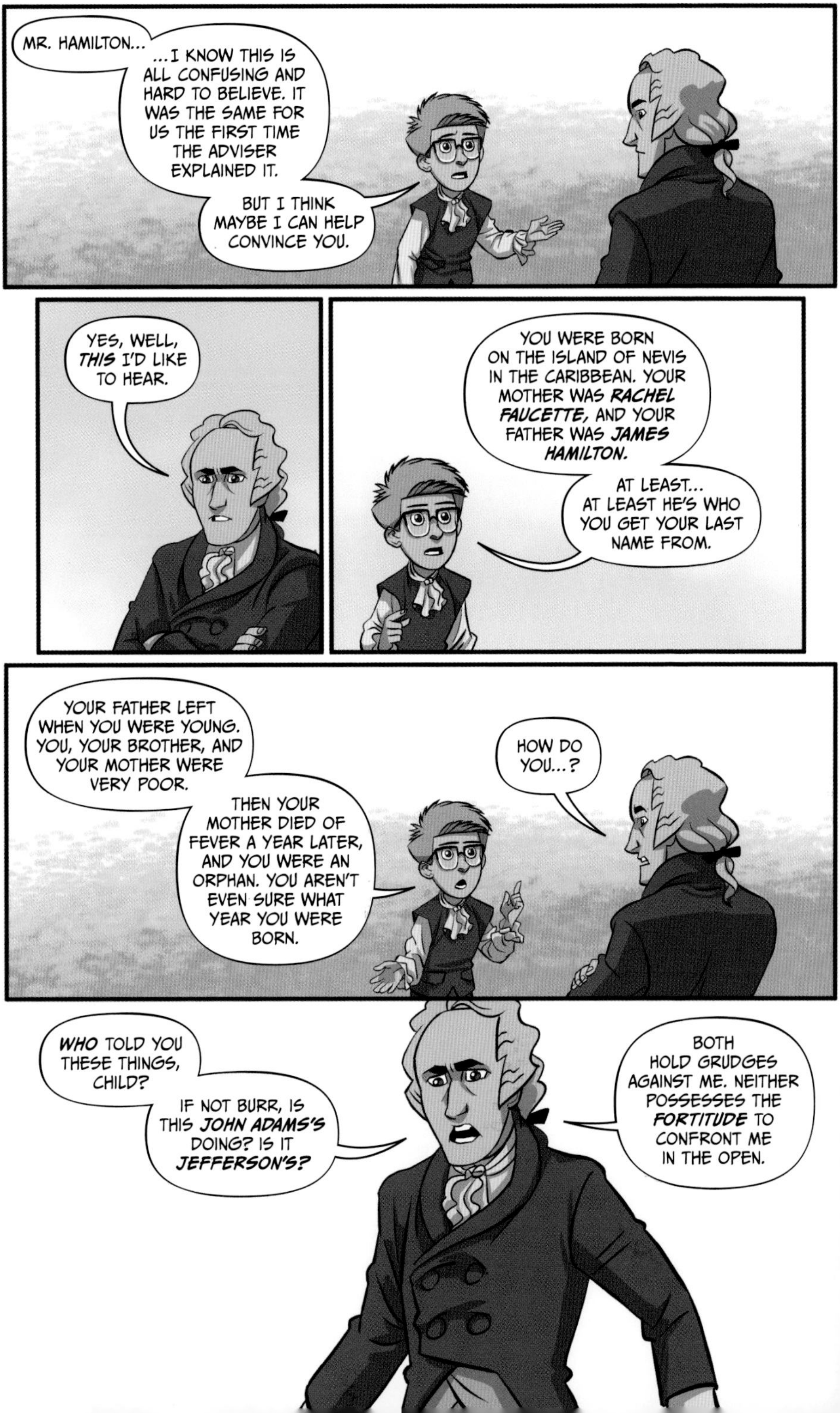
MR. HAMILTON...
...I KNOW THIS IS ALL CONFUSING AND HARD TO BELIEVE. IT WAS THE SAME FOR US THE FIRST TIME THE ADVISER EXPLAINED IT.
BUT I THINK MAYBE I CAN HELP CONVINCE YOU.
YES, WELL, *THIS* I'D LIKE TO HEAR.
YOU WERE BORN ON THE ISLAND OF NEVIS IN THE CARIBBEAN. YOUR MOTHER WAS ***RACHEL FAUCETTE,*** AND YOUR FATHER WAS ***JAMES HAMILTON.***
AT LEAST... AT LEAST HE'S WHO YOU GET YOUR LAST NAME FROM.
YOUR FATHER LEFT WHEN YOU WERE YOUNG. YOU, YOUR BROTHER, AND YOUR MOTHER WERE VERY POOR.
THEN YOUR MOTHER DIED OF FEVER A YEAR LATER, AND YOU WERE AN ORPHAN. YOU AREN'T EVEN SURE WHAT YEAR YOU WERE BORN.
HOW DO YOU...?
WHO TOLD YOU THESE THINGS, CHILD?
IF NOT BURR, IS THIS ***JOHN ADAMS'S*** DOING? IS IT ***JEFFERSON'S?***
BOTH HOLD GRUDGES AGAINST ME. NEITHER POSSESSES THE ***FORTITUDE*** TO CONFRONT ME IN THE OPEN.

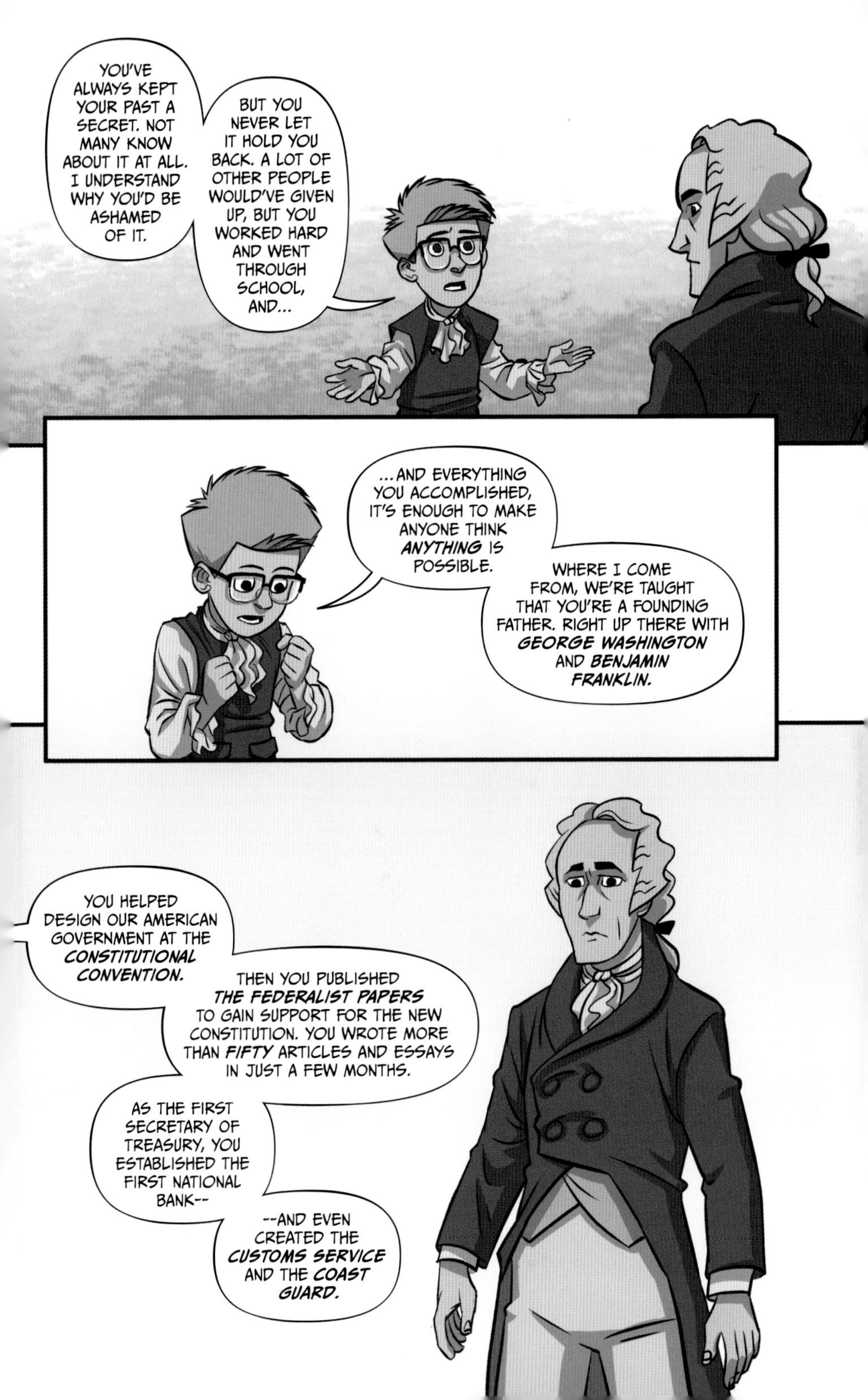
YOU'VE ALWAYS KEPT YOUR PAST A SECRET. NOT MANY KNOW ABOUT IT AT ALL. I UNDERSTAND WHY YOU'D BE ASHAMED OF IT.
BUT YOU NEVER LET IT HOLD YOU BACK. A LOT OF OTHER PEOPLE WOULD'VE GIVEN UP, BUT YOU WORKED HARD AND WENT THROUGH SCHOOL, AND...
...AND EVERYTHING YOU ACCOMPLISHED, IT'S ENOUGH TO MAKE ANYONE THINK *ANYTHING* IS POSSIBLE.
WHERE I COME FROM, WE'RE TAUGHT THAT YOU'RE A FOUNDING FATHER. RIGHT UP THERE WITH ***GEORGE WASHINGTON*** AND ***BENJAMIN FRANKLIN.***
YOU HELPED DESIGN OUR AMERICAN GOVERNMENT AT THE ***CONSTITUTIONAL CONVENTION.***
THEN YOU PUBLISHED ***THE FEDERALIST PAPERS*** TO GAIN SUPPORT FOR THE NEW CONSTITUTION. YOU WROTE MORE THAN *FIFTY* ARTICLES AND ESSAYS IN JUST A FEW MONTHS.
AS THE FIRST SECRETARY OF TREASURY, YOU ESTABLISHED THE FIRST NATIONAL BANK--
--AND EVEN CREATED THE ***CUSTOMS SERVICE*** AND THE ***COAST GUARD.***

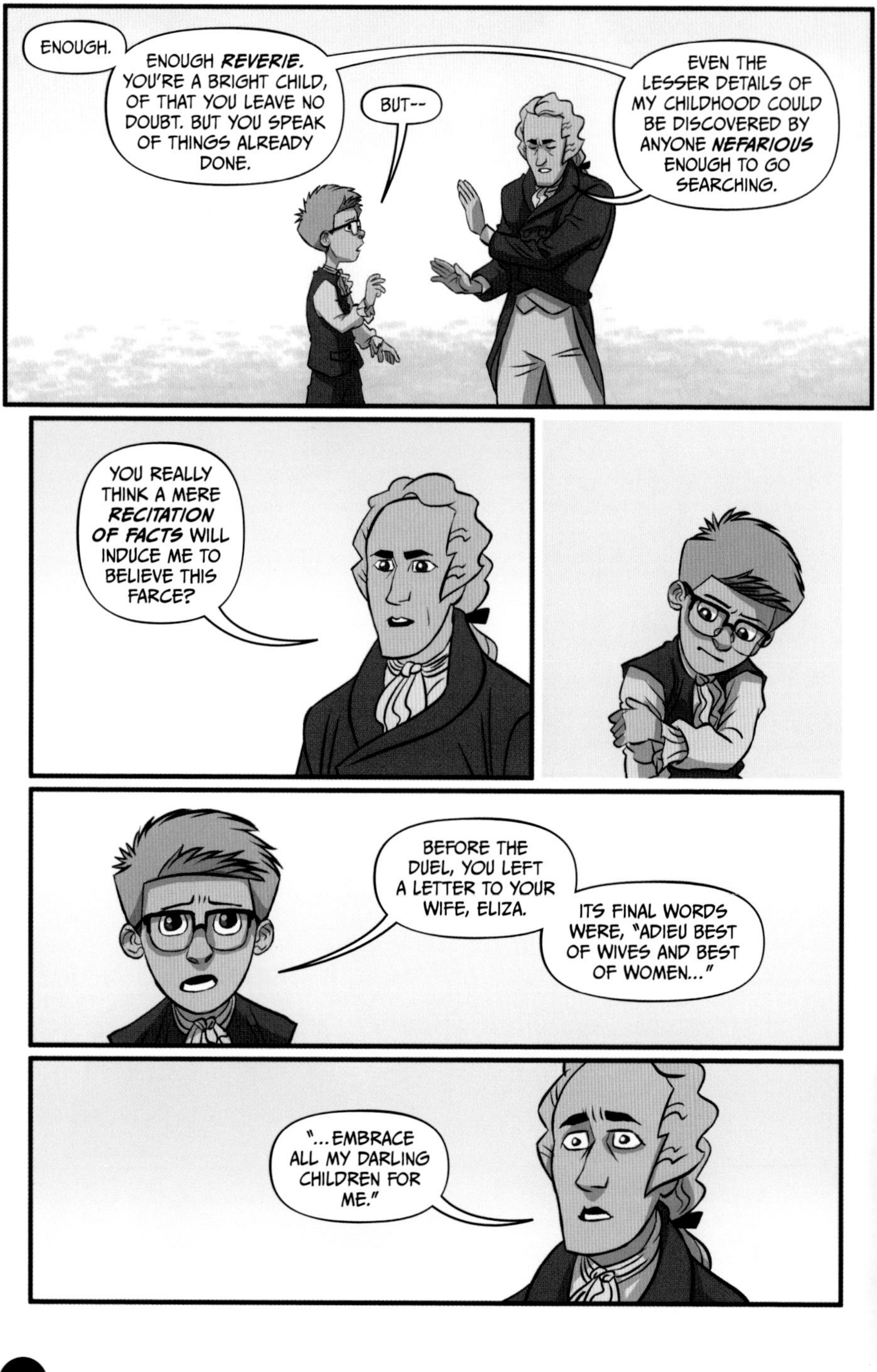
ENOUGH.
ENOUGH *REVERIE.* YOU'RE A BRIGHT CHILD, OF THAT YOU LEAVE NO DOUBT. BUT YOU SPEAK OF THINGS ALREADY DONE.
BUT--
EVEN THE LESSER DETAILS OF MY CHILDHOOD COULD BE DISCOVERED BY ANYONE *NEFARIOUS* ENOUGH TO GO SEARCHING.
YOU REALLY THINK A MERE *RECITATION OF FACTS* WILL INDUCE ME TO BELIEVE THIS FARCE?
BEFORE THE DUEL, YOU LEFT A LETTER TO YOUR WIFE, ELIZA.
ITS FINAL WORDS WERE, "ADIEU BEST OF WIVES AND BEST OF WOMEN..."
"...EMBRACE ALL MY DARLING CHILDREN FOR ME."

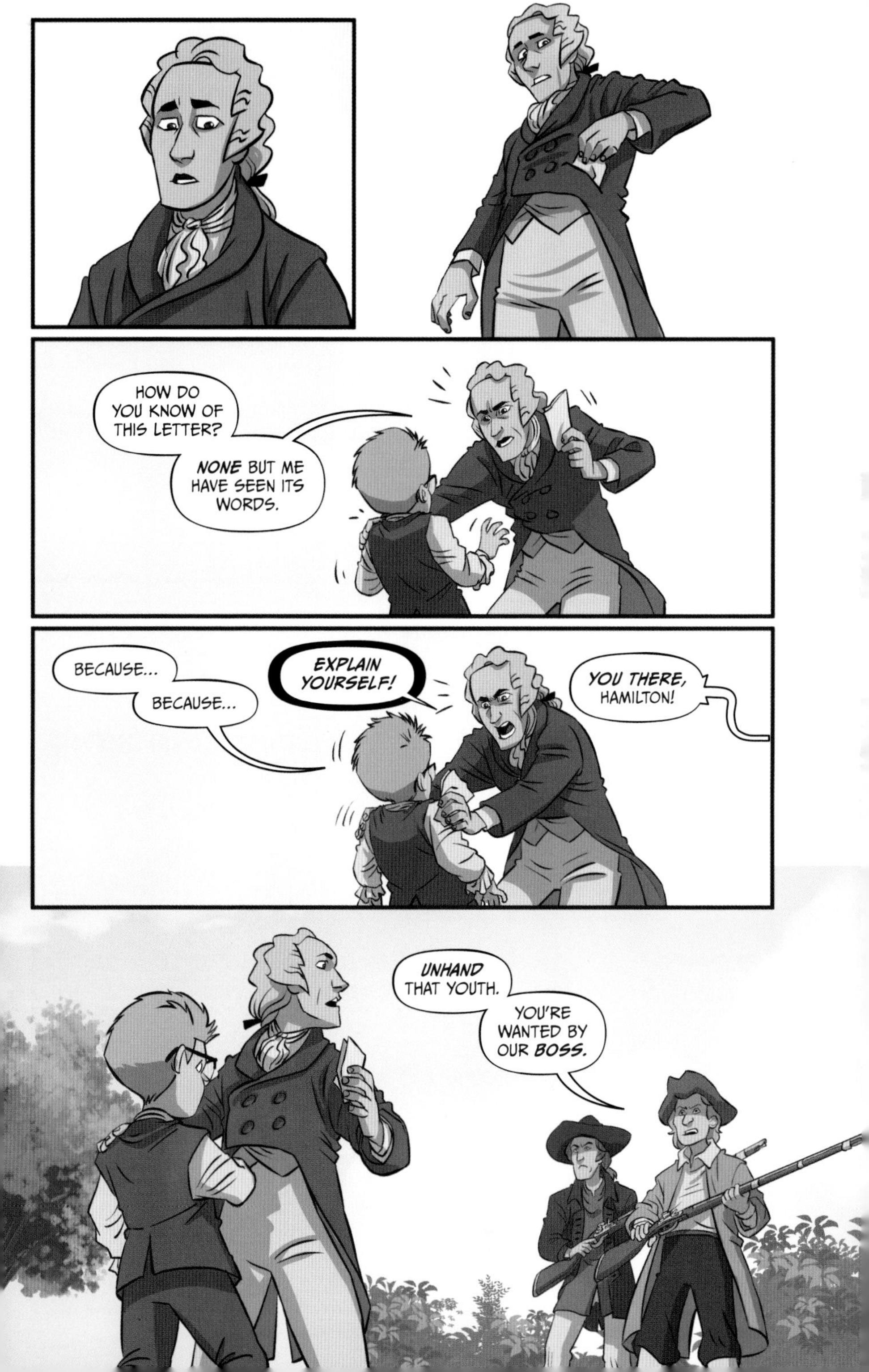

HOW DO YOU KNOW OF THIS LETTER?
NONE BUT ME HAVE SEEN ITS WORDS.
BECAUSE...
BECAUSE...
EXPLAIN YOURSELF!
YOU THERE, HAMILTON!
UNHAND THAT YOUTH.
YOU'RE WANTED BY OUR BOSS.

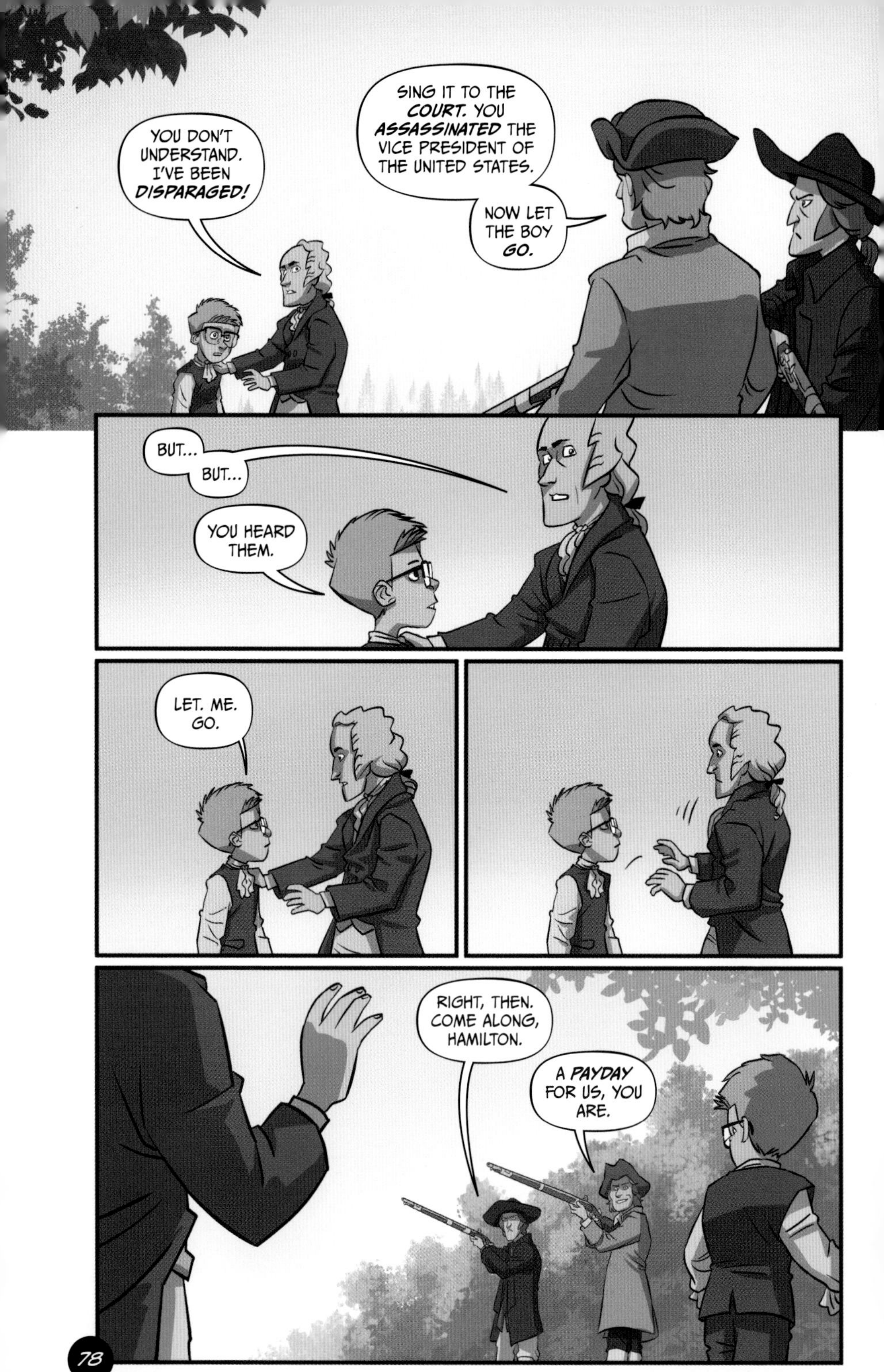
YOU DON'T UNDERSTAND. I'VE BEEN DISPARAGED!
SING IT TO THE COURT. YOU ASSASSINATED THE VICE PRESIDENT OF THE UNITED STATES.
NOW LET THE BOY GO.
BUT...
BUT...
YOU HEARD THEM.
LET. ME. GO.
RIGHT, THEN. COME ALONG, HAMILTON.
A PAYDAY FOR US, YOU ARE.

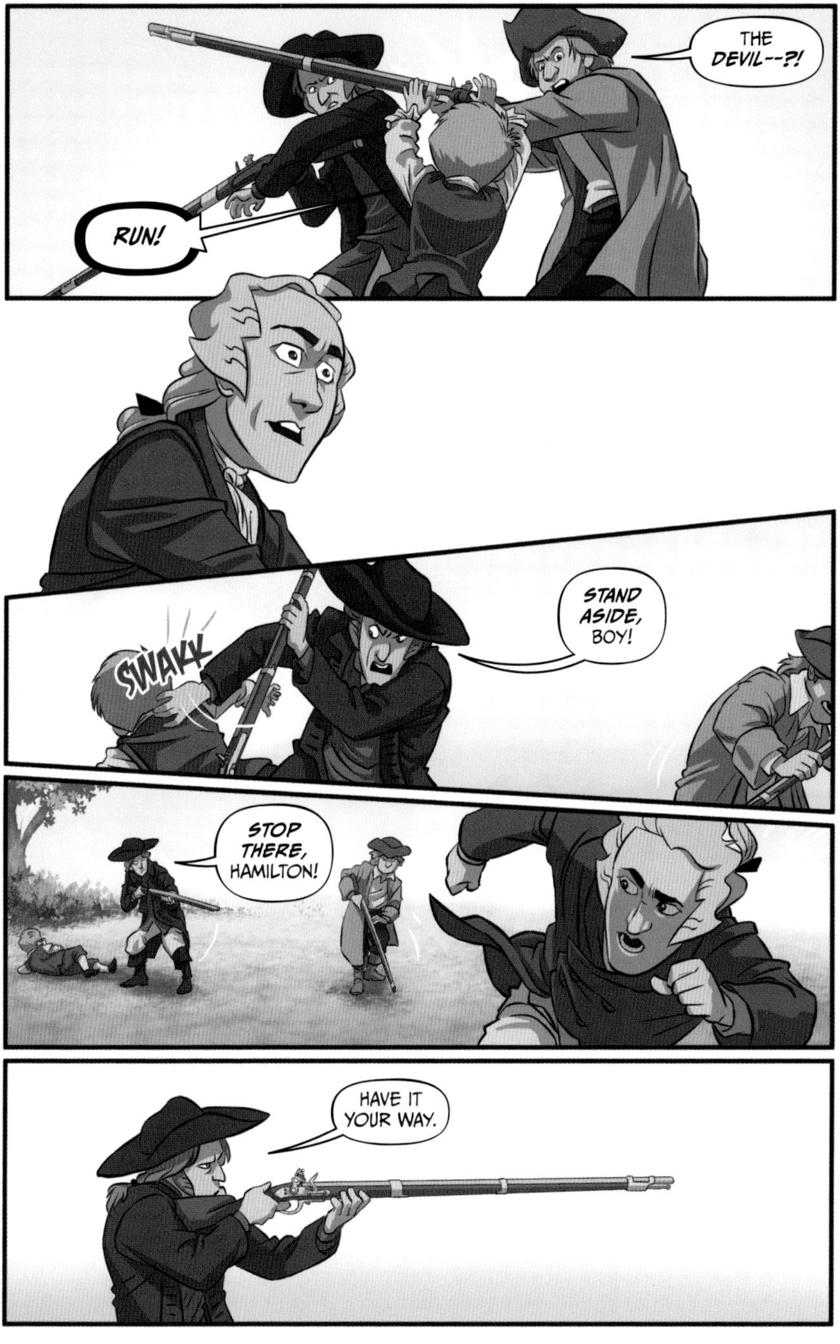
THE DEVIL--?!
RUN!
STAND ASIDE, BOY!
SWAKK
STOP THERE, HAMILTON!
HAVE IT YOUR WAY.

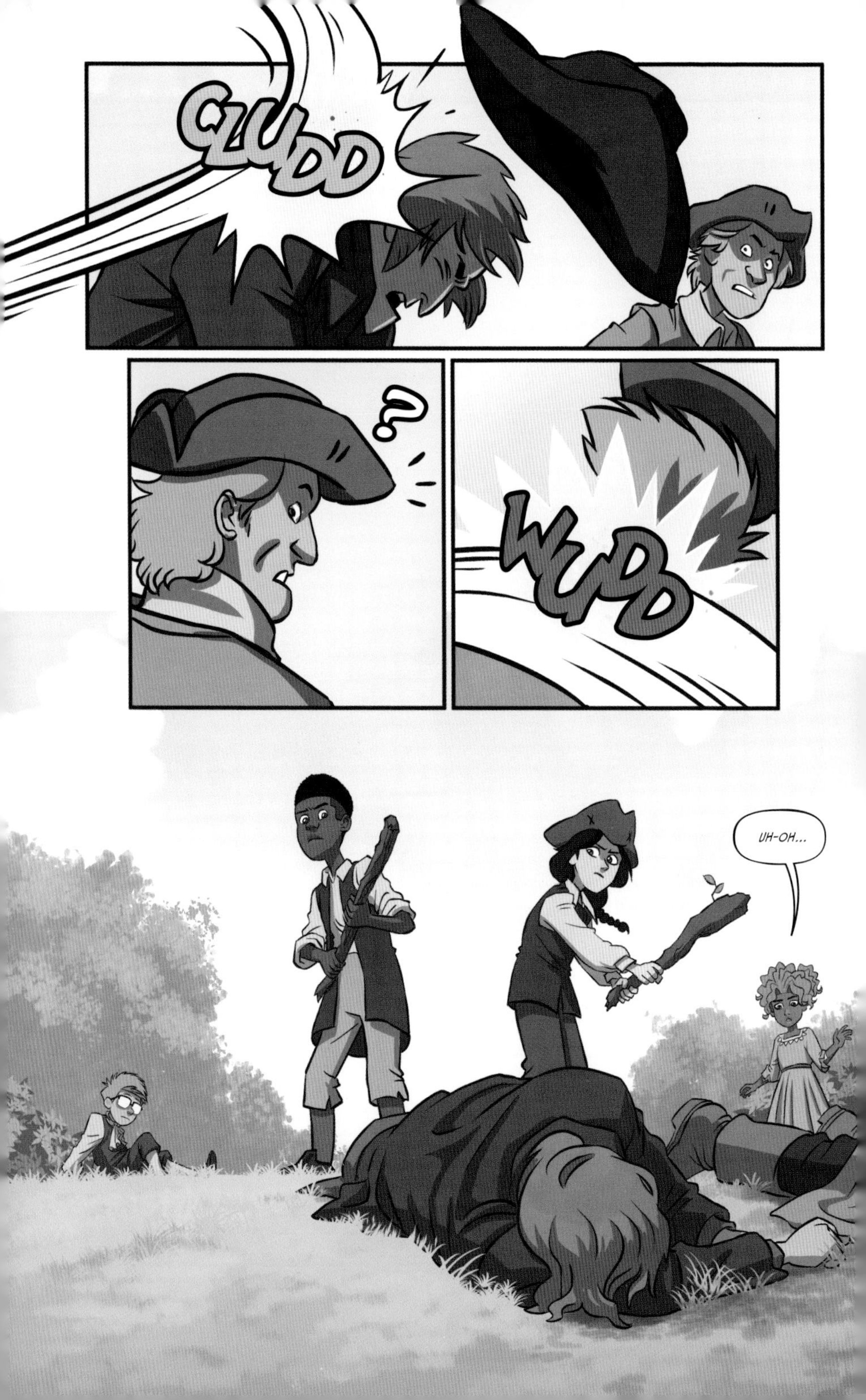
CLUDD
?
WUDD
UH-OH...

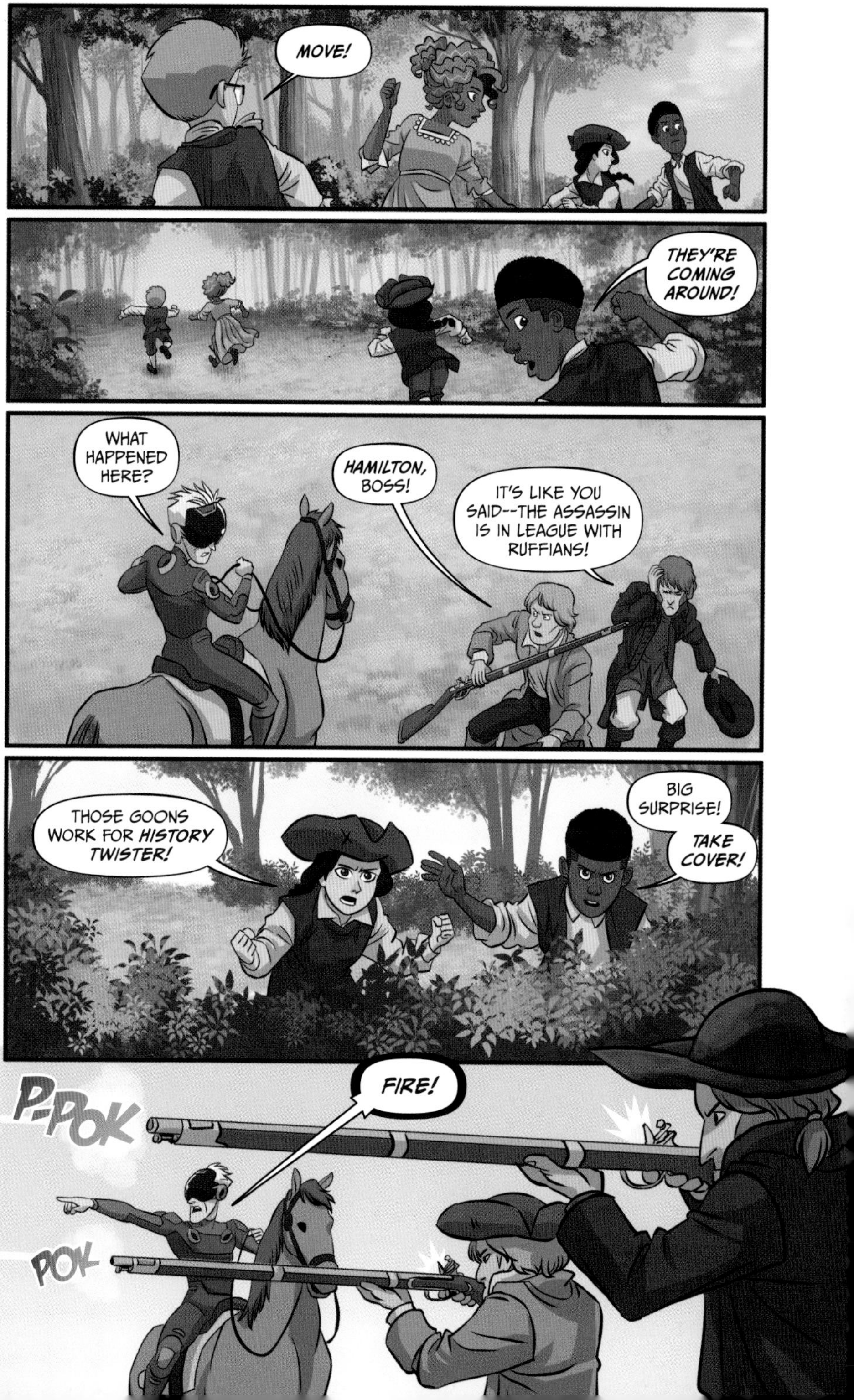
MOVE!
THEY'RE COMING AROUND!
WHAT HAPPENED HERE?
HAMILTON, BOSS!
IT'S LIKE YOU SAID--THE ASSASSIN IS IN LEAGUE WITH RUFFIANS!
THOSE GOONS WORK FOR HISTORY TWISTER!
BIG SURPRISE!
TAKE COVER!
P-POK
FIRE!
POK

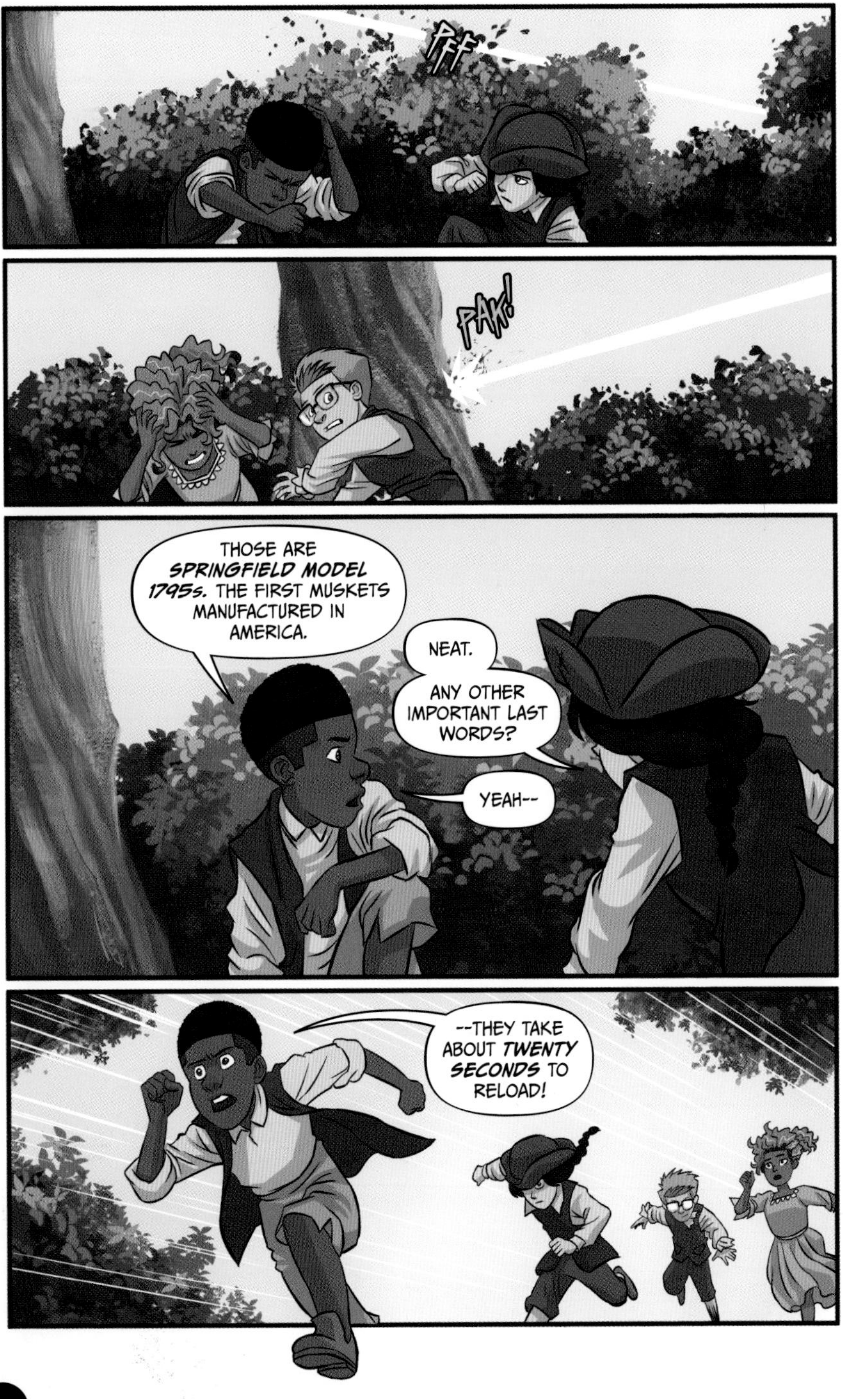
PFF
PAK!
THOSE ARE SPRINGFIELD MODEL 1795s. THE FIRST MUSKETS MANUFACTURED IN AMERICA.
NEAT.
ANY OTHER IMPORTANT LAST WORDS?
YEAH--
--THEY TAKE ABOUT TWENTY SECONDS TO RELOAD!

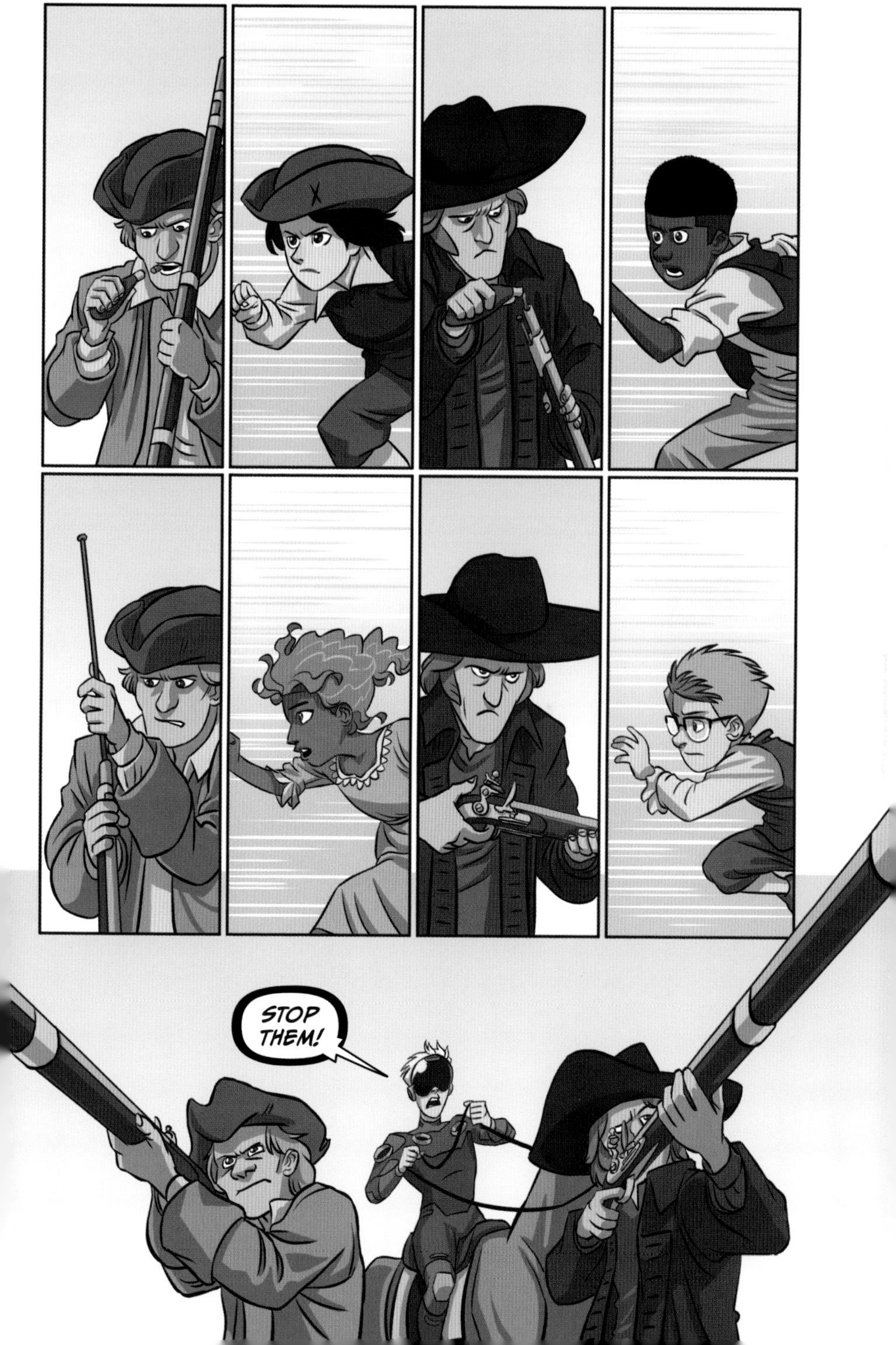
STOP THEM!

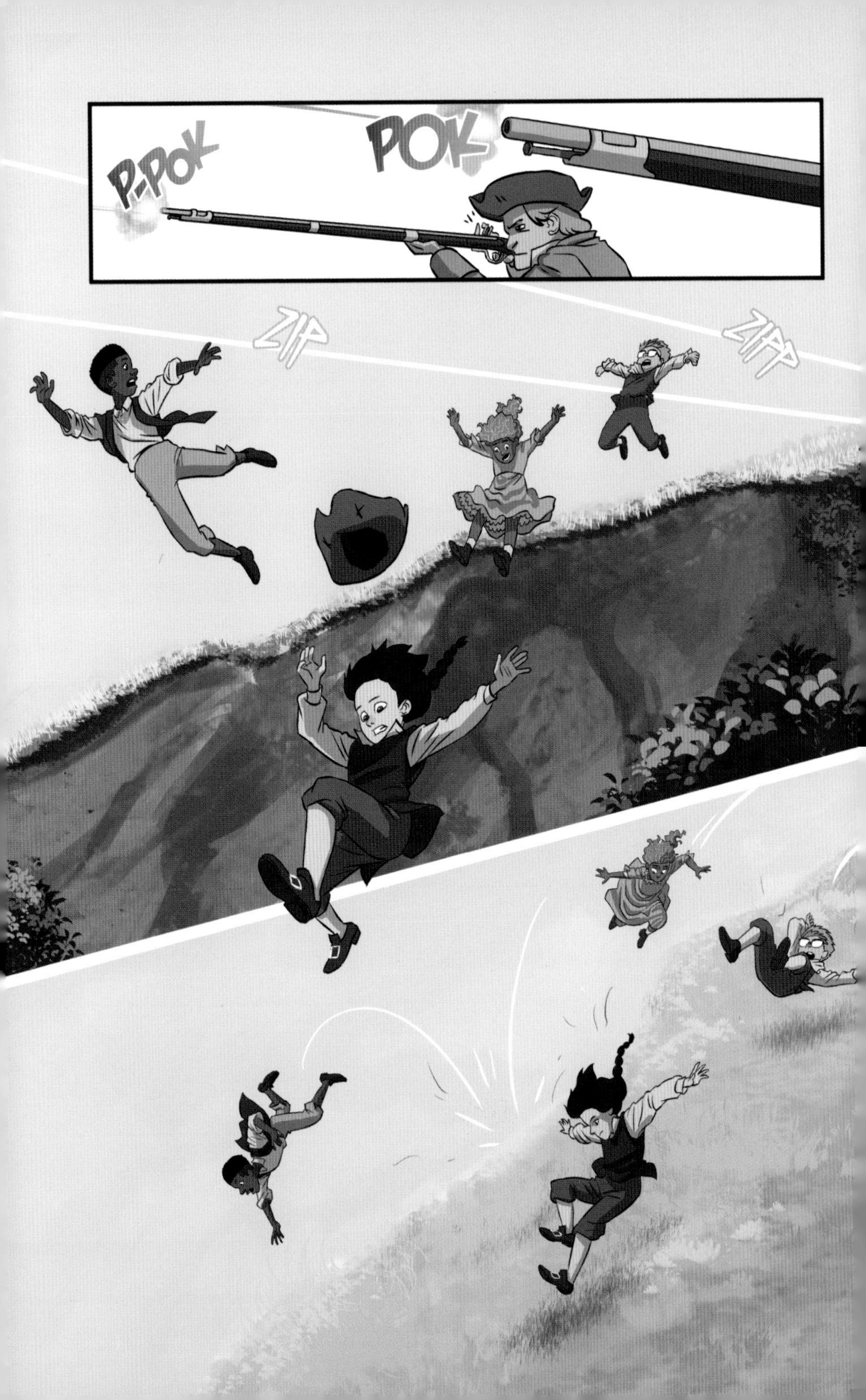
P-POK
POK
ZIP
ZIPP

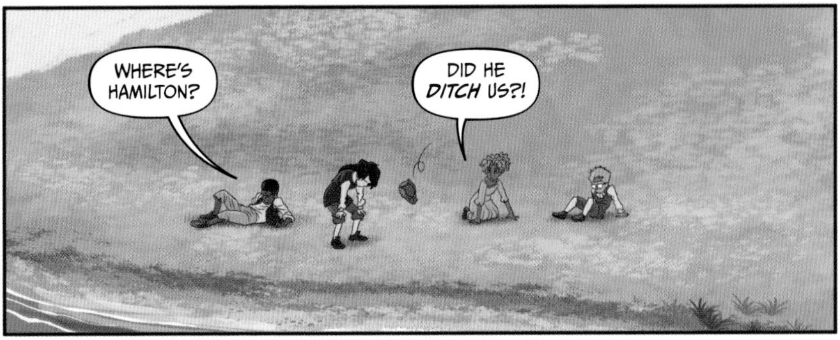
WHERE'S HAMILTON?
DID HE *DITCH* US?!

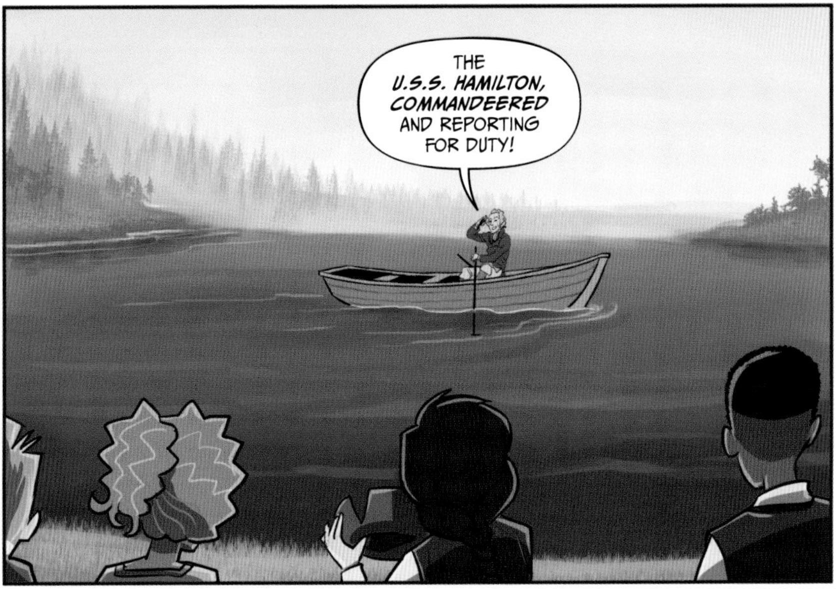
THE *U.S.S. HAMILTON, COMMANDEERED* AND REPORTING FOR DUTY!

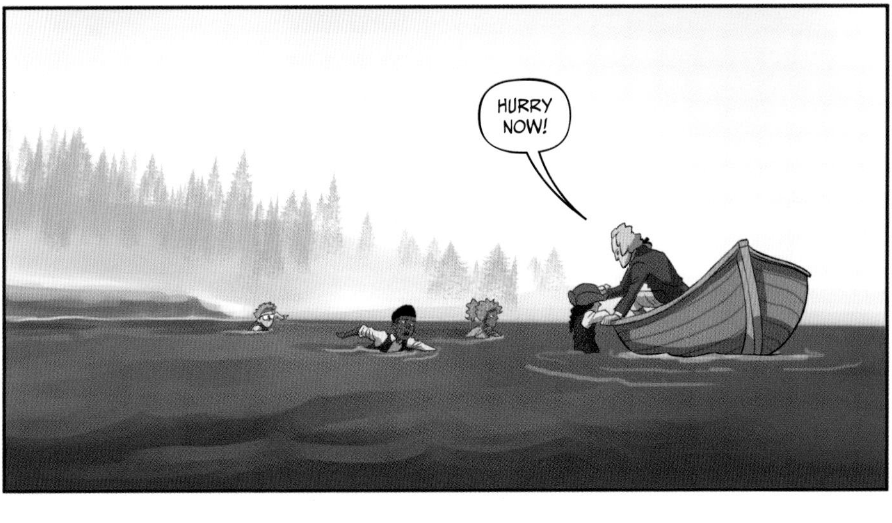
HURRY NOW!

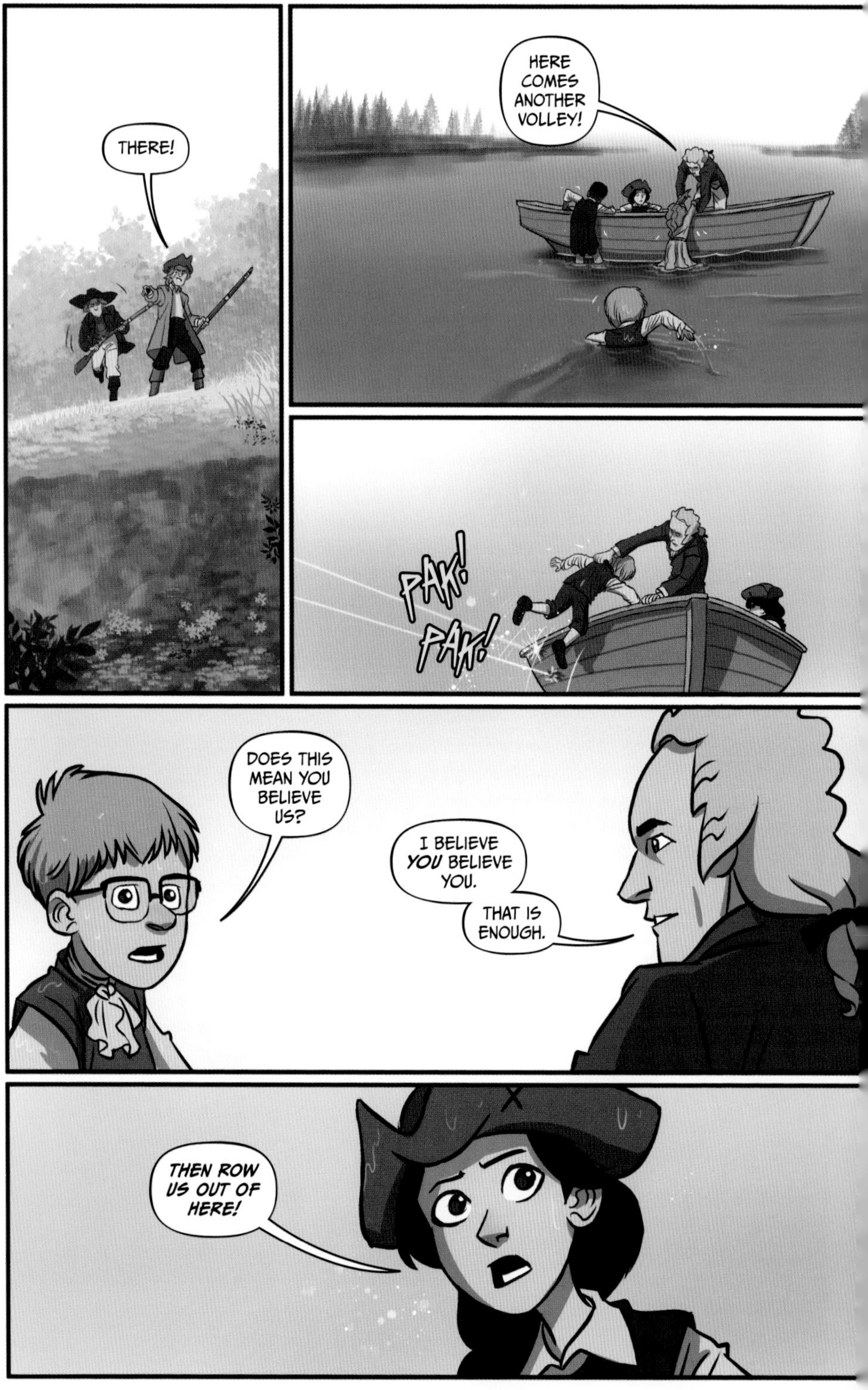
THERE!
HERE COMES ANOTHER VOLLEY!
PAK!
PAK!
DOES THIS MEAN YOU BELIEVE US?
I BELIEVE *YOU* BELIEVE YOU.
THAT IS ENOUGH.
THEN ROW US OUT OF HERE!

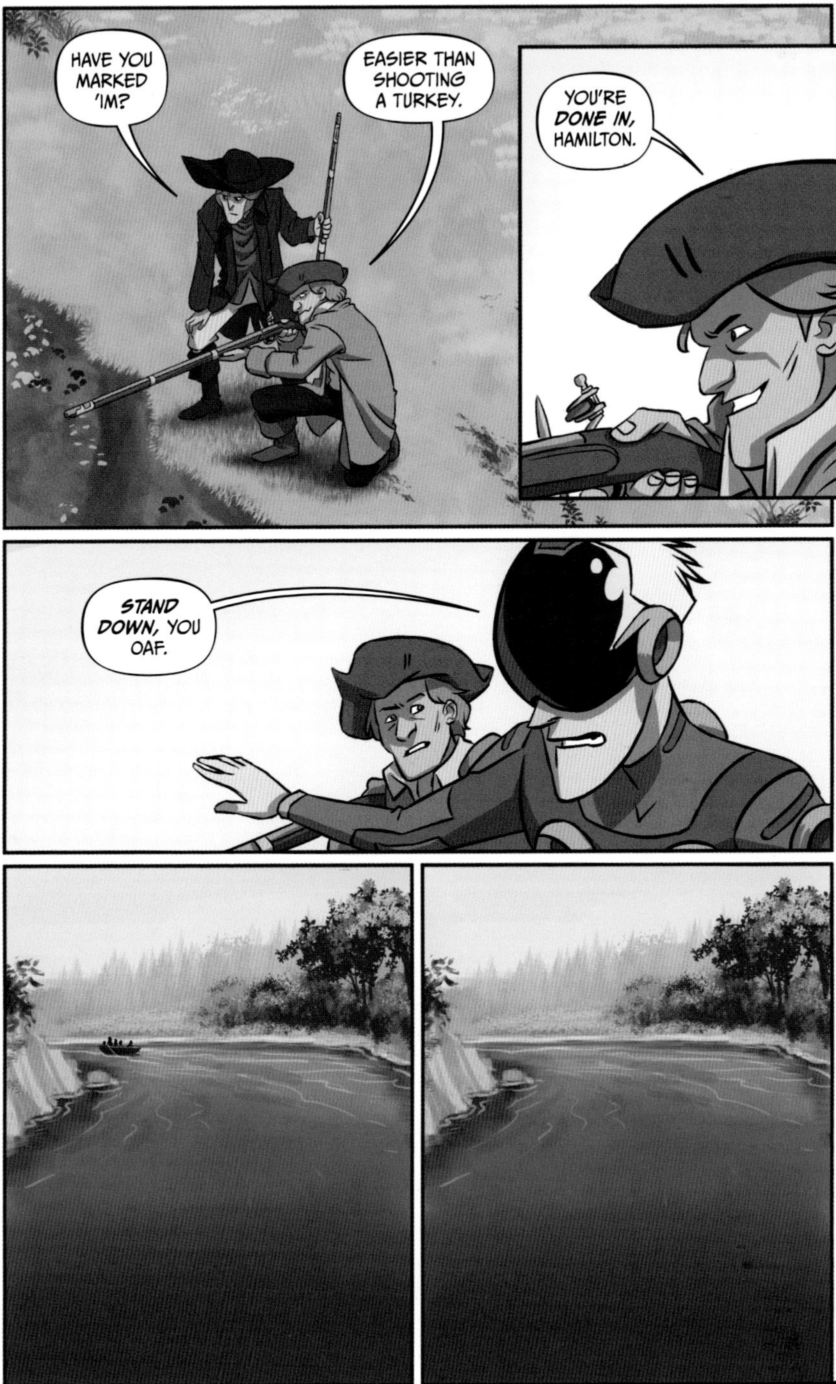
HAVE YOU MARKED 'IM?
EASIER THAN SHOOTING A TURKEY.
YOU'RE DONE IN, HAMILTON.
STAND DOWN, YOU OAF.

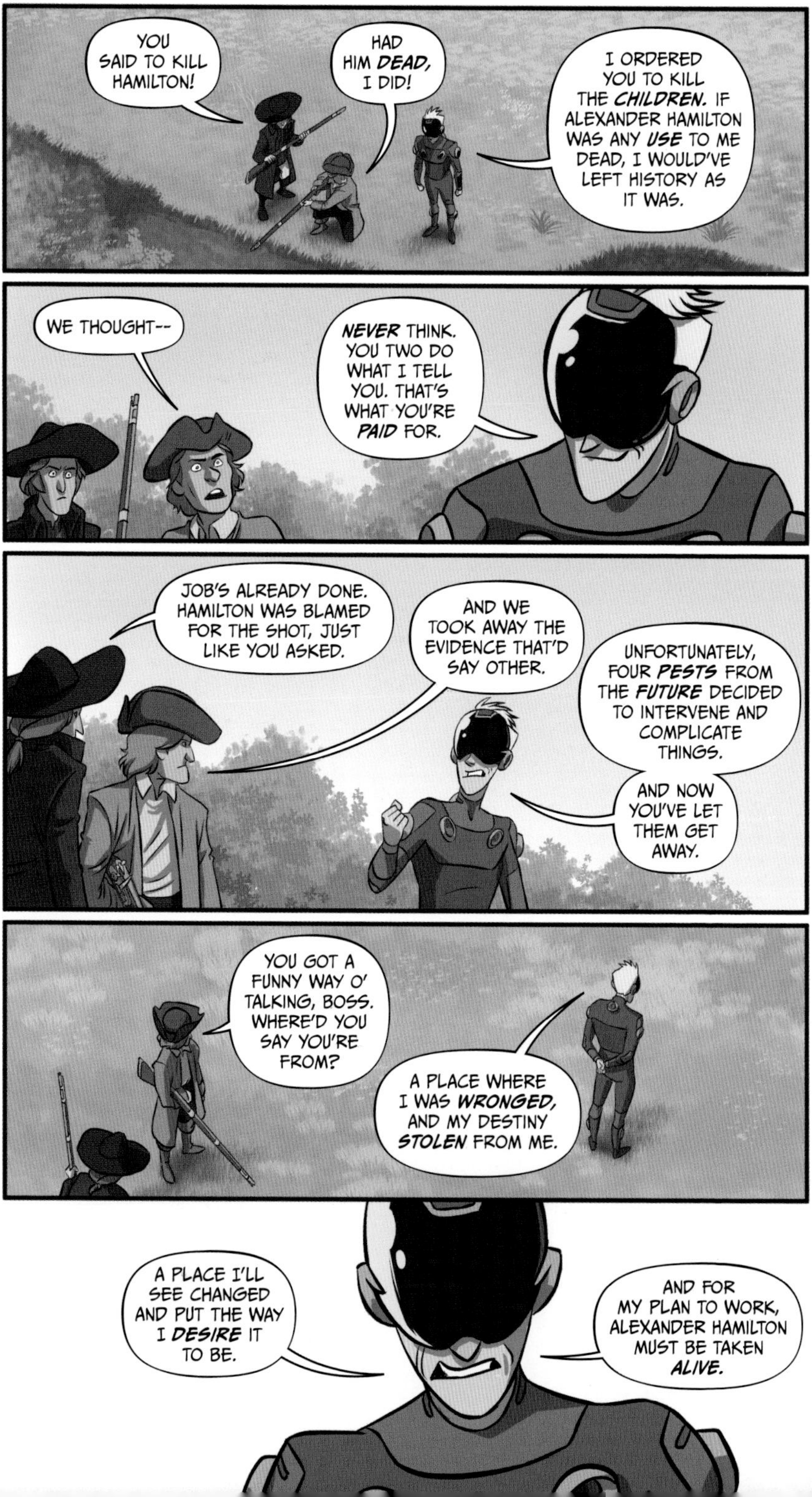
YOU SAID TO KILL HAMILTON!
HAD HIM DEAD, I DID!
I ORDERED YOU TO KILL THE CHILDREN. IF ALEXANDER HAMILTON WAS ANY USE TO ME DEAD, I WOULD'VE LEFT HISTORY AS IT WAS.
WE THOUGHT--
NEVER THINK. YOU TWO DO WHAT I TELL YOU. THAT'S WHAT YOU'RE PAID FOR.
JOB'S ALREADY DONE. HAMILTON WAS BLAMED FOR THE SHOT, JUST LIKE YOU ASKED.
AND WE TOOK AWAY THE EVIDENCE THAT'D SAY OTHER.
UNFORTUNATELY, FOUR PESTS FROM THE FUTURE DECIDED TO INTERVENE AND COMPLICATE THINGS.
AND NOW YOU'VE LET THEM GET AWAY.
YOU GOT A FUNNY WAY O' TALKING, BOSS. WHERE'D YOU SAY YOU'RE FROM?
A PLACE WHERE I WAS WRONGED, AND MY DESTINY STOLEN FROM ME.
A PLACE I'LL SEE CHANGED AND PUT THE WAY I DESIRE IT TO BE.
AND FOR MY PLAN TO WORK, ALEXANDER HAMILTON MUST BE TAKEN ALIVE.

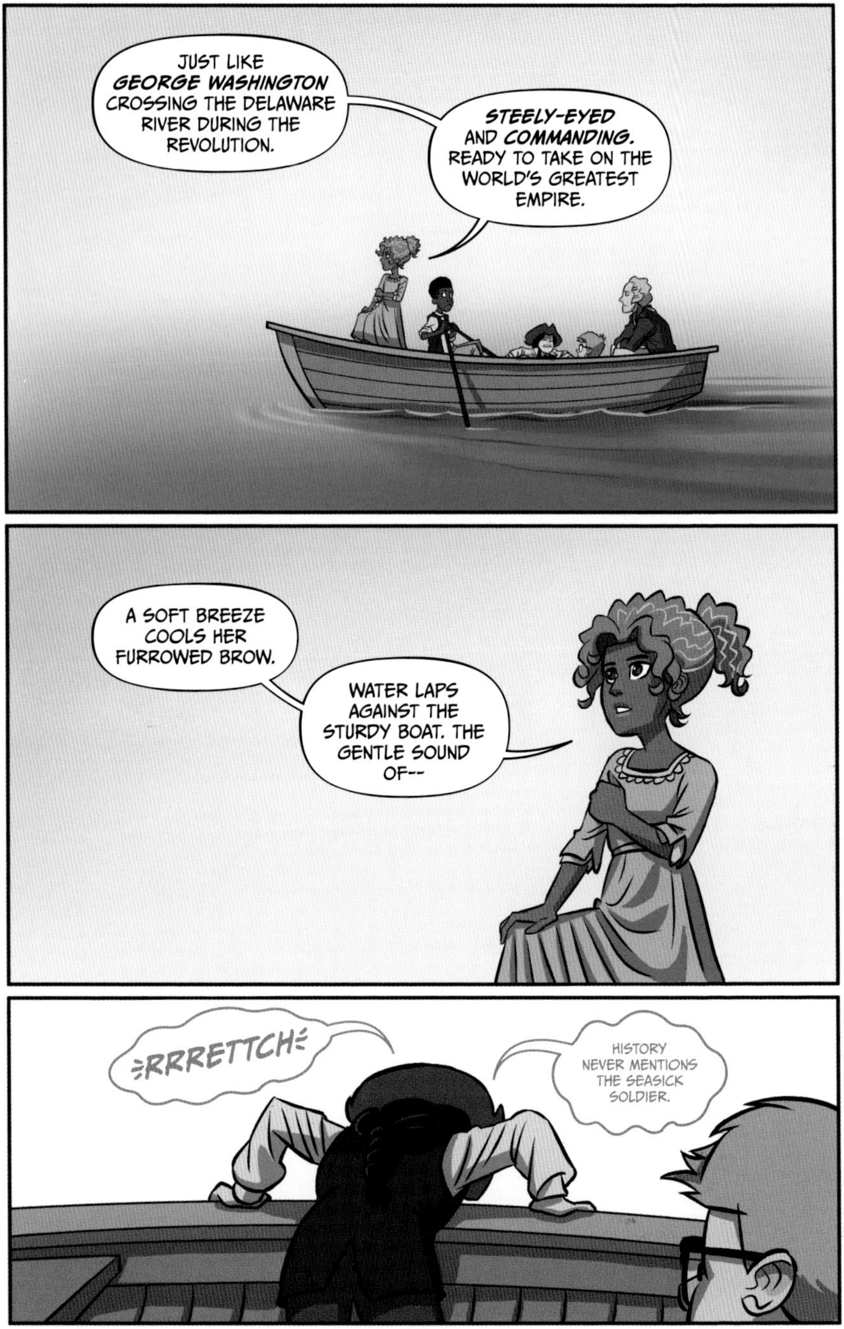
JUST LIKE GEORGE WASHINGTON CROSSING THE DELAWARE RIVER DURING THE REVOLUTION.
STEELY-EYED AND COMMANDING. READY TO TAKE ON THE WORLD'S GREATEST EMPIRE.
A SOFT BREEZE COOLS HER FURROWED BROW.
WATER LAPS AGAINST THE STURDY BOAT. THE GENTLE SOUND OF--
RRRETTCH
HISTORY NEVER MENTIONS THE SEASICK SOLDIER.

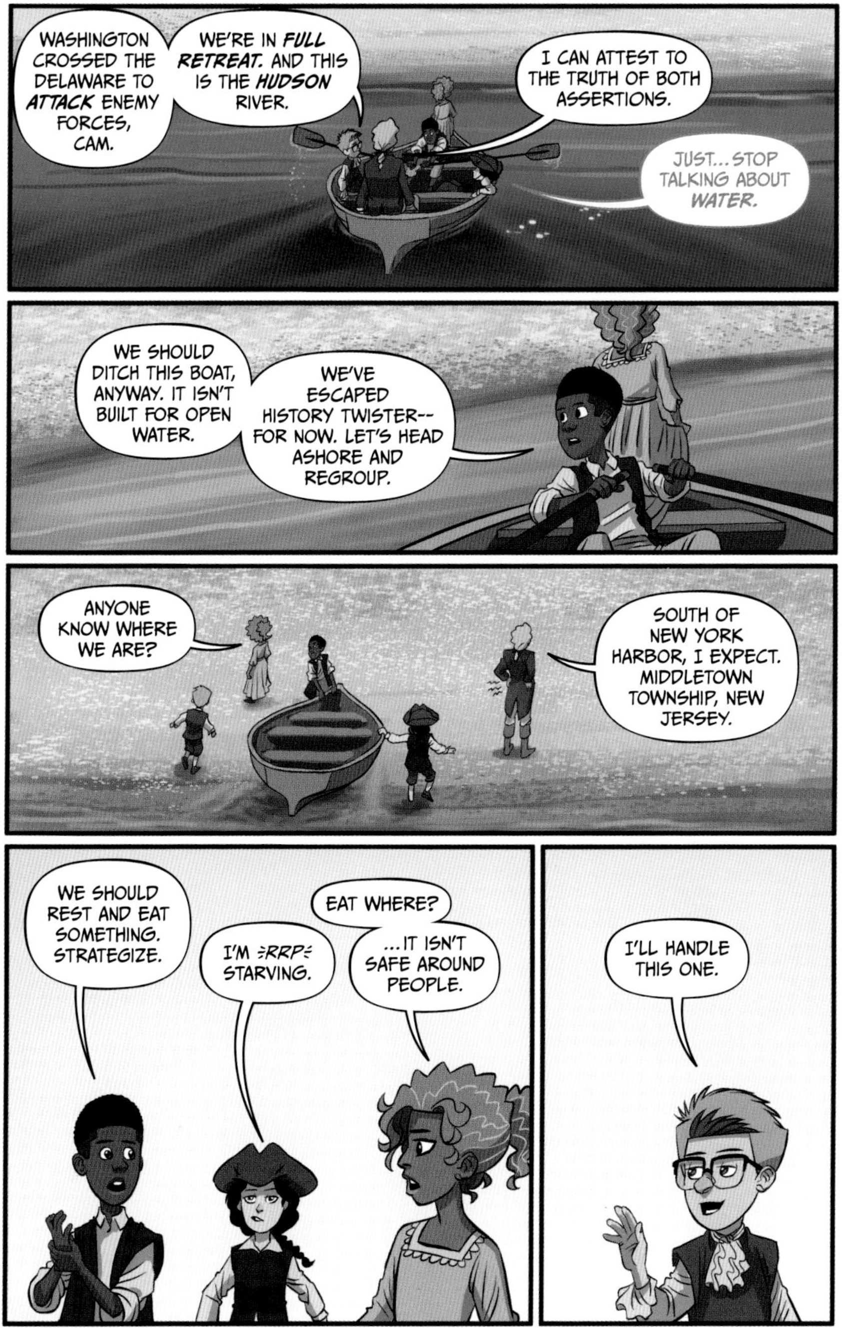
WASHINGTON CROSSED THE DELAWARE TO ATTACK ENEMY FORCES, CAM.
WE'RE IN FULL RETREAT. AND THIS IS THE HUDSON RIVER.
I CAN ATTEST TO THE TRUTH OF BOTH ASSERTIONS.
JUST... STOP TALKING ABOUT WATER.
WE SHOULD DITCH THIS BOAT, ANYWAY. IT ISN'T BUILT FOR OPEN WATER.
WE'VE ESCAPED HISTORY TWISTER-- FOR NOW. LET'S HEAD ASHORE AND REGROUP.
ANYONE KNOW WHERE WE ARE?
SOUTH OF NEW YORK HARBOR, I EXPECT. MIDDLETOWN TOWNSHIP, NEW JERSEY.
WE SHOULD REST AND EAT SOMETHING. STRATEGIZE.
I'M RRP STARVING.
EAT WHERE?
...IT ISN'T SAFE AROUND PEOPLE.
I'LL HANDLE THIS ONE.

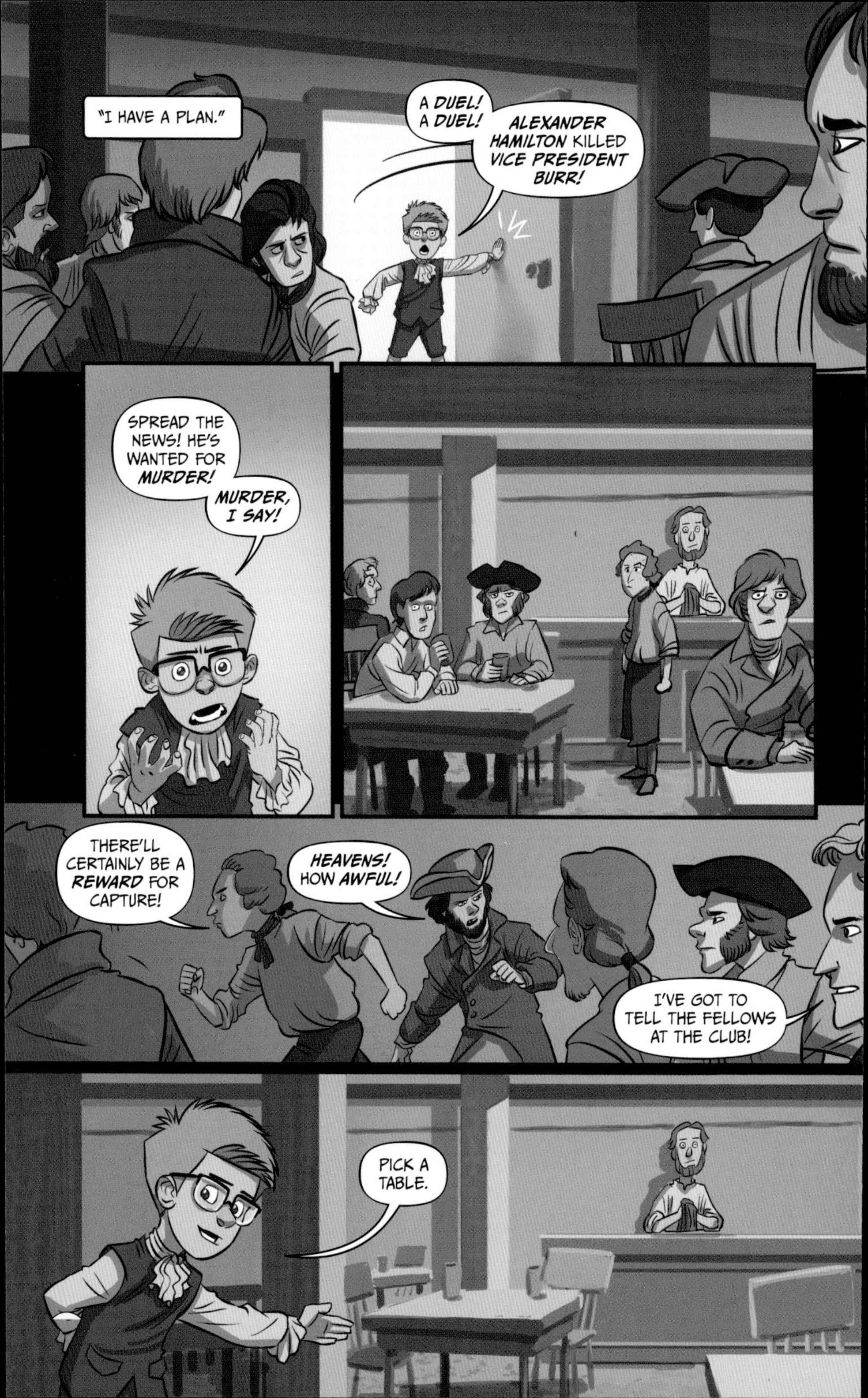
"I HAVE A PLAN."
A DUEL! A DUEL!
ALEXANDER HAMILTON KILLED VICE PRESIDENT BURR!
SPREAD THE NEWS! HE'S WANTED FOR MURDER!
MURDER, I SAY!
THERE'LL CERTAINLY BE A REWARD FOR CAPTURE!
HEAVENS! HOW AWFUL!
I'VE GOT TO TELL THE FELLOWS AT THE CLUB!
PICK A TABLE.

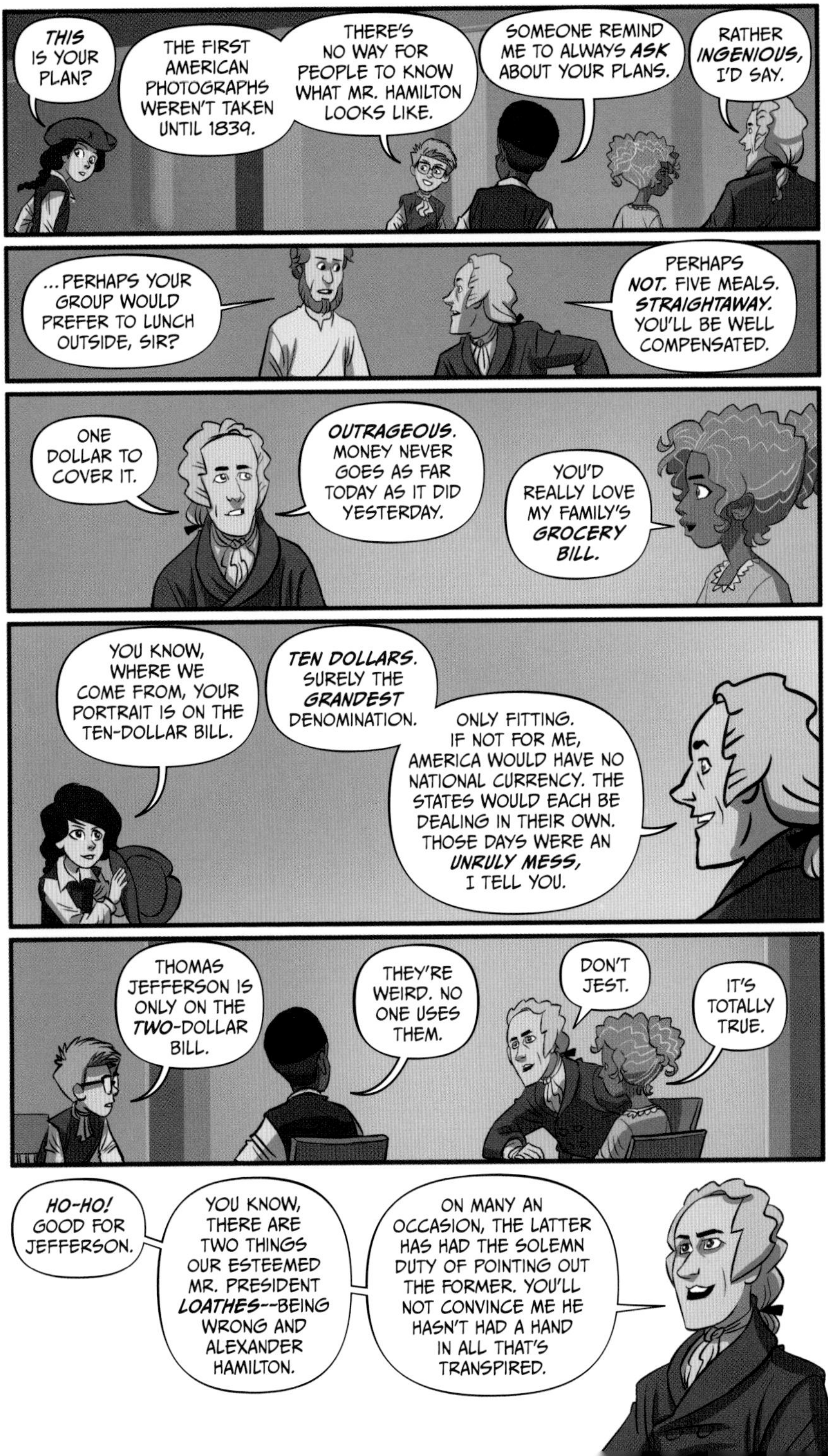
THIS IS YOUR PLAN?
THE FIRST AMERICAN PHOTOGRAPHS WEREN'T TAKEN UNTIL 1839.
THERE'S NO WAY FOR PEOPLE TO KNOW WHAT MR. HAMILTON LOOKS LIKE.
SOMEONE REMIND ME TO ALWAYS ASK ABOUT YOUR PLANS.
RATHER INGENIOUS, I'D SAY.
...PERHAPS YOUR GROUP WOULD PREFER TO LUNCH OUTSIDE, SIR?
PERHAPS NOT. FIVE MEALS. STRAIGHTAWAY. YOU'LL BE WELL COMPENSATED.
ONE DOLLAR TO COVER IT.
OUTRAGEOUS. MONEY NEVER GOES AS FAR TODAY AS IT DID YESTERDAY.
YOU'D REALLY LOVE MY FAMILY'S GROCERY BILL.
YOU KNOW, WHERE WE COME FROM, YOUR PORTRAIT IS ON THE TEN-DOLLAR BILL.
TEN DOLLARS. SURELY THE GRANDEST DENOMINATION.
ONLY FITTING. IF NOT FOR ME, AMERICA WOULD HAVE NO NATIONAL CURRENCY. THE STATES WOULD EACH BE DEALING IN THEIR OWN. THOSE DAYS WERE AN UNRULY MESS, I TELL YOU.
THOMAS JEFFERSON IS ONLY ON THE TWO-DOLLAR BILL.
THEY'RE WEIRD. NO ONE USES THEM.
DON'T JEST.
IT'S TOTALLY TRUE.
HO-HO! GOOD FOR JEFFERSON.
YOU KNOW, THERE ARE TWO THINGS OUR ESTEEMED MR. PRESIDENT LOATHES--BEING WRONG AND ALEXANDER HAMILTON.
ON MANY AN OCCASION, THE LATTER HAS HAD THE SOLEMN DUTY OF POINTING OUT THE FORMER. YOU'LL NOT CONVINCE ME HE HASN'T HAD A HAND IN ALL THAT'S TRANSPIRED.

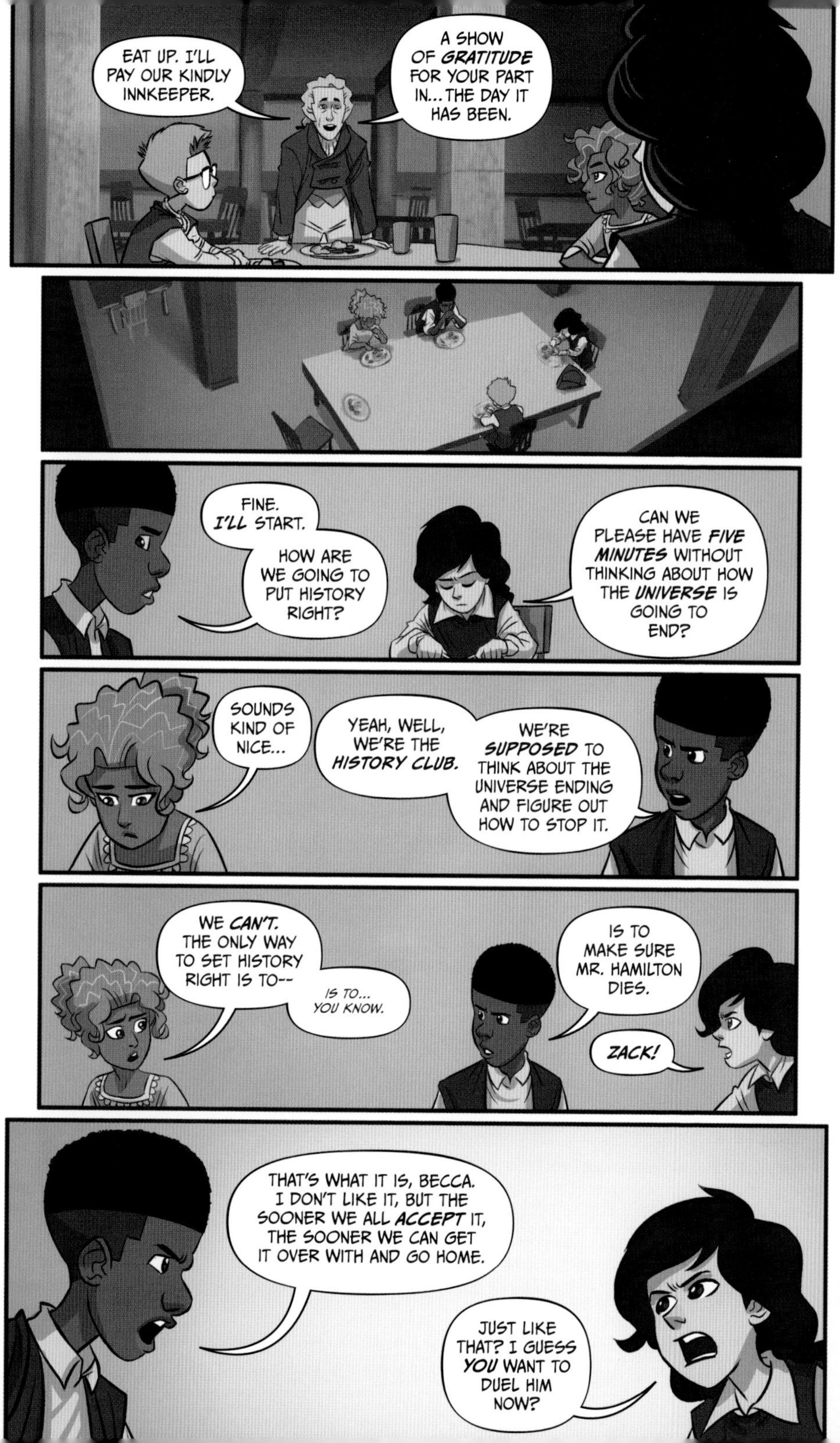
EAT UP. I'LL PAY OUR KINDLY INNKEEPER.
A SHOW OF GRATITUDE FOR YOUR PART IN... THE DAY IT HAS BEEN.
FINE. I'LL START.
HOW ARE WE GOING TO PUT HISTORY RIGHT?
CAN WE PLEASE HAVE FIVE MINUTES WITHOUT THINKING ABOUT HOW THE UNIVERSE IS GOING TO END?
SOUNDS KIND OF NICE...
YEAH, WELL, WE'RE THE HISTORY CLUB.
WE'RE SUPPOSED TO THINK ABOUT THE UNIVERSE ENDING AND FIGURE OUT HOW TO STOP IT.
WE CAN'T. THE ONLY WAY TO SET HISTORY RIGHT IS TO--
IS TO... YOU KNOW.
IS TO MAKE SURE MR. HAMILTON DIES.
ZACK!
THAT'S WHAT IT IS, BECCA. I DON'T LIKE IT, BUT THE SOONER WE ALL ACCEPT IT, THE SOONER WE CAN GET IT OVER WITH AND GO HOME.
JUST LIKE THAT? I GUESS YOU WANT TO DUEL HIM NOW?

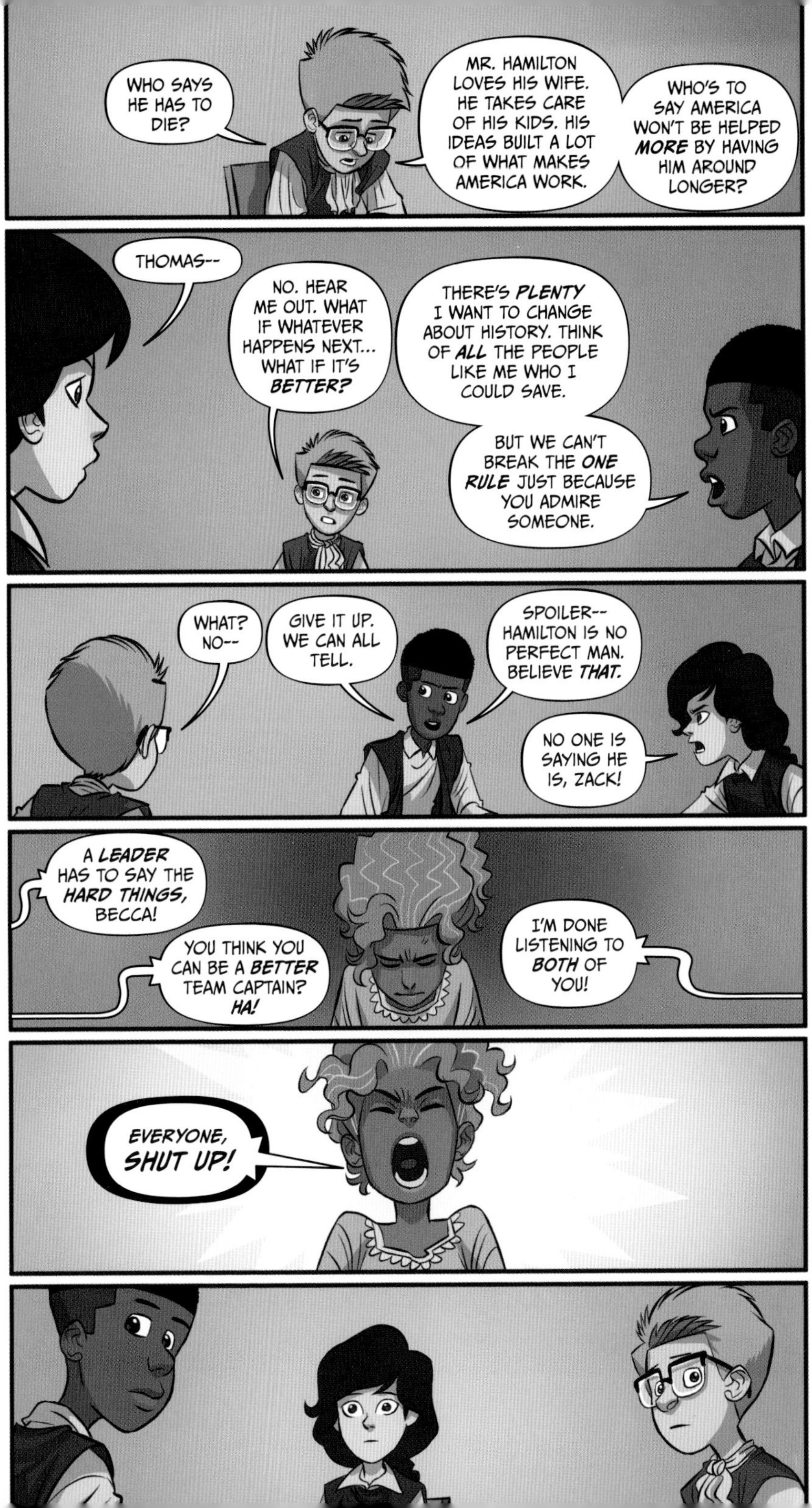
WHO SAYS HE HAS TO DIE?
MR. HAMILTON LOVES HIS WIFE. HE TAKES CARE OF HIS KIDS. HIS IDEAS BUILT A LOT OF WHAT MAKES AMERICA WORK.
WHO'S TO SAY AMERICA WON'T BE HELPED *MORE* BY HAVING HIM AROUND LONGER?
THOMAS--
NO. HEAR ME OUT. WHAT IF WHATEVER HAPPENS NEXT... WHAT IF IT'S *BETTER?*
THERE'S *PLENTY* I WANT TO CHANGE ABOUT HISTORY. THINK OF *ALL* THE PEOPLE LIKE ME WHO I COULD SAVE.
BUT WE CAN'T BREAK THE *ONE RULE* JUST BECAUSE YOU ADMIRE SOMEONE.
WHAT? NO--
GIVE IT UP. WE CAN ALL TELL.
SPOILER-- HAMILTON IS NO PERFECT MAN. BELIEVE *THAT.*
NO ONE IS SAYING HE IS, ZACK!
A *LEADER* HAS TO SAY THE *HARD THINGS,* BECCA!
YOU THINK YOU CAN BE A *BETTER* TEAM CAPTAIN? *HA!*
I'M DONE LISTENING TO *BOTH* OF YOU!
EVERYONE, SHUT UP!

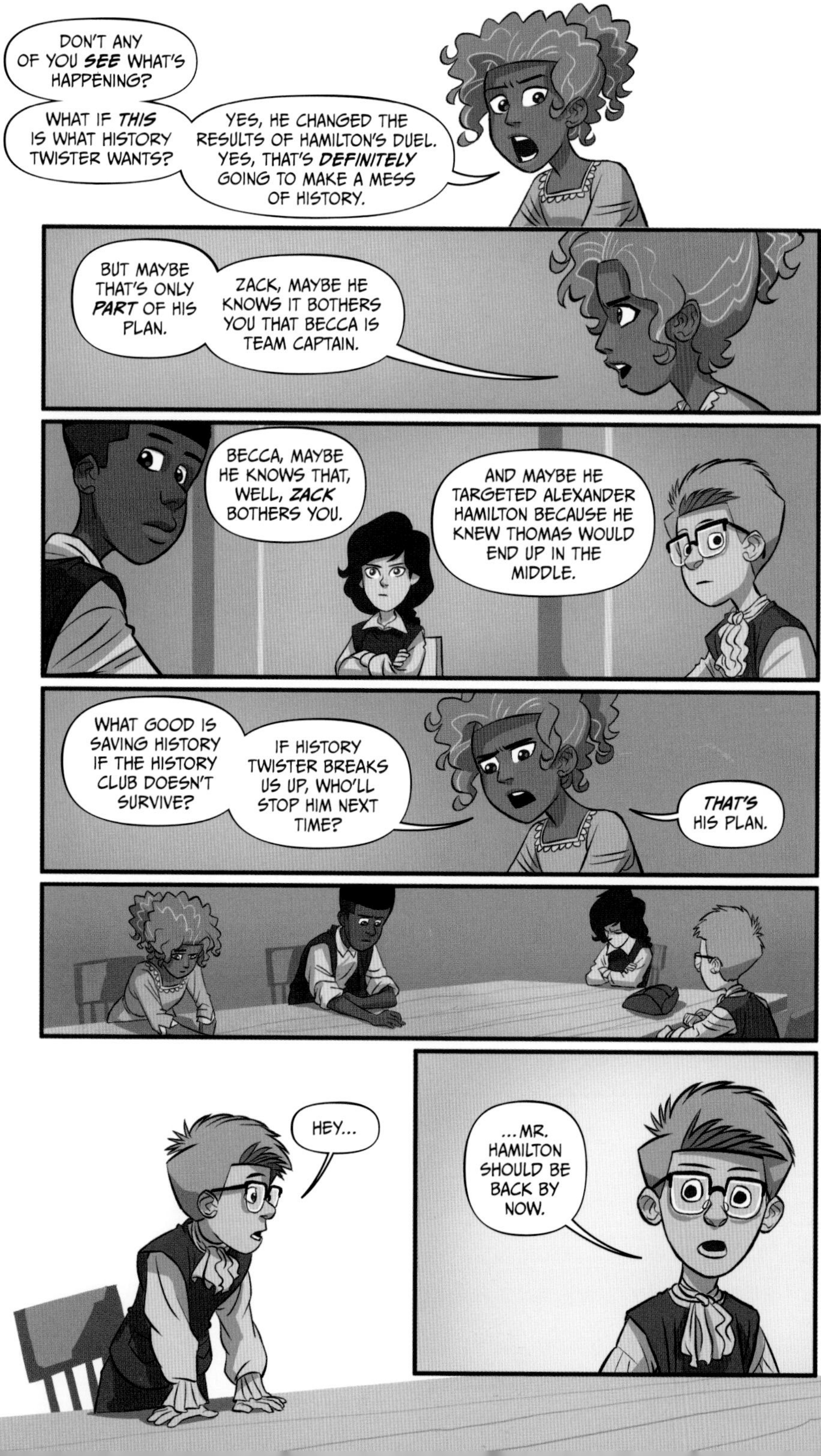
DON'T ANY OF YOU **SEE** WHAT'S HAPPENING?
WHAT IF **THIS** IS WHAT HISTORY TWISTER WANTS?
YES, HE CHANGED THE RESULTS OF HAMILTON'S DUEL. YES, THAT'S **DEFINITELY** GOING TO MAKE A MESS OF HISTORY.
BUT MAYBE THAT'S ONLY **PART** OF HIS PLAN.
ZACK, MAYBE HE KNOWS IT BOTHERS YOU THAT BECCA IS TEAM CAPTAIN.
BECCA, MAYBE HE KNOWS THAT, WELL, **ZACK** BOTHERS YOU.
AND MAYBE HE TARGETED ALEXANDER HAMILTON BECAUSE HE KNEW THOMAS WOULD END UP IN THE MIDDLE.
WHAT GOOD IS SAVING HISTORY IF THE HISTORY CLUB DOESN'T SURVIVE?
IF HISTORY TWISTER BREAKS US UP, WHO'LL STOP HIM NEXT TIME?
THAT'S HIS PLAN.
HEY...
...MR. HAMILTON SHOULD BE BACK BY NOW.

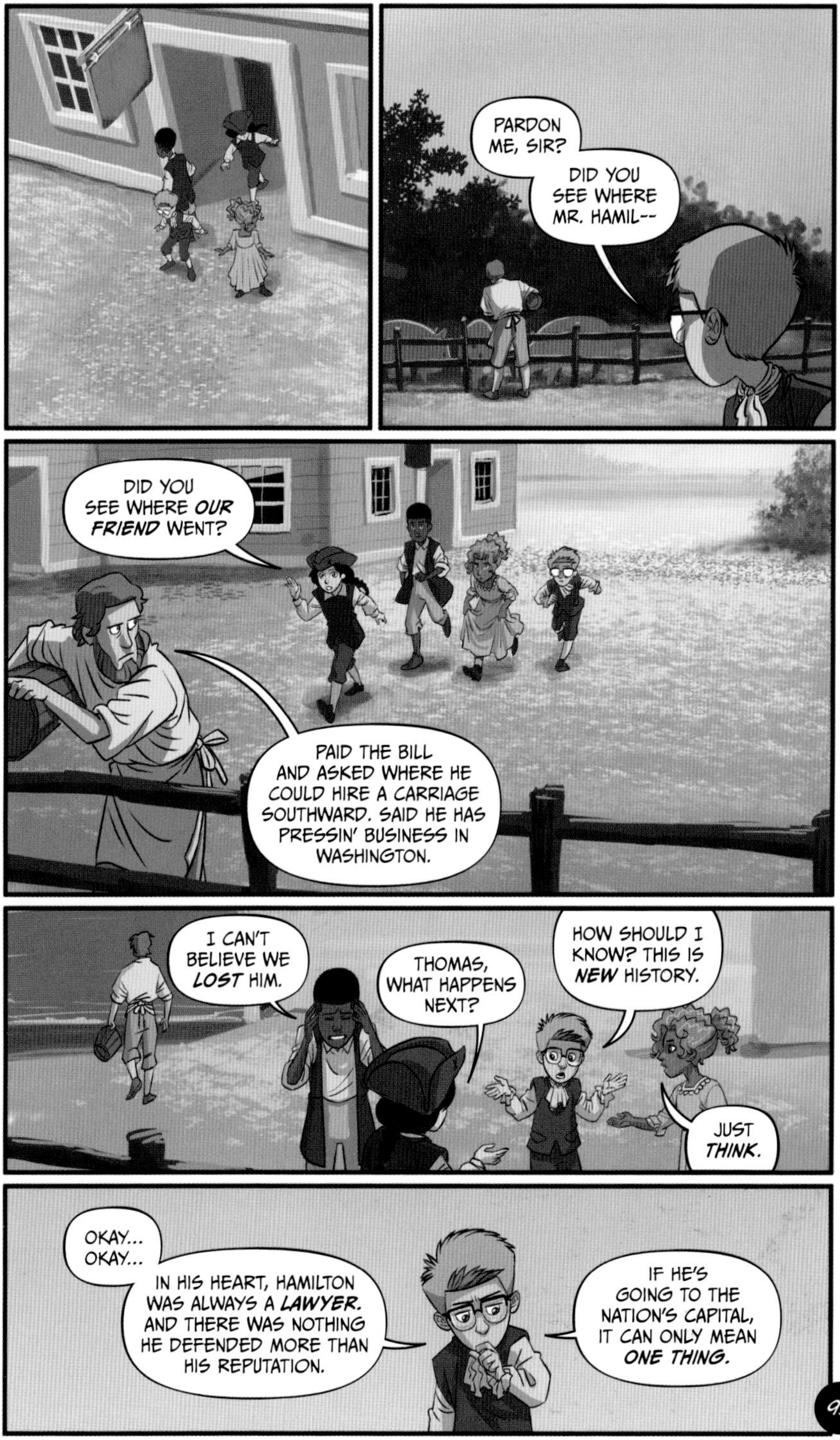
PARDON ME, SIR?
DID YOU SEE WHERE MR. HAMIL--
DID YOU SEE WHERE *OUR FRIEND* WENT?
PAID THE BILL AND ASKED WHERE HE COULD HIRE A CARRIAGE SOUTHWARD. SAID HE HAS PRESSIN' BUSINESS IN WASHINGTON.
I CAN'T BELIEVE WE *LOST* HIM.
THOMAS, WHAT HAPPENS NEXT?
HOW SHOULD I KNOW? THIS IS *NEW* HISTORY.
JUST *THINK.*
OKAY... OKAY...
IN HIS HEART, HAMILTON WAS ALWAYS A *LAWYER.* AND THERE WAS NOTHING HE DEFENDED MORE THAN HIS REPUTATION.
IF HE'S GOING TO THE NATION'S CAPITAL, IT CAN ONLY MEAN *ONE THING.*

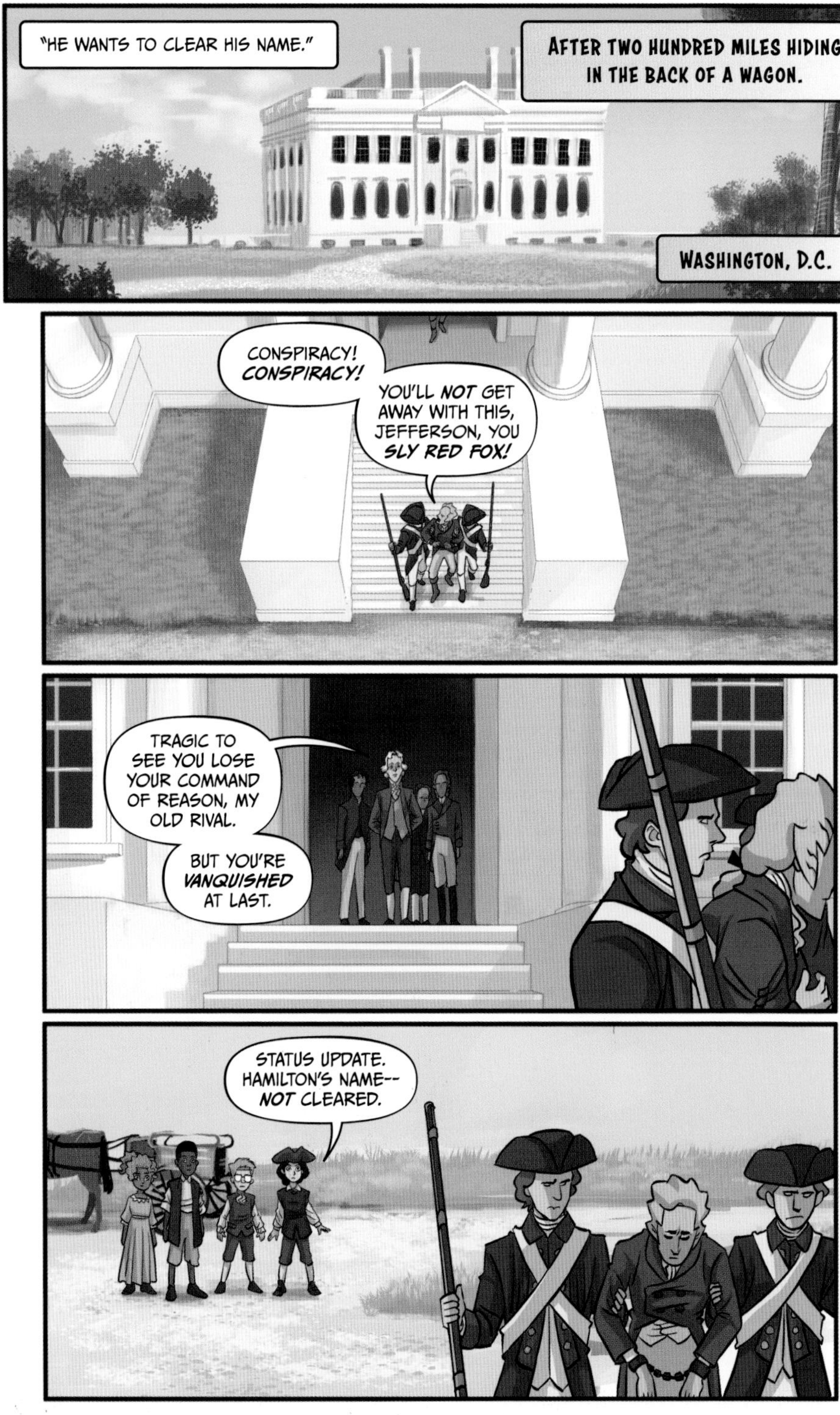
"HE WANTS TO CLEAR HIS NAME."
AFTER TWO HUNDRED MILES HIDING IN THE BACK OF A WAGON.
WASHINGTON, D.C.
CONSPIRACY! CONSPIRACY!
YOU'LL NOT GET AWAY WITH THIS, JEFFERSON, YOU SLY RED FOX!
TRAGIC TO SEE YOU LOSE YOUR COMMAND OF REASON, MY OLD RIVAL.
BUT YOU'RE VANQUISHED AT LAST.
STATUS UPDATE. HAMILTON'S NAME-- NOT CLEARED.

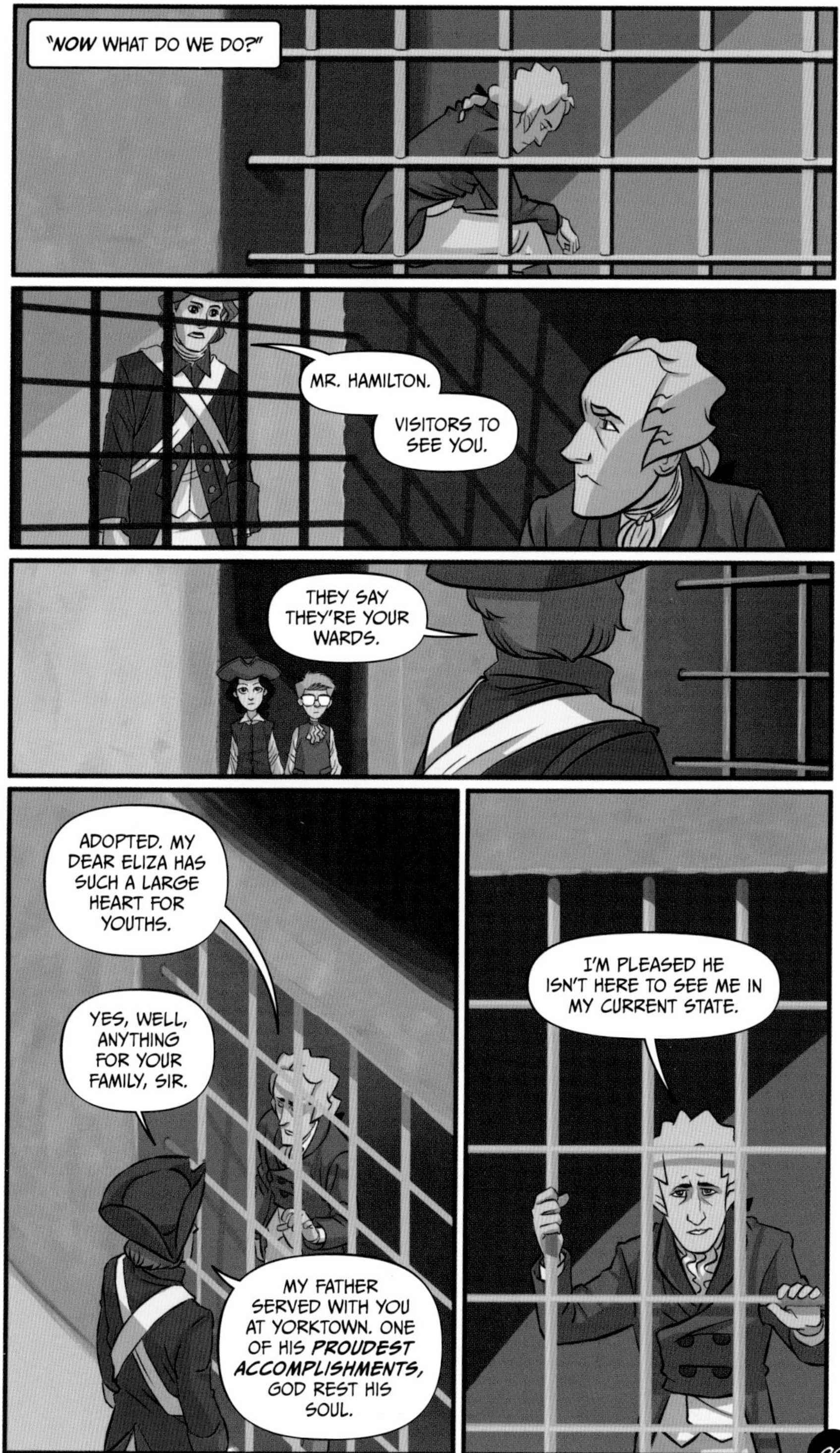
"*NOW* WHAT DO WE DO?"
MR. HAMILTON.
VISITORS TO SEE YOU.
THEY SAY THEY'RE YOUR WARDS.
ADOPTED. MY DEAR ELIZA HAS SUCH A LARGE HEART FOR YOUTHS.
YES, WELL, ANYTHING FOR YOUR FAMILY, SIR.
MY FATHER SERVED WITH YOU AT YORKTOWN. ONE OF HIS ***PROUDEST ACCOMPLISHMENTS,*** GOD REST HIS SOUL.
I'M PLEASED HE ISN'T HERE TO SEE ME IN MY CURRENT STATE.

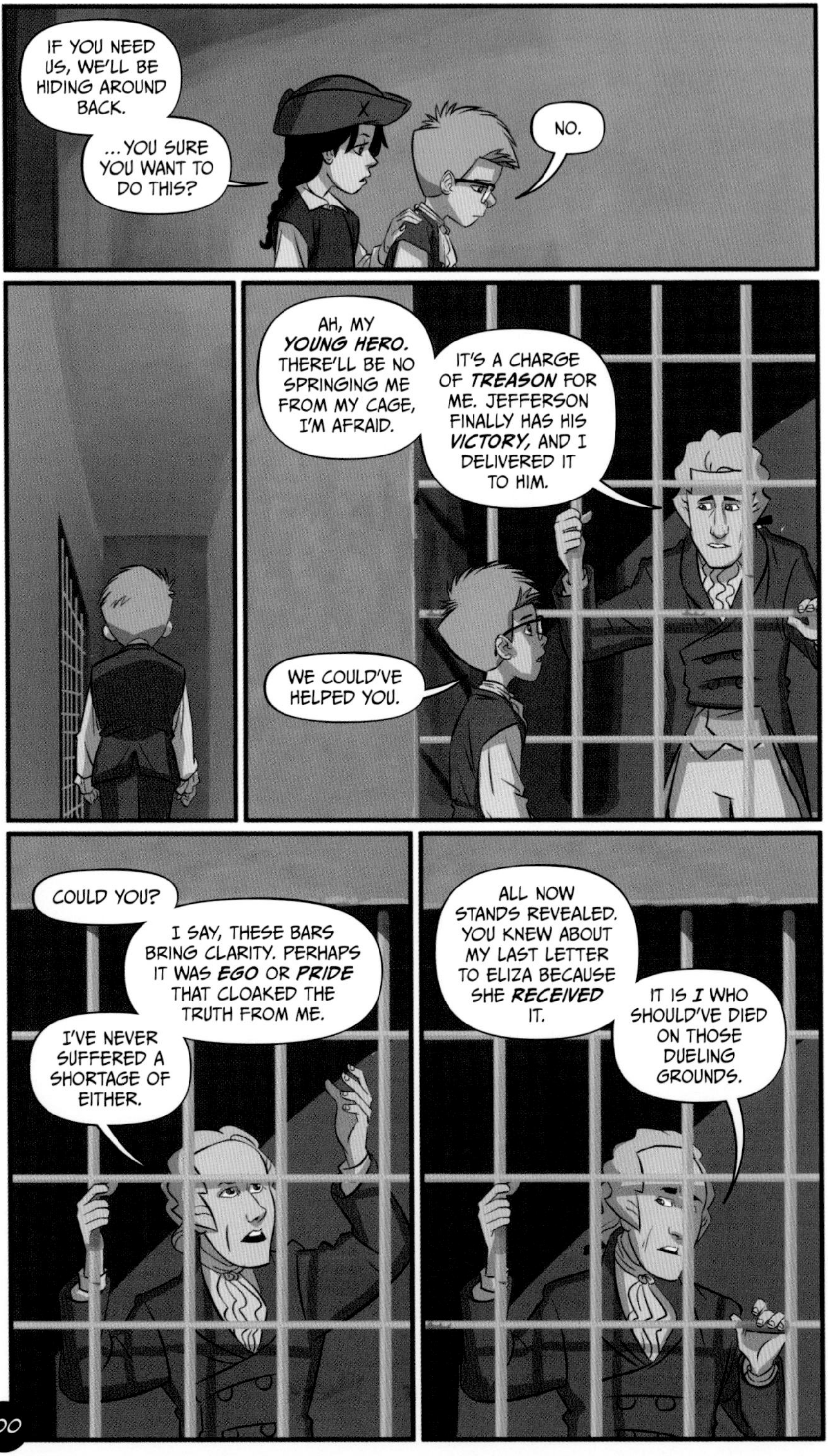
IF YOU NEED US, WE'LL BE HIDING AROUND BACK.
...YOU SURE YOU WANT TO DO THIS?
NO.
AH, MY *YOUNG HERO.* THERE'LL BE NO SPRINGING ME FROM MY CAGE, I'M AFRAID.
IT'S A CHARGE OF *TREASON* FOR ME. JEFFERSON FINALLY HAS HIS *VICTORY,* AND I DELIVERED IT TO HIM.
WE COULD'VE HELPED YOU.
COULD YOU?
I SAY, THESE BARS BRING CLARITY. PERHAPS IT WAS *EGO* OR *PRIDE* THAT CLOAKED THE TRUTH FROM ME.
I'VE NEVER SUFFERED A SHORTAGE OF EITHER.
ALL NOW STANDS REVEALED. YOU KNEW ABOUT MY LAST LETTER TO ELIZA BECAUSE SHE *RECEIVED* IT.
IT IS *I* WHO SHOULD'VE DIED ON THOSE DUELING GROUNDS.

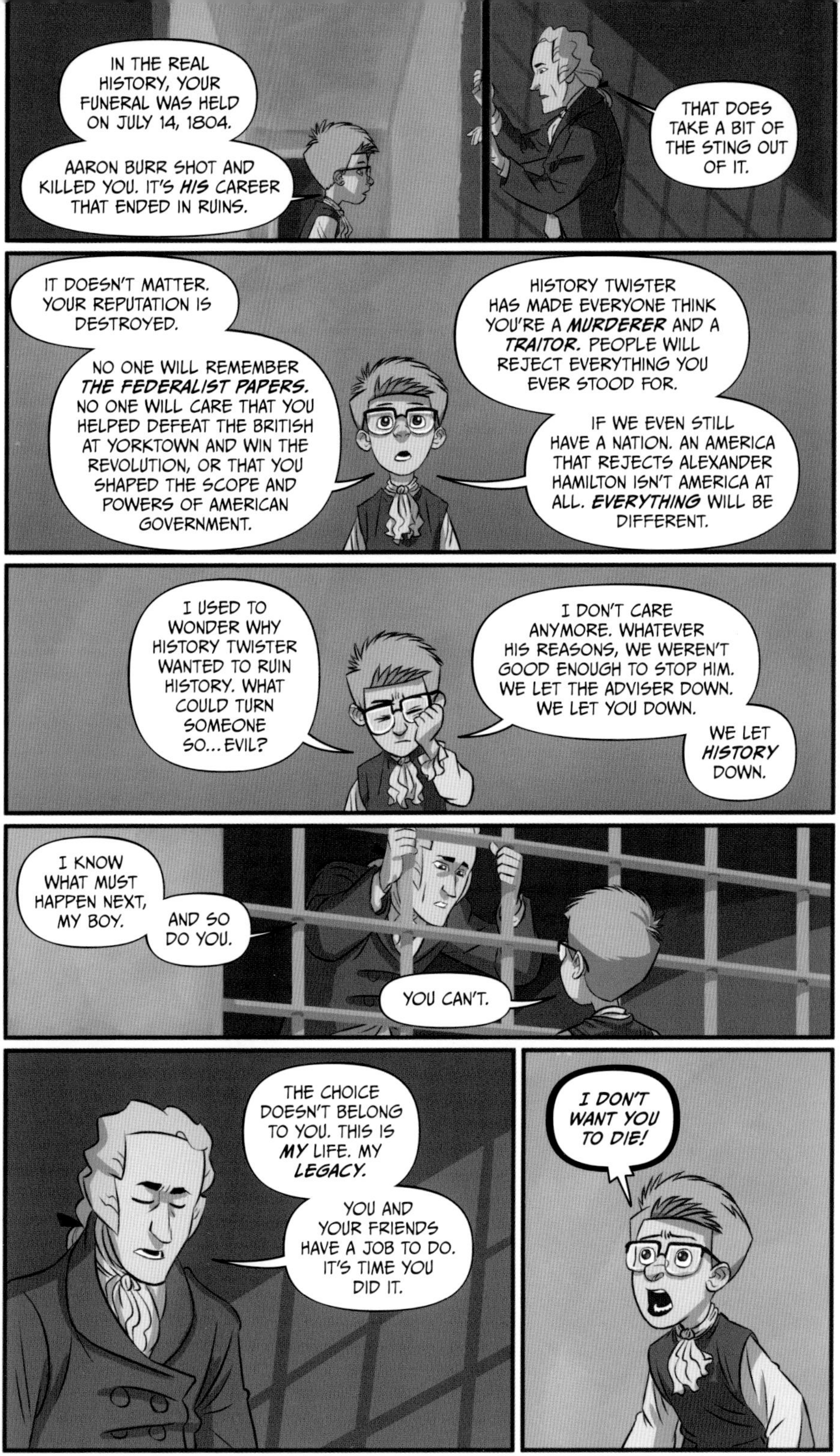

IN THE REAL HISTORY, YOUR FUNERAL WAS HELD ON JULY 14, 1804.
AARON BURR SHOT AND KILLED YOU. IT'S *HIS* CAREER THAT ENDED IN RUINS.
THAT DOES TAKE A BIT OF THE STING OUT OF IT.
IT DOESN'T MATTER. YOUR REPUTATION IS DESTROYED.
NO ONE WILL REMEMBER *THE FEDERALIST PAPERS.* NO ONE WILL CARE THAT YOU HELPED DEFEAT THE BRITISH AT YORKTOWN AND WIN THE REVOLUTION, OR THAT YOU SHAPED THE SCOPE AND POWERS OF AMERICAN GOVERNMENT.
HISTORY TWISTER HAS MADE EVERYONE THINK YOU'RE A *MURDERER* AND A *TRAITOR.* PEOPLE WILL REJECT EVERYTHING YOU EVER STOOD FOR.
IF WE EVEN STILL HAVE A NATION. AN AMERICA THAT REJECTS ALEXANDER HAMILTON ISN'T AMERICA AT ALL. *EVERYTHING* WILL BE DIFFERENT.
I USED TO WONDER WHY HISTORY TWISTER WANTED TO RUIN HISTORY. WHAT COULD TURN SOMEONE SO...EVIL?
I DON'T CARE ANYMORE. WHATEVER HIS REASONS, WE WEREN'T GOOD ENOUGH TO STOP HIM. WE LET THE ADVISER DOWN. WE LET YOU DOWN.
WE LET *HISTORY* DOWN.
I KNOW WHAT MUST HAPPEN NEXT, MY BOY.
AND SO DO YOU.
YOU CAN'T.
THE CHOICE DOESN'T BELONG TO YOU. THIS IS *MY* LIFE. MY *LEGACY.*
YOU AND YOUR FRIENDS HAVE A JOB TO DO. IT'S TIME YOU DID IT.
I DON'T WANT YOU TO DIE!

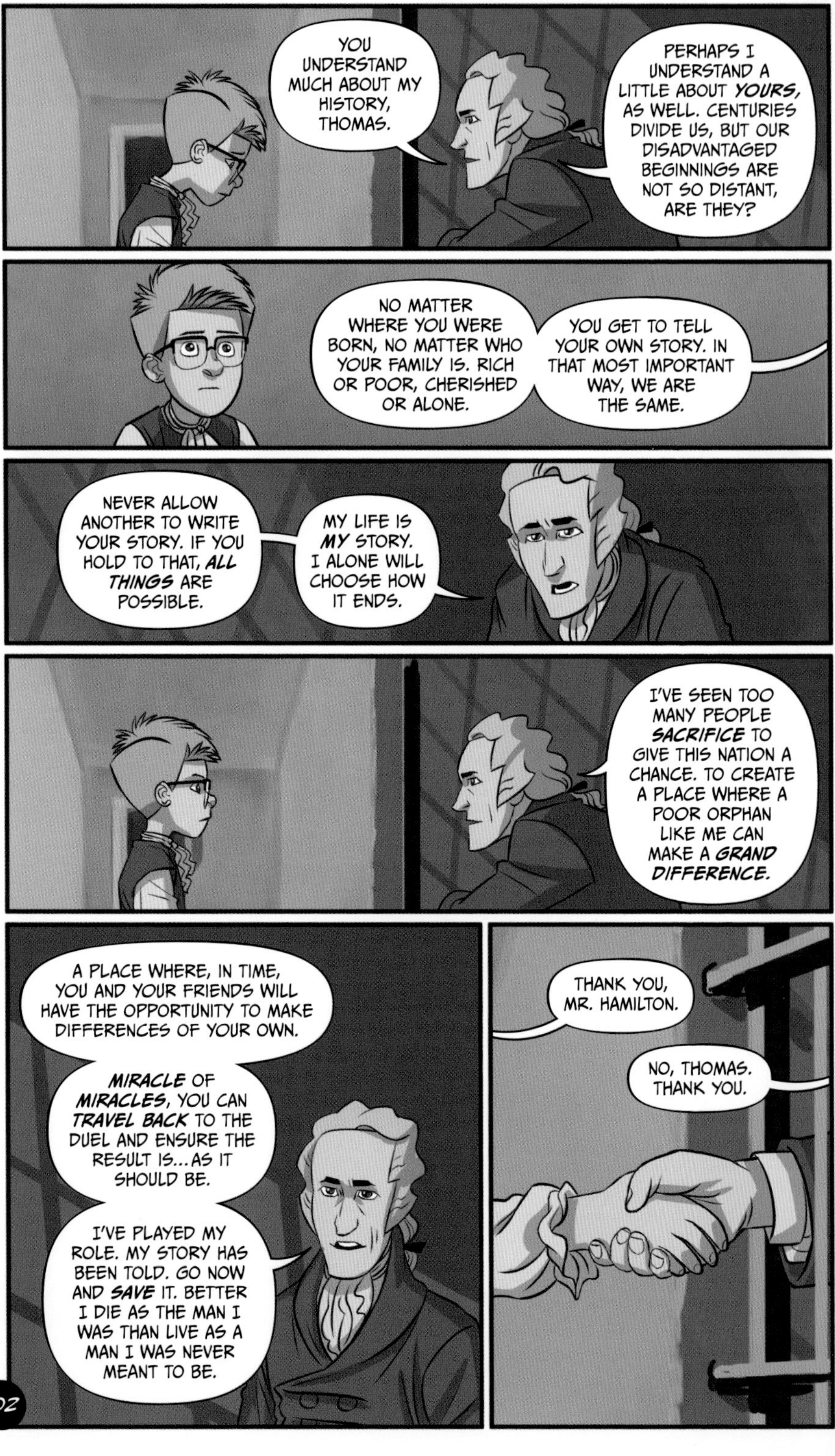
YOU UNDERSTAND MUCH ABOUT MY HISTORY, THOMAS.
PERHAPS I UNDERSTAND A LITTLE ABOUT *YOURS,* AS WELL. CENTURIES DIVIDE US, BUT OUR DISADVANTAGED BEGINNINGS ARE NOT SO DISTANT, ARE THEY?
NO MATTER WHERE YOU WERE BORN, NO MATTER WHO YOUR FAMILY IS. RICH OR POOR, CHERISHED OR ALONE.
YOU GET TO TELL YOUR OWN STORY. IN THAT MOST IMPORTANT WAY, WE ARE THE SAME.
NEVER ALLOW ANOTHER TO WRITE YOUR STORY. IF YOU HOLD TO THAT, *ALL THINGS* ARE POSSIBLE.
MY LIFE IS *MY* STORY. I ALONE WILL CHOOSE HOW IT ENDS.
I'VE SEEN TOO MANY PEOPLE *SACRIFICE* TO GIVE THIS NATION A CHANCE. TO CREATE A PLACE WHERE A POOR ORPHAN LIKE ME CAN MAKE A *GRAND DIFFERENCE.*
A PLACE WHERE, IN TIME, YOU AND YOUR FRIENDS WILL HAVE THE OPPORTUNITY TO MAKE DIFFERENCES OF YOUR OWN.
MIRACLE OF *MIRACLES,* YOU CAN *TRAVEL BACK* TO THE DUEL AND ENSURE THE RESULT IS...AS IT SHOULD BE.
I'VE PLAYED MY ROLE. MY STORY HAS BEEN TOLD. GO NOW AND *SAVE* IT. BETTER I DIE AS THE MAN I WAS THAN LIVE AS A MAN I WAS NEVER MEANT TO BE.
THANK YOU, MR. HAMILTON.
NO, THOMAS. THANK YOU.

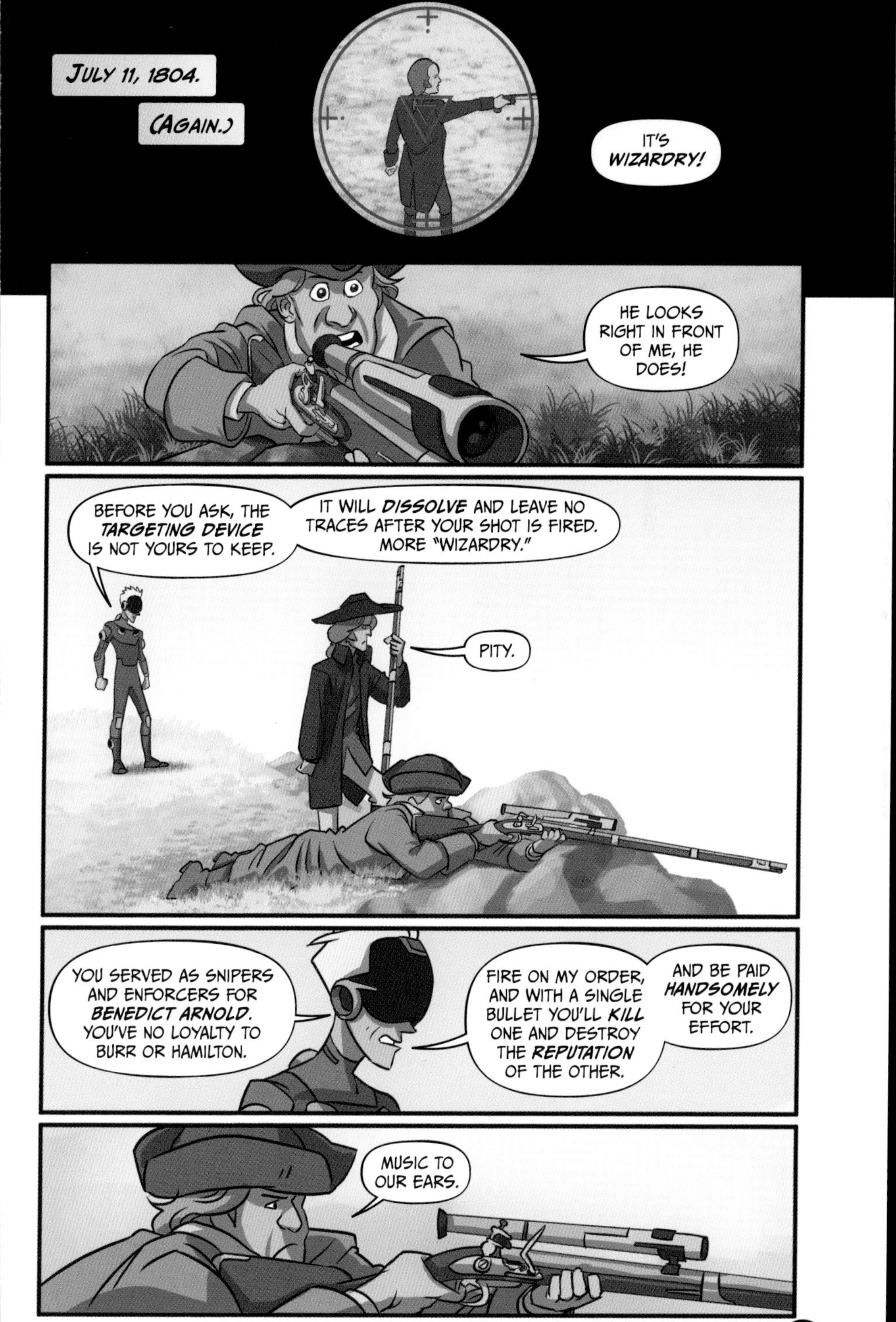
JULY 11, 1804.
(AGAIN.)
IT'S WIZARDRY!
HE LOOKS RIGHT IN FRONT OF ME, HE DOES!
BEFORE YOU ASK, THE TARGETING DEVICE IS NOT YOURS TO KEEP.
IT WILL DISSOLVE AND LEAVE NO TRACES AFTER YOUR SHOT IS FIRED. MORE "WIZARDRY."
PITY.
YOU SERVED AS SNIPERS AND ENFORCERS FOR BENEDICT ARNOLD. YOU'VE NO LOYALTY TO BURR OR HAMILTON.
FIRE ON MY ORDER, AND WITH A SINGLE BULLET YOU'LL KILL ONE AND DESTROY THE REPUTATION OF THE OTHER.
AND BE PAID HANDSOMELY FOR YOUR EFFORT.
MUSIC TO OUR EARS.

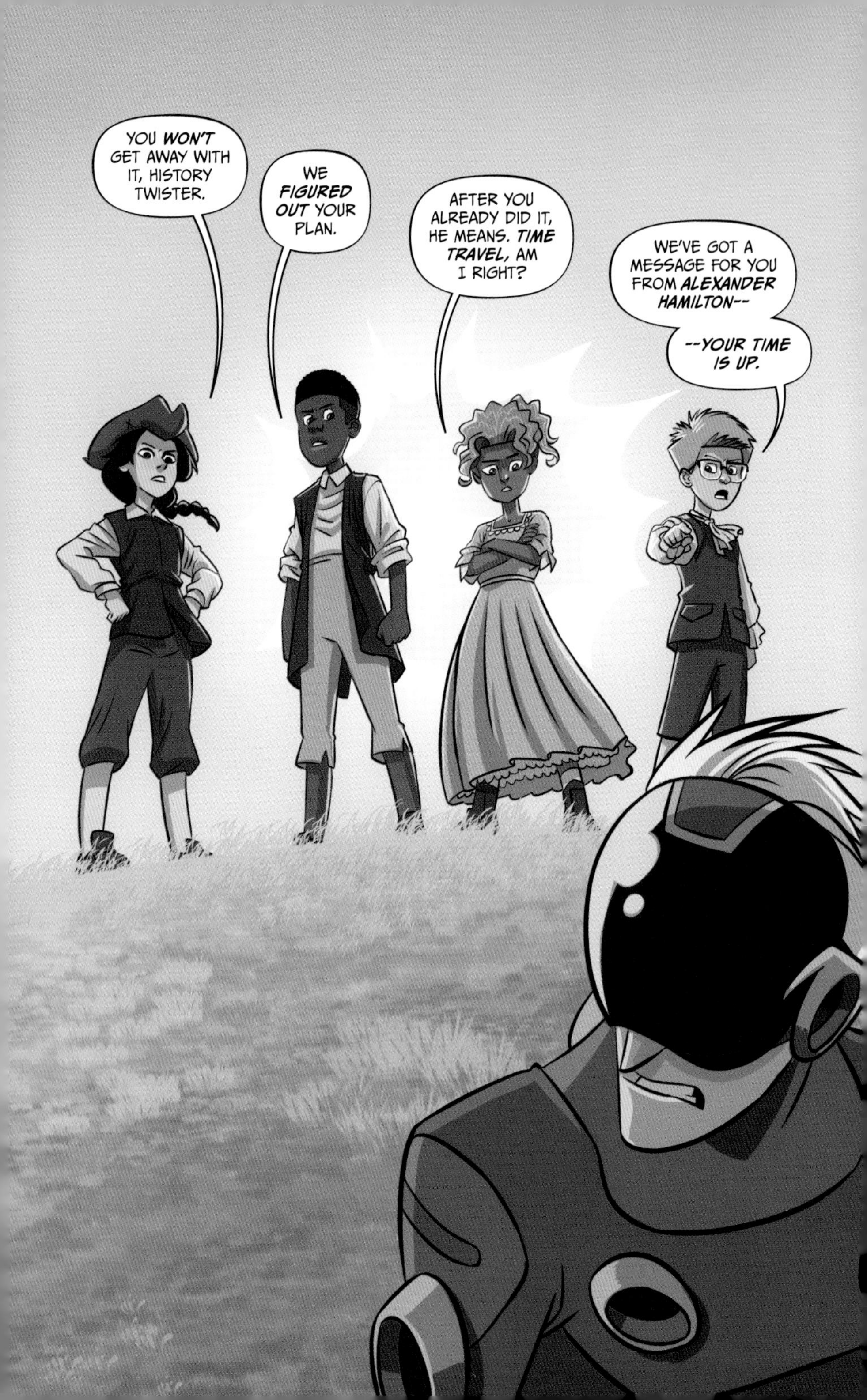
YOU WON'T GET AWAY WITH IT, HISTORY TWISTER.
WE FIGURED OUT YOUR PLAN.
AFTER YOU ALREADY DID IT, HE MEANS. TIME TRAVEL, AM I RIGHT?
WE'VE GOT A MESSAGE FOR YOU FROM ALEXANDER HAMILTON--
--YOUR TIME IS UP.

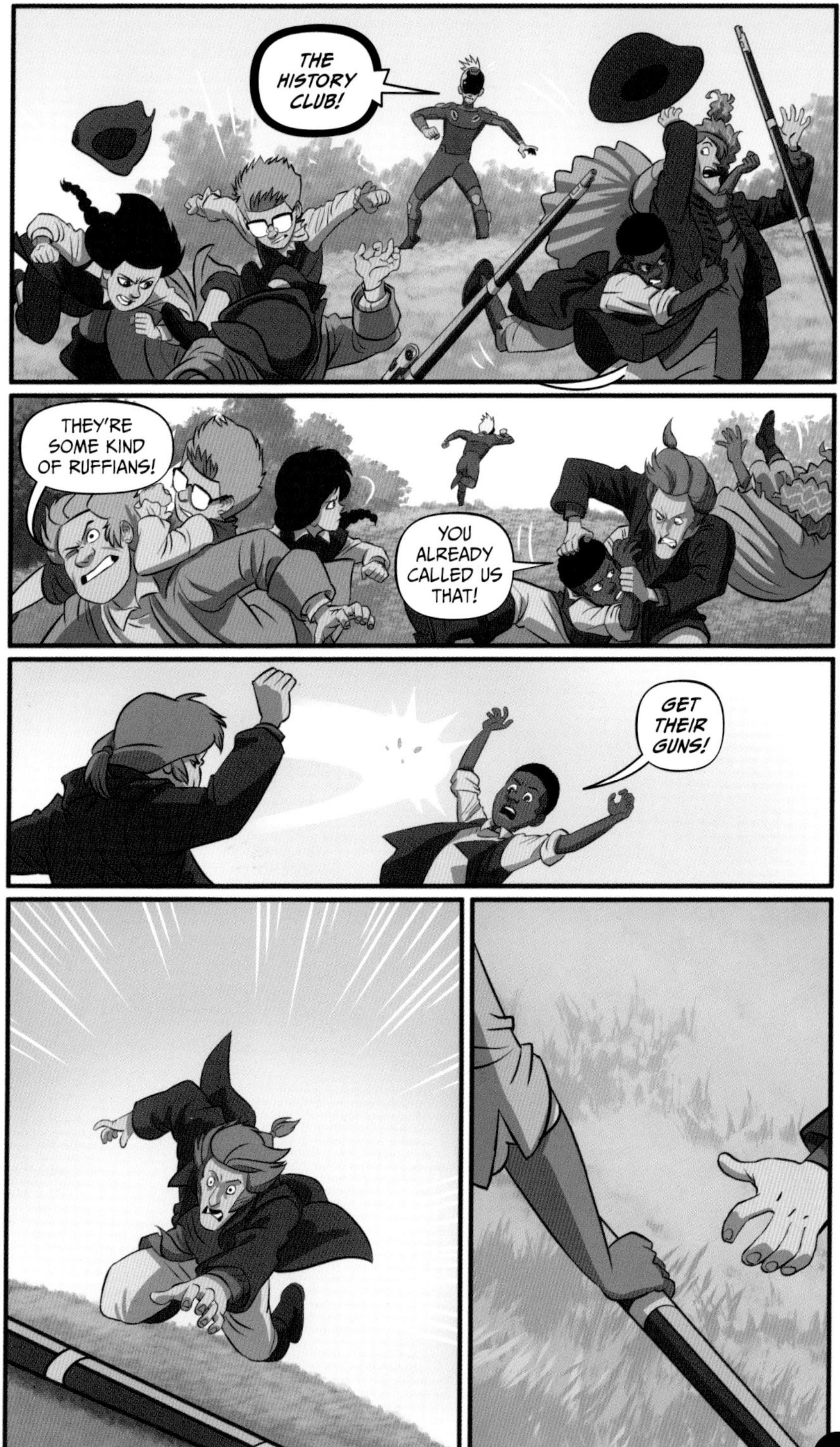
THE HISTORY CLUB!
THEY'RE SOME KIND OF RUFFIANS!
YOU ALREADY CALLED US THAT!
GET THEIR GUNS!

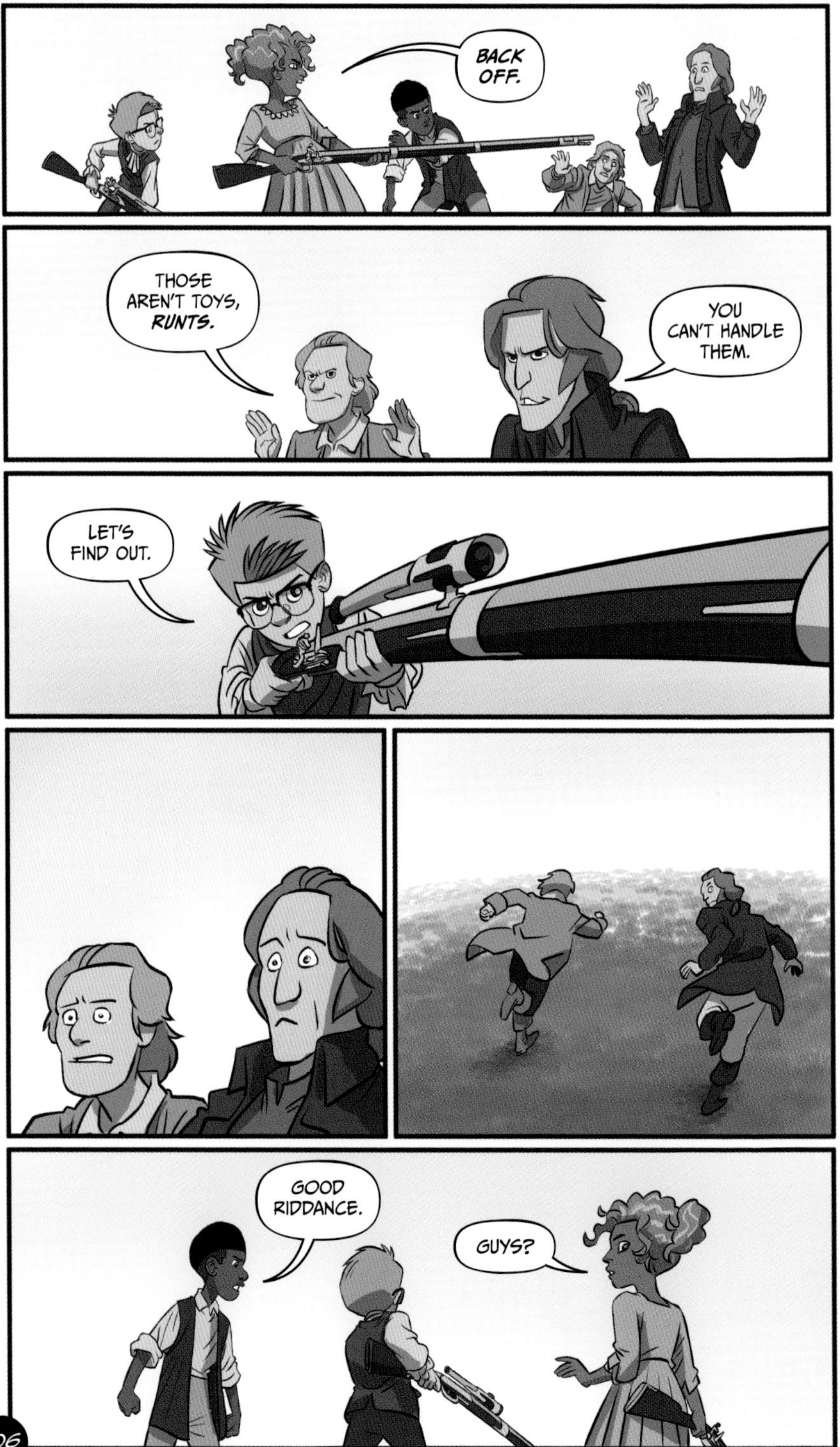
BACK OFF.
THOSE AREN'T TOYS, *RUNTS.*
YOU CAN'T HANDLE THEM.
LET'S FIND OUT.
GOOD RIDDANCE.
GUYS?

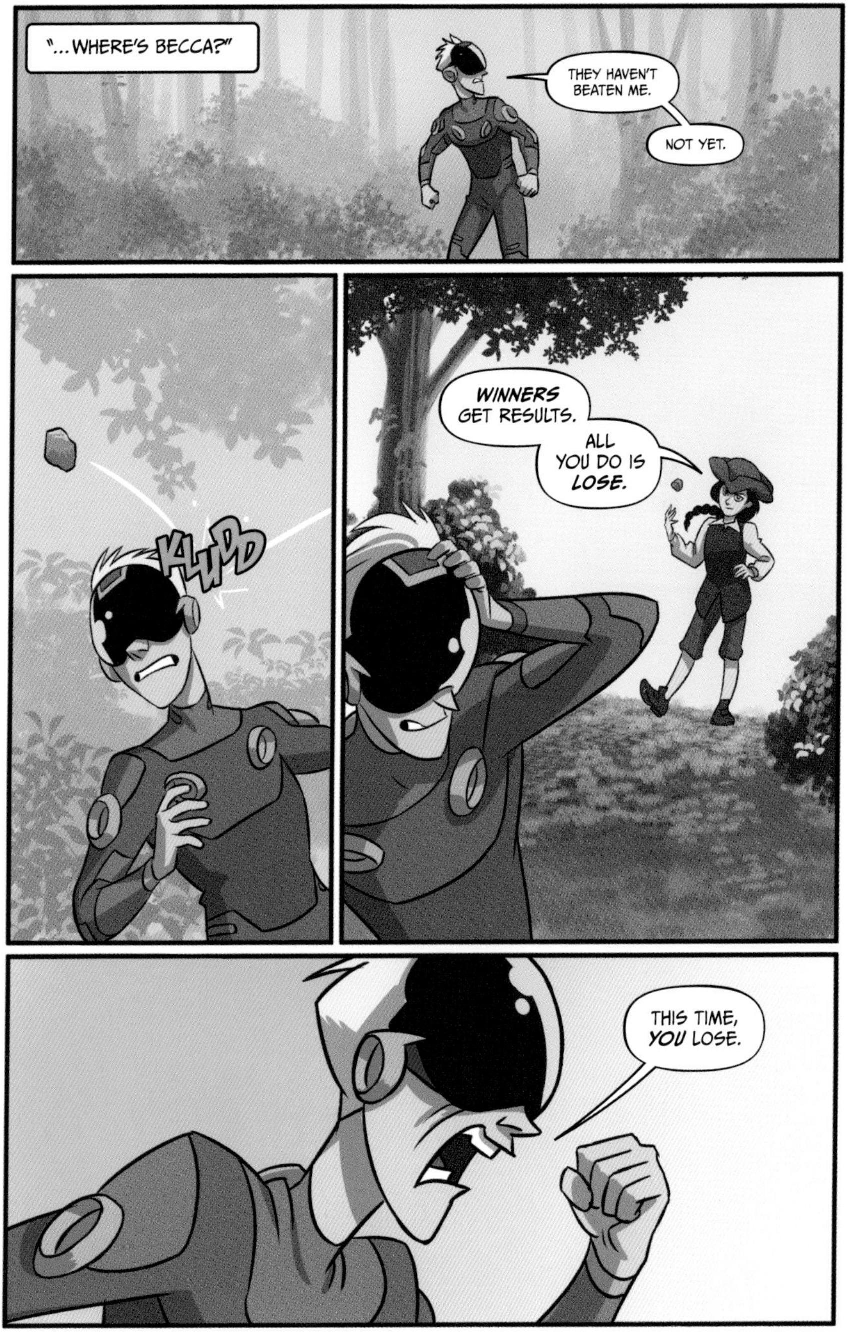
"...WHERE'S BECCA?"
THEY HAVEN'T BEATEN ME.
NOT YET.
KLUDD
WINNERS GET RESULTS.
ALL YOU DO IS LOSE.
THIS TIME, YOU LOSE.

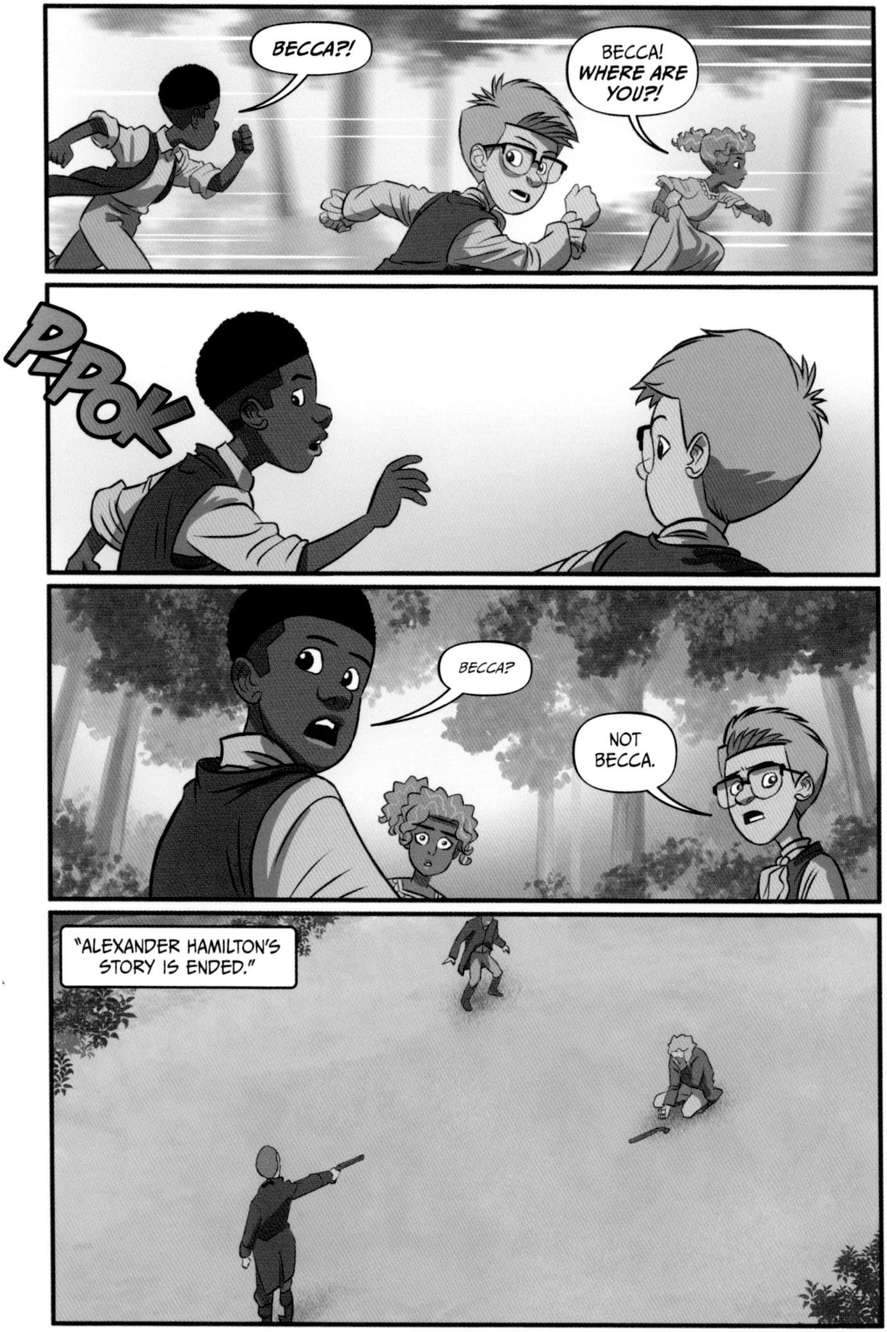
BECCA?!
BECCA! WHERE ARE YOU?!
P-POK
BECCA?
NOT BECCA.
"ALEXANDER HAMILTON'S STORY IS ENDED."

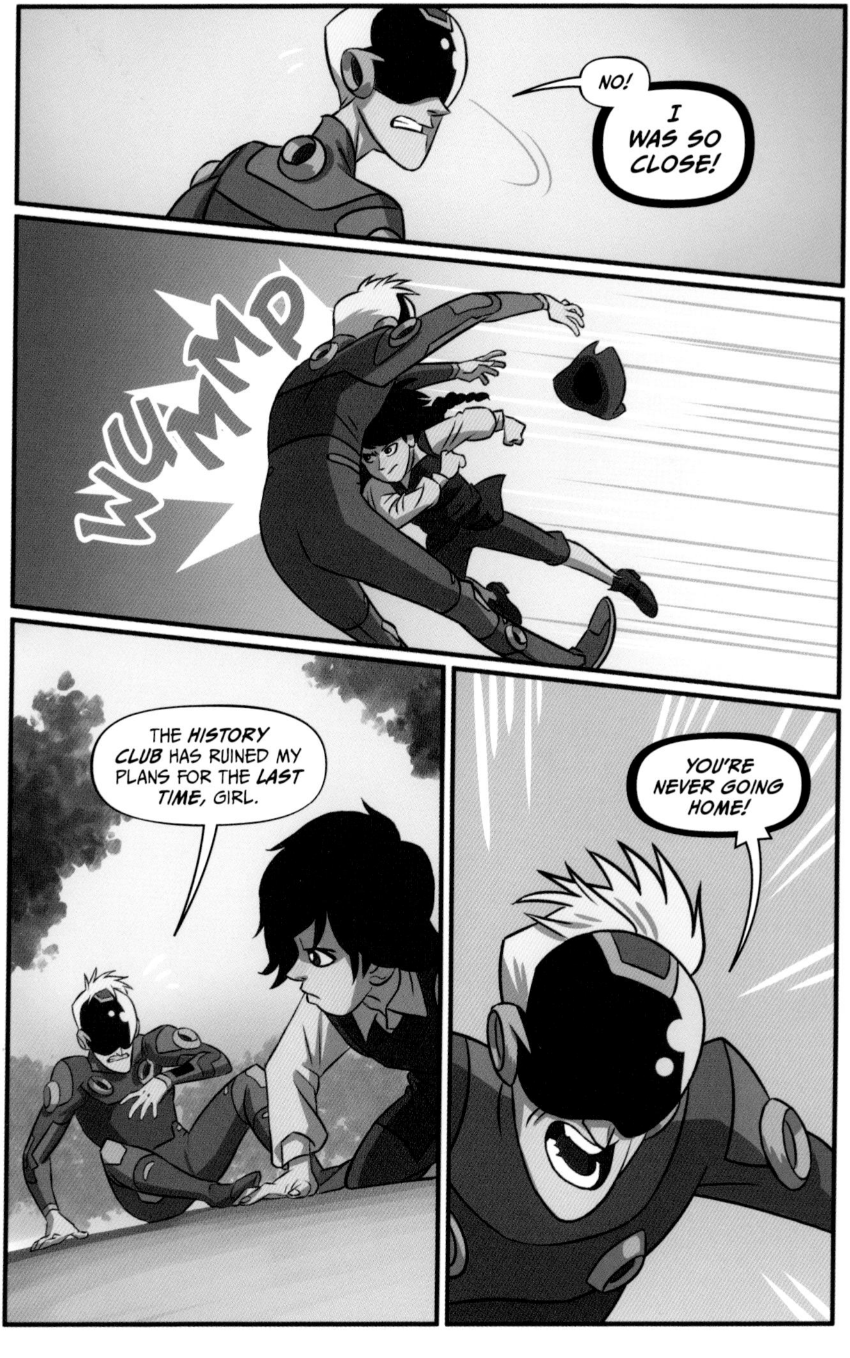
NO!
I WAS SO CLOSE!
WUMMP
THE HISTORY CLUB HAS RUINED MY PLANS FOR THE LAST TIME, GIRL.
YOU'RE NEVER GOING HOME!

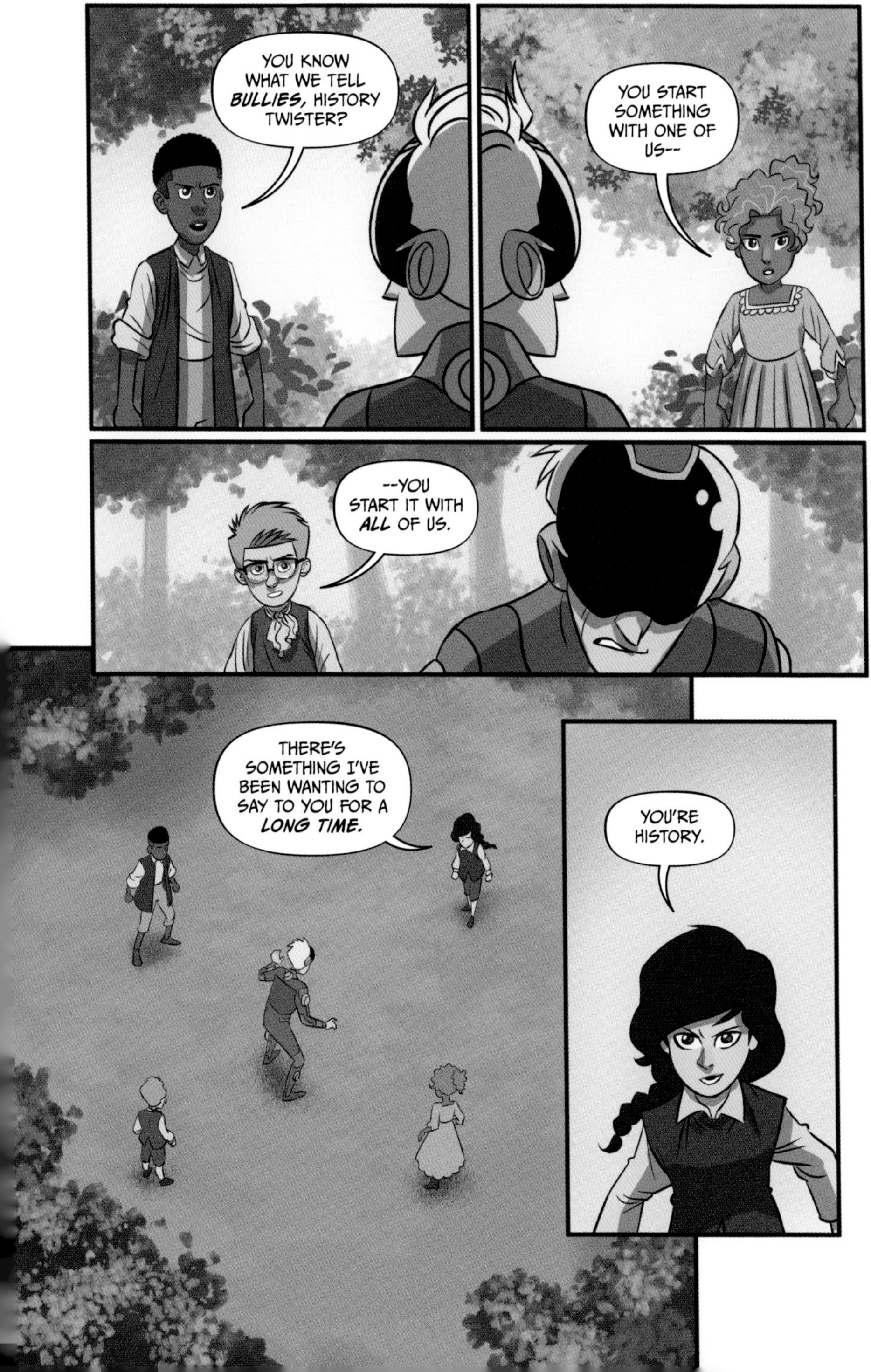
YOU KNOW WHAT WE TELL BULLIES, HISTORY TWISTER?
YOU START SOMETHING WITH ONE OF US--
--YOU START IT WITH ALL OF US.
THERE'S SOMETHING I'VE BEEN WANTING TO SAY TO YOU FOR A LONG TIME.
YOU'RE HISTORY.

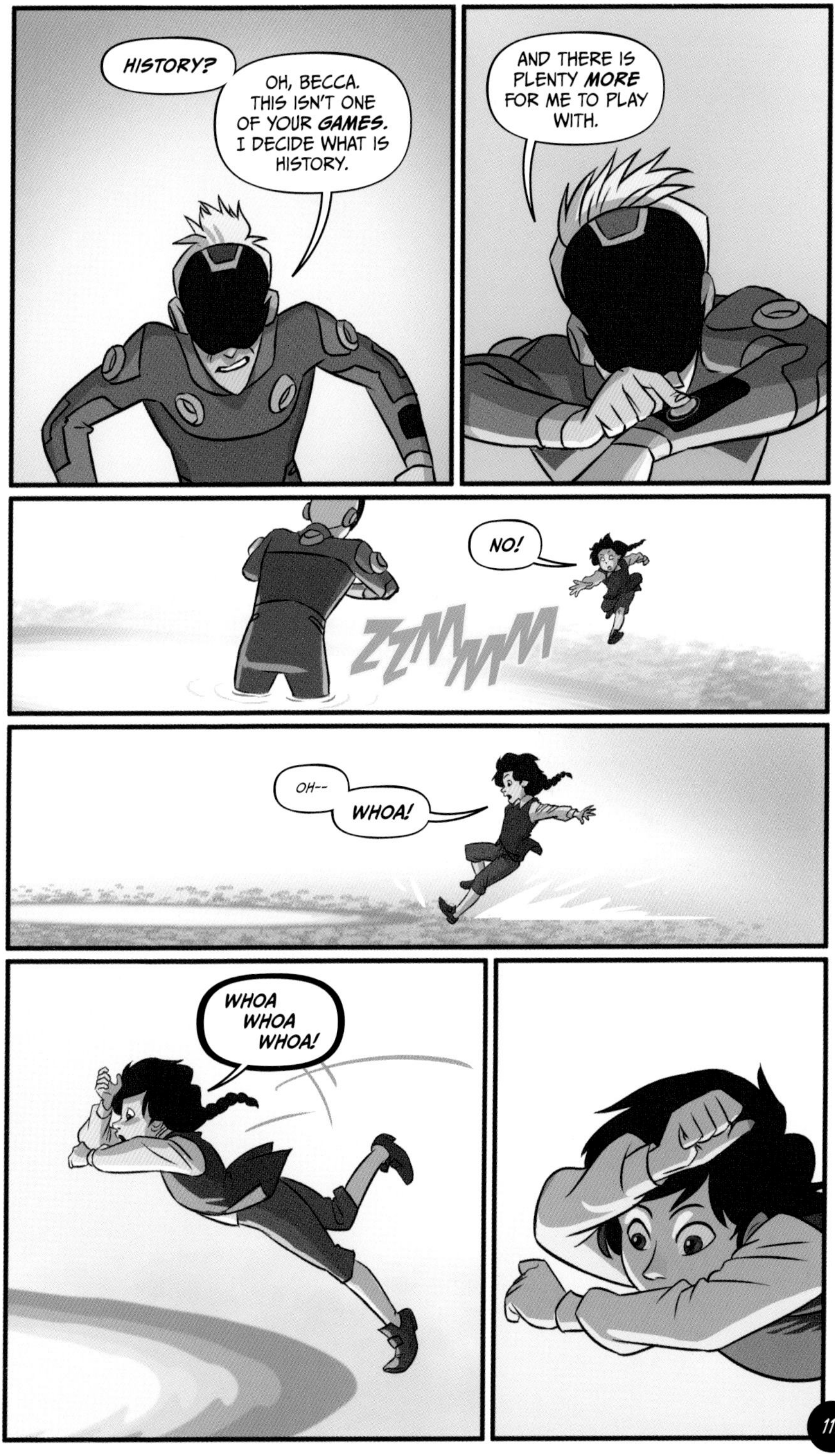
HISTORY?
OH, BECCA. THIS ISN'T ONE OF YOUR GAMES. I DECIDE WHAT IS HISTORY.
AND THERE IS PLENTY MORE FOR ME TO PLAY WITH.
NO!
ZZMMMM
OH--
WHOA!
WHOA WHOA WHOA!

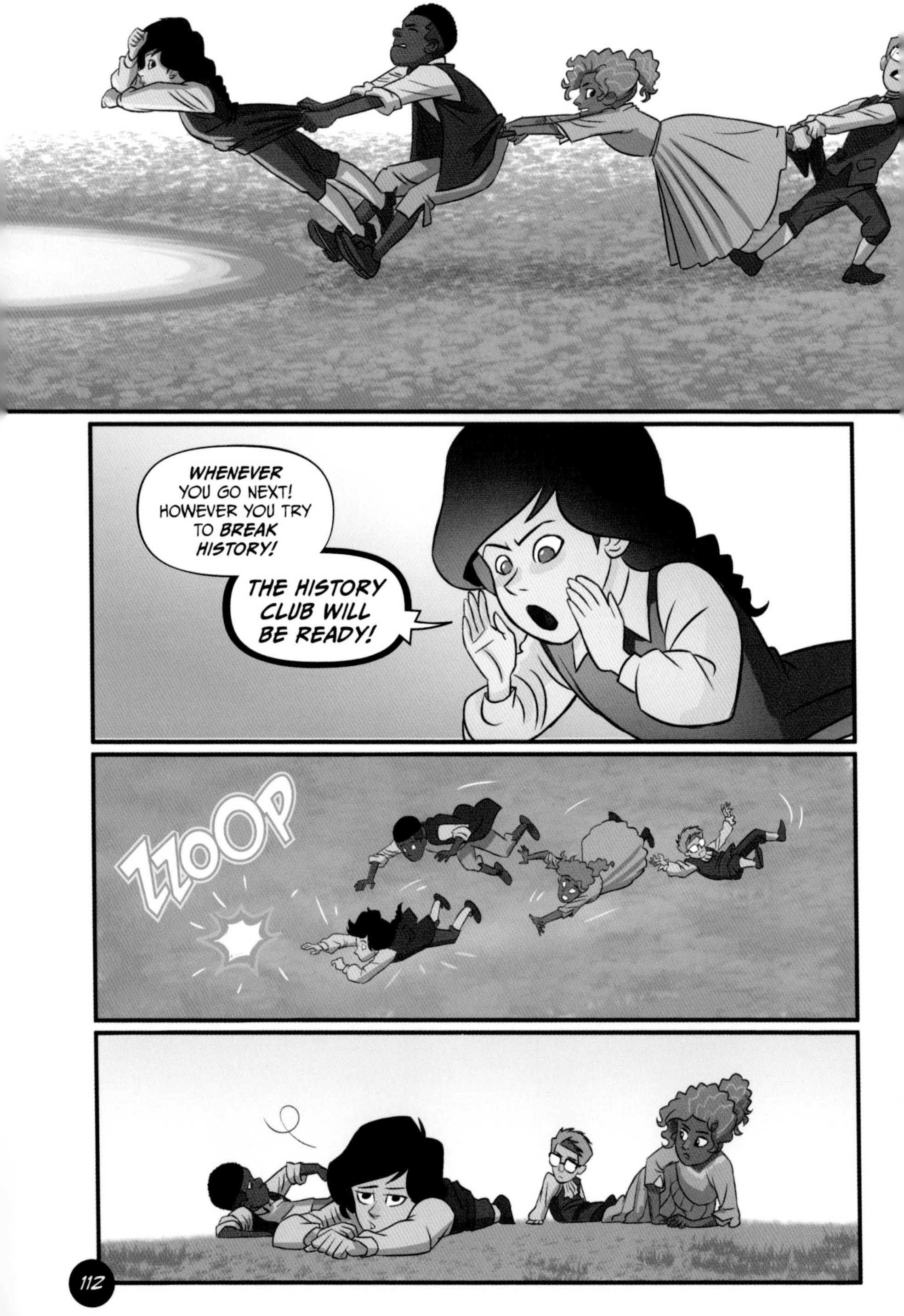
WHENEVER YOU GO NEXT! HOWEVER YOU TRY TO BREAK HISTORY!
THE HISTORY CLUB WILL BE READY!
ZZOOP

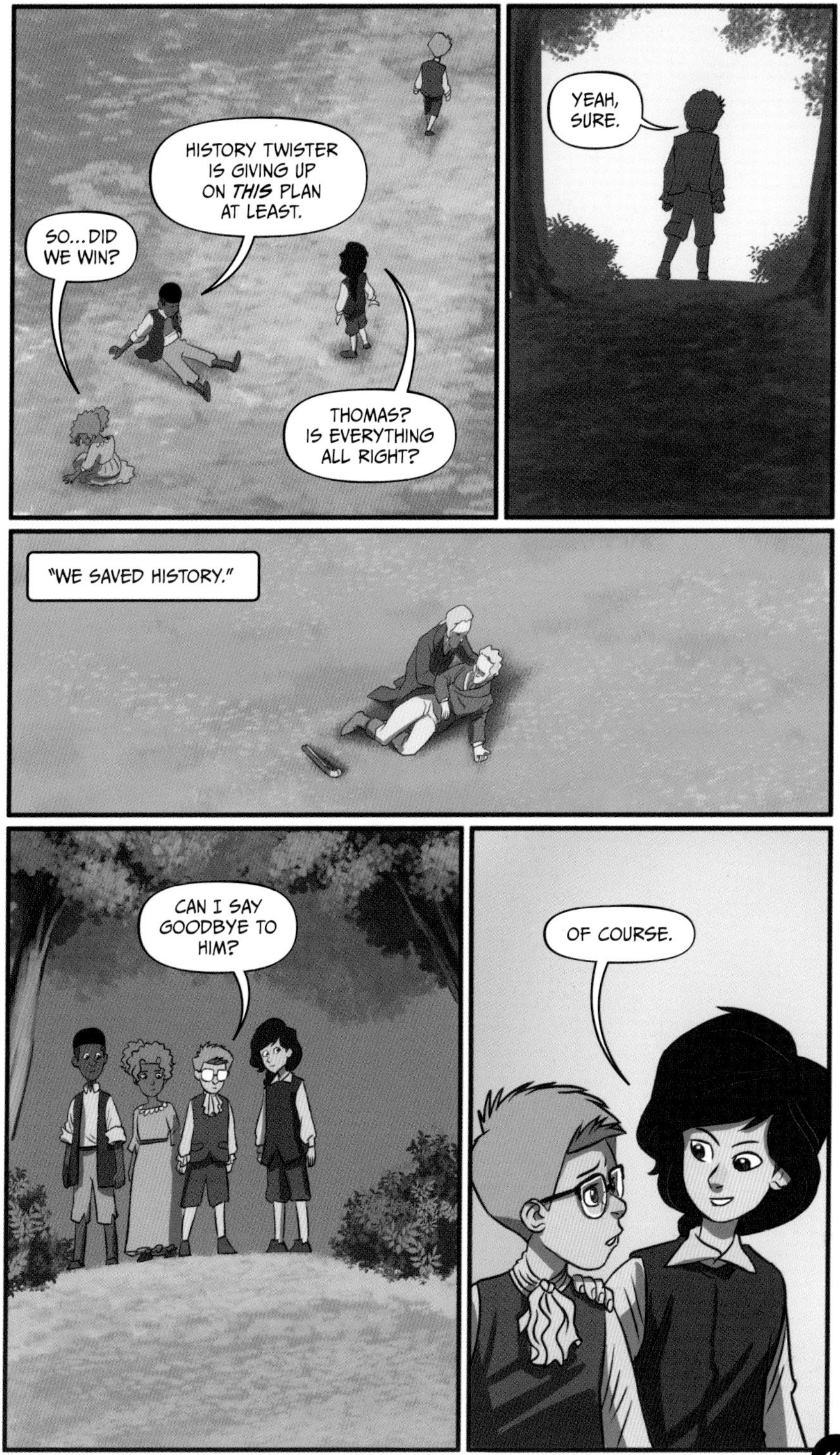
HISTORY TWISTER IS GIVING UP ON *THIS* PLAN AT LEAST.
SO...DID WE WIN?
THOMAS? IS EVERYTHING ALL RIGHT?
YEAH, SURE.
"WE SAVED HISTORY."
CAN I SAY GOODBYE TO HIM?
OF COURSE.

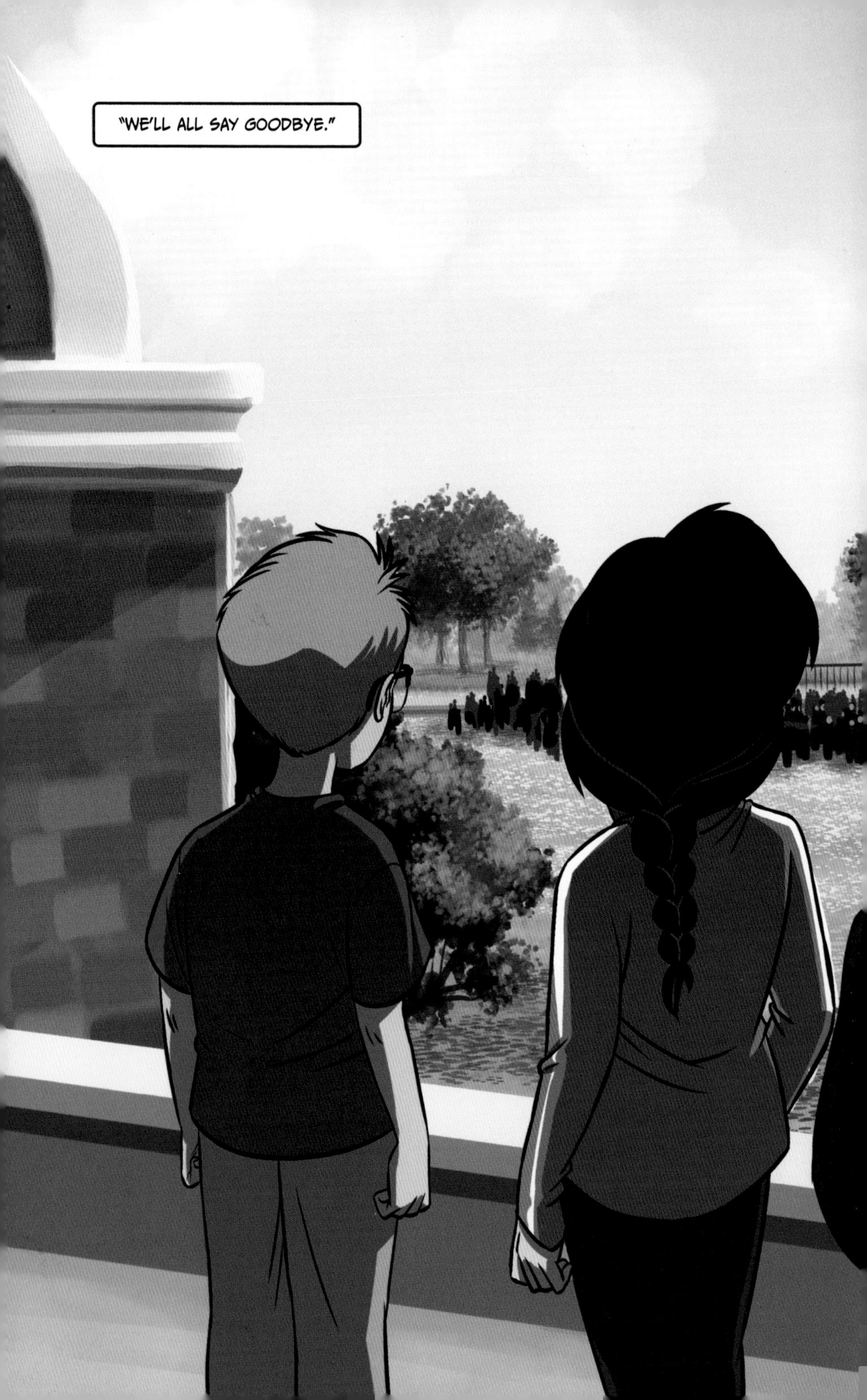
"WE'LL ALL SAY GOODBYE."

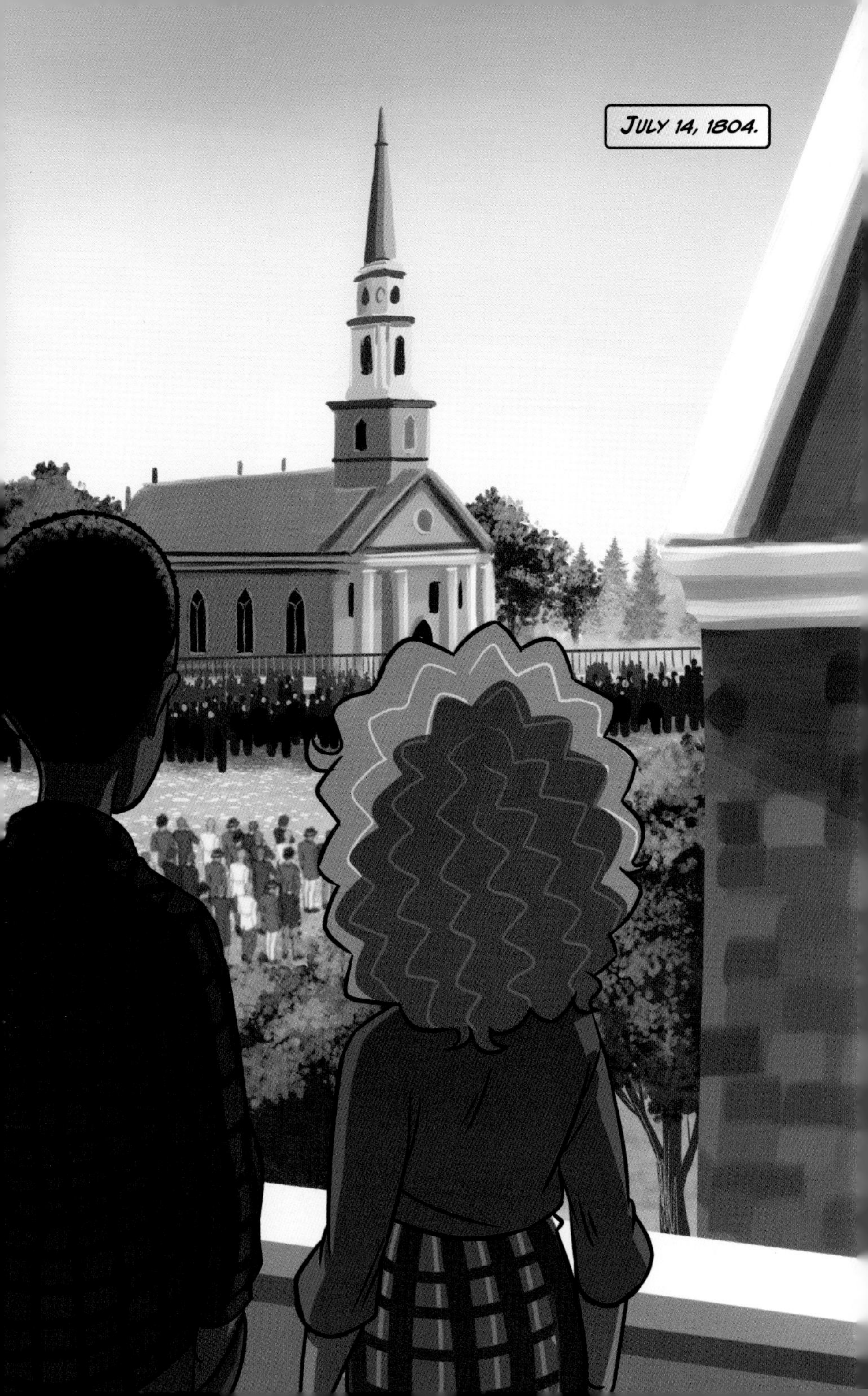
JULY 14, 1804.

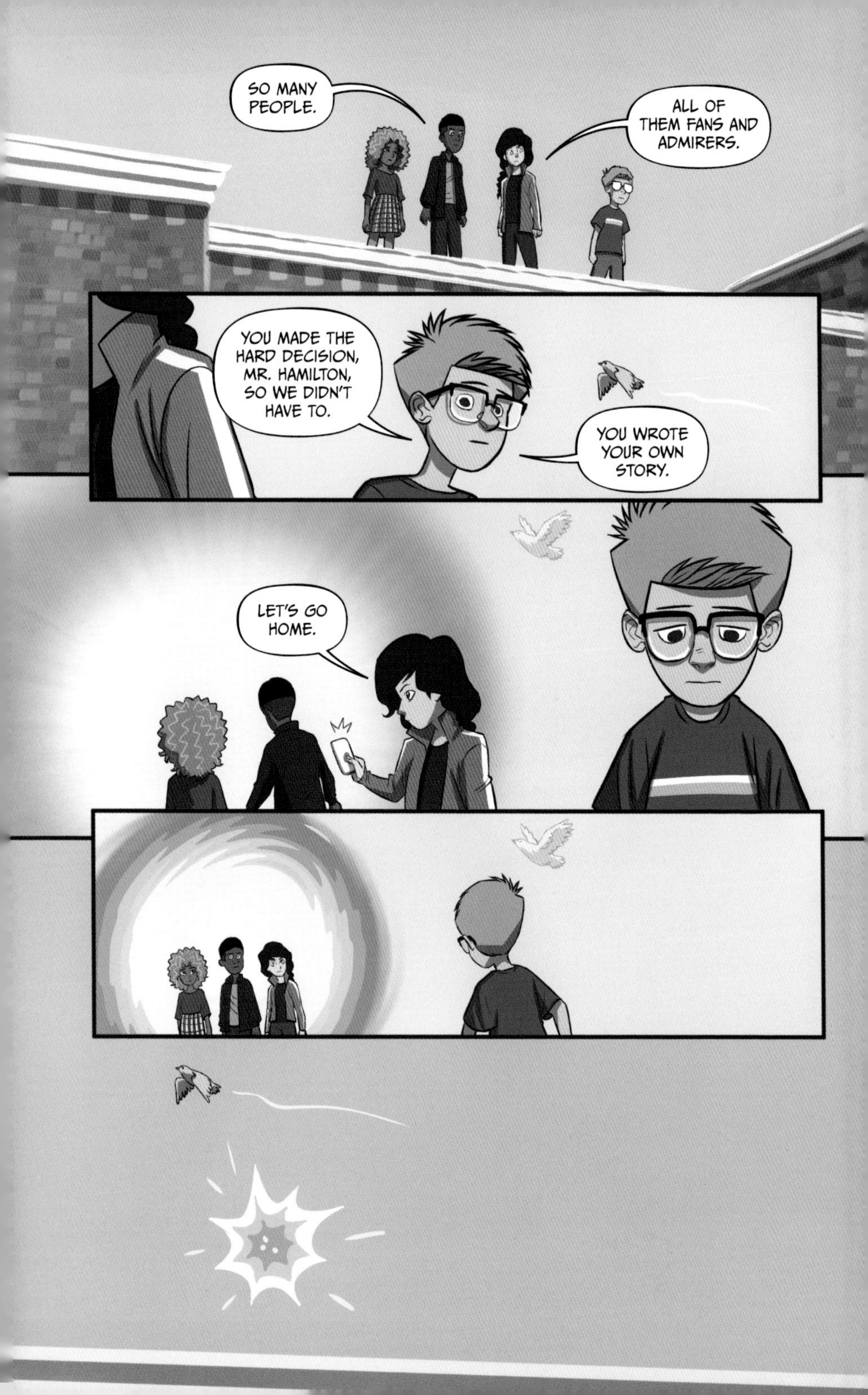
SO MANY PEOPLE.
ALL OF THEM FANS AND ADMIRERS.
YOU MADE THE HARD DECISION, MR. HAMILTON, SO WE DIDN'T HAVE TO.
YOU WROTE YOUR OWN STORY.
LET'S GO HOME.

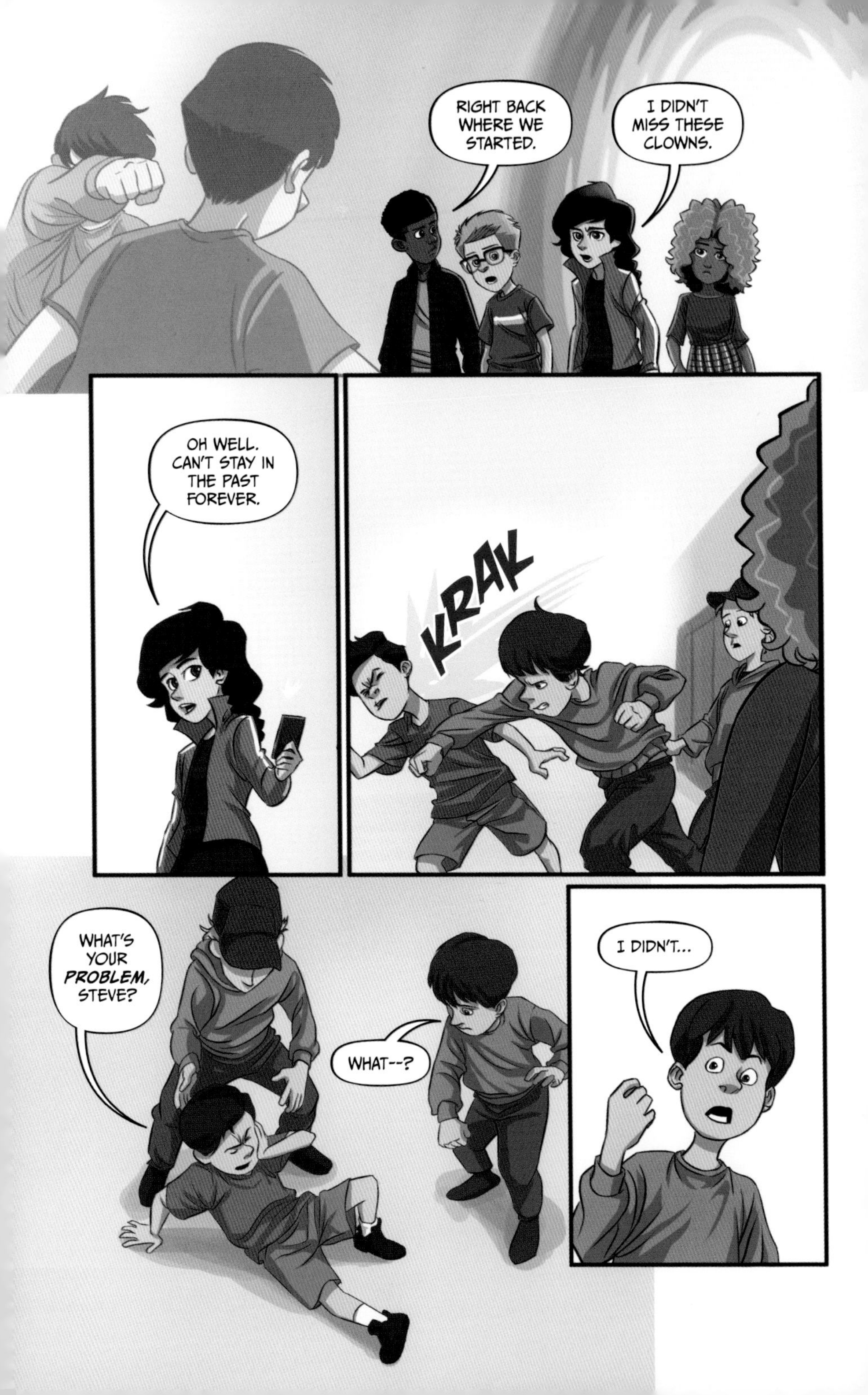
RIGHT BACK WHERE WE STARTED.
I DIDN'T MISS THESE CLOWNS.
OH WELL. CAN'T STAY IN THE PAST FOREVER.
KRAK
WHAT'S YOUR *PROBLEM,* STEVE?
WHAT--?
I DIDN'T...

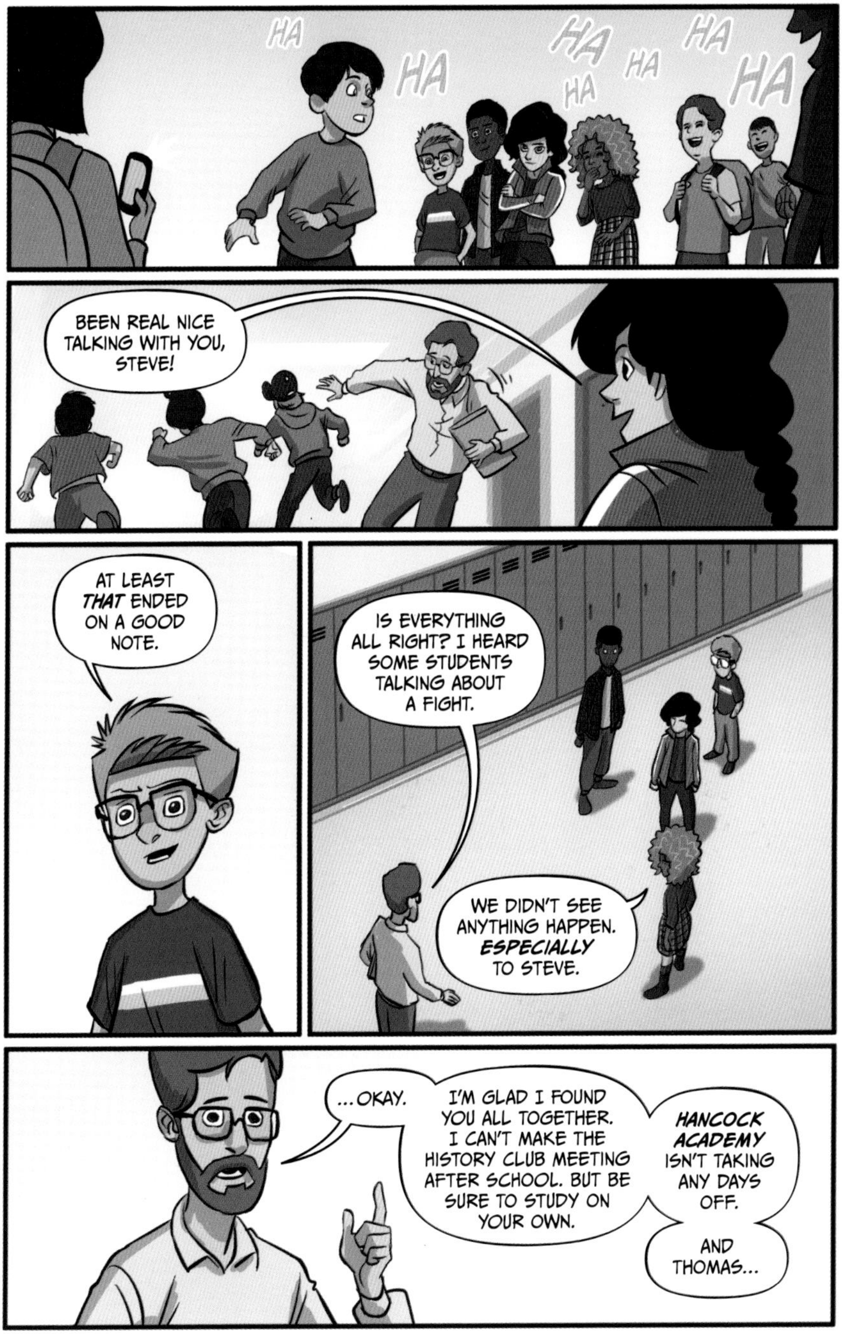
HA
HA
HA
HA
HA
HA
HA
HA
BEEN REAL NICE TALKING WITH YOU, STEVE!
AT LEAST *THAT* ENDED ON A GOOD NOTE.
IS EVERYTHING ALL RIGHT? I HEARD SOME STUDENTS TALKING ABOUT A FIGHT.
WE DIDN'T SEE ANYTHING HAPPEN. *ESPECIALLY* TO STEVE.
...OKAY.
I'M GLAD I FOUND YOU ALL TOGETHER. I CAN'T MAKE THE HISTORY CLUB MEETING AFTER SCHOOL. BUT BE SURE TO STUDY ON YOUR OWN.
HANCOCK ACADEMY ISN'T TAKING ANY DAYS OFF.
AND THOMAS...

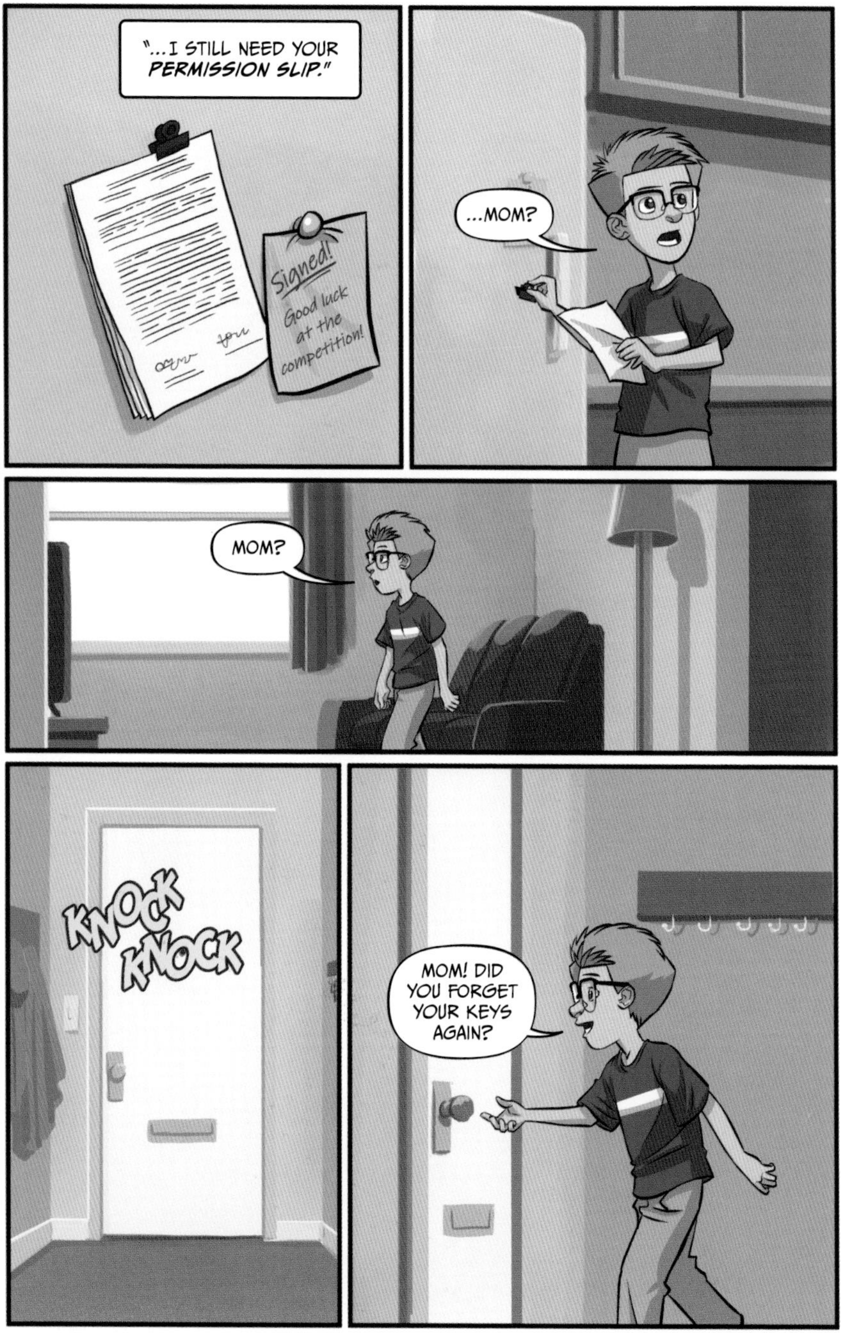
"...I STILL NEED YOUR PERMISSION SLIP."
Signed! Good luck at the competition!
...MOM?
MOM?
KNOCK KNOCK
MOM! DID YOU FORGET YOUR KEYS AGAIN?

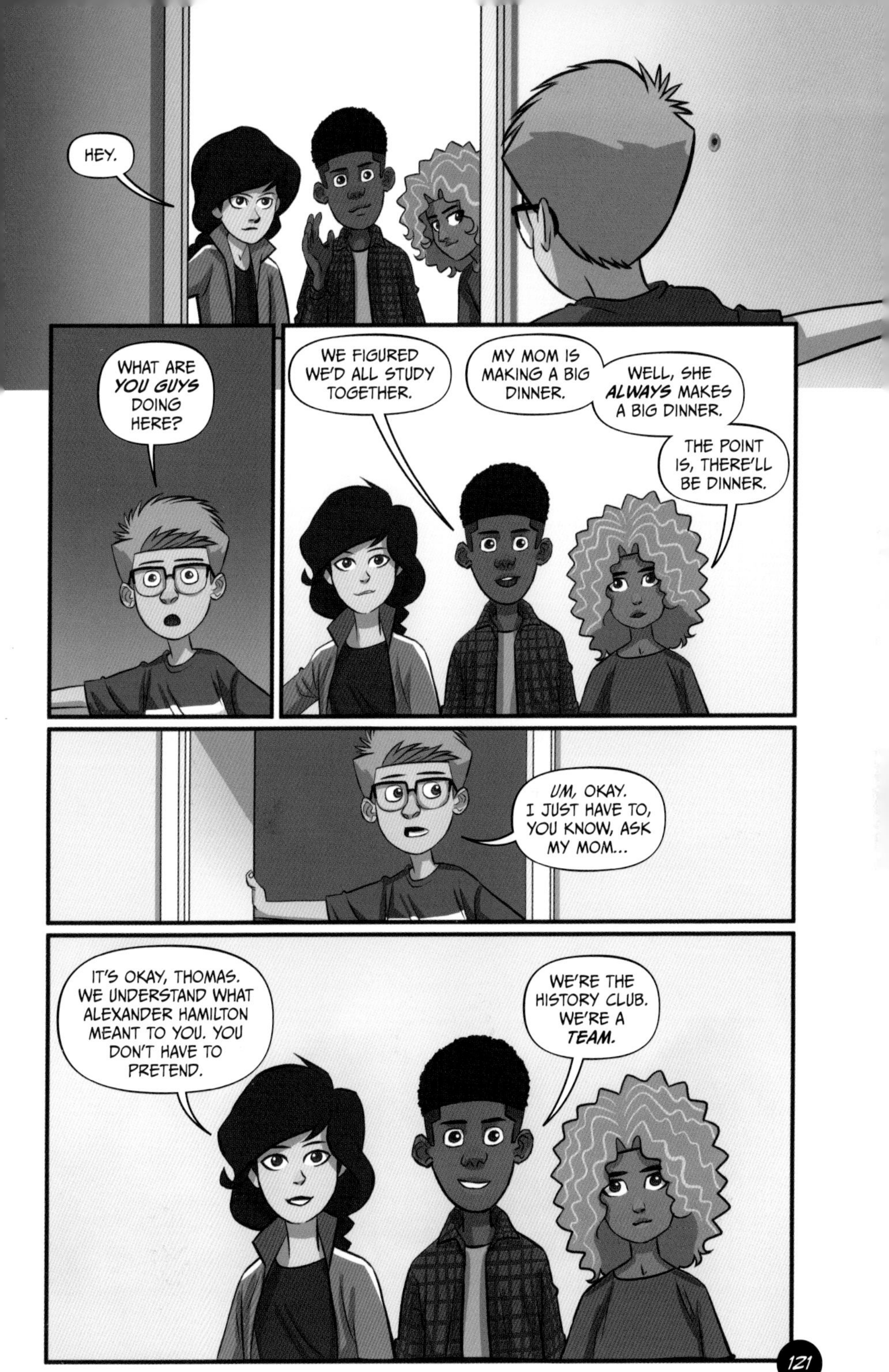
HEY.
WHAT ARE *YOU GUYS* DOING HERE?
WE FIGURED WE'D ALL STUDY TOGETHER.
MY MOM IS MAKING A BIG DINNER.
WELL, SHE *ALWAYS* MAKES A BIG DINNER.
THE POINT IS, THERE'LL BE DINNER.
UM, OKAY. I JUST HAVE TO, YOU KNOW, ASK MY MOM...
IT'S OKAY, THOMAS. WE UNDERSTAND WHAT ALEXANDER HAMILTON MEANT TO YOU. YOU DON'T HAVE TO PRETEND.
WE'RE THE HISTORY CLUB. WE'RE A *TEAM.*

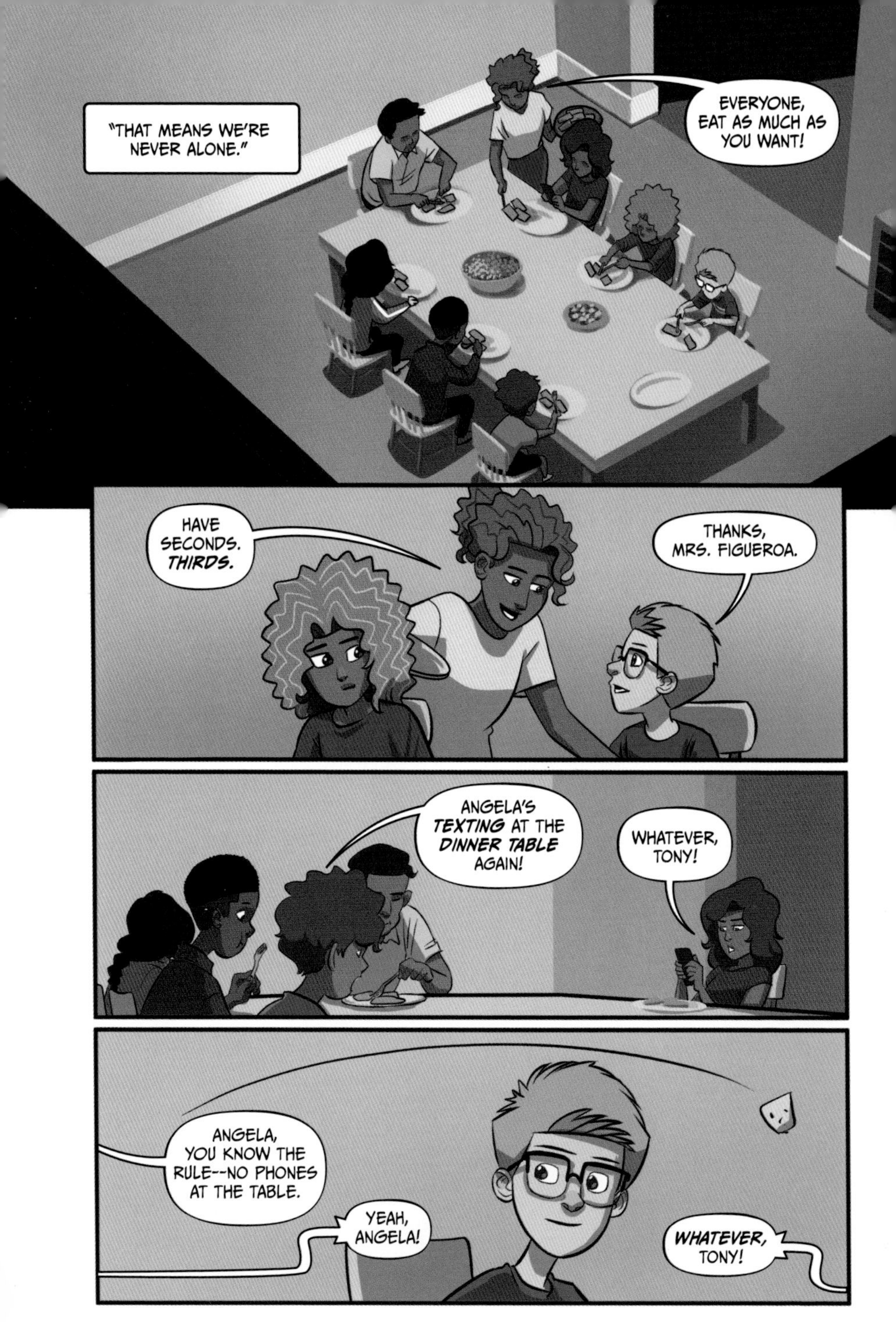
"THAT MEANS WE'RE NEVER ALONE."
EVERYONE, EAT AS MUCH AS YOU WANT!
HAVE SECONDS. THIRDS.
THANKS, MRS. FIGUEROA.
ANGELA'S TEXTING AT THE DINNER TABLE AGAIN!
WHATEVER, TONY!
ANGELA, YOU KNOW THE RULE--NO PHONES AT THE TABLE.
YEAH, ANGELA!
WHATEVER, TONY!

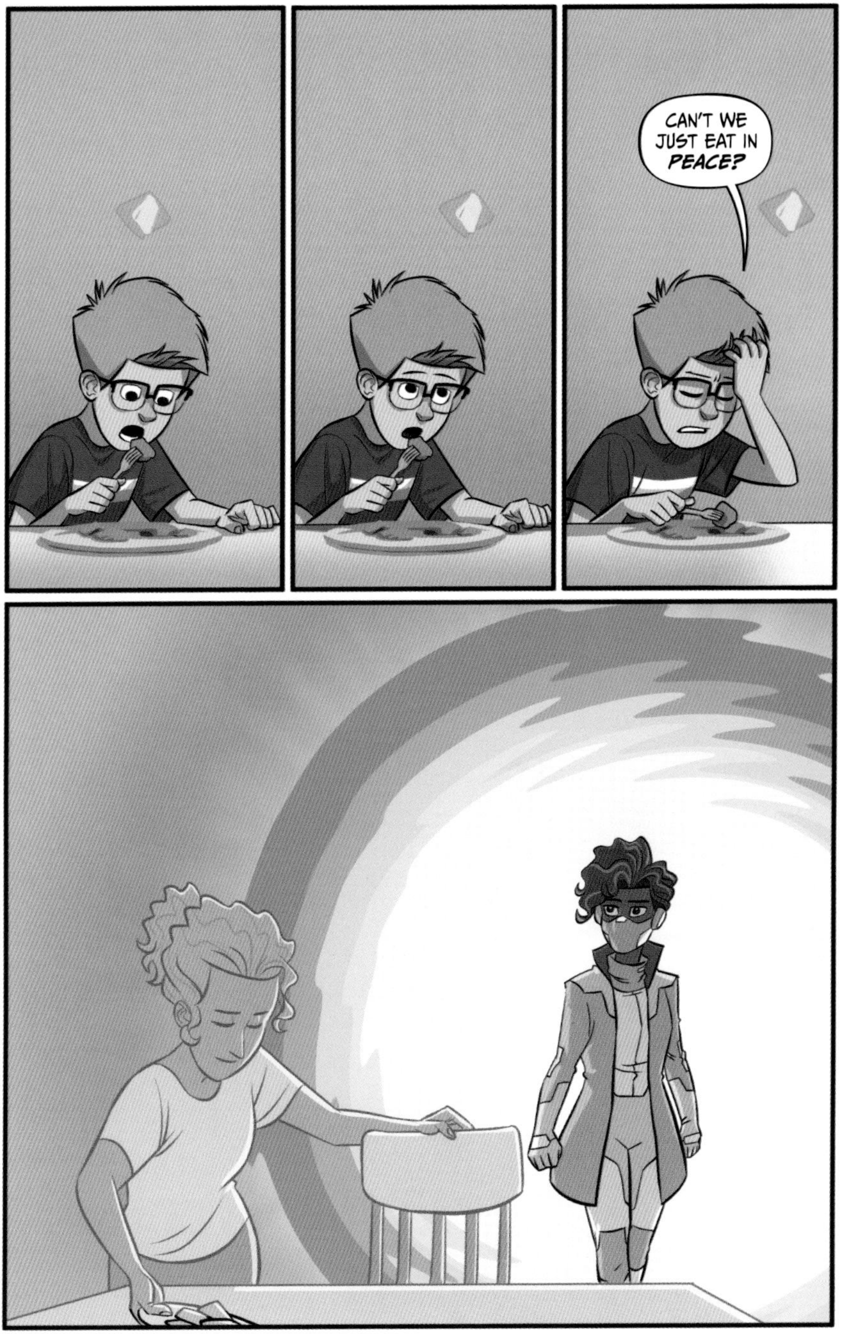
CAN'T WE
JUST EAT IN
PEACE?

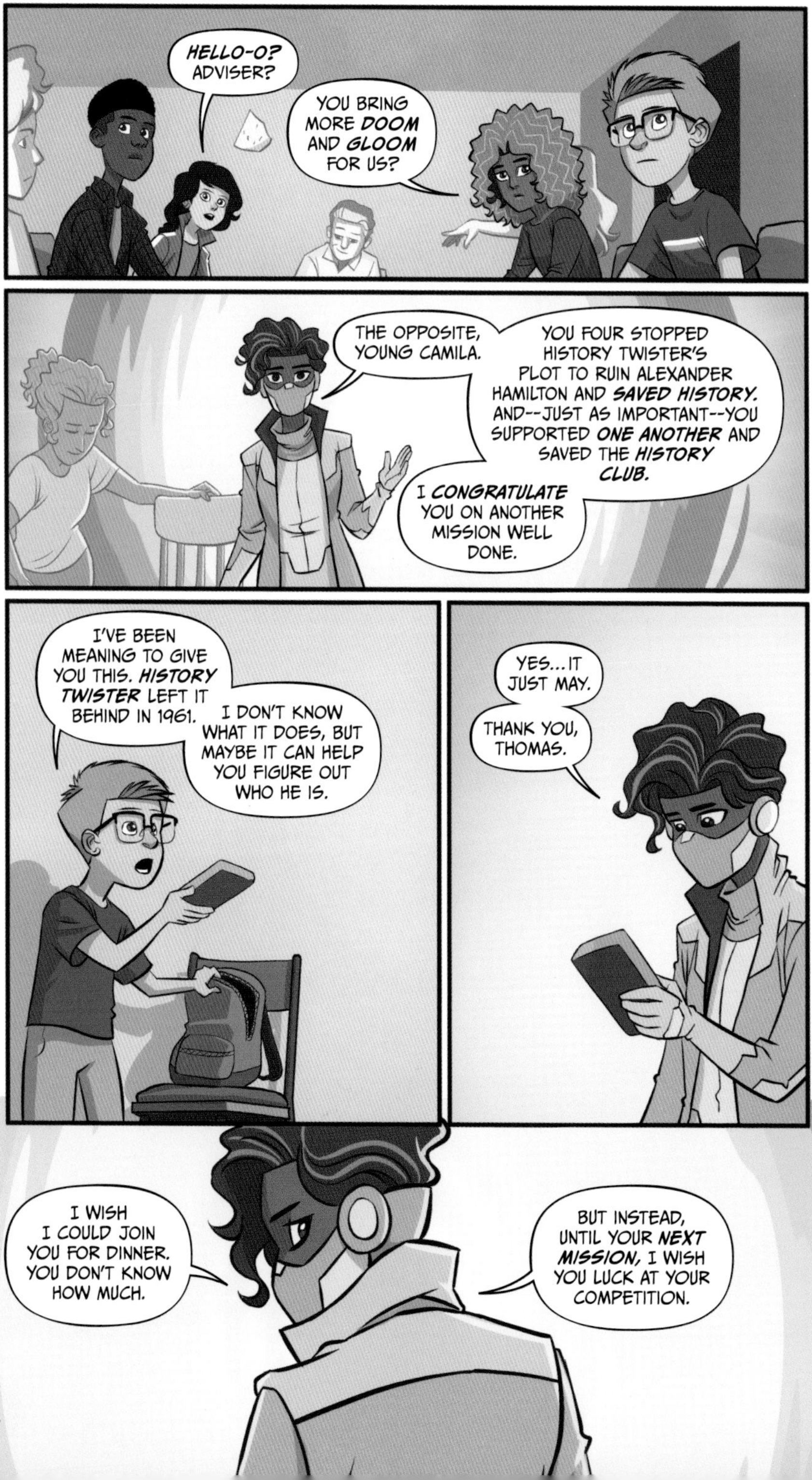
HELLO-O? ADVISER?
YOU BRING MORE DOOM AND GLOOM FOR US?
THE OPPOSITE, YOUNG CAMILA.
YOU FOUR STOPPED HISTORY TWISTER'S PLOT TO RUIN ALEXANDER HAMILTON AND SAVED HISTORY. AND--JUST AS IMPORTANT--YOU SUPPORTED ONE ANOTHER AND SAVED THE HISTORY CLUB.
I CONGRATULATE YOU ON ANOTHER MISSION WELL DONE.
I'VE BEEN MEANING TO GIVE YOU THIS. HISTORY TWISTER LEFT IT BEHIND IN 1961.
I DON'T KNOW WHAT IT DOES, BUT MAYBE IT CAN HELP YOU FIGURE OUT WHO HE IS.
YES...IT JUST MAY.
THANK YOU, THOMAS.
I WISH I COULD JOIN YOU FOR DINNER. YOU DON'T KNOW HOW MUCH.
BUT INSTEAD, UNTIL YOUR NEXT MISSION, I WISH YOU LUCK AT YOUR COMPETITION.

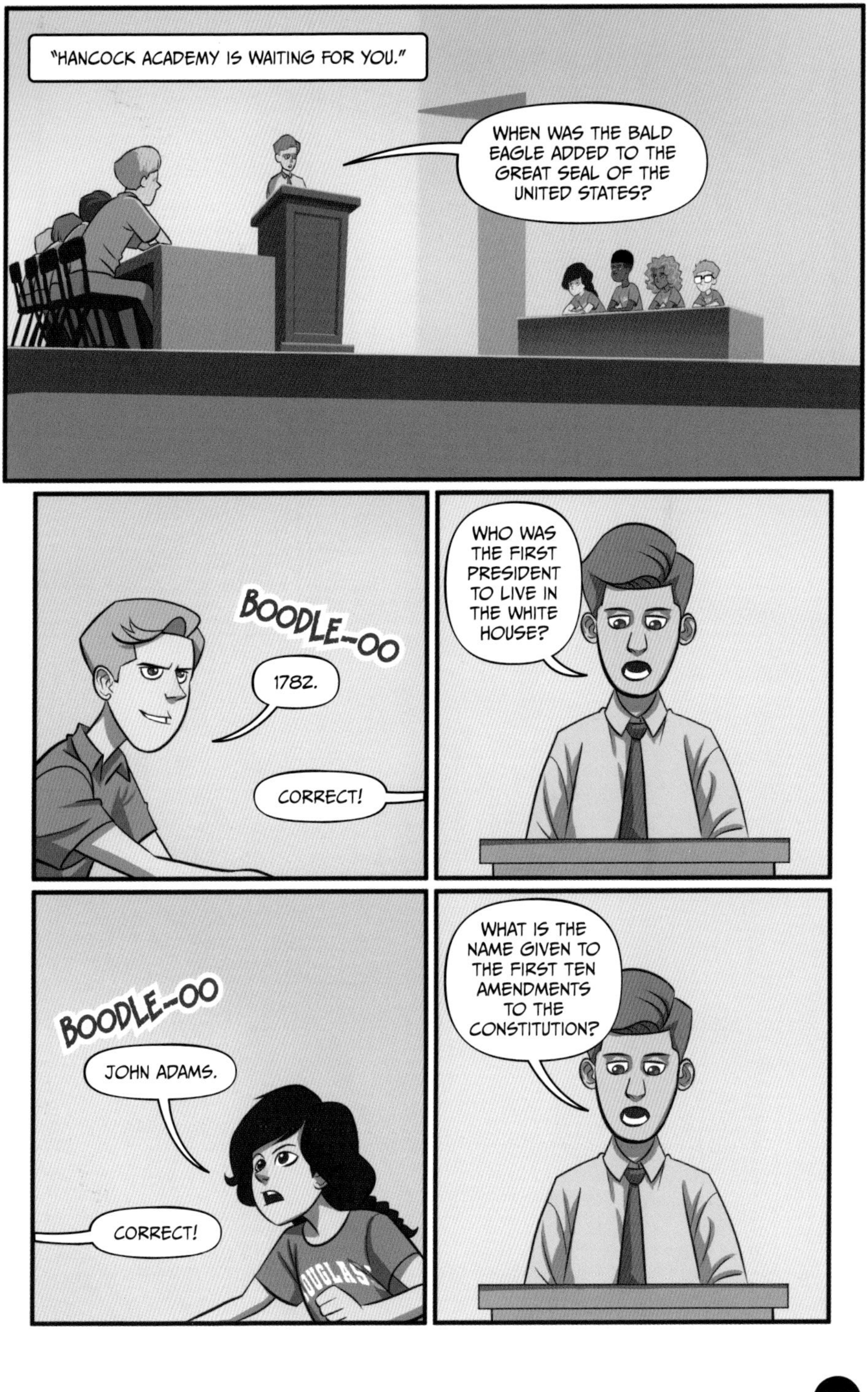
"HANCOCK ACADEMY IS WAITING FOR YOU."
WHEN WAS THE BALD EAGLE ADDED TO THE GREAT SEAL OF THE UNITED STATES?
BOODLE-OO
1782.
CORRECT!
WHO WAS THE FIRST PRESIDENT TO LIVE IN THE WHITE HOUSE?
BOODLE-OO
JOHN ADAMS.
CORRECT!
WHAT IS THE NAME GIVEN TO THE FIRST TEN AMENDMENTS TO THE CONSTITUTION?

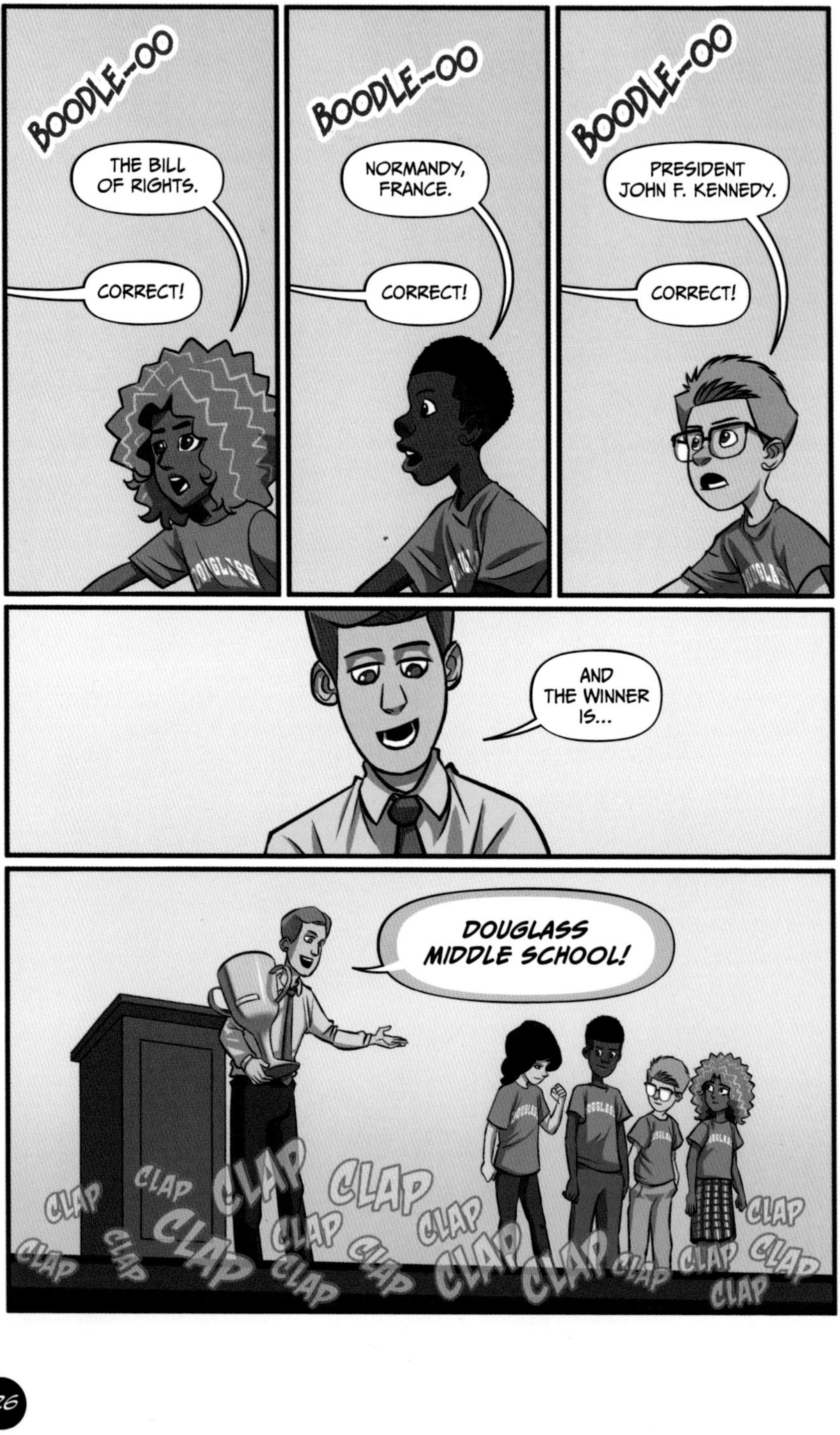
BOODLE-OO
THE BILL OF RIGHTS.
CORRECT!
BOODLE-OO
NORMANDY, FRANCE.
CORRECT!
BOODLE-OO
PRESIDENT JOHN F. KENNEDY.
CORRECT!
AND THE WINNER IS...
DOUGLASS MIDDLE SCHOOL!
CLAP CLAP CLAP CLAP CLAP CLAP CLAP CLAP CLAP CLAP CLAP CLAP CLAP CLAP CLAP CLAP CLAP CLAP

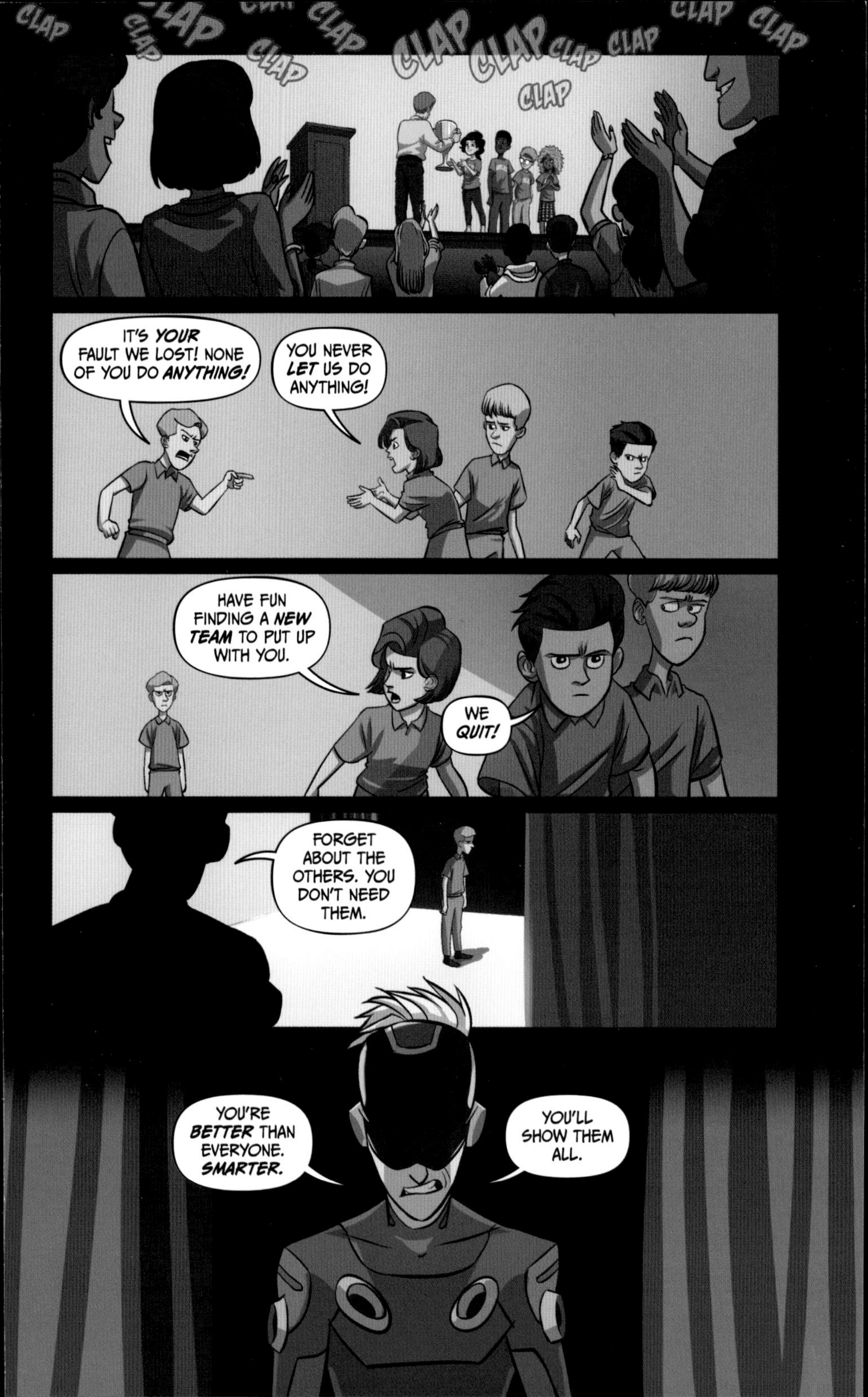
CLAP CLAP CLAP CLAP CLAP CLAP
CLAP CLAP CLAP CLAP CLAP CLAP CLAP
IT'S YOUR FAULT WE LOST! NONE OF YOU DO ANYTHING!
YOU NEVER LET US DO ANYTHING!
HAVE FUN FINDING A NEW TEAM TO PUT UP WITH YOU.
WE QUIT!
FORGET ABOUT THE OTHERS. YOU DON'T NEED THEM.
YOU'RE BETTER THAN EVERYONE. SMARTER.
YOU'LL SHOW THEM ALL.